DR. BROOKS

BILLIONAIRES' CLUB BOOK 3

RAYLIN MARKS

Contemporary Romance Author

CHAPTER ONE
COLLIN

*M*edical conferences usually intrigued me, but this one kicked my ass. Thank God it was finally over. This thing was as dull as they got. The only presentations that seemed to shed new light on the medical science industry were the lectures Jake and I had delivered. Everyone else's talks and presentations made it feel like we were back in freaking high school when the substitute teachers determined we'd watch videos from the 1970s in science class.

I guess the most irritating part of this conference was the fact that my best friend, Jake, Chief Cardiovascular Surgeon, and I were the only presenters who seemed to have done our goddamn jobs to share our research. Contrary to what I'd been bored to fucking tears by since this started three days ago, mine and Jake's presentations were current, not some rewind of known case studies from forty years ago.

Thank God I was born with the gift of unwavering patience, or I'd have left this final lecture of the day. I was at my limit, and I needed a drink. Tonight, Jake and I would attend the after-party event, something we'd passed on the previous nights. Maybe one reason no one was complaining about the boring lectures was that they'd all probably been nursing hangovers since they got here—one of many reasons not to hold business functions in Las Vegas.

Vegas came to life at night. I knew that, and I'd lived that on numerous weekend trips before. This trip, however, I stayed off of the strip and stayed safely at my hotel's pool. Granted, it was the biggest party pool oasis I'd ever seen before in my fucking life, but it was still less trouble than I was used to. The pool was lit up to create the ambiance of the nightlife, transporting and treating guests to an enchanting evening in a tropical paradise. Acres of water, palms, and any other treat you'd expect to find while vacationing in your own tropical world were present. What wasn't present was the gin I needed in my hand right about now. That's when I spotted Jake, sitting at a spot that was designed to impress our sizeable medical group and further this experience by bringing us into an enchanting Tahitian resort.

I stepped up to where Jake was already seated on a barstool. "Hey, sexy, looking for a date tonight?" I gripped my best friend's shoulder as I slid onto a stool next to him. "I'll have a Bombay Sapphire, on the rocks." I motioned to the bartender who'd moved my direction.

"I don't date pretentious assholes who drink gin," Jake said with a laugh while drinking his scotch. "Jesus, man." He rubbed his forehead and looked over at me. "Am I ever glad this shit storm finally blew the fuck out of here."

I took a large gulp of my favorite liquor and let the drink bring my mind back to life again. "Yeah, Obstetrics 101 was my favorite course."

"Obstetrics 101." Jake rose his glass to me. "That's certainly one way of looking at these fucked-up lectures."

"Well, this whole conference is easily compared to the nightmare of our college years. What the fuck was this damn thing for anyway? Hell if I know anymore."

Jake laughed. "My guess is a lesson to teach each medical professional about what others do for a living." Jake leaned his elbows on the polished wooden bar. "So, OB 101, eh? Did you learn how to deliver a baby today?"

I laughed, slowly unwinding with each sip of gin. "Yes, and it's a good thing I did." I brought the rim of my glass to my lips. "So, when you knock up Ash for a second time, she can use me as her midwife, and I can help deliver your next child in your bathtub."

Jake smiled. "The only in-home delivery you'll be doing for Ash is when she calls for Chinese takeout." He sighed. "Shit, this area is larger than I thought. Three fucking pools, waterfalls, palm trees?" He frowned. "Where are we, Tahiti?"

"I was actually looking for the exit to the beach when I walked out here," I said. "Though it's still not tempting enough to keep me here until morning."

That's when my eye caught the image of a vivacious and attractive young woman. She strolled out with a group of individuals, her beaming smile and the liveliness in her step instantly caught my attention, but it wasn't a minute before she disappeared through the crowd that surrounded the multiple pools.

I had no business letting my mind go in that direction with a woman while at a medical conference after-party, but I couldn't help but be taken aback when I saw her.

"Excuse me, gentlemen?" I was the first to look back and find a tall, hot blonde with bright red lips and a barely-there bikini, heading up a pack of what I quickly concluded were single women.

It didn't matter how fucking hot they were. Jake and I had drawn a hard line in the sand when it came to fucking around with women at medical conferences. That had nearly cost us everything while we were interns.

"Yes," I said, keeping the flirting at bay and smiling to be polite.

"We're from the Institute of Science medical internship," red lips started, "and we're looking to enjoy the night after this long conference. Do either of you mind if we join you?"

Jake's eyes met mine in warning, and this week had been such a disaster that I figured I might as well spice it up a little. My happily-married best friend was so in love with Ash that I didn't think he even noticed hot chicks anymore. His wild days were in the past, and so it was up to me to shake things up a little. The bastard had put me through hell enough times, and so I enjoyed repaying the favor now and then.

"Join us?" I answered the blonde. I eyed her red bikini and red stilettos, and I figured that if there were a Poolside Vegas Barbie doll, it would've looked exactly like this woman. I had to give her credit, though. She'd matched up her outfit—if you could call it that—to her lipstick. "You must be complimented on how you've coordinated all this red." I waved my hand toward her while the group of girls behind her giggled. "You'd make those hot chicks on Baywatch a tad bit jealous. I assume that was what you were aiming for?"

She laughed while Jake pointedly ignored the trap of women I'd been lured into. "Red is my favorite color," she said. "So, you guys are okay with us hanging?"

"Son of a bitch." I ran my hand through my hair. "I'm sorry. I almost forgot, and now I have to break your heart. You see, I'm married."

Jake looked at me while I slid my left hand discreetly to him, and he quickly picked up on my need to borrow his wedding ring so I could get out of this. These were interns—young, hot, and trouble. Being best friends since childhood, Jake and I read each other as twins would. Though, he had no idea what I was really up to, which made this situation that much more enjoyable.

I slid his ring on while using the distraction of ordering another gin. What the hell, did they water the liquor down at this place? Cheap-ass medical group most likely asked to have it served up that way.

"I didn't see a wedding ring on your hand," the shorter redhead in the bunch said. "Nice one."

"Oh, it's there, it just doesn't stand out so easily. Must be the onyx color of the band, but it's right here." I wiggled the fingers of my left hand and elbowed Jake. "If you want a hot and single doctor, this is your man right here."

"You're fucking joking, right?" Jake grumbled in a whisper.

It didn't matter how quietly Jake responded. These girls were tuned in and hanging on to every word.

"Well." I smirked at Jake, "I would be fucking joking if you weren't the best man at my wedding."

Jake turned back to the women, and his eyes widened when he took in Barbie and the whole Vegas gang. "Wow, you must like the color red…" he stopped himself, and I smiled. "Sorry. I thought my friend was fucking with you until now. You really did match up your lipstick to that bikini."

"You're awfully blunt," she snapped.

"It's why he's single," I chimed in. "You see, he's most likely already determining which one of you he's going to take back to his room and fuck before he sends you on a walk of shame." I met Jake's humored eyes. "You know I'm one hundred percent accurate on that one."

"There are plenty of women to back that up," he stated factually.

I looked back at the woman in red. "Does that lipstick rub off?" I pinched my lips, trying not to laugh.

The chick's face was now showing that she was fucking pissed at me and Jake for acting like dicks.

Jake held his hands up in innocence. "Hey, I'm just the single asshole." Jake gripped my shoulder. "It's Mr. Forever Guy who loves to cheat on his wife while we're out..." He eyed me as if to show he'd just kicked the ball back into my court. "If you're into the brilliance of a sexy brain surgeon," he gulped his scotch, "this is your boy right here."

"Then why would he wear a wedding ring?"

"It's kinky," I said. "I think chicks dig being home wreckers. Now, I'm curious as to how you'll look with those red lips and no matching bikini."

"Right," Jake feigned curiosity. "Like, would it all work without the matchy-matchy?" He shrugged.

"Exactly." I took a sip of gin, "Do the lips complement the bikini?"

"Does the bikini complement the lips?"

"Heels no heels?" I answered him.

"Maybe I do want to find out for myself too. You up for sharing after you find out?"

I held in my laughter. "I'm shocked you're considering sloppy seconds this time." I looked at Jake, both of us being dumbasses like we were known to be when we weren't interested.

"You deserve first dibs. This conference was harder on you than it was me."

"Truer words have never been spoken. I'll text you when we're done." I glanced back to be confronted with deadly looks. "You still up for it, Barbie?"

"Let's get out of here, Kimmy," another girl said, but my attention was instantly diverted from the women on the prowl.

"They always say the hot ones are pricks." I think it was Barbie who said that. I didn't know or care. I was locked in on the gorgeous woman from earlier. I was fully absorbed as I watched her dance, swaying her hips fluidly in a flawless salsa style of dancing.

"Yeah," I said in a dismissive tone while I glanced around Jake to keep my eye on the sexy woman. I gripped Jake's shoulder. "Who the fuck is that on the dance floor?"

"The entertainment?" he answered, looking past the bar where we sat and out to the dance floor. "The hell if I know."

"I'm about to go find out."

Jake grabbed my arm. "Bad idea," he said. "She was in one of my seminars. She's off-limits."

"The hell she is," I said.

"Coll." Jake looked at me as if I were crazy. "What the fuck are you doing? And give me my ring back, you jackass."

I absently gave him the ring. "Remember when we learned salsa years ago?" I smiled at him. "I'm about to cash in on that shit."

"That was a long ass time ago and in Florida, not Vegas." He sipped his drink. "It was also to get those two Cuban princesses in their thong swimsuits to dance with us and—"

"And into our beds," I finished his sentence. "Well, it looks like that was for the greater good because I'm about to put those skills to work."

"You still think you have those moves?"

I nodded. "I'm about to find out if all that money in lessons paid off."

"You're a horny idiot. Pull your shit together, and remember where the fuck we are. A medical conference shindig. Jesus, read the goddamn room or something."

"That's precisely what I'm doing," I said, watching every flawless dance step while she showed off her perfectly round ass in a fun and exuberant way.

Unlike everyone else who was out here, either dressed to impress or wearing bikinis that matched their stilettos, she was dressed simply and casually.

Jesus H. Christ, I was smitten as fuck by this woman. She wore a plain white tank that enhanced the glow of her naturally tanned skin. Her super short, cut-off denim shorts were frayed at the hem, highlighting the strong muscles of her gorgeous legs. Her tight ass moved and played along to the rhythm of the music that the live band played, making me believe we were actually in Florida. Florida, Vegas, heaven—I didn't even know where I was anymore. I just knew where I wasn't—out there on the dance floor, joining this woman.

Her smile was effervescent, and even though I couldn't hear her laugh, I could tell it was something I had to be close to. This wasn't about me wanting to fuck some hot chick I'd spotted who was shaking her ass out on the dance floor. This woman had fucking bewitched me with the way her hips moved to the music and the animated and cheerful way she lit up this whole place.

I stayed back and admired her from a distance, but I wanted more. No way in hell could I sit here and hide behind my rules of never pursuing someone in the medical field—not with this woman.

The more I watched her, the more I needed to be in her presence. I couldn't explain any of my behavior or the way I felt. All I knew was I was wasting time sitting here and debating right versus reason.

All sense left my mind, and Jake's warnings and reminders about staying away from females in our line of work—gone. All that was on my mind was cutting into her dance, pulling her against me by the small of her back, and guiding her in a more challenging dance—and into my arms from there.

"Fuck it. Just go get it." Jake laughed. "You're already consumed by this woman. Don't say I didn't warn your stupid ass."

I walked toward the crowd she'd drawn in, easing myself to the side and slipping out to where she teased the musicians by following the music—her movements fluid and sexy as hell.

I watched her feet, her style, focusing on her skill instead of that beautiful smile that I knew would trip my ass up. If I was going to interrupt her entertaining the group, I had to fall in perfectly. If she were the natural talent I was witnessing, she'd easily follow my lead.

As if it were meant to be, I stepped in behind her slowly-swaying hips and took the hand she held in the air and clasped it into mine. She reacted like someone who was expecting a dance partner, and she allowed me to clutch her hip with my other hand and spin her back to me. I dipped her for the hell of it, and that's when her golden-brown eyes met mine.

I pulled her up in one fluid motion, her hands molding into mine as if they were created to be held by them alone. She arched her eyebrow, her lashes emphasizing the chestnut irises I wanted to drown in.

"May I ask who you are, sir?" she asked, moving her hips, complementing each step I took to guide her in our dance that became more intimate with each movement.

"Your future husband." I grinned, spinning her away from me.

Her long, flowing hair breezed through the air while I spun her back, and I took her other hand, turning her back to mold against me.

"You're confident." She laughed as I twirled her out and dipped her to add to our little routine while bringing her to face me in our dance again.

"Goddamn, you're beautiful," I said, almost missing a step as I let her eyes and that bright expression of hers that had lured me out here take me as her victim.

"I could say the same about you," she said as we continued to move our dance into a more daring—after dark—routine.

"And what would you say about me?" I asked when I pulled her in close.

"I have no idea who you are."

"Collin," I gave her my real name.

"You dance well, Collin," she said, her lips full. My God, this woman's spark of delightful energy radiated from her. "Where'd you learn to dance like this?"

"Doesn't matter," I said, pulling my face down to her neck. She smelled like paradise. It was coconut, and some floral scent mixed together, assaulting my senses in the best of ways. "All that matters is that I'm out here with you."

She laughed again, and I never wanted this dance to end. Did someone slip me a love potion? What was going on with me? Who the hell was this woman?

After the dance was over, she thanked me, then tried to escape my grips. "I believe I owe you a drink?" I bit my bottom lip, watching her smooth her hair back into a ponytail.

"I believe you do." Her forehead creased in humor. "So," she said as I held her hand and guided her through the crowd as the music changed behind us to allow for more dancing, "are you a doctor or an intern?"

I grinned. "What do you think?"

"I don't think doctors are as handsome as you." She giggled and nudged my arm as if we were reunited friends from a past life. "And I also don't think doctors dance as well as you."

We arrived at the bar where Jake was in conversation with two older gentlemen and two younger women. He halted his conversation and eyed me and the woman I'd snatched up from the dance floor.

"You think I'm an intern then?" I asked. "What are you having?"

"Water for now," she said, sitting on the stool next to where Jake sat. "Hey, Mario," she smiled at the bartender.

"You looked great out there, Elena," he said. "It's going to suck around here after you leave tonight."

"I believe I have a question for you," I said, taking the stool to her left, Jake now fully facing the bar, listening in on us.

"Well, then, ask away, dance partner," she said, holding up her bottle of water. "Thanks," she said with a wink to the gentleman behind the bar.

"Seems like Mario knows you well enough." I kept my eyes locked on her. "Are you part of the medical group or the entertainment?"

Jake laughed. "Mario and I both think that she was doing well out there alone before your sneaky ass joined her."

She turned and smiled at Jake. "Well, if it isn't the famed Dr. Jacob Mitchell," she said with a laugh that could probably cure a lot of diseases in our industry.

"In the flesh. I see you've met my best friend and intern, Collin."

She turned back to me, and her expression was a dead giveaway that she read Jake's face well enough to know he was bullshitting her.

"Wait." She delivered the sexiest and most dynamic expression I'd seen from her yet. "You both are the two steamy and sexy docs from Saint John's, correct?"

"Don't tell me you know who I am from when the media followed my sorry ass around, documenting the lamest bullshit ever?" Jake said.

She giggled and tipped back her bottled water. My dick was joining in on the party now. Her full lips could've been viewed in so many better ways than wrapped around that water bottle.

"I didn't see that part." She laughed. "I felt for you when my dad told me what'd happened when your life was exploited." She shook her head. "But no, I just watched you in that docuseries. You were fantastic in your presentation here too. It makes me wish I looked more into becoming a heart surgeon now." She laughed then looked at me, "And *you*, Dr. Collin Brooks, the youngest neurosurgeon with a level of boldness and genius skill that is unmatched, yet you still find the time to be an arrogant asshole, or so your predecessor says." Her eyebrows shot up in humor while she and Jake laughed together. "Are the rumors circling this conference about you accurate?"

I arched my eyebrow at the sexy way she teased me. "Perhaps. It looks like Dr. Alvarez's parting words were sent in the invitations to everyone here at the conference. Not a very nice predecessor."

"Is that so?" She hit me with a toying look. "What exactly were Dr. Alvarez's parting words to you?"

"Well, as he gladly passed the torch to me in taking his place on our ward, his final words were mostly that I was the only arrogant asshole he trusted to stand in his place as neuro chief."

A laugh erupted from her in the most delightful way. "Seems like you've already met my dad, then? He's Dr. Alvarez."

That's when Jake nearly choked on his scotch, using the back of his hand to cover the fact he'd sucked the alcohol down the wrong pipe.

"Your dad?" I questioned in disbelief. This should have ended my fascination instantly, but instead, I couldn't give a shit who she was related to. I'd somehow mentally staked some claim on her and wasn't losing her over anything now.

"According to your introduction to me on the dance floor, he's your future father-in-law. I do hope you both get along. Life will suck if I have to pick between my beloved father and you, Dr. Brooks."

I grinned and ordered a beer. The gin had handled my nerves from earlier, and now, all I wanted now was to nurse the beer and enjoy the company of the woman who made every cell in my body come alive.

"Dr. Alvarez was quite the brilliant neurosurgeon. We were sad to see him retire. And you?" I questioned. "You never thoroughly answered my question."

"And which question was that?" she asked.

"Yeah, I think all questions are nailed into your coffin by now," Jake warned with a smile.

Damn, it was so intriguing how she blended in with Jake and me as if we were all old friends.

"You think my dad will kick his ass for hitting on me, Dr. Mitchell?" she asked Jake while studying me.

"I think Alvarez will definitely kick his ass," Jake said with a laugh.

"So the question is," she said, ordering a beer herself, "am I worth that ass-kicking?"

"Yes, and you're smartly avoiding my main question," I said, taking another sip of my beer. "What exactly is it that you do, and where the hell have you been all my life?"

Jake's eyes widened while he shook his head. "I'm going to need water and a Heineken, Mario," he called out to the bartender and then looked at me. "This is going to be a long, entertaining night."

Jake knew I'd already destroyed all our guidelines for playing it safe in this industry. Now here I was, pursuing our former Chief Neurosurgeon's daughter. Miguel could easily kick my ass even in his sixties. Was it worth it? To see this smile and be around the boisterous energy of this woman for the rest of my life, you're goddamn right it was worth it.

"Hmm, where have I been all your life?" she said with a devious laugh. "Well, I've been in Florida, busting my ass so I can work at Saint John's. Looks like you and I might be getting married after all, Dr. Brooks. Well, professionally, anyway," she teased.

I licked my lips after taking another sip of beer. "How so?"

"I'm working in Saint John's neuro ward and will have my own office outside of the hospital as well. Quite the dream that I worked very hard to achieve."

"What will you be doing exactly? Surgery? Research?" Jake asked, but I already knew.

She never pulled her eyes from mine. "I'll be the new—"

"Neuropsychologist," I finished her sentence.

"That's right, Doc," she teased me with those luscious lips.

"You're moving into my office building," I said, studying her. "And yes," I arched an eyebrow, taking another sip of my beer, "you and I will be joined at the hip mostly. I'm the one who requested a neuropsychologist to work closely with me, my patients, and even in some of my surgeries. I didn't know they'd already hired someone? I was supposed to have the final say in who took the new position."

"Looks like we both got screwed this week, missing my brother's board meetings," Jake said, shifting to face us both and leaning against the bar. "Looks like you and your new wife have a lot to iron out, and forgive me if I say that it looks like the honeymoon is over for both of you." Jake took a sip of his beer and smiled knowingly at me.

That's when I watched a tiny ounce of vulnerability flash across her face. "Holy crap." She softly giggled, pink coloring her cheeks, and her hypnotic eyes shifted the night's gears into another pace. She held her hand out to me. "Allow me to introduce myself formally. I'm Dr. Elena Alvarez," she said as I accepted her handshake. "Lovely to meet you, Dr. Brooks. I can already say I like your style."

"And I can safely say, welcome to Saint John's. Whether I hired you or not, those issues are irrelevant after meeting the woman who will make my job much more entertaining."

"Quite a compliment," she said. "I think we'll enjoy each other's company. I absolutely adore working with arrogant asses."

"Is that so?" I smiled.

"It is." She reached for her beer. "I love putting them in their place."

"Then, it's a match made in heaven." Jake raised his beer. "Though, I have to ask you, Dr. Elena Alvarez, do you think you'll enjoy working around this guy?" Jake chimed in, and I could tell my best friend was enjoying the collision course of career death I was on now.

"The question is, will he enjoy working around me?"

"As I mentioned when I met you on the dance floor, you'll be my wife —work partners or not."

I had no idea how to stop this when everything in my body was screaming that I should run this woman off to the closest wedding chapel and have fake Elvis marry us. It was insane. I never believed in any of that love at first sight bullshit. Ever. That was all crazy talk for sappy romantics and hippies who collected crystals—and yet here I was, staring this woman in the eyes and knowing I'd make good on the promise that I'd marry her—or at least ensure she was mine.

Was her dad going to kick my ass? Yes. He knew me all too well. Could my medical license be on the line? No. At least I didn't think so. There was no way I was going to let any of that get in the way. With the way she was flirting with me, and the way she treated Jake as if we were the three musketeers reunited, I knew this was somehow meant to be. She would be mine, and I would ensure that her gorgeous smile brightened more and more as each day passed with her in my life.

Thank God she had three weeks before her assignment began. I'd just taken two weeks of much-needed vacation for the first time in three years at Saint John's. So, get ready. All it took was seeing her on the dance floor to know that my days of playing women were over.

This was going to be the biggest mistake of my life or the best thing that ever happened to me.

CHAPTER TWO
ELENA

I walked through the open space of the condo my dad had taken me to view. I was a bit shocked that he had been so proactive in my relocation to California. He had lined up five places within my budget, but this one stole my heart from the second I stepped foot inside. I think he had already picked up on that fact as he eyed me carefully, looking for more positive feedback than I'd given at the previous two listings.

"It's got the ocean views," Dad started in, "but I don't like the commute."

"The commute is always worth it for a view like this," Mauricio, our real estate agent, chimed in, his smile directed toward me.

"Not when you work long shifts in the medical industry," I smirked.

Mauricio wasn't getting anywhere with his charms here. Dad and I were forces to be reckoned with in situations that required negotiating.

At the store where I was picking out a new mattress? Well, we sort of ruined that poor salesman's day when he started in on his sales pitch. And that was a mattress, not a half-million-dollar home.

This man was handsome with his dark hair, copper eyes, and deep brown skin. His smile matched his thousand-dollar suit too. There was no time to get caught up in Mauricio's dreamy eyes right now, though.

"Medical industry?" he responded.

Shit. I just gave him the bait.

"Yeah, and lots of student loan debt, too," I responded with a discreet wink to Dad.

"Listen," Dad said, "we need to think about the houses."

"This seller is extremely motivated," Mauricio answered, and I looked to the ocean view from the living room window to keep from smiling at how quickly the handsome man had caved. Hell, I would've caved by now. My father was nothing if not extremely intimidating.

It felt good to be close to my father again. I hadn't realized how much I'd missed the old man until I got off that plane a week ago and woke up in my old room in Beverly Hills. I felt like a teenager again without a care in the world. All of the fun memories from before my parents' divorce came back as if I were still a kid. Unfortunately, those times were long gone. It didn't take my mother long to realize that my father's true love would always be work.

Dad and I had spent our last few mornings together over coffee and laughs. No business talk, well mostly none. I had to admit to my father that I'd met and taunted the gorgeous and all-too sure of himself, Dr. Collin Brooks, making the confident man believe I had been hired as his neuropsychiatrist. The expression on Dr. Brooks' face when he thought I'd been hired without his final say was priceless. It's also probably why I hadn't seen him since that night.

The buzz around the hospital was this: *Due to a conflict of interest, Dr. Brooks will have Dr. Sinclair sit in his place on the hiring board for Saint John's new neuropsychiatrist.*

After I had told Dad about meeting Dr. Brooks and Dr. Mitchell at the medical conference—our dancing, his confidence, and my attraction for the man—Dad was certain I wouldn't have a shot in hell at becoming Dr. Brooks' new psychiatrist. Thank God Dr. Brooks didn't hunt me down after learning I'd left the conference to go through an entire week of interviews. As of yesterday, I had been narrowed down to the final three applicants, and I was the first one offered the job—as if I would turn down this dream opportunity.

My father was the best neurosurgeon in the country before he retired, and he'd sparked my interest in neuroscience at a young age. I'd watched him fight for his patients, care for them, devote hours upon hours of his time to research diseases, and do whatever he could to help people who had no hope. That's what drove me into the psychology specialty of this field. I was the one helping these patients cope and learn to live and love life again, and most of all, to never let a disease defeat them.

With Dr. Brooks being the one my father had spoken so highly about as the new Chief of Neurology at Saint Johns, I had to wonder how this man had captured my dad's attention. I mean, this poor real estate agent who was *talking turkey* with Dad was taking a beating; how the heck did Dr. Brooks survive with my dad as his superior? The only answer to that was that he was passionate about what he did—douche bag or not.

Tomorrow, I was set to observe Dr. Brooks' live surgery from the observation room, and something gave me the feeling that he would be just like my father. He would most likely push everyone in that room to their limits, act like a total asshole, and make the job hell for everyone who worked with him. He would do all of that if he were like my father because it wasn't about them. It would be all about the patient.

Why did I have such a strong feeling about this? Because my dad still liked the guy even after I told him that he'd hit on me at the medical conference. That spoke volumes, and that told me I was about to work with a doctor who was equally as passionate about neuroscience as my father. I was glad the man was most likely too drunk to remember flirting with me and dancing with me that night in Vegas—and *proposing* that I would be his future wife. What an arrogant ass. Either way, if he really was like my father, one thing was absolutely sure: I would *never* date the guy. Never.

I was not a woman who rode second best to anything, especially a job, no matter how important that job might be. Surgeons were married to their professions, and that's why my mom has been happily remarried to a real estate developer in Miami for the last nine years—she found herself a man who could appreciate her and give her his time. If and when I settled down, I would find the same in my guy.

"So, Laney?" Dad snapped me out of my daze. "What's it going to be? You've been staring out that window like you're not sure if you're ready to leave Florida for good."

"The family is willing to come down on their asking price by ten percent," Mauricio smiled.

"Make it twenty percent, they cover closing costs, and I'll take the condo. My financing is stellar and already in place, and since the house is empty, we can close this in lightning speed."

"Closing costs?" Mauricio stared at me in shock. "How about we offer half the closing costs."

"I don't need this place, but it seems like they *need* to sell. If the sellers are as motivated as you are making it seem, they'll take my offer."

"I'm not sure they won't be offended by this offer," Mauricio said, a bit thrown off by my resolve.

"I think it's a compliment." I smiled and folded my arms. "The house has been empty and on the market for six months, which brings up another issue for me. Things have been neglected. Let them know I also want them to pay for a warranty as well."

"You heard her," Dad smiled with pride.

"I'll give them a call and let you know what their answer will be. I guess that's it, then."

"I'm actually wondering if you could find out that answer now?" I batted my eyelashes at him. "I'd love to leave here," I waved my hand toward the oversized square window, "and imagine that in two weeks, this will be my morning view and a place where I may enjoy sunsets on my days off from long hours at the hospital."

"I'll see if they answer," he acquiesced.

"You really need to stop doing that," Dad said when the agent walked into the back room.

"Doing what? Acting like you?"

"No." He chuckled. "Flirting your way into a deal."

I smirked at my dad. "Just because I have that leg up on you doesn't mean I'm not going to use it, Papi. I want this place."

"Well, let's hope you didn't insult the sellers."

"It's negotiating." I briskly ran my hand over my dad's back. "That's all."

"They'll do it. Fifteen-day closing," Mauricio said with the same excitement as I felt jolt through my body. "Welcome to Los Angeles, Miss Alvarez."

"Thank you, Mauricio." I extended my hand to shake his. "Let's get the ball rolling on this place. My Papi already has my deadbeat baby brother living at home with him. He doesn't need me lounging around too." I arched my eyebrow at my dad.

"That's an understatement," Dad added. "Esteban hides out in the pool room now that his sister has come home to rule the roost."

"Stevie loves his sister being home, and you know it," I teased.

"Let's go sign some papers. We'll get this moving and get you in your new home fast."

"Thanks, Mauricio," I said with a smile. "We may have been obnoxious, but we had fun."

"I'd say I owe you a date for this sale, but I think you owe me." He smirked.

I laughed along with my dad. "Tell you what, if you can bust your ass and get me in my new place soon, I'll take you out," I offered. "For now, I'm starving. I saw a few taco trucks on our way here. I've so missed Southern California food and most definitely the taco trucks. Let's call this a business lunch, and I'll be one happy gal."

"Let's go, Laney," my dad said with a grin.

It was a done deal. My new job was in the bag, this beautiful condo was mine, and now I needed to see if I could handle the job and the doctor who'd opened up this position to make it all possible in the first place.

CHAPTER THREE
ELENA

I had just finished pulling my hair into a loose bun and prepping for my first day to observe Dr. Brooks at Saint John's Hospital. I should've been nervous, but I wasn't. I was eager to learn more about this side of the doctor whom I'd heard so much about.

"Laney," my brother hollered my name from downstairs.

One last slide of lipstick over my lips and a few pops and smacks of making sure it was evenly spread out, and then I snatched my purse on my way out of my room. I hopped down the stairs, my brother repeating my name as if I were still fourteen, and he was four.

"I'm right here," I said as he grumbled my name with impatience for the hundredth time since I'd pinned up my hair.

"About damn time," he said before continuing in a quieter voice. "Dad's lost his fucking mind."

"Easy on the language." I arched a big-sister eyebrow at him. "Seriously."

"Well, when Dad fills *you* in on his bright idea, my *perfect* sister might say a few choice words herself."

"We'll see about that." I reached over to poke his arm playfully. "Where's Dad? Or should I be more concerned about where his brain is?"

"He's eating breakfast by the pool."

I stopped walking and looked up at my brother's concerned

expression. Steve had grown to be such a handsome young man. More importantly, he was incredibly smart, so an average person could imagine how frustrating it was that his goal in life had morphed into pursuing his dream of becoming a full-time nightclub DJ. The kid had manipulated my mother into letting him move to California with Dad under the guise of attending better schools, and it seemed like no one could see his con except for me.

My older sister, Lydia, had given up on dealing with this particular subset of family drama when she was in grad school. Now, she was a hotshot lawyer at a top firm in Chicago, and she was on the fast-track to becoming a partner. The chances of her caring about Steve's lackluster goals for the future now were even smaller than before.

Part of me didn't know if I should cut the kid a break or not. He was no more than nine or ten years old when mom moved us to Florida, and her guilt for moving us from our father presented itself in allowing Stevie to slack off. Couple that with her starting to date and then eventually getting married, and maybe it was a fair assessment to say that Steve had slipped through the cracks more than a few times.

Who knew, maybe I was hypercritical, but it was hard being the one who begged her kid brother to at least take a couple of classes in community college until he found his true passion. Neither Mom nor Dad helped in getting Stevie motivated, and it drove me batshit crazy. How did Lydia and I work so brutally hard in college for so many years, and yet baby brother got to wake up at noon after stumbling through the door at dawn—much like this very morning—and wear Adidas sweatsuits all day?

"I can tell you're judging me and not saying anything, Laney," Steve said smugly.

I chewed on my bottom lip. "I'm just wondering why you're so upset with Dad. The look on your face tells me that whatever is up, you're not okay with it because it's not going to work with your professional tracksuit lifestyle," I said, waving my hand over his outfit.

"He's selling the house," my brother seethed in a low voice.

"Right." I cocked my head, studying his reaction. "You do realize that Dad retired at a relatively young age, and he has every right to do what's best for him, correct?"

He ran a hand through his thick black hair. "I've heard you say at least a million times that you love the memories of this house. You love being home and waking up in your bed, you love—"

"Stop right there." I reached for his arm and smiled. "I love all of this, yes, but I also bought my own home. I'm moving out as quickly as I moved in here. You haven't. If you're going to live on Dad's dime, then you have to deal with whatever comes with his decisions." I pinched his cheeks as I'd done since he was a baby. "Let's go find out if Dad's moving out of the country and if the nightclub life will work for you overseas."

I started toward the living room that overlooked the massive infinity pool. Dawn was displaying its painted hues for us to see on this glorious morning. The city lights muted the skies, but we could always see a soft pink color displayed with a sunrise on the west coast.

"Morning, Papi," I said, kissing his cheek. "Stevie isn't happy with you, so why don't you get straight to the point? I have to leave in fifteen minutes. Dr. Brooks' surgery is planned for seven, and I'm not missing out on my first day to watch this highly-esteemed surgeon do his thing."

Dad smiled after sipping his coffee. "Knowing Dr. Brooks, you probably should have been at the hospital hours ago. He's always there early. Which surgery is he performing?"

"Selective peripheral neurotomy," I answered with a smile. "Dr. Brooks is quite the daring doctor."

Dad smiled. "That he is; however, the man's arrogance is what drives him to work for medical breakthroughs. You will enjoy this."

I sipped on the coffee that Steve brought out and placed in front of me. "Let's wait until after this medical breakthrough has happened to praise the man."

"As a surgeon," my dad said, eyeing Steve sitting down, "it's always something to be praised when a patient wakes from surgery."

"Can we get to the real issue here?" Steve cut into the conversation, obviously annoyed.

I slid both hands around my coffee mug and let the warmth of it add to the soothing poolside sunrise. "Yes," I smiled at my flustered brother, then looked at Dad's stern expression. "What is this news that has Stevie staying up past his bedtime? Make it quick, Papi. The sun is rising, and your vampire son might burn in the daylight."

"I'm selling this house and moving to the ranch in Malibu," Dad answered with a challenging look to my brother.

"Really?" I asked, then looked at the watch on my wrist. "Well, this is not going to be a quick, five-minute conversation. Why don't we table this? I have to get out of here if you're right about Dr. Brooks starting surgeries early."

"It figures." Steve sat back in his chair and gripped the armrests as he looked at our father. "You cannot sell this house!"

"I'll do what I deem best for this family and myself," Dad growled as I stood.

I leaned over and kissed my dad on his forehead. "No fighting." I looked at Steve. "That includes you. We'll talk about this like adults when I get home tonight. It's not like my opinion matters in this, though. It's Dad's home to sell." I looked at Dad and smiled with some shock. "The ranch in Malibu? You really are concerned about your health, aren't you?"

"Doctors' orders were no more stress and to retreat to a quieter lifestyle."

"And no better place than our precious Manico Ranch."

"Go to work," Steve said in a whiny voice.

I walked over and kissed my brother on his head. "Be smart with your words, Esteban. You know what Dr. Mitchell and Dr. Xi said about Papi's health. He didn't retire because he *wanted* to. His health comes first."

Stevie reached up to pat my hand that I held on his shoulder. "We can't sell this house."

"We'll talk it all out later," I said.

"You two talk about me as if I'm not sitting right here," Dad smirked.

"Just like the old days." I shouldered my purse. "I'll see you both tonight."

To say I loved the atmosphere of Saint John's Hospital would have been an understatement. This place was like a five-diamond hotel, enhanced with waterfalls and walls illuminated with a soft light that gently changed colors.

When you walked through the entrance, you were greeted by a beautiful crystal chandelier that should have been entirely out of place, but instead, it was the focal piece that projected the richness of Saint John's. Indoor pillars lined the walls as if you'd walked into a palace.

There were elevators further down past the guest lobby and behind the square columns positioned throughout the large and open lobby.

In each of the square columns were holographic images that showed the hospital's exquisite outdoor grounds and different floors and wards. The other side of the column displayed numerous doctors, nurses, and staff, talking about Saint John's—those were on a loop and played facing where private seating was set for each area. This was all state-of-the-art architecture, and from what I'd learned since my first day here, Saint John's was remodeled and renovated by Dr. Brooks' father's architectural firm, so I wasn't surprised at the high-tech, modern nature of it all.

I smiled at the ladies who were hidden in the admittance and information alcove as if this were a grand hotel. I gave them a friendly wave, and then I was waiting with a group to get into the elevators that were fashioned to match the walls and disappear into them. It was a fun feature for a new person on their first day, especially when they were looking for the elevator, and the frigging wall opened up in front of them.

Now, four days in, I had it all down. And by now, I think it was abundantly clear to everyone that I was a smiley individual. So much so that it sometimes flat-out annoyed people. Strangely enough, in my opinion, when someone smiles a lot, it can tend to irritate the hell out of people with particular personality types. I couldn't help it, though, and so here I was, smiling at people in scrubs and a handsome yet cranky-looking older man, wearing his white doctor's coat.

The doctor held himself with great superiority over the rest of us who were *beneath* him and stood directly in front of the doors, hands in his pockets as if he held the greatest secret in the world and us little guys only dreamt that we were in on it.

As we filed into the elevator, Dr. Murdock—as the ID pinned to his lab coat stated—took his place at the front, my eyes drifted toward the doors. That damn smile of mine came back when the door opened, and he stepped out in front of me, his brisk and long strides carrying him through the long hallway that overlooked the atrium below on one side and walls of scenic images were backlit on the other. This place was enchanting.

"Off to snatch up Dr. Brooks," I softly said out loud as my badge let me into the gallery where I would find my place with two other colleagues and watch Dr. Brooks go to work.

"Good Morning, Dr. Alvarez," a chipper voice said from behind me. "Dr. Brooks is scrubbing in now."

"Thanks, Lacey," I said, knowing I wouldn't be changing into scrubs yet.

Today was going to be a full day, and I wasn't going to let the silence of this observation room let my mind drift to the fact that Dad was selling our home. The gravity of his decision was sinking in, and it was the last thing I needed on my mind. I began to wonder if there was something more about his health concerns that he wasn't telling us, but it was something I'd get to the bottom of later.

"You're the new neuropsychiatrist, aren't you?" an older man to my left greeted me.

"Only if she wishes to work for the haughty Dr. Brooks," a man said with humor from behind me.

I glanced back at the deep, confident voice and found it belonged to Dr. Mitchell, Saint John's cardio chief, and Dr. Brooks' best friend. The man was gorgeous, and that was an understatement, and he stood next to a man in an expensive suit who could've been his twin. *Must be his brother, Mr. Mitchell,* I thought. The Mitchell family owned Saint John's, and I knew the CEO of Mitchell and Associates was Mr. Mitchell, so this guy couldn't have been anyone else.

"Dr. Mitchell," I said, standing and turning to reach out and shake his hand.

"Dr. Alvarez," he smirked that same handsome smile I remembered from that night when I first met him and Dr. Brooks. "I see you're here bright and early."

"I am," I answered, his deep blue eyes a contrast to those beautiful sky-blue eyes of Dr. Brooks.

Great. I was standing in the company of the man who helped bring back all the memories I had erased from the night that I met Dr. Brooks. I had a feeling that if Dr. Brooks' flirting would've led me back to his hotel room, I probably would have signed a deal with the devil to experience one night with the man who was—hands down—the most handsome man I'd ever met in my life. Present company included.

Don't get me wrong, Dr. Mitchell and his brother, who was in conversation with another man in a fashionable suit, were gorgeous. Still, there was something about Collin Brooks that never left my mind, and I had to force that damn smile of his away, or I wouldn't have made it this far at Saint John's with his face lighting up every holographic wall.

"Dr. Alvarez," Mr. Mitchell said.

I looked over at him, and holy cow, this guy with his bright green eyes, black hair, and commanding air was too much for one girl to handle. My eyes couldn't help but drift to the man with dark blond hair sitting to his right. There was no way there could be this many gorgeous men in one area. Not even science could make something like this possible. Yet here I was being introduced to Mr. James Mitchell and Mr. Alex Grayson. Two of the youngest top executives in America.

"I guess this is Dr. Brooks' big day," I smiled at the three handsome men. "Not only are the executives who run the hospital here, but an ultra-famous, world-renowned cardio surgeon is here for this too."

"That's right," the man who'd introduced himself as Mr. Grayson said. "Though, I believe our opinions will pale in comparison to yours."

His smile was mischievous, leading me to believe that these three were in on some joke I didn't know about, but his eyes never wavered from mine.

"Yes, and I'm quite sure I'll be thrilled to work with and for Dr. Brooks after our interview today," I said, turning to sit, hearing the commotion of the surgical teams and the patient being brought into the room.

"I guess you're not one to judge the doctor by his extracurricular fun at conferences, then?" I heard the humorous voice of Dr. Mitchell say.

"That I can judge outside of the professional realm." I looked back at the teasing face of Dr. Mitchell. "And let's just say I hope that Dr. Brooks is as exciting to work with as he was a great entertainment for us when we first met."

Dr. Mitchell smirked, and his deep blue eyes twinkled. "What happened to that vibrant young woman who tricked him into believing you were hired already and without his consent?"

"She's sitting right here and ready to watch this man turn water into wine."

Dr. Mitchell laughed. "If only I could take a crash course in neurosurgery and be on this team."

"He wasn't too upset that I lied to him, was he?"

I had no idea why I asked the question.

"Well, he wasn't too happy when he learned the truth of your trickery."

His eyes widened semi-dramatically as he crossed his leg over his knee and leaned back.

My stomach sank. I felt the eyes of Mr. Mitchell and Mr. Grayson on me now, and I felt a bit foolish. What if I'd pissed off the chief neurosurgeon and was just now finding out about it? I'd find out after the surgery when I finally met with Dr. Brooks professionally this afternoon.

Just like that, I smiled, lifted my chin, and turned to watch Dr. Collin Brooks as he entered the surgical room. Heaven help me. The handsome men behind me prepped me so I wouldn't drool over the man who made surgeons' gear look good. His smile greeted those in the room, yet his piercing blue eyes told a different story.

He was there for his patient, and everything had better be pristine as he went to work in this particular spinal surgery. Beyond the man's beauty, I was captivated by how he commanded his surgical team and room. He didn't talk like an asshole. He talked like a surgeon who was determined to complete this surgery in a manner unlike any other doctor.

Maybe there were other doctors out there like Dr. Brooks, but I hadn't met one. Most were dry and a bit boring, mostly treating the patient and then moving on to the next subject. Not this surgeon, though. He was focused, and he filled us in on what he was doing with each cut, suction, and move he made. He explained why he did what he did, and he was captivating to watch.

I understood why my dad had passed the torch to him. Dad felt the same about his patients, and the knowledge that my dad's health was the reason I was watching Dr. Brooks and not him made my heart ache. There was no way in hell I was going home tonight and giving my dad crap about wanting to move to the ranch in Malibu. All it took was seeing the passion and care in Dr. Brooks to let me know that Dad didn't want to retire early, but he was forced to. Dad deserved to be happy and content, and I thanked God for allowing me to see my own father's passion play out in the surgical room through Dr. Brooks.

CHAPTER FOUR
ELENA

*T*he surgery lasted four hours, and it was phenomenal. As of right now, my assessment was this: Dr. Brooks was an absolute genius and a surgeon who was worthy of the praise he'd garnered. He complemented the refined nature of this institute. The family eagerly waiting for their loved one to wake from surgery would undoubtedly have a long recovery road ahead. Still, the execution was flawless.

The documentary makers in the observation gallery and I were left to wonder if this breakthrough surgery would work to give back the movement of the fifty-six-year-old man's legs after his accident. Time would tell.

Being a psychiatrist, I had to be grounded in the fact that experimental surgery may not work. I hoped with all my heart that this family was prepped for that possibility as well. Dr. Brooks may have done a stellar job today, but was this particular surgery ultimately going to be successful? Would it help this patient gain feeling again, let alone be able to walk? These were the things I would work on with Dr. Brooks. It was my job to help them cope with their outcomes and set realistic goals.

It was a matter of Dr. Brooks and me seeing eye-to-eye on these topics. I didn't need a doctor with a God complex destroying my voice of reason because of his ideas to move neuroscience forward. If Dr. Brooks and I were going to work together, I would have to be assured that he would not undermine my work while we consulted with future patients.

I would never know why they were leaving my willingness to work with Dr. Brooks up to me. It really should have been the other way around. I would never sit idly by and let a greedy doctor risk a patient's mental state all for the betterment of his reputation and in the name of science, but maybe that was the balance the administrators were hoping to achieve.

I had just sat down in the dining commons of the hospital. It wasn't as crowded today as it had been on previous days, but then again, it was one in the afternoon, and this must've been the time that this five-star restaurant place didn't see too many hungry families and staff.

I crossed my arms and looked up at the glass dome ceiling that added a beautiful light and airy feel to the restaurant. I had to give it up to whoever had a hand in designing this place. Ordinary hospitals had cafeterias, but I couldn't bring myself to refer to this place as such. It was as lovely as any nice restaurant I'd ever been in. I hadn't seen it at night yet, but I'm guessing they put candles on the tables and that the lights strung throughout the area twinkled and sparkled with magnificence. The designers had to be congratulated, and the chefs awarded something.

"Sis," I heard my brother call out, "why are you all alone?" He pulled out a chair across from me and sat in it. "Of all the people I know, you make best friends in minutes, but here you are, sitting by yourself like a loser."

It wasn't like my brother to volunteer to bring me lunch from my favorite taco truck, but there was no way I was going to argue with him when he texted me and suggested dropping by.

"That's because I told everyone that my hot date was on his way to meet me for lunch." I smirked as I grabbed my tacos, unwrapped the foil they were wrapped in, and examined the different salsas that he brought.

I decided on the extra spicy red sauce, doused my taco, and bit into the carne asada masterpiece, nodding my head while pointing at the taco to confirm how delicious it was. "Perfection," I said, smiling at Steve as he bit into his burrito.

He swallowed as his eyes drifted over my shoulder. "Holy shit," he said with wide eyes.

"Keep your mind out of the gutter, Esteban," I said. "There are gorgeous men and women all over this hospital, but don't get caught up in the façade. Remember, beauty is in the heart."

"Beauty? I guess I know what's on your mind." He shifted in his seat like he was ready to jump up.

I turned to see who my brother was gawking over. What do you know, Dr. Brooks had just joined Mr. Mitchell and Mr. Grayson at a corner table.

"Who are you looking at? What is wrong with you?" I asked, confused by the way Steve was acting. It was like he'd just ran into Al Pacino, and he didn't know if he should run over and ask for an autograph.

He looked at me in frustration. "You see that tall guy with the black hair? The businessman-looking guy in the blue tie? I've been waiting for like a year to speak with him, but I can't seem to get past the gatekeepers at that locked-down building he works in downtown."

"Get past the *gatekeepers?*" I questioned, finishing taco number one. I sat back in my chair, wiping my mouth with a napkin, and I folded my arms. "Now I know why you were so eager to bring me lunch. Spill it. I'm dying to know how you even know about Mr. Mitchell. Do you think someone like him wants to be stalked and harassed by someone like you?"

Steve's face fell, and I felt like I went a little too hard on him. Maybe I did.

"Earth to my little brother," I said, trying to snap his eyes away from looking up and over my shoulder. "You're *not* interrupting that man. Now, let's get back to why you showed up with my favorite tacos. What exactly did you come for, Stevie?"

"Yes, why would you dare interrupt the almighty Mr. Mitchell from his royal lunch?" I heard the voice I'd been focused on for the last four hours say.

I watched as Collin walked around, pulled out a chair, and sat next to my brother. Steve looked over at him in his dark blue scrubs and smiled broadly.

"If it isn't the amazing Dr. Brooks," he said, turning to shake his hand. "My dad's talked a lot about you. It's nice to meet you. I'm Steve."

"The pleasure is all mine, Steve," he said, then looked over at me. "You mentioned that your dad has spoken a lot about me, but has your sister?"

"Laney hasn't told me anything, actually," Steve responded with a knowing grin.

Collin arched an eyebrow at me, highlighting how impossibly gorgeous he was. "Laney, is it? I remember a young, vibrant woman named Elena. She was quite deceitful."

I wanted to shrink in my chair, but hell no. Not in front of him or my brother, both of whom seemed to be on the same team suddenly. "I prefer Dr. Alvarez, Dr. Brooks."

He smirked. "Very well, Dr. Alvarez." He looked over at my brother. "I overheard the word gatekeeper come from your mouth regarding my buddy's building. I can get you into the upper floors and seated directly in front of Mr. Mitchell," he glanced over my shoulder and smiled, "who does not seem to be impressed with his raw vegetables at the moment."

"You can?" My brother shot up.

I was stuck in stupid hormone land, gazing at Collin's eyes in the light of this room, the dark and light blond in his hair, highlighting some textured thing he did with it to make it look messy and youthful. It all worked. Everything about him worked. His sharp jawline, his biceps on full display with the way medical scrubs seemed to climb up and not stretch over muscles like regular shirt sleeves. He was glorious, and my lust for this guy was out of control. You could see he was in excellent shape, his features were perfection, and his smile was going to be the death of me.

"It's a deal." My brother shook Collin's hand as he stood, snapping me to attention after I'd tuned everything out while I was fantasizing like a fifteen-year-old.

"Wait, what's a deal? What are you two talking about?" I stood to try and meet the tall height of Dr. Brooks. "Hey, I'm sorry I tricked you or whatever I did in Vegas. It was all in fun, and I was enjoying the last night there. I knew I didn't have the job, and you would have the final word. It was just too much fun saying that I'd gotten the job, especially after you were so confident in dancing with me and stating I would be your future wife. Now, it's professional."

He smiled, and my stomach swarmed with butterflies. "Of course, it's professional, *Doctor Alvarez*," he acknowledged with a look that tinted my cheeks pink. "However, I'm still professionally acknowledging that whether or not you desire to work with me after our interview in thirty minutes, I made you a promise."

"And that was?" I was shocked the man didn't hate me for tricking him.

"That I am the man I proclaimed to be that night."

"And who was that?" I sat down in my seat, crossed my arms, and smiled.

Dr. Brooks' eyes glistened as he bit on the corner of his mouth. "Your future husband." He exhaled. "You see, Dr. Alvarez, you may have been enjoying the quirks and fun in teasing me with a little white lie that you were my new neuropsychiatrist that evening, but I wasn't playing around."

"Okay, then," I said carefully. "You're still willing to commit the rest of your life, and do the whole death shall part us thing after a salsa dance?"

"You'll see. Twenty more minutes, and your brother and I have an agreement." He leaned down, and I felt the coolness of his breath tickle my neck, "Help the poor boy buy a suit, won't you? Mr. Mitchell won't be as easily won over with a young man who's dressed like he's a groupie for Run-DMC. He may want to spice it up a little. If I have to—to make good on our deal—I'll have my designer help him out."

I glared at my conniving brother, and then at Dr. Brooks. "I have no idea what kind of lame deal you discussed while I was—"

"Lost in thought over me, I'm sure. I am quite attractive in scrubs." He chuckled.

Busted.

"I'll admit that yes, you are. However, I'm not spending a dime on my brother, no matter what ridiculous agreement you've come to."

"I think it's a fine idea," Collin said.

"I have no idea what the idea is, but if it requires you putting my brother in front of Mr. Mitchell for whatever crazy idea he might have, then I want no part of this. You can tell Mr. Mitchell that too."

"So, you'll lie to the chief neurosurgeon—"

"I let you down." I smiled at him.

"Imagine how depressing that was. I thought we'd be planning our wedding this week, and yet, here I am, about to get grilled by the most beautiful woman I've ever met in my life." He winked. "See you in fifteen minutes."

"Future wife?" My brother broke my gaze on Collin's shapely backside and brought it back to him.

"You know what they say about neurosurgeons," I said with a shrug.

Steve laughed. "He's coming over for dinner next week."

"Coming over? Stevie!" I sat up straight. "We need to figure out why our father has decided to up and sell our childhood home and move to the ranch. If there's anything I learned in surgery today, it's that he isn't going to be a happy man if his health is the real reason he retired early. Something else has to be up, and we aren't going to have Dr. Brooks over for dinner as a distraction."

"He's best friends with Dr. Mitchell, Laney. That's Dad's heart doctor," Steve answered. "Maybe Collin can fill us in?"

"With Dad sitting right there?" I shook my head. "And when did you start referring to him as Collin?"

"Since we made our deal."

"Good God." I rolled my eyes. "If Dr. Brooks wants to play into your dream of whatever it is you need from Mr. Mitchell, then he'll deal with me for giving you a false sense of hope."

"It's to start my new company."

I held my hand up. "Don't." I eyed him. "Now, thank you very much for my tacos. You're not going anywhere tonight. We're sitting down with Dad and getting to the bottom of his health issues and why exactly he wants to move to Malibu. Dad comes first just like I said this morning."

"Good luck with the interview," he said with a smile.

"You should have wished your luck to your new friend, Collin, not me. Right now, our interview may be going off-topic and a lot longer than I expected."

"Chill out, sis. He's cool."

"That's what worries me." I smiled. "Someone needs to kick your butt in the right direction, and I have a feeling Dr. Brooks just made my job a whole hell of a lot more difficult."

"And she cusses."

"Because you pissed me off," I snapped. "And for the record, I'm no saint. I use profanity. I just don't spew it everywhere, and especially in Papi's house. That's disrespectful."

"Love you, sis."

"You too."

Steve was way too jubilant for me not to leave this cafeteria in search of Collin's office to find out precisely what *Mr. Wedding Vows* said to strike a deal with my brother. Was I up against a mess with this man already? Time would tell. The last thing I needed was some cocky doc giving my brother insane ideas about overnight success. My brother needed to be grounded and have a healthy mindset. Collin seemed to balance both well. Who knew, maybe a few Cuban sandwiches would help the doctor talk sense into my brother.

CHAPTER FIVE
COLLIN

I sat in my office, going over the medical charts for a young woman that I had been trying to persuade to hold off on a craniotomy. For now, anyway. The brain lesions weren't life-threatening, and even though they were the cause of Jamie's mild headaches, they weren't something that called for surgery at this time.

I hated debating with patients when they were in pain and just wanted the fuck out of it. I understood their frustrations, and I was the first person in line to help fix that problem, but this patient was not a candidate for surgery. I only hoped she wouldn't seek out another, greedier doctor who would do the surgery. Some surgeons could get so distracted by seeing their success that they didn't consider the patient's aftereffects. I wasn't that surgeon. I believed myself to be the most patient man on the planet, and situations such as these proved that.

Knock. Knock.

"Come in," I said, knowing it was most likely my assistant, informing me that the woman who'd stolen my heart and soul that night in Las Vegas was here to learn more about me and determine if she would take the job as my neuropsychiatrist.

"Am I interrupting you?" Elena's voice—filled with sass and also professionalism—forced my eyes up from the CT scans I had been studying and to her flawless body that filled her business suit perfectly.

Damn that smile and those lively eyes. I was going to be lucky if she didn't eat me alive in here because the only question that I had for her was whether or not she'd go out to dinner with me tonight.

I offered a smile in return, and this was the second time I watched as our eyes locked, and then her cheeks turned the most beautiful shade of pink in response. Thank God I did *something* to her because she had no idea what being in her presence did to me.

I rose and waved my hand over my office chair. "Looks like you get the boss's seat, and I get the hot seat, Dr. Alvarez."

"I'll sit here," she smirked as she sat at the seat on the other side of my desk.

I cleared my throat—and my head—and reached over to her file. "So, I suppose this is to be our first official interaction since you blatantly deceived me at the medical conference," I said. I thumbed through her resume and notes from staff before I ended at her handwritten statement as to why she would be a perfect asset to my team. I folded my arms, sat on the corner of my desk, and watched her squirm.

"Again, I am really sorry about that." She tried to cover a smile.

"Imagine my disappointment and rage to learn that we are expected to begin our working relationship with little white lies," I said.

"And imagine my disappointment and rage to learn that you're going to use my little brother to get back at me for that too."

I chuckled and walked over to sit—more professionally—behind my desk. "You played the wrong man, Elena."

"Dr. Alvarez," she corrected me, crossing her legs and clasping her hands together around her knee.

"May I ask why you're so insistent upon me referring to you as a doctor, *Doctor*?"

"Professionalism."

I pursed my lips. "Curious. I have read through all your previous interviews with the hiring panel, and you insisted upon them calling you Elena." I looked up at her from the papers I pretended to scan over, "Am I to understand that, out of all of the respected doctors and administrators in this hospital that you've interviewed with, *I* am the only one you deem to be a professional? I have to say that I am utterly flattered that you show me such a level of esteem."

She smiled, and her bronze eyes lit up. "I only insist upon that level of professionalism for doctors who run around with a crazy idea that they're my intended husband."

I laughed and tossed her folder on my desk, something very unlike me. Everything in my office, surgical rooms, staff, ward, and every other single thing I touched was in order and placed in an orderly fashion. That fundamental aspect of my personality seemed to have faded from the moment this little ray of sunshine sat across from me.

"Well, I'm thoroughly impressed with all I've read, and now it's time to answer some of the questions you might have for me," I said.

She straightened up in her chair. "Yes. My first question is about the patient you operated on today. Did you do so knowing that man would walk again?"

She was cutting right to the chase, and I liked it. I clasped my hands together and leaned forward on my desk. "I operated on Mr. Hawthorne after he came to me and wished to have a better outcome in life. His car accident wasn't something he would allow to continue to rob him of the normal life he once had. Numerous rehabs weren't helping, either."

"You didn't answer my question." She arched an eyebrow. "Will he walk again, or—"

"I'm ninety percent sure that in three days, you and I will walk down to his room and see that he has muscle movement in his legs. We removed the damaged nerves, allowing Mr. Hawthorne's brain to receive signals from his healthy nerves so that he can have muscle movement in that location again."

"Fascinating," she answered.

"As much as I enjoy hearing that come out of your mouth and in such a beautiful way, I believe you understand very well that, in neuroscience, there's not an immediate answer with what we do. Especially when we are working with the nervous system and most definitely the peculiar way every brain works differently. It's always a waiting game."

"No, I understand that. That's why you'll have me at your side. I'll be the one sharing what we can do together to help patients who've undergone surgeries, such as the one you did today. I would help them accept their new lives and give counsel if the surgery didn't help change their current predicament."

"So, if Mr. Hawthorne wakes to find that he still cannot feel his legs despite my best efforts today in the operating room?"

"I'm willing to help him accept his current situation."

"Wrong answer." I smiled. "We fixed his current situation, but time must be waited out, or we fail in helping our patients recover."

"You're that sure of yourself?" she questioned with some irritation.

"I wouldn't have performed the surgery if I weren't. I've studied this for years, and the science behind it makes perfect sense."

"But it will take time, and I will be there for him, encouraging him every step of the way to not give up."

"And now we have two minds thinking on the same level," I answered, relieved that she was as brilliant, open, and understanding as she was captivatingly stunning. "Any other questions?"

"When you are working with your patients or when a neurologist calls you in for a surgical consultation for their patient," she paused, eying me as I studied her, "is your answer always surgery?"

I laughed. "Funny you should ask." I pointed to the chart I had set aside. "Those records belong to a young woman who moved from Colorado to Southern California to be in my care. She's been my patient for two years, and I have put off surgery that she's all but begged me to perform. She was twenty when her accident happened. She hit her head on the playing field in a soccer tournament. After studying her initial charts, I saw that this particular injury caused multiple lesions to continue to appear throughout her brain. Up to now, I have only done stereotactic brain surgery to remove the threatening lesions and keep her recovery minimal. Her minor headaches do not make her a candidate for a craniotomy at this time, no matter how much she begs."

"Wait a minute, awake brain surgery?"

"Yes." I knew she understood the term, but her adorable expression had me silent and waiting for the comment that I knew was coming next.

"No human in their right mind *begs* for that."

"Agreed."

"Yet your patient is begging you, Dr. Brooks."

"She is. Her fiancé cradles her, she sobs, and I have to watch all of that after I reveal that her latest CT scans still do not make her a candidate for the surgery."

"You and I both know that's heartless."

"Is it?" I questioned, seeing this issue cause my future neuropsychiatrist some discomfort.

"It's what the patient moved here for, right? So, the world-renowned neurosurgeon can help her? If she's begging for this type of surgery and cries in defeat when you tell her no, what good are you to her?"

"And what if I make the greedy mistake of trying to eliminate one of the small lesions, then something happens, and she can never walk again? Will that have been worth her craniotomy to get rid of minor headaches?"

"Minor headaches don't always feel so minor to those suffering with them." She sat back and studied me. "I've never met a surgeon who isn't willing to put their patients under the knife to fix their problems. Usually, surgery is *always* the answer."

"Yet here you sit in front of the *world-renowned* neurosurgeon," I grinned, "and he's telling you that surgery isn't always the answer. Even if it's heartless for me to refuse them their wishes concerning surgery."

"Intriguing."

"I care about each patient I have. Even if they think they know what's best for them, I believe it to be my responsibility to guide them in the safest direction. For now, anyway. Jamie is twenty-six, and her boyfriend, Paul, just proposed to her. She will continue to be my patient, but I plan to revisit her charts monthly unless the headaches worsen. I have new scans coming to me today—" I glanced up at the clock. "If the damn things arrive before her appointment this afternoon. I guess Saint John's is suddenly understaffed, and I wasn't informed."

"Damn, I wish I could be with you for that," she said, ignoring my apparent frustration that I didn't have my patient's current scans yet, and I wanted a bit of time to go over them before I walked in and broke Jamie's heart...again.

"If I were to bring you in when I meet with Jamie and her family this afternoon, what would the stunning Dr. Alvarez say to her that I already haven't?"

"Well, I would do my best to work to keep her mindset positive and reinforce that she is in the hands of a doctor who is helping her, even though her headaches are telling her that he isn't. That she needs to trust that you have her best interest in mind, and that there is more at risk than I think she knows." She pursed her lips. "You are sure that she isn't a candidate for surgery? You're willing to avoid something that could change her life for the better because you're not the surgeon who believes surgery is always the answer?"

"Trying to use my words against me, Dr. Alvarez?"

"I need to understand it all completely," she answered confidently. "Forgive me for saying this, but neurosurgeons are known to be arrogant assholes. My dad passed the torch to you, saying you were the greatest arrogant ass out there, too. I'm just trying to ensure that you're not completely on the opposite end of the spectrum with your judgment in preventing this young lady from having a better chance at life."

"Is that so?"

"Or perhaps you're doubtful of your ability to perform this surgery with no complications, and that's why you don't want to take more risk than necessary."

"I'm not sure if you can tell, but I'm hardly doubtful of my skill, myself, or much of anything else."

"Like I said, an arrogant ass." She grinned.

She wasn't wrong to push me about Jamie because the truth was that I had been going back and forth with myself about doing the craniotomy for quite a while. Elena was making me admit to myself that, like it or not, it was time to make a move.

"The lesion on Jamie's frontal lobe is the largest of them all. This one concerns me the most, but there is another one on the parietal lobe that I've been monitoring closely, and when I heard she was experiencing numbness in her right hand, I called for this meeting today. I ordered more scans; barring some unforeseen act of healing, I think I will be confirming her candidacy for surgery today. Now, I hope you accept the offer to work solely as my neuropsychiatrist because you are the reason I have concluded that I will be performing these surgeries at all. That is, of course, if you agree to be my psychiatrist and work with her and me as I map her brain and repair these lesions."

I stood, and she stood with me. "I did what? Wait. What?" she asked, looking confused as hell.

"Are you second-guessing your decision to help me help this young woman?"

"No, but you made a decision based on *our* conversation?"

"You gave me the nudge I needed. There's nothing wrong with me being on the fence about something and having a beautiful and intelligent woman like yourself push me off, is there?" I walked past her and licked my suddenly dry lips when I made eye contact with her stunning bronze irises. "Let's agree that Jamie will have you to thank for becoming a candidate for surgery today."

"I didn't say anything," she said in some bewildered tone.

"Well, you need to *say something* now. Will you or will you not be my personal neuropsychiatrist? I have a patient who is waiting for me to deliver some good news."

"Of course, I will. When will you perform the surgery?"

"I will allow the family to determine that, given we have the holidays coming up, and she may not want to be in a recovery unit when Santa comes," I teased.

I glanced back at her confused expression, and I couldn't blame her bafflement. I'd surprised myself by making the decision without looking at Jamie's new scans. Unfortunately, one thing was certain; the lesions were growing. Elena was intelligent in her questions, and she'd pressed on the one point I had been avoiding myself—Jamie's quality of life was suffering, so why not fix these lesions and be done with it? I just needed a small push in the right direction, and Elena gave that to me.

"I believe that you and I will make a fantastic team," I said, opening my office door.

"I still can't believe it took you sitting down with me to figure this out."

"I suppose it just took me meeting the right person, Dr. Alvarez, a doctor who I can trust, to give me the willpower to stop putting this off. Now to confirm, are you willing to perform this surgery with me?"

"I haven't proven anything to you that I would be a great help."

"Ever heard of trusting one's instincts, Dr. Alvarez?"

"Marriage again?" she teased with a smile.

I grinned. "As I said, I'm a patient man. I will wait for you to come to your senses about me and our future," I teased, loving the new facial expressions and reactions I got from her over that. "It's just a matter of time. I believe that, with your will and determination, we'll work together in a perfect balance to consult Jamie this afternoon." I held a hand up, "No jumping to the other side of the table if she cries, though."

She chuckled. "I'll do whatever I believe is in the best interest of the patient."

"Our patient," I informed her. "And that's why I'm willing to do this surgery. We will be successful together, and I look forward to having you at my side."

"I look forward to seeing a patient—who's waited a year for you to fix this issue—hear that you will help them, giving them the best news of their lives."

"Her name is Jamie," I said. "Unlike you, she's entirely comfortable with using first names."

She laughed, and the delightful sound sent a shiver through me. Her radiant smile, her genuinely happy laugh, her body language—she was completely open, light, and cheerful, and she sent blood rushing to every part of my body.

"So, before I leave to find out where Jamie's current scans are, I must know, are you excited to become the arrogant ass's personal neuropsychiatrist?"

"I am!" she proudly said.

"Good." I raised my eyebrows in humor. "I have some charts that need to be filed away. You can start there." I pointed to the file cart that my secretary, June, had rolled to the corner of my office, and I winked and walked past Elena. "Good to have you on the team, Dr. Alvarez."

After my office door closed behind me, I withheld my laughter and kept my composure.

"June," I said after she got off her phone call.

"Dr. Brooks," she answered with a smile. "Well, is Elena going to stick around?"

"She lets you call her Elena too?" I questioned in disbelief.

"She's told all of us that she prefers it."

I strummed my fingers on the high desk that June hid behind. "Interesting." I sighed. "Well, she'll be quitting on us soon enough if you don't get in there and clean up your filing mess."

"Oh, fairy darts!"

"Fairy darts?" I asked my jubilant assistant, who was majorly in the Christmas spirit, as her Grinch-themed scrubs and flashing Christmas pins showed. "That's a new one."

"Fairy darts," she said as she rolled her eyes. "It's part of the lore."

"A lore I want no part of it would seem. And find a new term, please, or *Elena* will quit on us for sure. I don't think she realizes you are secretly obsessed with woodland creatures."

June laughed and nodded. "I need to bring those files downstairs. I'm sorry I didn't get around to it before your appointment today, Dr. Brooks."

"No worries, June-bug. It was a good way to get Dr. Alvarez back for a little prank she played on me before we met professionally."

"Oh?"

"Oh, indeed," I said in a mischievous tone. "Sorta like throwing a fairy dart and hitting the bullseye on that one."

She frowned. "That is not a fairy dart, Dr. Brooks."

"God forbid I upset the fairies for insulting whatever the hell a fairy dart is." I feigned fear. "Can you please tell Dr. Alvarez to get Jamie Peterson's file off my desk and meet me in conference room five? My patients are due there at any time, and I have a feeling she's scrambling to figure out where the filing cabinets are for the cart of files you *hid* in my office."

"I'll get on that."

I loved June immensely. One would naturally pin her for being the nutjob on the floor, but she was a hard-ass worker, and I wanted for nothing when it came to her. However, I did feel that she and her fairy darts—whatever the hell that was about—coupled with pranking Elena would have me on my toes.

CHAPTER SIX
ELENA

I sat in awe of Dr. Brooks as he spoke with the Peterson family. I watched Paul, Jamie's fiancé, tear up along with Jamie and her parents as Collin delivered the good news. The whole situation was an emotionally charged experience and a perfect reminder of why I entered this work field.

"In moving forward," Dr. Brooks said as he glanced toward the charts he'd intently studied on our way down to this conference room, "those charts make me truly grateful that I listened to our new neuropsychiatrist's advice today.

"The lesions have put me in a position not to be able to give you an option to wait until after the holidays. For this, I am sorry, but we'll get you on the road to recovery, and that's all that matters." He subtly smiled at the family who sat across from us around the long, polished table. "Now, I won't be using the 3D images and devices that I used in stereotactic brain surgery." He nodded toward where I sat at his right. "This surgery requires my neuropsychiatrist to guide me instead of computers."

"Dr. Collin," Jamie said, sniffing and taking tissue from the box Dr. Brooks picked up and extended toward her, "I'm not worried about this surgery interfering with the holidays. This is the best Christmas gift I could have asked for."

Dr. Brooks softly laughed, and I couldn't help but smile. "I'm happy to hear that I was able to one-up your handsome fiancé for gift exchanges this year." He grinned over at the ecstatic young man. "I know we are all grateful this is moving forward, and I'm quite sure," he slowed down those last three words as he eyed at Jamie playfully, "you've done all the research under the sun *and* the moon to understand exactly what will happen while we perform this surgery. Even with what I've already explained—and your own research—I'd like to turn this part over to the one who will be at your side during the surgery." He shifted to face me, and his twinkling blue eyes locked with mine. To prevent me from falling victim to the gorgeous man's gaze, I carefully pulled my eyes from Collin's and smiled at Jamie.

"Thank you so much, Dr. Alvarez." Jamie looked at me eagerly. She blotted the corners of her eyes with her tissue as she choked up again. "I'm sorry. This is just overwhelming and such great news, especially since my headaches have gotten worse."

"I'm so very happy for you, Miss Peterson—"

"Jamie, please. Call me, Jamie," she sniffed again and smiled at Dr. Brooks before bringing her attention back to me.

"And if it makes you more comfortable, you may call me Elena."

"You see?" Dr. Brooks interrupted with a broad smile. "This is why she'll be an amazing asset to my team. She is comfortable using her first name instead of being one of those super uptight physicians who always want to be called *doctor*."

"Yeah, those kind sound like the worst," Paul said as Jamie and her family laughed.

"Oh, you have *no idea*. So obnoxious, right, Elena?" Collin said as he glanced at me with a hint of smugness that was wildly charming and almost irresistible to me for some strange reason. "All of us being on this first-name basis is fantastic. What a wonderful way to be comfortable together in the OR. I would have it no other way."

"I agree. I really appreciate that, thank you," Jamie answered both of us with a smile.

"Absolutely," I said, keeping a smile on my face through Collin's buffoonery. Aside from wanting to roll my eyes and elbow the man in the ribs, I was a bit shocked the young woman was happy at the idea of awake brain surgery. I'd never met anyone who was *okay* with this. "As Dr.

Brooks mentioned, I will be the one at your side during your surgery. Dr. Brooks revealed earlier the details of using the electrical probe to ensure that he will not be anywhere near the good tissue and causing any damage to any part of your brain." I paused to ensure I was on track with the doctor and the patient. "That is where I come in. After you are pulled out of sedation, you will have enough medication to keep you relaxed. Since your brain has no pain receptors, there will be no need for sedation or heavy drugs for him to fix the problematic lesions. You and I will have lots of time to talk in that room." I smiled at her. "Dr. Brooks will rely on our communication and me to relay information about your responses to him, and he will be able to maximize his pursuit to fix the lesions. Does this make sense?"

"I've probably read everything ever written about this procedure, so I think I've got a grasp on it." She chuckled. "But I'm delighted you'll be there."

"So, now that is all cleared up," Dr. Brooks chimed in. "If you lose your ability to recite the alphabet backward or you forget how to make pancakes," he pointed his thumb toward me, "it's all on this beautiful doctor who you'll have the privilege to talk to during your surgery."

"Dr. Brooks!" Jamie scolded him as she and her family nearly roared with laughter—not a response I would've expected, but at least they had a sense of humor. "I can think of no better person to have at my side. When are we doing this?"

"As much as I know you'd love to walk out of the room right now and run into the OR, we're not doing it today," Dr. Brooks said while I laughed at this woman's cheerfulness. "Once I have all the consent I need —" He paused, looked at her parents, fiancé, me, then the patient, "which I believe we're all in, yes?"

"All in," she said, crying tears of happiness again.

"Very well, then. I will begin freeing up mine and Dr. Alvarez's schedules, and I believe I can push out my Thursday appointments this week. I will inform my secretary that this Thursday will be dedicated to taking care of the young woman who has been eagerly awaiting getting back the quality of life she once had before these lesions began interfering with it."

Dr. Brooks stood, and the rest of us followed his lead.

"I really don't know what to say. I'm so grateful," Jamie said.

"Have patience with me. I need Patty to clear up this Thursday, and from there, I will have Patty call you to confirm the time and dates of pre-op."

"Patty hasn't had the baby yet?" Jamie's mother asked while Jamie and her fiancé fell into a tight and loving embrace.

Dr. Brooks grinned that sexy smile of his. "Not yet. I tried to get her to take her maternity leave two weeks ago," Dr. Brooks said as he picked up Jamie's files from the table, "given it's her first child, and her husband is serving the country overseas. I wish for her to be comfortable and fully prepared for the little one's arrival, but she's not budging. She probably hopes she'll go into labor while she's on the clock and in walking distance from the hospital." He chuckled.

"She probably feels safer, knowing there's a doctor around," Jamie's dad said.

"Hey, I've told her time and again that I'm a neurosurgeon, not an OB. She knows me better than that." He laughed.

"You're not just a neurosurgeon, Dr. Collin. You're a miracle worker," Jamie's mom laughed along with the rest of us.

A miracle worker who will probably get me into a lot of trouble, I thought as we said our farewells and left the room.

After we walked away from the Petersons, Dr. Brooks whipped out his cell and called his office. I listened as he handled the call and followed him as we returned to his office.

He took the files that June handed him while he worked out the details of opening up his schedule with Patty on the phone. I watched as other staff around the area appeared to look over at him as if he were some kind of god.

He missed nothing and no one. He shot a smile at those who greeted him in passing, he gave a quick punch to a young doctor's arm as we passed the nurses' station, and even gave a nod or two toward the interns who gawked at him—gawking like I must've been doing since we left the meeting with Jamie Peterson. It reminded me of those teen shows where the star of the football team walks through the hallways of his school and everyone is high fiving him or smiling. His charisma radiated to everyone around him, and he knew it.

I watched him ease his right hand on his taut waist as he continued discussing moving his patients around to free up Thursday. His voice was calm yet assertive as he worked with another doctor to take one of his patients due to a scheduled surgery that the two would be doing together next week.

With his white lab coat removed, I had a perfect vantage point, standing behind him and enjoying his firm ass in his scrubs. I was beginning to wish I didn't have female hormones that suddenly loved to betray me with this man around. I couldn't take my eyes off of him. His perfect back muscles flexing nicely through his scrub top. Don't get me started with the forearms, broad shoulders, and biceps. There was nothing but beautiful perfection built there. I wouldn't expect anything less, though. He was a neurosurgeon, and he needed the steady hands— and so, he had the arm muscles to keep that all in check. Yes. That's it. That's the reason he was built so muscularly perfect, and I was feeling those stupid butterflies flooding my stomach again while I imagined him taking off his shirt so I could get a glimpse of how well he was defined.

He hung up the phone, and that's when I felt the heat blaze across my cheeks. *Shit!* What was I supposed to do, fan myself like an old lady who'd caught the Holy Ghost in an Alabama church service?

He slid the phone onto his desk, picked up the files June had given him, and turned to face me. He leaned back against his desk, and his eyes went to the charts he held.

"So, *doctor*," he started, my cheeks cooling down just in time for his icy blue eyes to meet mine. "Oh, I forgot, we're on a first-name basis now, right, Elena?"

"No," I said, my palms sweating.

What the hell? This was a problem I'd never experienced before unless Dad was grilling me about something.

He arched an eyebrow at me. "Well, I feel more comfortable calling you Elena."

"I don't," I said, honestly. God, the way my name rolled off his tongue. The way he said it was sexy, even if he was only teasing me. I couldn't do sexy with this man. I couldn't do *anything* with this man so long as I got butterflies in my stomach around him, my cheeks heated up to a feverish temperature, and my palms started sweating.

"May I ask why that is?" he asked, and I could sense that the flirty side of the man, Collin, had vanished, and I was left to stare at Dr. Brooks and his solemn and curious blue eyes. "I sincerely do not wish to make you uncomfortable in my presence or my ward. We need to come to some kind of agreement outside of this Dr. Brooks and Dr. Alvarez nonsense. Even if you don't return my feelings," he started thumbing through his charts as if this were any other conversation, "which you eventually will," he looked up at me and flashed that irresistible cheeky grin of his and then looked down at his charts again, "you and I need to be a bit more comfortable in each other's presence, wouldn't you say?"

"I say we keep it professional and move in that direction as we get to know each other," I answered with a smile, finding my bearings.

His phone buzzed, and all he did was smirk as he answered it, put it on speaker, placed it aside, and continued looking at his charts again.

"Dr. Mitchell?" he answered. "You're on speaker. Talk."

"Pull me off speakerphone if you're in the company of a group of staff, please," Dr. Mitchell answered with annoyance in his voice.

"You're in the company of Dr. Alvarez and me. We're alone in my office," he said.

"Dr. Alvarez? Ah, Elena," Dr. Mitchell said, realizing Collin wasn't referring to my father. "How are we enjoying the cocky neurosurgeon? Are you going through with this professional marriage agreement?"

"Hold up." Collin's eyes met mine after setting the charts to the side and picking up his phone. "She *allows you* to call her Elena? I thought she preferred Dr. Alvarez?"

Jake started laughing then was cut off when he was interrupted on his end of the phone. Collin folded his arms as he studied me with a look that made me swallow the instant lump that formed in my throat. Trying to keep it professional with him was starting to backfire on me. If he only knew why I would rather keep it to professional names.

He hit the mute button on his phone. "You mean to tell me that you're more comfortable with Dr. Mitchell than the guy you'll be helping to guide through a brain-mapping craniotomy?"

"Dr. Mitchell? You mean Jake?" I teased, now able to hold my own under his humored yet somewhat baffled expression. Something told me that working with Dr. Collin Brooks was going to be highly enjoyable.

"Yes, I mean Jake. Dr. Mitchell. Jacob Mitchell." He pulled his phone off mute as he narrowed his eyes at me teasingly, and Jake came back on. "Jacob Allan Mitchell," he said with a shit-eating grin.

"Hey, now," Jake came back. "Who the hell are you suddenly, my dad? Or has my brother taken full possession of my best friend?"

"It's the name that Elena—pardon me, *Doctor Alvarez*, just informed me that you prefer. Is this shit true too?" Collin said, pinching his lips and closing his eyes.

"You're lucky as hell that you're still in the process of trying to keep Elena working for you."

"So, what shall we all call each other then?" Collin looked at me while I heard Jake sigh on the other end of the phone.

"I told you, Dr. Alvarez. Jake can call me Elena if he's comfortable with it. We already had that conversation earlier."

Collin's lips rose dangerously sexy on one side, "Very well, then, Dr. Alvarez."

"Listen, I hate to interrupt you two already bickering, but I have a very thrilled Mrs. Irene Waller down here. She's getting ready to leave the cardiac unit today, and I told her I'd see if her second favorite doctor would like to come down and say his goodbyes."

"You tell my spicy little Irene I'm on my way and that I have a good friend I'm bringing with me. A doctor that I'll be putting her in contact with too."

"Should I inform her that it's Dr. Alvarez or Elena who will be joining you in sending her off today?"

Collin rubbed his forehead. "You see the madness this is causing the entire hospital, don't you?" he seemed to feign annoyance while Jake laughed.

"I see the madness it's causing you." I found my game and rhythm again and was so grateful to God I had. Collin was fun, and his reactions were priceless. I seriously never expected a neurosurgeon to be this enjoyable.

"Let's go before we hurt ourselves."

"Work out your kinks before you both walk onto my hospital floor, please?" Jake laughed then the line died.

"I believe I told you that you are playing the wrong doctor," Collin said as he picked up the charts on his desk.

"You did," I answered as we walked out of his office.

"June-bug," he handed her the charts. "Keep these out, please. Dr.

Alvarez and I have a quick visit to make on the cardiac floor, and we'll return in about thirty minutes to make these rounds together."

"Yes, doctor."

"Dr. Brooks," I said.

"I prefer Collin," he said as we walked through the nurses' station, prompting heads to pop up and look at him like he'd lost his damn mind.

No, he hadn't lost his mind. He was making me probably the most entertained I'd been working in any hospital with and around doctors since my intern days. The man was fun, quirky, and highly intriguing. And even though this whole Dr. Alvarez thing was getting old to even me, I figured it was more enjoyable than not to watch him get a bit flustered that everyone got to call me Elena except for the one man I loved hearing say my name the most.

If he only knew I was struggling to keep my professional composure with these sudden hormonal rushes around him, he'd understand exactly why we needed to steer clear of him saying my name in his youthful, sexy voice—his voice that had a certain raspiness that turned me on by that alone. Time would tell how long I'd be able to keep up the *doctors and professionalism only* basis with him.

I was a down-for-whatever kind of gal, and there was undeniable chemistry between us. I could feel it without needing to have more than these small interactions. I could see it in his eyes. Though he teased me with the professionalism stuff, I could tell he wanted more, but how much more? I wasn't afraid of commitment, but who knew how the handsome doctor who turned heads everywhere he went felt about that. That's why I was going to keep him at arm's length and enjoy this for now.

CHAPTER SEVEN
ELENA

*D*r. Brooks and I walked onto the cardiac floor. We were greeted by an extravagant outer waiting room—one of the ones where families could comfortably sit if they were not dealing with a family emergency.

I was more than impressed with how the hospital atmosphere at Saint John's was fashioned to be relaxed and carried with it a soothing ambiance to keep visitors comfortable and most likely to feel like they were in the atrium of a large, exquisite hotel. I'd seen most of this in pictures, but to be here and experience in person was unreal.

We walked down the hall opposite the intensive care floor and turned into a hospital room that matched the exquisite feel of this place.

"There's my hot tamale!" Dr. Brooks said when the patient came into sight.

"Dr. Collin," the elderly woman who sat on the side of her bed, dressed and ready to leave, said with a smile. "You're as handsome as the day you saved my life."

I followed Collin and smiled over at who I assumed were her children in the room.

"That was over a year ago, Irene," he said, sitting next to her on the side of her bed. "As I told you then, I'm like a fine wine. I just get better—"

"With age," she chuckled and patted his leg.

Very original for the witty doctor, I thought with a smile.

All this *professionalism* and hardcore doctor stuff I'd learned in school and experienced in hospitals as an intern faded when I watched Collin bring his arm around the sweet and tiny elderly woman. I could almost imagine this woman to be his grandmother or a great aunt, but she wasn't. His warmth drew everyone to him, and he was such a natural at being a star.

I grew more curious by the second about what had happened to her and why she was the patient of both a neurosurgeon and a cardio doctor.

"She wouldn't budge until she had an opportunity to see you one more time," a woman in her fifties added from across the room.

Collin grinned, and Irene's sharp eyebrow arch validated what the woman had said about her. "Well, I'm not surprised, Gail," Collin said, glancing to the woman behind him and back to Irene. "I believe I told my young crush here that I was owed at least a small turn on the dancefloor if she promised to allow Dr. Mitchell to fix her up and get her back on her feet again."

Irene smiled over at me. "Before I grant you that dance, young man, is this beautiful young lady my new doctor?"

Collin's humored expression met mine. "She is," he said, and I kept my cool, trying not to fall victim to his eyes and smile again. This sweet interaction between Collin and Dr. Mitchell's patient was enough to make my heart swell. I'd never witnessed a doctor *this* close and caring of a patient before. It was endearing, to say the very least.

"She's not talking because she has these moments, you see," Collin said, pulling my mind off of the elderly woman whose makeup was done, complete with bright pink lipstick and matching blush.

"Moments?" I questioned with a smile and walked over to Irene. "Hello, Irene." I reached out to shake her frail hand. "I'm Dr. Alvarez, but you can call me Elena if you'd like." I eyed Collin and smiled. "Dr. Brooks has informed me that I am going to be quite fortunate to have you as one of my new patients."

"Elena," she smirked, eyeing Collin, then bringing her attention back to me. "I am happy to meet you. Dr. Mitchell explained a bit about what you'll be doing as my doctor, and I have to say, I might not be your favorite patient."

"What makes you think so?" I asked, teasing back to the sass in her voice.

"Well," Collin interjected as he arched an eyebrow at the lady, "she doesn't like to follow the rules. She was supposed to stay on her medications, but one day she decided she didn't need them anymore. That executive decision led to multiple TIAs and me having to call in the cardiac doc to have a stint put in on top of the shunt I'd already placed so we can keep my favorite lady around."

"I just get to the point where it's hard to imagine that I'm eighty-three," she said in defeat. "I guess that's why I ignored my doctor's orders."

"And imagine my despair to know I was about to lose you again." The family remained quiet as Collin and Irene sat side-by-side on her bed, talking more seriously. "I can't go through this again, and if you end up breaking my heart and making me a patient of Dr. Mitchell's, I don't think he or I will ever forgive you."

"I guess this is where I come in," I said, listening to Collin and Irene communicate. Collin used a serious yet teasing method of trying to keep this sweet woman on her medication and out of the hospital. I could instantly sense her depression when she admitted to accepting that she wasn't a young woman anymore. "We'll work together. I want you to remember that it doesn't matter how old we are when it comes to taking medication. Age is most certainly just a number, and that medication is going to keep you feeling great, strong, and as youthful as you believe yourself to be."

"No, age is *not* just a number, Dr. Alvarez," she came back, still sad and with a hint of annoyance.

Collin frowned and studied me, waiting for my response after I seemed to piss off his patient. This was my specialty, though. My job was to ensure people could psychologically understand and accept a positive outcome to any adverse situation that may have altered their lives. Whether it was the sinking feeling of allowing one's age to spin them out to depression, injury of a car accident, or even paralysis, it was my job as their psychiatrist to help them cope. Helping a neurosurgeon perform a craniotomy was just a bonus of being at a patient's side while helping the surgeon and his patient through that particular process.

"Perhaps you are correct," I said with an unwavering smile. "Some, even younger than I am, believe that they're older than they appear. They even act like it too."

"That's impossible."

"Oh, it's quite common." I smiled at Irene, who was looking to Collin for whatever reason. "You'd be surprised at how many young people have wasted their days, plopped onto a couch lost in the television, napping all day, never wanting to leave the house for some reason or another."

"Absurd," she sat up and stared at me. She looked back at her family, then to me again, "Before this last incident, my kids back there couldn't even keep up with me."

"I bet," I said. "Let me guess. You're not the type to sit around the house and act like you're over a hundred years old like a lot of middle-aged people do?"

She gave me the most adorable smug grin. "Not a chance," she cackled. "I've been all over the globe. I just returned from a trip to Australia to see my oldest boy. I go to Reno all of the time to gamble, and I never miss square dancing nights."

"That's why age is just a number," I reaffirmed. "Maybe one day I can join you on a square-dancing event when we get your doctors to approve it."

"The first square dancing partner she's going to have will be me," Collin said, standing up and turning to offer her his hand.

I wanted to take in the reactions from her family behind her, hoping they didn't think I was some crazy psych doctor who was going to have their eighty-year-old mother sky diving as soon as the doctors cleared her, but I couldn't take my eyes off the sight before me.

Collin stood perfectly erect and held Irene as she stood as his ballroom dance partner. "It was *Can't help falling in love,* wasn't it?" Collin asked as he took his phone out.

"Oh, Elvis Presley. I saw him in Las Vegas once." She looked at me. "Dr. Brooks promised me a turn around the dance floor if I followed his orders in the hospital." She smiled, "This was mine and my late husband's song. The only man I'll allow to take Clancy's place is my sweetheart, Collin, here."

As Collin set his phone to play the song, I smiled as I watched him ease her around the small area next to her bed. The rest of us in the room must have vanished, leaving the doctor and his adorable patient dancing together in their own world. I watched as Irene held onto Collin's hand and waist, closed her eyes, and began to sing her and her husband's song.

I could tell she must've been imagining dancing with her husband and not the handsome neurosurgeon who was leading her to the beautiful love song.

"She's a firecracker," the woman who walked around to me said. "I'm Janice, her youngest daughter. This is my oldest sister, Gail." Both women were meticulously dressed and coifed, and their air told me they were a very proper and wealthy family. "This is our little brother, Wyatt. Our oldest brother, Miles, left before you both arrived. He's working with the medical staff to make sure mom's place is set up for in-home care with her new nurse."

"She won't move in with family?" I softly asked as the two continued to dance in a way that made me want to learn more about Collin, not just inside of work but outside of the hospital too. I mean, who wouldn't fall hard for this man? He had the looks to call for that alone, but this softer and more loving side, I would have never imagined.

"She would never move in with any of us," Gail chimed in. "She's far too independent for that. We interviewed numerous in-home health nurses who would be willing to stay with her, and we finally settled on one that mom fell in love with.

"That's nice to hear," I said. "Do all of you live here locally?"

"Only me," Janice said. "I live about twenty minutes away from Mom in Burbank. Our dad passed fifteen years ago. He worked in television, and Mom loved every bit of that crazy life they had with the after-hours parties, award shows, you name it. She's still in the house where we grew up and has friends who still like to *cut the rug* with her." She chuckled.

"I don't want her to lose that youthfulness in her spirit," I said. "How do all of you feel about her still holding onto that?"

"It's the best thing for her," Wyatt interjected. "This last round of mini-strokes that sent her to the ER gave all of us a scare. Thank God that Dr. Brooks was on-call since she was already his patient from before."

"My God, that's terrifying," I said, truthfully. "And how did he determine she stopped taking her meds?"

Gail laughed and nodded toward where Collin finished their dance with a graceful twirl and a dip. "That man can get her to spill the beans on just about everything. He's truly the best."

"Outside of me, of course," Dr. Mitchell said as he entered the room in his scrubs, and fresh out of some surgery given the medical cap he was wearing.

"The two heartbreakers," Irene giggled. "Get over here, Jacob." She held out her hands as Dr. Brooks walked over to Jake, took her charts, and pulled out his pen. "I'm going to miss these handsome faces. Thank you, sweetheart," she said as Collin intently studied her charts, then flipped the page and started writing his notes.

"Let's keep it at this: if you want to see your favorite doctors again, invite us over for dinner," Jake said, accepting her hug. "My son just celebrated his first birthday, and I'm sure he'll love tearing up your place like he does mine."

Irene laughed as her kids walked over to grab their purses and Irene's personal belongings. "Well, Dr. Collin," Jake said, "is she able to go home and be transferred into the care of the lovely Elena?"

"She is," Collin said, scribbling more on the charts before looking up. "You and I will have another turn on the dance floor next week on a follow-up appointment in my office. At that time, I will work with *Doctor Alvarez* as her schedule will start filling up fairly quickly. Her office is still under a small renovation, but she'll be right next to mine if, for any reason, she may need my assistance with any of the patients we share."

"Which means, Irene," Dr. Mitchell said, his dark blue eyes mischievous, "if you give Elena any trouble, then your *mean doctor* will come rushing in to bust you." He crossed his arms and smiled, "I'm the nice one, remember?"

"Hospital gossip," Irene said. The five-foot-tall woman stood in front of these two GQ model-looking men, their muscular build highlighted by their scrubs. "That's all. I love you both." She grew serious. "And I thank you both." She looked at me, "I think you and I will have fun together, especially if your office is close to Collin's. Maybe we'll give him a hard time together." She winked, and then her family helped guide her from her two favorite surgeons.

"I'm finishing up on the release orders right now," Dr. Brooks said. "Follow them, please. I look forward to meeting your new in-home nurse next week at your follow-up. Any questions for me or Dr. Mitchell before we turn you loose and back into the human population again?"

As Irene and her kids asked a few questions to both doctors, I stared at Collin. At this moment in time, I didn't know what to think of the man.

Never before had I been at a loss for words, my heart somehow feeling it would take the lead over my mind.

Relationships happened between medical professionals often, and so did fun and straightforward affairs. I wished I thought the man was only flirting with me after his constant teasing and the way his smile broadened and eyes sparkled when we were playful from our day of interacting, but I wasn't foolish or naïve. I felt Collin might have seen something in me that night we first met, the night that I first lost myself in the most striking set of blue eyes I'd ever seen when he spun me around to face him after coming from out of nowhere on the dance floor.

I would be a fool to turn the man down after witnessing what I had today, and I knew it. Was I afraid of him breaking my heart? Well, no one wants to be crushed after allowing themselves to take a chance on someone, but I was raised to get up when I fell and to walk off the pain. My parents didn't raise their children to be sensitive and crumble—they raised the three of us to be bold, daring, and live every day as if it were our last, and that's how I saw life. I loved life, and I wasn't afraid of loving hard, no matter the cost.

Was I in love with Collin Brooks? No, but I was fascinated by the man. Right now, I wanted to be a good, close friend with the doctor. I loved this part of first meeting people—the fun, less complicated side of everything.

I knew these thoughts were only in my head because of how we both seemed to *fit* together. I could see it in his eyes as solidly as I felt it in my mind. We clicked, and we would work well as a team. One thing was sure, though: he would continue to refer to me as Dr. Alvarez until I was able to hold my own against the way my name sounded coming out of his mouth.

We didn't need me drooling over the doctor or like I was now, watching him and Jake banter back and forth, lost in these thoughts. I had to get all of this out of my system and get myself under control, or I wouldn't be an asset to his team. I'd be the giggly-goof, sitting there in surgery while Dr. Brooks depended on me to help him during high-pressure surgeries. Here I was putting Collin in his place by insisting we keep it professional with the doctor formalities—little did he know, it wasn't Collin who I couldn't trust on the first-name basis stuff. It was myself.

CHAPTER EIGHT
COLLIN

The day had finally ended, and if it weren't for Jake's *heads-up* text, I would've completely forgotten that I was supposed to meet up with the guys at Kinder's tonight. Since being in Elena's presence on Monday, the fact that I'd lost two days in the week was somewhat strange to me. The time flew by, and here I was on the eve of Jamie's surgery, and mine and Elena's first surgical experience together since she accepted the job.

She was already stacked with appointments, and that didn't surprise me in the slightest. Elena was charming and a brilliant light that couldn't be put out. Everyone wanted to be in her presence, and that included me. I took a step back, though, after having her at my side all day on Monday. I knew she needed to shine on her own, and she did that without even trying.

Did I still fantasize about the woman as I had since the day I met her? Hell yes. In fact, I hadn't turned my attention toward another woman since the first dance we'd shared in Vegas. I guessed that my best friends believed I was taking some personal challenge in not dating, but the reasoning for it, they'd never believe, and I didn't give a shit.

"That's the file on Mrs. Johnson," I said to Patty. "I'm out until Monday. Thanks again for moving my patients around for the surgery tomorrow."

"Never a problem, Collin," Patty answered with her dimpled smile. "I bet Jamie is nervous, but I know she's elated to have you fix the issues finally."

"She deserves the freedom from the pain and the pain meds she's been living on," I answered, signing off on one last prescription for Mrs. Johnson. "This needs to be sent off, and I want Mrs. Johnson to call the hospital if she feels the slightest dizziness after taking her first dose. She understood that after I talked to her, but make sure the pharmacist relays that vital information for me, please."

"I hope this helps with her seizures," she said.

I leaned against the counter that faced the center of the office floor. Ten doctors shared this common area, and all of us worked the neuro floor in the main hospital of Saint John's. I'd previously spoken with the hospital board about closing things off a bit to allow our patients and personal secretaries a bit more privacy. Things could easily get chaotic in this open environment, whether the neurologists, psychiatrists, surgeons, or therapists were sort of our own unit or not. Some days—like today—this place was more congested than the hospital, and it made for a tense environment for patients whose diseases varied and required a quieter and calmer atmosphere.

Don't get me wrong, I loved this spot, the teams I worked with, and my office, but we needed to do something with patients being called back on intercoms and staff being called out the same way. It was a goddamn circus at times, and today was one of those days that all of us were in here working with only two up in the hospital. It was a madhouse, and I was shocked that Patty didn't go into labor just juggling shit around all day. Not only was she dealing with my patients, but until Elena hired herself a secretary, she was dealing with Elena's too.

"You need to go home and get your feet up and stop worrying about our friends, Miss Tao," I teased. "I swear you worry more about the patients than you do little Collin." I eyed her large stomach and grinned at her.

"You think it's a boy, eh?" she asked, swiveling around in her chair. "And that I'd actually name my first-born son after you?"

"Of course, I do," I teased. "He's heard nothing but my wisdom for the past nine months. You might as well name the little fellow after the most intelligent man he's ever had the privilege of listening to."

"You're too much, Dr. Brooks," Patty answered, typing the script in her computer to send off to the pharmacy. "And if it's a girl?"

"Collin seems to love the name Elena," I heard the voice of the one woman who found a way to speak straight to my heart without even knowing she did. "I say, if he's all about naming your baby, we stick to his selfish ideas, Patty."

I twisted to lean and smile at the beautiful ray of sunshine that filled this part of the office. "Selfish? Me? You've lost your mind, Alvarez."

"You are a selfish man." Elena raised her eyebrows at me and filed her papers off to the side. "Patty, don't worry about these until tomorrow. Go home, put your feet up, and relax."

"I believe I already gave her that order." I arched an eyebrow at the bronze eyes that stole my breath away.

"Then she's under two doctors' orders." She grinned, and I was done.

I pulled my bottom lip between my teeth and enjoyed taking in the portrait of perfection, beauty, and cheer. God, I was a patient man...until her.

After leaving Patty to finish up her work and Elena, giving me the privilege of watching her float down the hallway to her office—conveniently located next to mine—with poise and grace, I decided to pack it up and head out to my car.

After tucking away Jamie's file and most recent scans, I pulled on my suit jacket, shouldered my leather work bag, and left the office through the side door.

While I fiddled with my keys, I went back in my mind to Elena's and my previous meeting with Jamie and her family. We'd fully prepped Jamie for her craniotomy. I'd be back at the hospital at four in the morning and ready to do what I did best—go after issues most doctors would naturally shy away from. This surgery would be a challenge, but instead of allowing challenges to play with my mind, I welcomed them, heart and soul—case and point: Elena Alvarez. Aside from the woman who was testing my patience more than I imagined possible, I had to admit I thrived on situations that those in neuroscience referred to as breakthroughs for our work field.

Brain lesions weren't necessarily a *breakthrough* in science, but any form of a craniotomy while being so close to the brain's vital areas was critical. These lesions were seemingly too close to her memory receptors and her fine motor skills. One small fuck up, and I could wreck Jamie's life, and my new neuropsychiatrist would be working with Jamie on a whole new level.

Like anyone, neurosurgeons made their fair share of mistakes, but in all my years, one case would never leave my mind. The act was perpetrated by a chief surgeon from a previous hospital while I was an intern, and it made me sick to recall how greedy the doctor was. He was so sure of himself and so fucking cocky that he stopped listening to the doctor who was working with his patient during the craniotomy, and he kept going after the poor woman's tumor as if it were *his to conquer.*

The mother fucker ruined that woman's life that day. And instead of allowing that man to destroy my outlook on being a neurosurgeon, it pushed me harder to become a better one—one who wouldn't put my aspirations of being the best above the well-being of my patient. I wanted to be the kind of physician who could put his ego aside and know when to quit, and especially when to listen to those helping me in surgeries like a craniotomy.

Did I want Jamie's lesions never to return? Abso-fucking-lutely. I also wouldn't dare go farther than Elena would guide me and risk any damage to my patient. If I removed these damn things entirely, Jamie would never have to return for a craniotomy again.

"Nice car," I heard Elena say when I finally reached my vehicle.

I glanced up to see her smile beam under the lights of the covered garage.

"Damn, you are beautiful," I said, finally outside of a professional environment and alone with the woman who stole my heart away and seemingly had no plan to give it back, either.

She playfully pulled her hair out of the loose bun she always wore, giggled, and flipped her long black hair around like she was being filmed for a shampoo and conditioner commercial.

"I get that a lot." Her eyes widened playfully as she walked up to where I'd reclined against the newest car I'd added to my sports car collection.

"Only a fool would think otherwise. So," I folded my arms, mirroring the sassy way she stood in front of me, "when are you going to finally let me prove that I'm the man of your dreams?"

"Who says you already haven't, Dr. Brooks?" she teased with her smile.

"The fact that we're still on this doctor nonsense," I smirked. "You're wasting precious days without being able to come home with me each night."

She covered her smile, and I loved it when I said something that painted her cheeks pink. "What if I wanted you to come home with me?"

"And get my ass kicked by your dad? Hard pass," I returned.

She rolled her eyes. "A man who's all talk and no walk."

"Bullshit." I lifted my chin and held her gaze. "I believe you've seen the walk, Alvarez."

"Nope," she answered. "You may be the best and most attractive neuro-doc I've ever met, but you're scared shitless to come home to see what my dad has to say about you as my boyfriend."

"Your brother and I have an agreement, and I'll be there next week," I returned.

"That's cheating, Brooks," she said. "You're coming over as my brother's *friend* and not Miguel's daughter's strappingly hot doctor boyfriend."

"All right. You got me there," I answered. "Why can't we just start slow?"

"Slow?" she answered. I swear this woman did nothing but smile and vibrantly interact with everyone she came across, and it made me crave her presence. Talking to her again made me feel like an addict getting their fix.

"Yeah, like eating at a taco truck or something?" I asked.

Her eyes widened, "You know taco trucks are my thing, right?"

"Then I'm your man," I answered truthfully, hoping to rope her into doing *something* with me.

"Possibly, but I don't do the whole," she waved her hand over my new McLaren, "you know, the car is making up for *something the dude doesn't have.* Overcompensation, I believe, is the proper term."

I choked out a laugh. "What the hell does that mean?"

"This car is obviously one that you bought for performance, correct?"

"And I have quite a few others you might disapprove of as well. This one I enjoy for commuting."

"But its performance is why you bought it?"

"It's the only reason I drive sports cars."

"Yeah, makes sense, Dr. Brooks," she smirked. "Your car is making up for your performance issues."

"Now, that's something you'd have to judge after riding in my car and back to my place."

"I don't date doctors," she finally said.

"I don't either. Never have."

"Then why all the games?"

"Because they're not games, Dr. Alvarez. I don't see you solely as a doctor; I see you as the woman I *will* spend the rest of my life with." I studied her as she almost nervously ran her thumb over her bottom lip. It was a gesture I noticed two days ago—something she did when I brought her into consultations, and she was deeply considering the answers. "Does that scare the shit out of you?"

She twisted her lips up and recovered the slight nervousness I'd sensed. "No. Nothing scares me," she boldly proclaimed.

"Then what's the hold-up? You and I have chemistry, and you know it. I see it in your eyes."

"Good God, man," she laughed loudly, that lovely, delightful laugh that lit her her face. "We hardly know each other."

"That's why I want to take you on a date to a fucking taco truck!"

She exhaled, cocking her head to the side as she looked at me with the most adorable face. It was like she was loving every second of this, and she had no intention of turning me down. I could sense that from a mile away. "Tempting because I'm starved, but Dad texted me, and he's making one of his Cuban delights for dinner tonight."

I stepped forward, enough of the silly back and forth. I had to do something to stop this woman from being hung up on me being only a doctor when, even though that was true, I was also a human man—a man who had been shot by cupid's arrow and had mysteriously fallen for this Cuban goddess.

She stood completely still as I reached my hand up and gently took a piece of her soft hair in my hand and tucked it behind her ear. I was keenly aware, watching and hearing everything, that her breathing had fallen out of rhythm as I gently allowed my fingertips to run down the side of her neck.

"I'll see you in the morning, Alvarez," I said, trying to win her over with a touch of charm. She had no idea how desperately I wanted to pull her into my arms. The soft moan from her and her eyes—which were now dazed—made this interaction more torturous for me than her; my cock could attest to that. "It'll be a big day for you, me, and our patient."

"It will," she answered. "I will be ready."

"I do not doubt that," I answered, stepping back, needing to cool it down for my own good. "Where's your car? I'll drive you over to it. Or walk you."

"On the other side of yours. I get doctor parking too." She chuckled.

"Then, get plenty of rest. Give your dad and brother my best. Perhaps you and I will celebrate our first successful surgery tomorrow night at the taco truck of your choosing."

"You're that sure of yourself with this brain surgery?" she asked.

"I'm sure of you," I answered and then turned to get into the car. "Tomorrow night, Alvarez."

She smiled, shook her head, and then walked in front of my car and over to hers. I took a glance at the vehicle she had been more impressed with than mine, and I smirked to see it was a white Land Rover. *Overcompensating, indeed,* I thought with a laugh. She enjoyed some fine luxuries herself, and here I was starting to feel like somewhat of a douche with my *high-performance* sports car.

I backed out and called Jake, knowing I was late to meet up with the guys. These nights were pretty much our mid-week, guys-blowing-off-steam sessions. A nice dinner, a few drinks, and teasing the hell out of each other is what we lived for.

Tonight was probably going to be the discussion about the when's and where's of Jim and Avery's wedding. Who knew, our conversations lately ranged from the mundane to news none of us ever saw coming. This night would be no different.

CHAPTER NINE
ELENA

$\mathcal{M}$y night was restless, and it wasn't because I was anxiously awaiting Jamie's surgery. I was more eager than I expected to help that young woman get her life back, but that wasn't what was weighing on my mind. What started my spiral into a sleepless night was my little brother, acting like a spoiled four-year-old about Dad selling the house.

Dad wouldn't divulge any extra information about his particular reasons for moving, and the truth was that he was a grown-ass, retired man who could move to Japan if he so wished. He certainly didn't deserve to be questioned by anyone in his family—especially his son, who wouldn't just fall out of the damn nest and learn to fly on his own. Mom and Dad let Stevie get away with too much shit, and now, Dad was dealing with the fallout.

Stevie didn't have the memories that Lydia and I had from the Malibu ranch. That was where we learned to ride horses—forced to ride, in Lydia's case—and participated in equestrienne events. We enjoyed every second of our slice of paradise, with countless acres to explore and play. It was every kid's dream, but why would an aspiring DJ care about any of that? My brother was such a little idiot sometimes, and I certainly wasn't in the mood to stay up late and calm down the two bulls who were locking horns about this topic all night. So, I left them grumbling in the living room while I headed to bed, and that's when the last three days of falling harder and harder for Collin's charms decided to plague my mind.

Watching the man, even in passing, was enough to make me drool. I watched him on the hospital floors and then spent the last two days watching him move around our beautiful office. Collin was cocky as hell —that was certain—but what was surprising was that he was even more compassionate than he was arrogant. That was a hidden gem that I wasn't anticipating, and I couldn't get past it. Something was sparking up between us; he knew it, and I knew it, but I was the one pumping the breaks on him—until tonight.

Tonight, I finally had given in and allowed my feelings, which were growing more rapidly than they should have, to come to the surface. It was true that we hardly knew each other, and we'd only started working together three flipping days ago, but I'd never felt more drawn to a man in my life. This was different than all of my other romantic experiences. I couldn't explain how, but it was one-hundred-percent undeniable. And every time I wanted to shut off the emotions, Collin and I wound up face-to-face, and he conjured them right back up again.

Oddly enough, it felt like the brain surgeon was already in my brain and manipulating it in ways I couldn't understand. So, on my path to destroying a perfectly solid night's sleep, I decided to press him, to flirt back with him, and to feel the gentle touch of his fingertips as they slid down the side of my neck. That, coupled with his eyes, his seriousness, and being half a second away from reaching up to feel his full lips on mine—finally letting the crisp scent of his masculine cologne seep into my senses—was the reason I woke up every thirty minutes throughout the night. Hornier than hell, too. Jesus, what I wouldn't do to feel his fingertips soothing my clit that seemed to throb at the thought of how it would all go down, having him in bed with me. I'd been single long enough, and I was dangerously close to thinking that if we just had sex and got it out of the way, maybe we could both get on with our lives as usual.

Unfortunately, the fantasies that'd held me hostage all week told me that getting on with life, as usual, was not in the cards for either one of us. Now and then in life, we come across someone we know is meant to be a significant part of our lives, and Collin was one of those people for me.

Call it kismet, fate, or fortune—whatever it was, it was beyond either of our control.

I'd had plenty of coffee before arriving at the hospital. I wanted to quickly check on Jamie before I worked with the staff to help set up the OR for Dr. Brooks to do the craniotomy with his attending neurosurgeon Dr. Nathan—and the entire team we met with yesterday afternoon to prep for Jamie's surgery this morning.

Thank God for this line of work and today's surgery because it wasn't less than three seconds on the floor, and I was in surgery prep mode. As I expected, Jamie was nervous and ready to get this over. It was a typical reaction to having an awake craniotomy, and I reassured her that Dr. Brooks would ensure that this six-hour, give or take, surgery would move safely, and she'd be walking out of here tomorrow after Collin cleared her.

Once again, I was highly impressed with how efficiently and smoothly this team worked to prepare the surgical room and the patient for the doctor to do his job. Collin's voice announced his entrance to the room, and I was greeted with a confident smile as if this critical surgery was like everyday walking and talking for him. His presence kept the room's atmosphere calm yet charged with an energy of confidence that radiated through everyone.

I watched the image guidance screen that Collin had used to make his marks. He used the equipment to help lock Jamie's head in a vice to prevent her from moving when the anesthesiologist was ready to wake her to work with me. He made smaller than usual cuts with such precision that there would be no scarring when he was done. Collin—the surgeon—was a completely different individual in his OR.

I could quickly tell this man didn't bullshit his way through or around anything. He had the most advanced technology giving me *and* him the 3D images of Jamie's brain to watch as well as the functioning MRI, which was telling me and the doctors in the room precisely where certain areas were being stimulated. At the same time, he would probe around on her brain while she and I would talk. Everyone's brain was different, and that's the fascinating thing about brains and the human mind. One's speech may be in a particular area of the frontal lobe, and it could be in a completely different area of another person's frontal lobe. That's why we were in

DR. BROOKS   67

here, and Collin was now calling for the anesthesiologists to wake up our sweet Jamie.

I smiled, holding different picture images for her to tell me about when her eyes fluttered open, and she stared at me in confusion.

"Hey, Jamie," I said. "It's nice to see you again."

Her eyes widened with a bit of fear. That was normal, given she would still be a bit loopy, and her head was locked in a vice as opposed to how she was positioned before they put her under.

"Where's Dr. Brooks?" she asked with some paranoia as I reached for her fidgeting hands.

"Right behind you," Collin said, eyes staring through the computer magnifier and working on probing around the troubled lesion in her brain. "I know you want to see my handsome face, but Dr. Alvarez, sitting at your side, has decided to do all the easy stuff."

She smiled and calmed some, her eyes sliding back over to where I stood. "That's right," she answered. "I'm having brain surgery."

"That you are." Collin looked at me as my eyes flicked from Jamie to the computer screens the neurologists were carefully studying, displaying each cut, clip, and electronic probe Dr. Brooks was doing on Jamie's brain.

"And I'm looking at Elena." She smiled sweetly at me when my eyes went back to hers.

"That must be wonderful. I have to know something, Jamie," Collin said as I watched him probing around the frontal lobe area. "What does it feel like to wake up and the first thing you see are the beautiful eyes of Dr. Alvarez? I forgot the color, remind me, would you, please?"

Her glossy eyes dazzled as I looked at Dr. Brooks to shake my head for him to stay clear of the area where he was working.

"Hazel?" she said, somewhat confused.

"Hazel, it is. Just like my great-grandmother's name," Collin answered.

I held up a card showing a picture of a shoe and asked Jamie if she could tell me what she saw. I could instantly recognize her discomfort. This was a blatant reminder that we were in brain surgery. Dr. Brooks was doing so well in ensuring everyone in the room was comfortable and moving through this surgery flawlessly, and here I was, acting like a robot fresh out of an internship with the basic cards to keep our patient talking.

"Good grief," Collin said with a laugh. "Why are we looking at oversized flashcards, Dr. Alvarez?"

Jamie laughed. "Her name is Elena. Elena?" she questioned while I watched Collin, working extremely close to her temporal lobe where the largest lesion had grown toward. The area bordered the frontal lobe, where Collin worked with her cognitive skills a moment ago.

The frontal lobe was where he had to be extremely careful, given I was mapping him around these two areas where her speech, cognitive skills, and responses were located—not to mention her memories. Now, we needed to get her talking about something while Collin worked within millimeters of where her memories could be altered if he got too close to that part of her brain.

"Yes, Elena."

"A beautiful name, even more beautiful than my great-grandmother's," Collin said.

"Elena," she repeated as I continued to nod and communicated with Collin to assure him we were in a safe area for him to work on this lesion. "You remind me of Elena from the Vampire—"

She stopped speaking, and I shook my head to Collin to let him know that his device had mapped the location of her speech, which cut her off mid-sentence. Collin nodded and moved away from that area.

"Vampires?" Collin asked. "Like Dracula? Are you saying that Elena reminds you of one of the Count's beautiful bloodsucking creatures?" He chuckled.

"The Vampire Diaries," she laughed too.

"Interesting," Collin said while I smiled at her.

"That's a huge compliment," I said after Collin gave me a look that he said he'd let me know when he was sure of the location where he could safely operate. "I love Elena in that show."

"I love her too," Jamie said.

"Why am I just now hearing about your love for vampires?" Collin asked. I found it fascinating that he could operate and hold an actual conversation instead of needing silence to focus, given how close he was to these critical locations in Jamie's brain.

"You would have laughed at me before," Jamie said with a grin.

"And you think I'm not laughing now?" Collin answered. "So that you know, you'll remember all of these confessions after you wake up from surgery."

"I love Damon," I added, knowing we had to keep Jamie talking because Collin was now making cuts and clamping off certain blood vessels.

"I love how Damon loves Elena."

"So, who's the vampire?" Collin asked. "The lovely Elena or this Damon joker?"

"Damon," Jamie said. "Sometimes Elena."

"Sometimes a vampire, sometimes not? Interesting," Collin added. "And does this lovely Elena share Damon's love in this vampire show?"

"No spoilers. You'll have to watch it someday," Jamie laughed.

"Maybe he can binge-watch it on a day off and find out. I love Damon's icy-blue eyes," I said.

"Icy-blue eyes?" Collin asked.

"Like yours," Jamie answered.

"Ah," Collin answered, and I certainly wasn't disagreeing with our patient, who was confessing that she loved a vampire television show. "Given this vampire has the same beautiful eyes as I have, and we have an Elena in the room, I might have to ask her out."

"Elena doesn't like Damon in the beginning," Jamie said as Collin continued to work, and the room chuckled to her response.

"He's too pushy, I think," I said. "Though extremely handsome."

"Sometimes, it's not about icy-blue eyes and looks alone," Collin said, then turned to a nurse for suction and another tool.

He was moving to the area with Jamie's fine motor skills. "So, vampires are usually cold—since they *are dead*," Collin said with sarcasm. "Can you tell me if our Elena has deathly cold hands, Jamie?"

I reached over and held Jamie's hand and shook my head, knowing that somehow Collin was about to turn this talking and awake brain surgery experience into some Collin and Elena vampire show.

"Nice and warm," Jamie said.

"Go ahead and squeeze my hand." I watched Collin as he mapped around where her second lesion was on her parietal lobe. "Nice," I said, nodding at Collin and giving him the clear on this area.

"Can you hold your hand up for me, Jamie?" Collin asked.

She couldn't, and everyone in the room knew that was an area he had to stay away from.

"Nope. It doesn't sparkle, does it, Dr. Alvarez?"

"Sparkle?" Jamie laughed. "Those are different vampires."

"Aren't they all the same?" he questioned, working diligently in this area of her brain.

"Hardly," I answered with a wink to Jamie. "As we said, we like Damon and his icy-blue eyes. Like yours, Dr. Brooks."

Jamie smiled at me.

"Are you wanting to be in surgery all day, Dr. Alvarez?" Collin asked, working closely with the nurse to gather instruments. "I need the magnifier shifted to the left, please," he requested.

"She's doing a great job," Jamie said. "Ignore him."

Collin reached for another instrument, gave me a quick knowing look, and then looked back to Jamie's brain.

"Dr. Alvarez understands that if she distracts me, we'll be in here all day with me having great difficulty trying to focus."

"We're just down here, stating vampire facts," I said.

"I thought vampires sparkled."

"Twilight vampires sparkle. If you really want to be here all day, we can go into all the different vampires," I added with a laugh.

"You thought vampires were Dracula's ladies too," Jamie answered.

"That's how I always saw them. The Count was the reason they multiplied. I am just now learning that vampires aren't in love with the big guy with no heart? Strange."

Collin was back and working closely on the lesion where her memories were again. The brain was so complex, and each one of them so different. Being in here and helping a surgeon map one out for multiple lesions was even more fascinating.

"Vampires?" Jamie questioned.

"To the left," I said to Collin, seeing his attention was solely focused on fixing this last lesion.

"You remember we were talking about how hot Damon is, but he was too pushy with the beautiful Elena," I said, teasing Collin and knowing he was trying to get this lesion fully repaired, but it was too close to the memory location of the temporal lobe.

Collin remained silent while Jamie looked at me in confusion. "How is it a man can be too pushy when it comes to a beautiful woman? Especially when her name is—what was her name again?" Collin asked while I prayed that she remembered. This was the do-or-die moment for this lesion, and if Jamie couldn't recall things right now, he'd have to abandon that area completely.

"Elena," she finally said. "What happened?"

"Collin is jealous of Damon," I smirked.

"Oh," she laughed. "I thought I did something wrong."

"You're doing everything right. Just keep talking to *our* Elena, and we'll keep moving along," Collin said.

I could hear the nurse, Collin, the other surgeon, and the others talking, but I was fixated on the fact that—somehow—we got lucky. With Collin's steady hand and patience, he was nailing this lesion and repairing the most problematic one. He was a prodigy, and there was no doubting that fact—even if his broad knowledge of all-things vampire royally sucked.

Jamie and I talked about Vampire Diaries' episodes, and I laughed when Collin grew tired of hearing about Damon's eyes. I even tried to change the subject to her talking about her wedding plans, but she wouldn't have it, and I loved that.

"Well, I guess your fiancé is going to have to blame Dr. Alvarez for whatever I messed up in your surgery. It must've happened at the beginning," he teased with a laugh after Jamie refused to talk about her wedding.

"He didn't mess anything up." I laughed while he and Jamie argued about the wedding stuff.

"No?" Collin pressed, "I figured you two ladies would be filling me in on wedding plans for Jamie this entire time, but instead, I'm hearing about doppelgangers and witch weddings."

"The witch wedding happened," Jamie insisted. "I remember it."

"It was a horrible scene, to be honest," I added.

"The horrible scene will be when you wake up and your handsome fiancé—who doesn't have this *drop-dead gorgeous* vampire's icy-blue eyes—finds out you'd rather talk witchy weddings than your own."

"My colors are silver and blue," she told me with a smile.

"You're in trouble, young lady," Collin said. "You're marrying poor Paul while you're in love with a vampire. Wait, Paul isn't a vampire, is he?"

Collin nodded toward me to signal that he was finishing three hours ahead of time, after all of us going on and on for the last four hours. All Jamie's lesions had been repaired, and that was only due to Collin's steady hand and constantly watching me for locations he could or couldn't get anywhere near.

I don't even think my dad would have had the skilled precision of that man, pressing himself to the limits and trusting me to guide his hand by watching the computer models as well as talking with Jamie. Most doctors would have gone in hard and fast to repair the lesion in such a critical area, or they would've abandoned it and waited to see if the patient felt any different when they woke up.

Not once did I see either of those temptations in Collin. We mapped her brain down to the closest areas, and I wanted to jump up and shout in the victory that we'd done so well and pulled off what I would deem the impossible, but I kept my cool.

Just as Collin called for the anesthesiologists to return Jamie to sedation so that he could stitch her back up, I smiled over at the man who was hard at work and as cool as a freaking cucumber. This was second nature to him. I could sense that a mile away. Collin requested they turn on Bob Segar songs for what I assumed was his *wrap it up* music, and I couldn't wipe the smile off my face if I wanted to.

Dr. Collin Brooks was perfection, and I was definitely down for celebrating tonight at the taco truck he mentioned the previous night. This was my first surgery, and I was damn proud at how well we all did. It was crazy how I felt since it didn't match the vibes of the room. Everyone was still working on their ends of the craniotomy, and I was sitting here feeling an adrenaline rush as I focused on Jamie's vital monitors. I felt like confetti should fall from the ceiling, and I couldn't help but laugh at the fact that I was such a newbie. I didn't care. I knew this cheesy grin would stay plastered on my face for the rest of the day and night.

Hell, yes. We did it, Dr. Collin Brooks. We were a team, and I wouldn't change the fact that I worked with the best neuro-doc I'd ever seen. He made my love for this job grow to heights I didn't know existed. To see a calm, fun, patient, and skilled man work in perfection was simply amazing to me.

What a guy. That's all I could conclude. This man rendered me speechless, and after we walked out of this room, I knew I wouldn't be able to hold up this flirty front with him. All I knew was that adrenaline was pumping in my veins, and I couldn't be prouder to work with such an incredible neuro team.

CHAPTER TEN
ELENA

*S*trangely, the only thing to get a *stunned* reaction out of Collin after a day in the hospital, performing a highly-successful craniotomy was me asking him when he planned to take me on our date to the taco truck. The man reacted as I'd reacted in the OR when he managed to get both lesions fixed in Jamie's brain—his smile was plastered from ear to ear.

Unlike Collin, I remained in my scrubs since I didn't keep a change of clothes in my office, and I had to pull my shit together when he walked out of his, wearing a pair of jeans and a snug, V-neck sweater, the burgundy color making his blue eyes pop even more than usual.

I followed his badass sports car to Long Beach, shocked that we didn't stick around the downtown Los Angeles area, but Collin swore by this particular taco truck, and I wasn't going to argue.

We arrived and ordered our food before driving to a more secluded area where Collin found us a bench to share closer to the beach. We sat in comfortable silence, eating our food and listening to the waves rolling into the shore across the street from where we sat.

"Damn, these tacos are the best I've ever had," I finally said as I went in for another carnitas taco out of the bag.

"Told you," he said between bites of the large-ass burrito he ordered.

"It's the seasonings they use, and I love their green salsa. It makes it worth the drive to Long Beach."

"You live around here?" I asked.

"No," he answered with a smile. "I have a place in Malibu."

"Oh, yeah? My dad is selling my childhood home and moving to our family ranch in Malibu."

"When he retired, he said something about going to Malibu so he can enjoy the ocean again."

"Yes," I laughed. "That is the current family drama that I'm dealing with at home."

Collin crumbled up the foil from his now-devoured burrito and reclined back with his bottled water in hand. "Drama in the Alvarez family?" he questioned. "I definitely couldn't see that *ever* happening."

I nudged him with a laugh, my mouth full of the last bite of my taco. "Getting off the subject of *my family issues*, how'd you find out about this place? You don't seem like the Long Beach kind of guy. Did you date some hottie who lived here?"

Collin smirked. "Jake and I love to surf. It's our way of decompressing sometimes."

"You surf?" I asked, drinking from the glass Coke bottle I ordered.

"Have since I was a boy. You name the beach, and Jake and I most likely have surfed it." He draped his arm up over the back of the bench. "What about you, Miss Cuban Floridian Goddess of mine."

I practically choked on the carbonation I was downing from my soda bottle. "Pardon me?"

He chuckled. "It's what I call you," he stated factually.

"I'm not *yours*. Changing the subject *again*, Collin?" I exhaled, my eyes turned back to the beach because I knew that if I didn't look somewhere else, I was going to kiss him and prove how much I loved hearing that sentiment come out of his mouth.

"Collin, you say?" he perked up. "As in, we're finally on a first-name basis?"

"I'm in scrubs, so I'm still Dr. Alvarez," I teased. "You changed into civilian clothing, so I can call you Collin."

"Oh, come on!" Collin said, smiling over at me with a look of annoyance on his face. "I'm starting to believe your one of *those* obsessed doctors now."

"What?" I looked at him in confusion.

"Yeah, the assholes with a *doctor* complex." He poked my leg teasingly.

"That's not what I'm doing, and I don't have a complex," I answered. "Listen, another subject change, but I wanted to tell you that you were awesome today. Honestly. I wanted to jump up and scream with excitement at how well you performed a surgery that most doctors might not have handled as you did."

"Well, funny that you should say so because I usually prefer to end all of my surgeries with such fanfare, so you should have done so," he answered with a cheeky grin. "It would've actually made me believe I finally impressed you."

"Our taco truck date didn't prove that to you?"

"I knew that was going to happen," he said. "I already asked you on this date last night."

I shook my head. "What made you go into this profession? I know it wasn't money."

"I see you've stalked me out and found I was born with a silver spoon in my mouth." He smirked, and damn it if he didn't continue to look sexier and sexier with each passing moment.

"Possibly," I lied. Everyone knew about Dr. Collin Brooks, the famous neurosurgeon, and son of the late and gifted architect, John Brooks—well, everyone who was in our profession, I guess. Collin's father came from old money, as they say, and aside from John Brooks having a stellar reputation, his net worth of billions was well-earned. "I'm just wondering if Saint John's was named after the famous architect who designed its renovation."

Collin shook his head, smiled, and then looked out to the white foam waves in the ocean. "My dad was a lot of things, rest his soul, but he was no saint. However, he was arrogant enough to *wish* the hospital was named after him."

"I'm sorry for your loss, by the way," I said. "I heard about it from my dad. He said you seemed to accept it better than Dr. Mitchell, though."

"We all grieve differently," he said, becoming more introspective at that moment, and I instantly felt terrible for saying anything.

"I apologize. I didn't mean it to sound like Dr. Mitchell cared more about your father than you. That came out completely wrong. I spoke out of turn."

"No, please. Don't apologize for that," Collin said with a laugh and a look that made me tingle from head to toe, even through my embarrassment. "I understood what you meant. And to be clear, I was devastated about my father. There were many factors leading up to his death that didn't make his passing a complete shock to me, though. That is to say that some people die suddenly and unexpectedly. My father had been sick for years—which doesn't make his passing any less tragic to my mother or me—but, on some level, I had been slowly accepting that it was inevitable.

"That being said, his death affected Jake much harder because Jake lost him on his table. We were both on call that night, but when Dad stroked, he was going down faster than any paramedics could handle. Then, if that wasn't enough, the ER staff sent him straight to Jake's OR, and it was chaos."

"Oh, my God," I said in shock. "That's horrible."

"Dad had it coming, and we all knew it," Collin answered. "Jake knew it too. It was no one's fault. The ER didn't mess up by not sending him to me first. Dad's heart was failing and was the immediate killer in his situation. It just fucking sucks because Jake had him and saved his heart, but he went into renal failure and everything started shutting down. You know how it goes. It just all landed on Jake. He thought he could do more."

"Jake blamed himself?" I asked, confused.

Collin looked at me. "Jake is close with all of his patients, and if he loses them, he goes down pretty hard for a day or so. My dad was like a father to Jake and his brother Jim after their father died, so feeling responsible coupled with deep grief is never an easy thing to swallow. Jake may seem like he's solid as a stone, but he is deeply caring, and my dad's death rocked him hard."

"And you—how do you deal with the death of your patients? I've watched you this past week, and you are also extremely close to your patients."

"Jake and I are a lot alike in that regard, but when it comes to grieving, that's where we differ."

"How so?"

"Here we are talking about death, and this is supposed to be a nice, taco-truck date with an ocean view, Alvarez." He looked at me like I had grown three heads.

"Sorry." I zipped up my jacket, feeling the chill of the salty air hitting my scrub top and going right through, almost causing a shiver.

"Don't apologize to me unless you fuck up in my OR," Collin said as I crossed my arms and legs to keep my body heat at an even temperature.

"Speaking of which—or rather, going back to that." I looked at him. "How do you do it all so casually?"

"What, brain surgery? Is that supposed to be hard or something?" He nudged my arm and laughed.

"Shit." I laughed at the brilliance of his smile that I loved to be on the receiving end of. "Everything. All of it. You're a natural."

"I wouldn't call it that," he dismissed the compliment.

"Then what would you call it? You're a highly-educated, brilliant physician. I see it in how you work. I hear it in the way you talk. You had to have graduated at the top of your class, and now look at you, putting it all into play so effortlessly."

"Nice guess. And you're right about graduating at the top," he said.

"So that's it, then? A smart-ass and an even smarter doctor?"

Collin laughed. "Ever hear of the quote, *while wisdom dictates the need for education, education does not necessarily make one wise?*"

"Yes," I responded.

"I can have all the education in the world and graduate at the top of my class, but without wisdom, I'm just an educated fool."

"So, how did you gain your *wisdom?*" I teased him with the last word.

"Experience, mostly, but I'd like to think that my innate curiosity and ability to be ultra-observant is the real reason. Being in the OR like you were today—watching everyone and everything—was vital to me. I scrutinized every move that every person made, especially the doctors. I could see when a doctor was selfish in his methods or being a chicken-shit compared to the way another doctor worked. I absorbed all of those things in my internship days like I was a goddamn sponge. I knew the kind of doctor I wanted to be when I decided that I wanted to enter this field of medical science and that I was going to be wise in my methods, patient, and use my best judgment."

"That's why you got into this field of work?"

"I suppose I got into this field of work because there are so many fascinating obstacles to keep me challenged." He grinned at me. "I am *so* damn intelligent that I get bored easily, you know. Neuroscience keeps me guessing."

"Ah, of course," I answered. "So, how long before Collin grows bored of Dr. Alvarez?"

His eyes held mine at that moment. "I've already grown severely bored of *Doctor Alvarez*." He raised an eyebrow at me. "I'd like to enjoy some time with the lovely Elena for once."

I grinned. "Keep staring at me with your sexy, icy-blue eyes like that, and you may not know what hit you, doctor."

"That was a beautiful, extremely tempting statement until you killed it with the doctor tagline."

I laughed. "Okay, truth?"

"I've been nothing but honest with you since the moment I first spoke to you," he said without missing a beat. "I believe it's you who needs to gain my trust with your lying about being my new psych doctor when we first met in Vegas."

"I don't—I mean..." Shit. I couldn't think with the way he was casually leaned back and looking at me like he'd take me home and fuck me if I said the word. And that was the problem. I was back to wanting that again.

"Loss for words? Just come out and say it. You know that you and I work. There's something here. Just say the damn words, and I'll show you exactly what I've seen in your eyes this entire week."

"You act so sure that I'm not *just* your girl, but the first words that came out of your mouth were that you'd be my future husband."

"Glad that stayed with you since our first dance," he added.

"Then I get here, and you're acting as if I'm the woman of your dreams. How am I supposed to take you seriously?"

"Because I am serious."

I shook my head. "You have girls throwing themselves at you all day at work, and yet you settle for the one girl you hardly know?"

"I would never *settle* for anything, Alvarez," he answered confidently. Jesus Christ, I loved that confidence.

"It doesn't make sense." I laughed. "You don't make sense. I'm not one to be played, Brooks."

"Neither am I," he answered pointedly.

"So, you're going to marry me, then?" I thought I'd just hit him straight between the eyes. I'd love to pretend that I was as self-assured as I hoped I sounded, but the truth was that I was way past the point of no return with this guy.

He didn't flinch. "You're going to marry me," he corrected my statement.

"You're the most complicated man I've ever met," I said, more perplexed than before.

"Here's something that might help you understand me a bit more. I don't just *fall* for women, especially women in the medical field." His eyebrows rose. "If I'm honest—which I am, unlike you when we first met —I should have run the other direction that night. I should've never allowed myself to fall under some spell by your gorgeous smile and then walk out to that dance floor just to hear your laugh. I should have never gone anywhere near you—given you were a beautiful woman from our medical conference—because those are my rules. When you said who your father was, I should have had one of the Men in Black come to wipe your memories away so he wouldn't try to murder me for hitting on you. Even with all of those things that I shouldn't have done—wouldn't have done under any other circumstance—I didn't have a choice. There was no way that I could've stopped myself from doing all of those things. I crossed so many of my personal boundaries to get to you—I didn't just cross them, I did Olympic-level vaulting to get across them—and I'd do them all a thousand times over without a second thought." Our eyes were locked onto each other's at this enlightening confession of his, and I had a lump the size of Albuquerque in my throat.

I smiled, my cheeks burning with fire as his lips pulled up confidently on one side, his eyes mysterious, yet so beautiful. "I thought you told me you were a wise doctor, Collin Brooks. No self-control, huh?" It would've been lovely to form a statement that remotely covered his heartfelt sentiment, but that stupid response was all I could manage.

"I guess the heart overrides the brain," he confirmed and leaned closer to me. "You're not the only one questioning my wisdom, however. My friends think I'm sabotaging my career because I want a piece of ass, so that goes to show the respect I get from my loved ones." He laughed loudly, and I was grateful for the levity.

"Are they right?"

"Firstly, I would never sabotage my career, so on that count, no. They're very wrong about that." He pressed his lips together and studied me. "I'm not historically the kind of man to have his sights set on only one woman, especially if she makes me wait so long even to call her by her first name."

"So, I should feel lucky that you're giving me the time of day?" I teased.

"I would love to make you feel lucky all times of the day," he said with a devilish smile.

I instantly felt the throbbing between my legs and growing wet at the thought of what Collin was referring to.

"So, you haven't had a girlfriend or anything like that—" I paused while I watched him unashamedly shake his head as I spoke.

"I haven't been with anyone since I met you and realized that this whole soulmate shit is real. You've become the biggest test of patience ever to challenge me."

"Soulmates?" I half-smiled. I felt like a lunatic entertaining the thought, but maybe this was the connection I was feeling with him. It was kind of hard to make heads or tails of anything when I was so busy lusting over his beautiful face and body on top of his personality and his genius in the OR.

"I see it in your eyes right now," he said, narrowing his eyes at me. "You're questioning it."

"Perhaps."

He grinned and chuckled. "It's much easier if you just fucking go with it."

I thought I'd test him and play with him because, well, why not? If not now, then when? Without giving him a chance to react, I straddled him and cradled his face in my hands. I studied Collin's eyes, sexier and more serious than I'd ever seen them. "If this is the case," I said, feeling a charge of emotions I'd never felt with a man before, "then I guess we should both hope I accept this fact and soon."

Collin's hand slid down my sides and over my ass. My body froze after a violent shiver surged up my spine in reaction to his graceful touch and somber expression. I wanted to do so much more with him tonight, but something deep inside told me to hold off for now.

He licked his lips, and the fresh, crisp scent of his cologne was potent with our faces so close. I wanted to taste his kiss, to feel the urgency of him kissing me. I wanted all of him. I closed my eyes and exhaled.

"Are you going to let me kiss you, or is tormenting me high up on the things you enjoy doing, Alvarez?"

I smiled at the way he always said my last name as if he were a high school basketball coach. My eyes pulled from his, and the wind blowing away his delicious scent helped me come back to hold my own against the man I desperately wanted. If he wanted me like he said he did, I would find out soon enough, but not tonight.

"You're one intriguing man," I said, my eyes studying his. "Thank you for an incredible day at work, reminding me why I love my job, and this delicious dinner."

I slid back to see Collin's face flustered and filled with bewilderment. "What the hell are you trying to do to me, Elena?"

I bent over and kissed his forehead, my eyes closed and inhaling deeply of the man I knew deep down inside I'd fallen blindly in love with somewhere between when we first met and this moment. I let my lips linger as I ran my fingernails through the sides of his short hair. "It's Dr. Alvarez to you, and I'm trying to say thank you."

I don't know how I did it, especially since I heard him let out a breath as he ran his hands over my forearms, but I managed to stand and leave the man sitting and staring as I smiled at him and then turned to walk away.

If he did believe we were soulmates, as I was starting to believe myself, then we'd see how he would treat me after that. Most men would tell me to kiss their ass for wasting their time, most would call me a bitch and probably a cock-tease, but if Collin and I were going to play the *soulmates* game, well, that went farther than screwing and flirting. That was hardcore. That meant our souls were created to find each other one day, and they finally did.

I knew I wouldn't be able to keep Collin at arm's length for much longer. I wasn't *that* strong, and I didn't know if I even wanted to. I wanted more, and I wanted it right now, but I wanted to relish in this feeling. It was the beginning of something immense—something epic— and I knew nothing was going to stop this.

CHAPTER ELEVEN

COLLIN

I walked into Kinder's to meet up with the guys, and, for the first time, I was the last one at the table.

"If it isn't the man of the hour," my best friend, Jake, said as I sat at our usual table.

"And I'm all smiles," I said, sitting down and grabbing my menu.

"Always," Jim, Jake's older brother—and CEO of the company that owned Saint John's—added.

"How's the relationship moving along with Dr. Alvarez?" Alex, our close friend and the vice president of Jim's company, asked.

"Well, after she decided to kiss me on the forehead a few nights ago," I started, setting my menu aside after deciding on blackened salmon, "I figured I'd give her a taste of her own medicine during our lunch break."

Jake chuckled. "As fond as I've become of the woman you're obsessed with, I have to say, I loved watching her squirm with that one."

"What the hell are you two talking about?" Jim asked after the waitress quickly took our order and left.

"Elena, Jake, and a few others were sitting in the cafeteria, eating lunch, and I got paged to go to the OR." I reached over to the gin and tonic that had been ordered for me, took a sip, and shrugged. "So, before I got up, I kissed her in front of everyone, and then I left."

"That is *not* how that shit went down." Jake laughed and took a sip of his usual scotch. "We're all sitting around the table—it happens to be one of those rare occasions that we're all having lunch in the cafeteria together." Jake shook his head as he gave me the side-eye before continuing. "Coll gets paged and becomes distracted with the scans that were sent to his email on his phone before he determines it's a *go for surgery.* Then—in front of every gossiping hen that lives and breathes hospital drama—Collin gets up," Jake dramatically raises his hands, to create the full visual, "turns to Elena, who is sitting at his side, and kisses her cheek before he walks away from the table."

I watched Alex—the one that every chick we've ever met claimed was a younger Johnny Depp look-alike—nearly choke on the Manhattan he was casually drinking. "Spit that shit out on me, and you'll pay." I raised an eyebrow at him, sitting across from me.

"God in heaven," Jim said as he elbowed Alex's arm. "Here come all the jealous women complaints from Saint John's again."

"That's an understatement," Alex added with a laugh. "Are you sure this chick is worth all of this trouble?"

"More than," I assured the table.

"That's not even the best part," Jake chuckled. "Poor Elena was rendered speechless—"

"Because the poor gal probably knows that every woman who has been eyeballing the *sexy* neurosurgeon is going to be talking shit about her," Alex interrupted. "She's only been there for what, a little over a week now?"

"I told you that wasn't the best part, right?" Jake continued without skipping a beat. "So, it's obvious that Collin realizes the position he just put Elena in because he stops in his tracks, turns around, and gives me, Dr. Brandt, Dr. Chu, and Dr. Brown all the same farewell he gave Elena."

"Cheek kisses all around?" Alex burst out laughing as Jim slowly shook his head, trying not to smile.

"*Have* we been sent over complaints that Dr. Brooks is kissing doctors in the cafeteria now?" Jim asked, looking at Alex.

"Nothing about the French farewells yet," Alex said, swallowing the last of his drink. "You are a fucking lunatic, Collin. You know that, right? You either need to get somewhere with Elena or just let it go."

I shook my head and remained firm. "Nope. She's my girl, and she knows it, too. She's just playing me right now. She'll come to her senses soon enough." I looked over at Jim, who undoubtedly saw his fair share of sexual harassment complaints. He was lucky Jake and I were close friends with each of the doctors I'd laid lips on so I could move the gossip off of Elena and onto the fact that I was working on seventy-two hours of on-call sleep deprivation. "Most people know that Elena and I not only work closely together but also—"

"You both walk around with constant *fuck-me eyes* toward each other," Jake interrupted. "Even if I didn't know you, I could easily see that you're obsessed with the new neuropsychiatrist—a woman who's been hit on by practically every male and some female staff at Saint John's, by the way."

"Whatever you idiots do, just keep this ball out of my court," Jim said. "Seriously, Coll. You and Jake have enough goddamn complaints working their way up to Alex and me since you're both hotshots."

"It's the burnouts who are constantly making bogus complaints, and you know it," Jake said, defending both of us. "And what about Brandt? He's Mr. GQ of pediatrics. He's getting this shit too."

Alex rolled his eyes. "Brandt is different. That guy needs to quit messing around with the new nurses who are hired on."

"Dude actually blamed *us* for that. He said it was our fault for hiring hot nurses," Jim chuckled. "I guess that's one way to spin it."

"It's the fact that you have a new documentary running on him now too. He's easy on the eye, and we're sending these things off to universities with, shall we call them, *eager* young interns," I added. "Not that I keep track—nor am I defending him because I have my own problems, *and* I don't care all that much—but last I heard, Brandt was in a relationship with that pediatric nurse, and he broke it off with her. Word has it, she was fucking pissed and determined to make his life a living hell. I'm just saying what I hear in passing. As you all know, I don't listen too much to the gossip brigade. This job is hard enough without finding out there's a complaint against your ass every other week. He's too good at what he does to be dealing with that shit."

The waitress arrived with our food, and this conversation was doing nothing but starting to piss me off. I hated that unqualified, bitter associates scrutinized everything we did. People's lives rested in our hands, and you would think that should've been the most stressful part of the job. Dealing with HR grievances was not what any of us signed up for.

"The frivolous complaints seriously need to stop, Jimmy," Jake said, taking the words right out of my mouth. "You guys need to put a pin in that shit. If the hospital board can't kill this nonsense, then what the hell are they good for?"

"It comes directly to me when I have highly-esteemed doctors who could be fired by the board, dipshit," Jim said, cutting into his steak. "I request it from the board and then deal with the board. Your asses would have been fired long ago if I didn't oversee this shit."

"Then hire someone to take it on," I added. "You both know it's mostly bullshit. The legitimate harassment complaints are being overshadowed by the people making shit up."

Alex laughed. "You think we can't see through it all?"

"Every time we get together, you both act like this is all you get on your desks," Jake added between bites.

"That's because you and Collin get so fucking pissed that it makes for a great dinner," Jim mused.

I rolled my eyes at the two jokers sitting across from Jake and me. "Okay. So, once again, we're the subjects for your entertainment. Let's change the topic, shall we? You're going to ruin my fish."

"All right," Jim said. "Moving on to more important things. We're throwing the hospital Christmas Gala this weekend."

I closed my eyes in annoyance. "The one weekend I'd planned on going over to Elena's new place and helping her move in?" I looked at Jim and sighed. "Can I *not* catch a break in my pursuit of this woman?"

"What the hell are you talking about?" Jake questioned. "This is news."

"Not breaking news, obviously," I said, rubbing my forehead. "This gala that we are always forced to attend—what is it, *four weeks early* this time?—that, my friend, is breaking news."

"I'm curious. Do you honestly believe that unpacking boxes with Elena this weekend is going to be the start of a relationship with her?" Alex asked with a laugh. "God, you are *off* your game these days, man."

"I don't give a shit how our *relationship* begins. Whether it's cleaning toilets or unpacking boxes, the bottom line was that I would be *alone* with her for the first time since taking her to Long Beach. Better than that, alone in her new home." I raised my eyebrows. "I figured it was a gift from God that she got her keys early and actually invited me to help her move in."

"Take her with you to the gala then, drama queen," Alex said. "That way, we can all experience your true love through your cheek and forehead kisses."

"More than that, if you think that shit is going to get real between you two, it's best to have the CEO and VP of Mitchell and Associates in attendance while you show up with her on your arm," Jake added.

"Great point. It's just a matter of convincing Elena of that. At the moment, we're *just friends* and are working on acting on our feelings." I pinched the bridge of my nose. "I truly don't know how she feels. She smiles radiantly at everyone, has this beautiful, infectious laugh..." I took another sip of my gin and tonic, my frustration rising and really for no reason. Goddamn, what was going on with my obsession with her? "All I have is that her cheeks turn bright pink when I flirt with her."

"And that ever-loving kiss to your forehead." Alex chuckled.

I pursed my lips and kept my gaze on Jim's grin. "What's the reason for the last-minute gala? Aside from it interfering with my plans with Elena, this was my only weekend off before I planned on taking the Friday before Christmas off for the time that we *usually* have this jamboree."

"Well, you'll have two weeks off the day after Christmas and through the new year now too. We have to move things around because Avery and I decided to get married the week after Christmas...in Hawaii. I expect you still plan on being one of my groomsmen?" Jim said with a broad grin.

"You're shitting me, right?" I questioned. "You two have waited almost six months to finally marry, and now that you've decided on this, and it's all last-minute? And—" I stopped myself.

I had to shut my fucking mouth because I was happier than hell that Jim and Avery had finally settled on a date to tie the knot, so if everything needed to be scheduled around that, I shouldn't have been bitching about it. It was just so annoying because I'd been looking forward to spending the entire day this Saturday—and hopefully *through* the weekend—with her. What the fuck ever. I couldn't seem to have anything go *my* way when it came to Elena. For God's sake, she still mandated that I call her Dr. Alvarez, and that was more maddening than anything. Mostly because I wasn't a fool, and I knew she had feelings for me as well, but she seemed to hold back for some reason. A reason that was driving me batshit crazy while trying to figure it out.

Fuck it. I needed to stop acting childish about Avery and Jim's spur-of-the-moment planning.

"And?" Jim pressed.

"Dude hasn't been laid in months, and now he's all caught up with Elena. I can only imagine how blue his balls really are." Jake laughed.

"That's completely true," I said.

"How long has it been, loverboy?" Alex asked.

"If it was your damn business—which it's *not*," I smiled at Alex, a storm of an idea brewing in my head as we talked, "I might tell you. I should have all you dip-fucks know that I was never the one to just screw around with women. I dated them and enjoyed them while I did."

"Says the chump who got all of us labeled the goddamn Billionaires' Club?" Jim said while rolling his eyes at that fact. "If I recall correctly, *you* were the one who was too drunk to think and fucking around with that real estate heiress. Thanks to her, we have to explain that to anyone who finds out."

"That was years ago, and I ended shit like that then, too." I smirked at the three who all had their hellish histories—fucking women and breaking hearts in their own particular and selfish ways.

"So, that Kaci girl was the last woman you seriously dated?" Jim asked, trying to keep his demanding CEO composure that didn't work worth a damn around the three of us. He turned to face me. "You haven't been laid in how long?"

"Laugh it up, assholes," I said with a smile of my own. "I'll be making up for the lost time when my little sparkplug finally realizes that I'm her guy."

"Anyway, moving on." Jim put to bed the topic of my seriously needing to get laid. "We're flying out three days after Christmas. Schedules are cleared, and I had my assistant check for both your and Jake's scheduled surgeries. It appears there are none planned during that time; is that right?"

"I'm clear." I smiled at Jake, who narrowed his eyes at my grin. If anyone could tell that I was up to no good, it was my best friend.

"As am I. Any urgent surgeries that come up always go to Chi in my absence," Jake added.

Jim had just finished texting Avery, and I reached for the phone that he was dumb enough to set between our plates.

I held the phone to his face and unlocked it, knowing Jim would keep his composure given the expensive restaurant we were in. I now had the world of Jim and Avery at my fingertips.

"What the hell are you doing?" Jim asked as the waitress returned with a new round of drinks.

Perfect timing, I thought, eyeing Jim with an unwavering smile.

"Handling an issue with your fiancé," I said. "Try not to act like a teenager and tear the phone from my hands, please?"

Jim rolled his eyes after I punched the button to dial out to his most recent call—Avery—and she answered in three rings.

"Shit. That was a quick dinner," she answered, and as usual, Avery's sailor mouth made me smile.

"Actually, it's been a painfully long and hellish one," I said. "It's Collin."

"Oh, hey," she said with a surprised laugh. "What happened to Jim?"

"Well, he's devastated, if I'm honest," I said in a voice that had all eyes on me now.

"Oh, fuck. Here it comes. What is it now?" she answered, likely hearing the smile in my voice.

"Well, I'm not going to make it to the wedding. I just can't do this to you and Jim," I said.

"Do what?"

"Well, Jim informed me that I'm to be a groomsman in the *aloha* wedding he just popped on us."

"And that's a good thing, right? He said your and Jake's schedules were clear for this time. Where is he?"

"Sitting right here, looking at me as if I've lost my mind."

"Which you have," Jim grumbled.

"Here's the deal," I continued, ignoring Jim. "Being a numbers guy—and the genius I am in *all* things—I've done the math, and this wedding will be a disaster. I'm assuming you're having Ash's best guy friends arrange it all?"

"Clay and Joe? Yes, and they're not worried about anything? Please tell me how a brainiac neurosurgeon has made this determination within the span of the evening," she said, humoring me.

I rested my elbow on the table. Jim went to reach for the phone, over my bullshit, but I wasn't making the point yet. I calmly held up my index finger to stop him and leaned away. "Does Clay and Joe realize that you have a groom with three groomsmen?"

"Yes."

"And how many bridesmaids to even out the beautiful wedding pictures—wedding pictures that I'm sure will be taken as you kiss while the sun sets on the ocean's horizon?"

"What the hell are you trying to—" Avery laughed. "I have my sister, Ash, and..."

The line went silent.

"Right. And who am I to walk with?" I questioned dramatically, which brought eye rolls from around the table and a laugh from Jake. "Imagine how Clay and Joe are going to view this nonsense? Seriously, Av? A billionaire gets married in a tropical paradise, and the whole thing looks like an offset, uneven calamity because I've got no partner. And sweet Jesus, if not me, I don't even want to think about Alex being the only one without a chick in some bright pink chiffon dress on his arm in the pictures."

"First of all," Avery started, "this wedding isn't taking place in the 1980s, so don't worry about the chiffon. Second of all, I really don't care what you guys look like so long as I get to marry the love of my life. I guess I should apologize for not taking *you* into consideration with my wedding plans," she added sarcastically and with a laugh.

"Apology accepted, and as long as you don't care, sweet Avery," I said in a teasing voice, "then you won't care that I'll be providing the missing bridesmaid for you. She is a woman who will enhance the photos with a smile brighter than the flash of the camera."

Avery laughed. "You think Elena will be down for something this crazy when she still won't even let you call her by her first name?"

"Do you and Jim gossip about everyone's shitty situations, or is it just my life that is the most fascinating?" I asked, looking at Jim's smile. "I must insist on this. I cannot in good conscience allow your wedding photos to be unbalanced. Good God, woman, you're a billionaire now. It's time to start acting like one."

"Oh, for the love of God," she said. I knew how much she hated all the money talk, but I couldn't resist. "You can bring Ronald McDonald for all I care. Just as long as it shuts you up."

"I don't care for his make-up, so Ronald is going to have to sit this one out," I said, hearing her laughing on the other end of the line.

"Hey, as long as Elena is comfortable and you aren't harassing the poor woman, then she is more than welcome to come and be a part of our wedding. I can't wait to meet her."

"You'll meet her," I said. "And you're welcome."

I ended the call and handed Jim his phone.

"Are you out of your mind?" Jim asked.

"As if you hadn't known that for years," Jake responded to his brother.

"I know what I want, and that's the lovely Dr. Elena Alvarez. This is the brightest idea I've had since," I paused and chuckled, "well, since I decided the woman would one day realize I'm the man of her dreams."

"You'd better hope to God the woman doesn't think you're some insane doctor and run *far, far, far,* away from your desperate ass after this *bright idea*," Alex said, shaking his head.

"It'll be fun," I added. "Of course, I won't force her to do anything she doesn't want to do. Hell, I'm not even forcing her to go to this Christmas party if she's busy unpacking. Elena is her own woman...we are all swiftly learning that."

"I guess this is the part where we all place bets on whether or not Collin gets Elena on a plane to be in a wedding for someone she doesn't know? Right?" Jim added.

"Place all the bets and wagers you've got, boys," I said. "All I needed was Avery's approval, and now all I need is Elena's."

"You mean, *Doctor Alvarez*," Jake teased. "Don't forget you still need her approval to call her Elena too. This should be the easiest shit you've ever pulled off."

"Exactly." I held up my glass and smiled confidently. "Here's to you all losing your lame-ass bets against me."

It was up to me to make it all work, and if I could perform brain surgery, I could pull this shit off too.

CHAPTER TWELVE
ELENA

I loved my office, this hospital, these patients…God, you name it, I loved it. I was happy and grateful for everything, and I was so relieved when my family drama finally started dying down at home.

My brother took his attitude down a few notches after some convincing, but Dad surprised us both when he announced that he'd decided to rent out the Beverly Hills home instead of outright selling it.

After coffee this morning, Dad admitted that he wasn't quite *there yet*, selling the home where we all shared so many fond memories. Maybe it would happen eventually, but for now, it would technically remain in the family. Either way, the time was here to juggle my moving out and Dad and Stevie needing to pack as well because Dad wanted to move to the ranch this weekend, and I'd gotten my new keys already. Thank God I was off until Monday after I finished work tonight.

"Dr. Alvarez," the RN working the floor acknowledged me as I passed her in the hallway.

"Hey, Katy," I said. "Everything going good today?"

"Long day," she eyed me with a smile. "It's good to see you up here today. Mr. Follows is almost ready to leave for the rehab center. You're just in time."

"Got it." I waved as she turned to continue walking away, "Have a good one."

I loved the staff here, every single one of them. They were all pleasant and lively to be around, making it enjoyable to come to the hospital and check on my patients. Sure, there were a few cranky RNs, techs, and doctors, but hey, sleep deprivation does that to people—well, to everyone but Dr. Brooks, of course. God only knew how that guy functioned, working nonstop on his on-call days. Another check in the box of a dream guy, a guy who had a bright outlook on everything even when functioning on zero sleep.

"Mr. Follows," I said, entering the room, seeing where his stroke had caused him to lose strength on the right side of his body.

I rushed to his bedside when he smiled and tried to get up. His wife was in conversation with the rehab doctor and Dr. Waters, who'd been his surgeon since he was rushed to the hospital.

I gently sat next to him, took the cloth from his hand, and dabbed the saliva that was dripping from the right side of his mouth. "I know you're excited to see me, but Dr. Waters will not be pleased if I'm the reason his patient is in rehab for longer than a month."

I watched him smile but then fall back into his pillows in defeat.

"Hey," I said, reaching for his hand, "look at me."

He did, and I saw the man I knew he was before this stroke caused him to suffer from hemiparesis. His pitch-black hair was sprinkled with gray, and his eyes showed lines that were evidence of what his family told me when I met with them yesterday—he smiled often, joked, and was a pillar of strength. I wasn't about to let him suffer or become a victim of this stroke.

"Dr. Varez," he slurred.

"Yes," I arched an eyebrow at him. "Listen, this is a new chapter—a new challenge. I've talked to your wife and kids," I gave him a knowing grin, "and they told me I was lucky to have met the strongest man they knew. Is that still true?"

He nodded.

"You're darn right it is. We talked about this yesterday. They told me that you've broken in the most stubborn young horses and even the mustangs that you and your wife rescue, right?"

He nodded. Talking wasn't going to be easy for him, even though he was already progressing well with his new speech therapist. I eyed his charts, seeing that he was ready to be released and in more appropriate, rehab-center care. My job was to prepare him for the road ahead mentally, so it would be a speedy recovery. There would be changes he would need to make to adjust to the lasting stroke damage, and it was my duty to bring him the facts and not talk down to him. I had to shoot him straight. He had to fight hard, and it was my job to make this fight worth something.

"Now, just like with the stubborn horses, you have to be determined and patient. Have you ever given up on a horse?" I asked, seeing this man was broken.

He tried to turn his head from me.

"Mr. Follows," I said, my voice a bit sterner, "when you leave Saint John's today, it's up to you if you want to give up and become a victim of this stroke. You can easily become that, but I don't think you're that kind of man. I think you're the kind of man who fights back with everything he's got—the kind of man who gets right back on that horse when he throws you from his back."

He looked at me in annoyance.

"There are statistics that show the body has a way of recovering through these strokes, and that the neuro pathways can open back up and reestablish nerve and muscle function." I squeezed his hand. "You can choose here and now to leave Saint John's as one of the statistics of a patient who has recovered from a stroke, or you can give up. I won't allow the latter. You will fight back, and you will work hard."

His expression grew curious. "Yes," he managed.

"Yes," I repeated. "I won't lie to you during this process, so I am going to tell you now that this will not be easy. This will probably be one of the most difficult things you've ever done in your life, but like the stories that I've heard about you, you're going to get back on the horse."

"One of those horses should have broken his neck at least three times," a young man no older than I interjected. "Dad was beaten up and bleeding from being thrown into the fencing time and time again, but he wouldn't stop. Would you, Dad?" I looked over and saw Mr. Follows' expression brighten, listening to his son, who stood at the foot of his bed. "You worked that horse until morning when I got up."

"Slept in," Mr. Follows mumbled with a husky laugh.

I smiled at the young man's beaming expression. "Slept in?" I teased and then looked back at Mr. Follows. "I have a younger brother who likes to *sleep in*. Drives me insane."

"If you call waking up at seven in the morning sleeping in, Dr. Alvarez," the young man stated, standing there, impeccably dressed—looking nothing like the slacker his father might've led me to believe.

"I do." I lifted my chin. "That suit you're wearing tells me that you know seven in the morning is sleeping in now too?"

He smirked. "Dad's always right. His stubbornness shows in everything. And yes, Dr. Alvarez, if I'm up at seven in the morning, I'm most likely missing a morning conference call, an important meeting, or losing a client."

"Your dad's going to come out of this just fine," I said. I looked back at Mr. Follows. "I want to hear that you'll fight to get your life back."

He nodded, his eyes still on his son. I could tell that even though the tough cowboy who lay in bed differed vastly from his businessman son, the two shared a close connection, and Mr. Follows would be in great hands with his wife and son.

I stood. "I love to check in on my patients before they leave for rehab. So, don't think for one second I'm letting you off easy by walking out of this room right now. You promise me that when I show up in a few weeks, you're going to be ready to get home and saddle up."

"If there's one thing I know about you, old man," his son said with a laugh, "it's that the only thing that will stop you from getting back on those horses is death itself." He looked at me. "My mom said we could consult with you for anything; is this part of Dad's recovery plan?"

"Yes. I'm here for anything. The rehab center is in the new wing and close to where I can make rounds on my lunch if needed," I said. "And I will. Your dad will recover; he just needs to be determined and fight when his body doesn't want to fight."

His son scratched the shadow on his cheek. I could see that it was difficult for the man to see his dad like this, but I also saw that same fire in his eyes. "So, I get to finally be the one to boss you around now, eh?"

"I wouldn't let him," I said, siding with Mr. Follows. "You show your son that Dad's strong spirit is alive and well."

"Thanks, Dr. Alvarez," his son said as the doctor and Mrs. Follows were wrapping things up.

The rehab doctor was ready to bring in his team to transport Mr.

Follows to their facility. It truly was up to him to fight, and I would be there to check in every step of the way. Discouragement was such a silent mental killer if you let it take over. In a stroke victim's case, that could easily happen. It was my job to help them.

"This won't be easy," I repeated, "but any success is monumental to progress in retraining your mind to do things. I will see you soon enough, Mr. Follows." I smiled at the family. "You all have my information on his discharge papers. It is in his care plan with Saint John's and our rehabilitation center for any of you to make an appointment for consultations. Please don't hesitate to make an appointment for anything."

With that, I took my leave with Dr. Waters, and we both walked back to our offices together. "You are an amazing doc, Elena," Dr. Waters said. "It's nice having you on the floor like this. I don't know how you make the time for it."

I looked over at the man who was number two on the cocky neurosurgeon list at Saint John's. Everyone knew who number one was. Dr. Waters was a bit older than Dr. Brooks, but still young, being in his mid-forties. I did find it strange that Saint John's was almost like a soap opera hospital—young, hot doctors and nurses floating around this extravagant place.

"I'm just grateful you trust your patients in my care. I'm still new and have a lot to prove. To have doctors trusting me with their patients is quite an honor," I answered as we turned toward the back doors that led into our offices outside of the hospital.

"What makes you think we trust you and aren't testing you?" he said in his dick-voice, something I was accustomed to with men like him.

"I hope you're testing me," I answered confidently, "because if I were getting things spoon-fed to me around this place, I'd probably suck at my job."

"Oh?" he smirked as we stopped, and I turned to open my office door. "I hardly think you'd suck at your job. Your smile alone is enough to rehab any patient."

I laughed, pulling off my lab-coat and turning to pack up my desk. "Amusing. If only that were the case, then I wouldn't have had to bust my ass in college, med school, and internships."

"Good night, Elena." He smiled and then left me to pack things up.

It was Thursday night, and my stuff should have been delivered and moved into my new place, ready for me to go through and unpack this weekend. I pulled out my phone to confirm the movers had shown up, and Stevie was there to let them into the apartment. God bless his little nightlife soul—he was taking the week off to help Dad and me clear the main house and move out for the cleaners to prepare the place for the new renters.

Part of me knew that Dad could hold off—and should have to save us all this crazy time crunch in getting out of the house—but he was ready to go to Malibu, and after talking horses and seeing the cowboy in Mr. Follows, I was excited to get out to the ranch and greet the horses.

"Dr. Waters, eh?" I heard Collin's lighthearted voice say.

I placed my briefcase on my desk and looked up at the man, leaning casually in my doorway. He had his arms crossed, and a leg smoothly crossed over the other one. Damn it. I had trained my eyes and brain to get used to this man by now, so why was I acting like it was the first time I'd seen Collin looking hotter than ever in his dark suit.

"Dr. Waters?" I questioned with a laugh. "I just finished up with one of his patients he's sending to rehab."

"Ah," Collin answered, eyes illuminating with his vibrant smile. "You realize that guy is so slimy that if you poured salt on him, he'd dissolve into a pile of goo, right?"

"Well, shit." I sat back in my chair and rubbed my forehead. "Too bad you're not a shrink like me, then."

"I could easily fix any problem you might have if your mind is leading you down a path to date some slimy geek of a man."

"I bet you could." I laughed, trying to cover up the fact that my body was aching for things to turn into *something* more than unpacking boxes and setting up my bed this weekend. "What makes you think he'd even be up for a date with me, Dr. Brooks?"

Collin glanced over his shoulder and then smiled back at me. "Unlike you, I've actually listened in on the gossip that is brewing around the floors of this hospital. It looks like you're the new hottie that the doctors and nurses—"

"Oh, God. Don't." I closed my eyes and held up my hand.

Collin laughed. "You seem a bit flustered, Dr. Alvarez." In the new Collin fashion, he seemed to know when things could work me up—like hospital gossip directed at me in such a way—and he diffused it with a smile. "And why the hell does that guy get to call you Elena?"

"I think you know exactly why by now," I said, somewhat annoyed. "And please don't tell me that people are talking like this about me?"

"Everyone adores you," he said, more sincerely this time. "You are quite the asset to Saint John's, and that's not just me, speaking as your future husband, either."

That was all it took, and I chilled out some. "Well, I love working here," I added. "Whether I'm speaking with my future husband or not, I am about to find out if the brain and spinal surgeon can put a bed together this weekend."

His lips tightened. "About that," he said in a lowered voice. "I'm sure you heard through the rumor mill that runs stronger than the white-water rapids through Arizona that we have a Christmas event this Saturday evening?"

"Yes," I said. "And those rapids in Arizona and Utah are both quite the adrenaline rush."

His face lightened, and that beautiful Collin smile spread broadly. "You enjoy white-water rafting, Dr. Alvarez?"

"Absolutely. Sort of an addiction." I shivered with excitement, remembering the many times we vacationed in Colorado, Utah, and Arizona just to take on the rapids. "I love the feeling of adrenaline coursing through my veins." I exhaled, feeling almost that same way as I noticed an expression I'd never seen on Collin's face before. God, it was as painful as looking into the sun right now. I could barely hold my own against his flawless face and this cursed smile that could be a superpower against evil if that were even possible.

"Wow." His forehead creased while his eyebrows shot up as if he'd just been slapped with the most enormous revelation of his life. "You really are my other half."

"Because I'm an adrenaline junkie?" I chuckled.

"Precisely because of that."

"You enjoy white-water rafting?" I asked, somewhat surprised.

"You have no idea the adrenaline me and my best friends chase—well, mainly Jake and me because the other two are boring, CEO work-a-holics." He laughed. "Listen, I have to go to this gala, and I promised James Mitchell that I would ensure his latest hire, the amazing Dr. Elena

Alvarez, would be there. So, how about we go to this Christmas thing together, and while we're in the holiday spirit, we'll hit up a Christmas tree farm. We can pick out a tree for your new place on Saturday morning, and we can manage the unpacking and moving in around…" He raised his shoulders in excitement, "Well, around this festive holiday season."

"You do have me figured out," I smirked. "All but the part where Mr. James Mitchell is requesting me to show up. Last I recall, this was to recognize the best through the year at Saint John's, celebrate the holidays, and give out special bonus checks. Me being here for less than a month says that I get to duck out of this event."

Collin's lips twisted. "Even after I offer to buy the Christmas tree for your home?"

"Even after all of that."

"Decorate it too?" he said in some playful voice.

"You're going to decorate a tree that you plan on randomly buying me?"

"Yep," he said resolutely.

"With what ornaments?"

"Whatever ornaments you have."

"I don't have any."

Collin grinned. "Well, then, that allows me to help buy our first Christmas ornaments together."

"Slow down." I stood, ready to leave. "You have fun at the Christmas party, and I'll text you my address if you still want to give me a hand unpacking."

Collin pulled up from reclining in my doorway and walked toward me. "What are you so afraid of with me?" he asked, almost as serious as he seemed curious.

"I'm not afraid of you," I said. "I have to get moved in."

"I already said that I'd help."

"I have no type of Christmas party outfit to wear," I finally admitted.

"Good God, Alvarez," he said, plopping into one of the seats across from my desk. "You're in Southern California *during party season*. I'll take you out personally to buy the dress. Then I say we make an appearance at this party and bounce."

I eyed Collin becoming more relaxed and casual. "If I'm honest, Collin—"

"Which, historically, is not your strong point when it comes to me," he interrupted, never missing a chance to rub my Las Vegas lie in my face. "Continue."

"Fine. I'll go," I said. "Let's give us a try, starting with a chaotic event that I'm not prepared for, a looming move that's hanging over my shoulders, and..." I stopped and smiled at him as he nodded along.

"And," his eyebrows rose, "the Christmas tree you'll be picking. That, in and of itself, should be enough to put a strain on *trying us out*."

"I'm picky with my trees," I said.

"I'm picky with who I invite to last-minute hospital Christmas parties."

"Then it's a date. You and me, the two pickiest people on the planet, trying out a date."

"You said you loved adrenaline, right? Addicted to it, I believe those were the words you used," he stood and said with wide eyes. "Crave it?"

"Live for it."

"Then I'm sure I'll find a way to satisfy your adrenaline addictions." He turned to walk out. "I'll have you addicted to me." He stopped and eyed me. "And I'm sure you're not afraid since you made it very clear you're a fearless woman."

My heart decided to take off at a rapid pace again, knowing exactly what he was talking about and me wanting him more than ever before. "I'll meet you there," I said.

"No, you won't." He smiled, "This isn't going to be a separate-cars situation. I'll drive you. Text me your address, Alvarez. I'm not going to be in the office tomorrow, so I won't see you until party night."

"Fine. I'll see you then."

"And it's about time," he smiled.

"Hey," I caught him before he left my office. I rubbed my forehead, knowing I needed to keep my priorities straight. "Seriously, I don't think I should go to the party. I really need to get up and help my dad unpack at the ranch."

Collin seemed to be unaffected by that. "Well, then we'll unpack two houses this weekend," he answered. "I don't give a damn. I'm not letting you back out of this."

I met his challenging grin with one of my own. "I'm off this weekend, and I'm headed to the ranch tomorrow. I shouldn't break up everything with a Christmas party."

"Well, it's a good thing I have the weekend off too, isn't it?"

"You seriously think you're going to go to the ranch and help me get my dad all squared away?"

"I seriously think I'm taking you to that Christmas party, and I'll do whatever it takes to make it happen." His smile broadened. "And here I had no idea you had the entire weekend off until now. It looks like we're unpacking *Papa Alvarez* tomorrow, making Christmas party appearances, unpacking your place on Saturday, and then," he pursed his lips, "we'll be a solid couple by Monday morning."

"Sometimes you're too sure of yourself." I narrowed my eyes at his confidence. "Okay," I let out a breath, "meet me at the ranch in Malibu. We'll see how sure you are of this *solid couple* thing by Monday morning after dealing with my dad."

"Best to get his kicking my ass out of the way now, instead of later. Give me your digits, Alvarez," he said, taking my phone number as I laughed in disillusionment that he was willing to do any of this. "Great. Now, here's mine." He smiled as he texted me. "See you bright and early at the Alvarez ranch." He winked and walked out of the room.

My phone buzzed and I glanced down at it.

555-230-8927: *Save this number as, My Future Husband.*

I COULDN'T DO anything other than smile at Collin's text, reminding me of the name he used when we first met. The man would most likely have his confidence shaken by my dad tomorrow. I sure as hell wouldn't want to be in Collin's position, anyway. Hell, I didn't even want to deal with Dad going off on my brother's lazy ass, but I was putting off unpacking my stuff until Saturday so I could get this out of the way. I wanted Dad settled, and God help me if Stevie had been sleeping all week and hadn't yet lifted a finger to help.

At least we had *my future husband* helping out. As far as I was concerned when it came to moving, the more help, the merrier. If I was honest with myself, I was excited about this. I was excited to be around this man who excited me so much. It was time to get to know Dr. Brooks better and see if he crumbled under pressure outside of work because he sure as hell didn't seem to let any form of pressure get to him otherwise.

CHAPTER THIRTEEN
COLLIN

J pulled up to the Alvarez family ranch and parked next to Elena's Land Rover. People were in and out of the front door, carrying boxes and working to help Miguel get this house moved in as fast as the man would call his surgical team into the OR for a trauma-related emergency.

I had to give Dr. Alvarez some credit; never in my life would I have imagined the man to have such a badass ranch in Malibu. The house was across the Pacific Coast Highway and hidden in the mountains that overlooked the beach. The rustic yet contemporary log cabin sat peacefully overlooking the ocean and was surrounded by small pastures shaded by the mountain bluffs beyond them.

This was undoubtedly any horse lovers' dream if they loved the serenity of the mountains accompanied by the ability to gaze at the ocean from their front porch. The barn and horse stables sat beyond the detached garage and matched the main house with their log and slate rock exteriors—definitely a place you couldn't easily find on the coast in Southern California. Hell, I lived on the beach twenty minutes down the road from this place, and it was an entirely different world from where I stood at Miguel's house.

I knocked on the knotty-pine double doors, and the one man I knew who may or may not be happy to see me answered it.

"Brooks," he said. He gave me a stiff nod, then his forehead creased in humor as the man brought me in for a hug.

What the hell? Didn't expect this.

"Damn it, it's good to see your ugly face again," I teased him like we were at the hospital. "I have to admit. The old battlefield isn't the same without you there."

"I already know that. Get in here," he said with some humor. "What brings you out here? A patient? Ready to resign that chief position already?"

"Funny," I said, glancing around and seeing the man was entirely moved in. "I was actually invited by another Dr. Alvarez." Elena came walking up, wearing a pair of overalls with a red and black checkered flannel over them. Her smile was mischievous and giddy, all at once. "You may know her. She's good at misleading me into believing her little white lies."

"My adorable and innocent, Elena?" Miguel laughed and draped around Elena, who held an open moving box in her hands. "White lies? Never."

She was more beautiful now than ever. She had a handkerchief tied around her head, holding her hair back from her face, and the red material made her bronze eyes pop more than when she wore makeup to enhance them.

"That's right, Papi," she said, leaning into her dad. "These are the first of the memory lane boxes you won't let that company touch. Collin and I will get them up into the attic."

"Collin and I were just about to catch up, kid," Miguel said. "I'm ready for a beer, and now that the boxes are unpacked and moved in, it's time to relax."

Elena bit down on her lower lip when my eyes met hers, knowing she'd lured me out here to spend time with her dad—but this time, he wasn't my co-worker. He was the father of the woman I was infatuated with. I could see it in her challenging smile, and I could sense it in Miguel, but at the moment, I was somewhat lost.

Was Miguel going to sit me down and tell me to keep my ass far away from his daughter, or was he poking back at Elena and on my side with the fact that the man didn't need help moving in as it was apparent he'd hired a company to do most of the work for him? Nah, there was no way Miguel was taking my side over his beautiful and tricky daughter.

"You told me you needed help moving in, and I dropped everything to show up and find out you hired a company to do most of the work. Collin offered to help too, and now look at us?"

"That's why I'm offering up a beer." He smirked.

"At eight in the morning?" Elena raised an eyebrow to her dad. "I don't think so. You need to unpack your office, Stevie needs to wake his ass up and help unpack his stuff, and there is a room full of boxes of stuff from us kids I need to get up into the attic," she challenged her dad. "You go wake Stevie up, and get back to your office. We'll relax with a beer later, old man."

Miguel shrugged. "And you think you can handle that one?" he asked as Elena turned to give instructions to a group of movers who had walked in with more boxes. "Good God, Brooks. You're in over your head with her."

"I see I've been the topic of conversation?" I smiled, following him into the house.

"Well, when my Laney comes home saying that a handsome fellow who goes by the name Dr. Collin Brooks proposed to her on the dance floor, then yes." He turned back and smirked at me before he clapped me on the arm. "Anyone who takes that kind of interest in my daughter becomes the topic of conversation in my family." He glanced over at his daughter as she spun around and walked toward us. "And allowing you to spend time with her might keep her off my butt for a while."

"Oh, Papi," Elena came back with a laugh. "Get to your office. Collin, you're with me."

Miguel nodded. "Gee, thanks for the help." He chuckled, then disappeared and left Elena and me to haul boxes up to a massive attic.

Elena was on a mission to clear the boxes out of the room where they'd been stacked. We worked to organize the boxes in sections, and I studied a picture of a strikingly-beautiful woman that'd slipped out of a box with the name Lydia scrawled on the side.

"It looks like the genetics of beauty run strong in your family," I said.

Elena chuckled and took the portrait of the woman from my hand. "This is my older sister, Lydia," she said. "She's gorgeous, right?"

I studied the sharp features of Lydia's face. Her piercing green eyes made me feel as if she were sizing me up through the picture alone, and her ruby red lips set off her thick, pitch-black hair. She was beautiful, that was certain, but I'd been around my fair share of beautiful women who had a similar, mysterious look in their eyes. I looked back at Elena's bronze eyes as she patiently watched me, and those feelings I felt the first night I saw this lively woman returned. She was perfect in every way and soothing to a soul that had been searching too long to find its other half.

"Not nearly as gorgeous as you," I said.

"Well, you'd be the first to think that," she responded with a laugh. "Lydia's even won some pretty fierce modeling competitions."

"That wouldn't surprise me at first glance," I pursed my lips, "but she's not as beautiful as my future wife."

Elena's cheeks tinted pink. "Get over here. I need some help with this heavy box."

I followed Elena over to her section and saw where she had a box open. "This one?" I asked, seeing ribbons and trophies in it.

"Yeah, I need it moved over here."

"Hold up." I knelt when I saw a picture of a teenage girl, dressed in an equestrian riding outfit and holding onto a stunning thoroughbred. "Is this you?" I asked, pulling out the old, golden picture frame.

Elena laughed. "That's Cookie and me. He was the best jumper around."

"I can tell. He won a hell of a lot of trophies and ribbons," I said, seeing *First Place* written on pretty much everything in this box.

"Hey, I did some of the work for us to get those too." She reached into the box, pulling out a picture of the horse standing alone. "I miss this guy," she said, running her fingers over the image.

"You enjoyed jumping, then?" I asked, intrigued to find out more about her.

"Well, the adrenaline part was mostly what kept me going. I would sneak Cookie out of the stables, and we'd race through the mountain trails so that I could feel his power surging through him."

"So," I smiled at her soft expression, "is the woman who has captivated me into horses?"

"I love them. They're therapeutic to ride. To feel that raw power come to life and turn the reins loose? I love every minute of it."

"I know how you feel. I grew up doing the same. Perhaps we crossed paths during a competition once?"

"Perhaps," she said playfully. "Maybe one day I'll find another feisty horse like Cookie and use my weekends off to come here to feel the freedom of being on the horse again."

I eyed her, seeing the look of wonder in her eyes, and the first and only thought that hit me was fulfilling her wish. "Hey, I saw that your dad had three or four beautiful thoroughbreds out in that pasture. Not good enough for you?"

Elena laughed and folded up the box top. "No," she said. "Two of those horses are being boarded here, and the other two are Dad's and Stevie's. I wasn't living in California when Dad and Stevie bought them. They got them from some ranch in the Central Valley. Great horses, but I would've saved up a bit more money and bought from Natsummers."

I laughed in response to that.

"What?" Elena returned my laugh.

"My old man knew Grant Natsummers. I knocked out his son in a fight in the seventh grade, but hey, I bet I could still get you a good deal on one of his horses. They are the best." I chuckled.

"Well, then," she rocked back and sat on her heels, "there's no hope for you and me for sure now. I *knew* there was a reason I couldn't date you."

"I'll make you a promise here and now." I smiled at her confidently.

"Another promise?" She smiled as she pointed to the box. "I need that over here, you goof."

I picked up the box and followed Elena to a darker corner of her section in the attic. Then I stopped her when I put my arm up on a stack of boxes, our bodies so close that I could hardly handle the energy between us.

"Okay, what's the promise?" Elena asked, crossing her arms and arching her eyebrow at me. "Another Christmas tree? A horse ornament?"

"No, let's call it a prediction." I pursed my lips at her challenging grin. "I'll get your Christmas tree and have you in my arms as my future fiancé, all while securing a chestnut stallion as your wedding gift."

She burst into laughter, the same as me, knowing it was ridiculous, but it was fun, and I was confident it would happen. I saw the way she looked at me, and I just needed to gain her trust.

"I'll hold you to that. Let's go get lunch." She ducked under my arm. "You said you rode?"

"Yep." I turned back to her. "How the hell else would I have gotten into a fight with that spoiled Natsummers kid?"

"Good God," she laughed. "All right, then. Let's saddle up Frisco and Brinks and take lunch out by the lake on the edge of Dad's property. Do you want to know where I get my little *white lies* from? It's that man. He made it seem as though he had no help to move, and Dr. Mitchell was going to come after all of us for allowing a man with his blood pressure to unpack his entire house." She rolled her eyes. "I could've gotten my whole house unpacked today."

"Well, let's make the best out of your dad misleading you, and then me, into coming out here. I'm curious to learn more about the woman I'm about to spend quite a lot of money on a horse for."

ON THE DAY that this woman walked back into my life at Saint John's, if someone had told me that I'd be on horseback, riding on my way to have egg-salad sandwiches with her by a lake, I would have told them they'd lost their minds.

Elena was becoming more intriguing to me by the hour. This fun yet strangely romantic affair was more consuming to me than trying to get her into bed. That was saying something for the type of man I'd always been, but I was adamant about locking down a relationship with her no matter what, and I wanted to know everything about her.

Elena and I managed to saddle Frisco and Brinks in record time, and as soon as we set off, everything came back as if I hadn't skipped a day of riding since my teenage years. I smiled and followed the feisty, spirited woman, who encouraged both horses into a race up through the mountainside on a dirt path.

This was as exhilarating as bringing my car up to top speeds on late nights when the freeways were clear, and it was as close as it got to bringing my street bike at an aggressive speed while cruising up PCH. It was freedom and an escape, and what better person to do this with than the woman who drew me in more every time I was with her?

We climbed up to the mountain ridge, and Elena slowed her horse when a pasture opened up, displaying a small lake with a canoe and dock.

All of it seemed like it was from another place. It was hard to imagine we were still in Southern California.

I LOUNGED ON MY SIDE, propped up on an elbow on the blanket Elena had laid on the grass, facing the serene pond, and I bit into the delicious egg salad sandwich that was more than fitting for our view.

"So, Alvarez," I said, looking at her where she sat, cross-legged and watching the horses graze without their bridles. "What's your story?"

"My story?" she smiled back at me.

"Yeah. I need to know specifics since I'm marrying you."

"Okay, future husband. My story." She gave me a teasing wink that only made me adore her more, and she gazed up at the sky, holding onto her sandwich. "I grew up here. My parents divorced when I was young. My mom easily got custody and moved us to Miami, where I graduated high school. Then, I went on to college. I was fascinated by stories I'd heard from Dad's profession. So, two years into that—"

"Good God, woman." I laughed. "That's a highlight reel."

"Well, what do you want to know? I seriously have no idea why you're on this crazy road to marry me anyway." She laughed the laugh that I'd fallen in love with from our very first conversation.

"You mentioned you were fascinated by your dad's profession," I smirked at her brilliant eyes, "which basically affirms that you're already fascinated by me since I'm doing that exact job."

"Then, I decided I didn't want to be a neurosurgeon," she challenged with a bite into her egg-salad, giving me a funny expression and crossing her eyes in a silly way that made me laugh.

"You wanted to be a shrink instead?"

She reached into the bag of chips she brought and tossed one into her mouth. "I don't know. I realized that doing such a high-risk job wasn't quite my style. I would rather be the one to help those who have to deal with the life changes that an injury could cause them. You know," she looked at me, more serious now, "it's devastating and could happen to anyone. One minute, life is normal, and you're dancing around or driving down the road, and the next minute, you're waking up in the hospital with a disability that you never saw coming. That's a difficult tragedy to deal with. I want to be their advocate when their minds see nothing but defeat."

"I watched the way you consulted Mr. Numen's family. You did a good job with them. That family was torn in every way possible after his accident. The irreparable damage that had been done to his spine is indeed a tragedy. He'll be paralyzed for life. Those things sit with me, knowing that I can't fix the problem in cases like his and give him his life back."

"From the medical records and your notes," she eyed me, "you did better than any surgeon I'd met in fixing the areas to help give him a fighting chance to use his hands."

"Sometimes, in surgery, a surgeon gets lucky and finds something he can repair. I instinctively knew there was something more. I managed to find and repair it, and I was grateful when I made my rounds and saw that he had some movement in his hands again."

"You realize that he can still overcome just by using the hope with the start you gave him?"

"I heard you loud and clear on that; however, I am a scientist, and scientifically speaking, he won't completely overcome the paralysis of his legs," I said, crumbling up my napkin and putting it in the trash bag we'd brought. "It's why, at first, I was concerned with you giving the family such hope and praising me." I arched an eyebrow at her. "Yet you remained firm on what you read on his charts and scans."

"You're out of your mind if you think I'm going to plant flowers and happy-go-lucky pictures in people's minds."

"I never said that, but it was one of our first consultations, and I was hanging on to how you would work as a team member on the neuro-ward."

"Well, Dr. Brooks," she eyed me, "I do study charts, and I see where the mind is one powerful thing. It will take work, but if he follows my advice of mentally overcoming what *science* says he can't, then you'll have a patient feeling better about his altered life."

"That's a tough one, doctor," I said. "He has to accept that he'll never walk again."

"So many people are crippled with disabilities that they mentally impress upon themselves, and for no reason too."

"How's that?"

"It's anything. It's waking up one day and asking where did the time go? Why did I lose my spouse? Why do I hate my spouse? What the hell am I doing with my life?" She sighed. "Believe it or not, that negativity can alter minds in ways to cripple a competent individual."

"That's very true," I said with a smile. "And how do you get through a situation that you don't *mentally* put yourself in?"

"Like being in a wheelchair?" she asked, crunching into another chip. "You find other methods to live happily and appreciate that you're living and breathing and waking up to a sunrise every day. You rode that horse today; how'd that feel?"

"Pretty fucking awesome," I answered truthfully.

"Therapeutic, wasn't it?" she asked.

"Yes," I grinned. "Are you trying to get into my head now, my sexy little shrink?"

She blushed, and I loved that she responded to my flirting like this in a fun way instead of getting pissed about it. "One day, I hope to have a rehab center with horses. They have them here in Southern California, but what a dream to have a place where I can treat my patients who can't easily recover and give them freedom and the thrill of the accomplishment of riding a horse. Many have broken through with their diagnoses for life in a wheelchair after equine therapy, you know?"

"Well, we'll call it Elena's Equine Miracle therapy?"

"Nice," she rubbed her hands together and folded up the chip bag. "How about you and I take a ride in that canoe?"

I looked to the lake and the canoe and laughed at the thought of us doing this. "I was hoping we could just call it what it is between us: you allow me to call you Elena from now on, and we make out up here in the middle of nowhere."

"Nice try, bud," she rose. "Let's go. I'll show you a little about *my story* that you asked about earlier."

Balancing and trying to get into the canoe without it tipping over was a laugh all on its own. Still, once we were in, Elena sat perfectly straight, gently pulling the water through her paddle, and we escaped life, finding ourselves together in this unique moment.

"So this is it, eh?" I asked, rowing my oar to the rhythm of hers. "This is Elena's story, riding in a canoe. Hell, I knew I fell for an adventurous woman for a reason."

"Getting bored back there?" she glanced over her shoulder.

"Well, we're rowing, and your ass looks sexy in overalls," I answered.

Elena turned and hit me with the smile I'd be hoping I'd see today. "All right. Don't move. Hold still," she said, moving closer to the middle of the canoe.

"Bout time you kiss me," I said.

"Don't move," she said with a smile. She exhaled, steadying her hands on the sides of the canoe, gripping the rim, and it wobbling in response. I watched in curiosity as she blew out another breath, and then my eyes went from her perfect cleavage to her feet as they started pointing toward the bottom of the boat while she began to bend her knees.

"What the hell are you doing?" I asked.

"Don't move, damn it." She laughed, froze, and then I watched in awe as she did some crazy acrobat shit and slowly brought herself to hold her legs up in the air, body completely erect. The woman was doing some crazy handstand by holding onto the rim of the boat.

"Jesus Christ!" I said, marveling at her and trying to figure out how the hell she'd pulled off this crazy yoga canoe maneuver.

"Pretty awesome, huh?" she said, her white teeth brilliantly shining through this upside-down Elena grin.

"You're insanely talented."

"Wanna try it?" she asked with a laugh that shook the boat. "Don't move! Don't Move!" I tried to steady the canoe but made it worse.

"Oh, hell," I said as Elena erupted into laughter, and the boat flipped both of us into the water when her weight shifted. Elena came up directly after me and pinched the water from her nose.

I smoothed my hair back and cleared the water from my eyes while I caught the canoe from drifting away. "And you *just* came up with that? That's some crazy, acrobat shit."

"I did it all the time up here as a kid. I got bored with floating on rafts and the canoe since the lake is so small, so I got creative and taught myself that stunt. I'm shocked I can still do it."

"You're pretty fucking amazing," I said as I pulled her closer to the canoe, and she pulled herself in before helping me up.

. . .

AFTER ENJOYING Elena's personality now more than ever, I was beginning to ache for the woman to allow me in more. She kept my sorry ass at arm's length, and I was as patient as I could be. I loved the challenge, and Elena Alvarez was my greatest challenge yet.

I was going to use a little bit of her advice in pursuing her as well. It was a mental challenge, and instead of being pissed as hell that I couldn't so much as seal a deal on a kiss tonight, I'd get that kiss and much more later. Now just wasn't the time.

I was about to take off after we got back to her dad's place, but Miguel insisted I stay for his *famous* Cuban sandwiches.

"Best damn sandwich I've ever eaten." I swallowed another savory bite after Miguel asked what I thought, then looked at Elena. "Aside from your delicious egg salad today, of course."

"She gets that from her mother," Miguel laughed.

"And I can cook as well as my Papi too," she teased back.

"So," Steve spoke up, eyes bloodshot from whatever he'd been smoking on all day. "Is James Mitchell going to give me a shot to pitch my idea or what?" he asked me, and I instantly felt the previously-happy atmosphere at the table disappear.

"The DJ thing, right?" I smiled. "Exactly what do you want Mr. Mitchell to fund?"

"Me, man," he answered as if he were the solution to every businessman's problems.

"Have you finished college?" I asked, wondering if the kid was serious. "What reason do you think a billion-dollar man and his empire would want to invest in—"

"A kid who smokes weed all day and sleeps until the afternoon?" Elena cut me off.

"Yeah. The weed thing isn't going to seal any deals for the big guy," I said. "I get you must love music, and I'm down with all of that, but you've gotta keep human hours, man."

"Exactly," Elena said.

"I'm at the club making a name for myself," he said. "I keep real human hours."

I could tell Miguel struggled with his son's life choices by his expression alone, and the way Elena fired up like she was about to eat her brother alive reaffirmed that.

"Oh, Stevie, please," Elena said, holding up her hand as if to shut him up before she looked at me. "I'm sorry about this."

"Don't apologize. I was once wild and carefree too. You have to be real with yourself, Steve," I said.

"You have to get your ass back into college. You want to milk Papi for everything and live here for the rest of your life?"

"Trust me, bringing chicks back to your parents' place isn't ideal?" I arched an eyebrow at him. "You've got some strong family genes in you; don't waste them."

"What's college going to do for me? It doesn't give me any life experience."

"Life experience, he says," Elena interjected, rolling her eyes. It was painfully obvious they'd had this conversation too many times.

"You like music and mixing all that up, right?" I asked.

"Yeah. I'm an artist."

"Then head into college, striving to learn more in an artistic field. You could even do sound engineering," I said. "At your age, a lot of people have no idea what they want to be. It's natural. But you've got to take a step in that direction, and it'll come to you." I took a sip of my beer.

"Yeah, I guess," he reluctantly agreed. Maybe just to shut me up, but whatever.

"Start small and work your way up. You can't get shit done without a degree these days, so life experience isn't going to help much in the long run. Not anymore. The sky is the limit with grounded dreams and goals. You'll get them."

"Thank God someone speaks sense, and hopefully, the boy listens," Miguel said.

Steve stood. "Thanks for dinner, Papi. Nice to see you again, Collin. Later, sis," he said, tapping her on her shoulder.

"In one ear and right out the other," Elena said as Steve walked out.

"Well, it's the first time he said thank you for dinner," Miguel laughed.

"I'm going to talk to him some more. I swear I will lose my shit if he goes out and clubs all night tonight," she said.

Elena left a smiling Miguel and me at the table. "She's been up his ass since she moved back." He laughed. "And here I have you at my table now too." He took a swig of his beer. "Damn it, Collin Brooks. I want to be pissed-off at you for going after my little girl, but I can't. I have to warn you, though. Elena is her own woman."

"She's made that clear, especially since I can't call her Elena; it's only *Dr. Alvarez* for me." I laughed.

"You know," he arched an eyebrow at me, "she wouldn't let you this close to her if she didn't have the slightest feelings for you. She's fun and tough all at once."

"Fire and ice," I smirked.

"One way to put it, and somehow that sweet daughter of mine thrills my heart to be around her." He leaned back in his chair, beer in hand. "Babies are usually born screaming their heads off," he said, and then his eyes became distant, "but not my Laney. That child came into this world with big, curious eyes and a smile as bright as the one she wears to this day."

"Yeah?" I shouldn't have been surprised. Of course, she'd be a perfect baby.

"Laney's eyes were always searching for something, always dazzling with wonder in them. I knew then we had a special little girl, and I can't fathom seeing her heart crushed." He looked at me with a half-smile. "Tread carefully with her, Brooks," he said with some warning in his voice. "She's a wild and free spirit that can't be tamed. She has a soul that strives to see the good in everything and find adventure anywhere she can find it."

"I have to say that's what has captivated me about her," I answered honestly. "From the first moment that I saw her, I knew she was a special woman."

"So long as you keep that in mind, I won't feel the need to kick your ass. She's an angel, so don't you dare try to clip her wings or break her heart."

I stood, knowing I only had an hour to meet up with Jake and Ash for Ash's art gallery Christmas presentation. "I enjoyed the day. It was really fantastic to see you again."

Miguel nodded. "You too, Brooks," he said, standing with me. "I'll tell Elena you took off. You're seeing her tomorrow, right?"

I smirked. "We have the Saint John's Christmas gala, and I promised to unpack her place," I said, making Miguel laugh.

"Glad those parties are all behind me."

"I wish I could retire just to get out of them." I chuckled. "Good night, Miguel. You have an impressive home, and I know Jake will be delighted with this location for your blood pressure issues."

"Give my best to Jake, and you keep doing what you're doing. I hear nothing but great things through the hospital grapevine."

"That's good to know." I smiled and took my exit, not knowing where the hell Elena went, but I wasn't about to get into the middle of her roasting her brother's ass for being stoned as fuck tonight.

THE NEXT MORNING, after falling asleep to images of Elena's face, I found myself excited to go to this Christmas gala. The threat of Miguel kicking my ass, especially after hearing him confirm his daughter was as special as I thought her to be, would probably hang over my head for the rest of my life if he had his way.

I didn't even have her yet, but I knew there was no way I would hurt that woman. If I didn't get close to anywhere with her tonight after the Christmas party, then my idea of buying a fresh-cut Christmas tree had better be the game-changer.

CHAPTER FOURTEEN
ELENA

$\mathcal{I}$ had just finished fastening the stubborn top button of my dress when I heard a rhythmic knock on my door. I smiled at my reflection in the mirror, knowing it was Collin, and my heart felt like it was going to beat out of the top of my simple, spaghetti-strap dress.

"Be right there," I called from my room, which was a maze of boxes scattered around the mattress that was lying on the floor.

The only thing put together in this disaster of a place was me, and I was on my way to walk out the door. I opened the door to the brilliant smile that'd officially smitten me, and I saw Collin was dressed in a dark navy, three-piece suit, looking like a million bucks. I expected no less, though.

"I see you brought your A-game," I teased.

"And I see you didn't even have to try to bring yours," he said, reaching for a piece of my hair that didn't make it into the stylish bun I'd twisted my hair into—which was being held together by a silver clip and a prayer. I tucked the loose strands into the back of my hair, hoping that would do the trick.

"Like the dress?" I asked, giving him a twirl with a laugh. The last time I'd worn this thing was underneath my cap and gown at my college graduation. I had no idea why I twirled around because there was nothing special to see. The dress was plain, blue, and form-fitting from my chest to my knees. Not exactly *hot-date* attire, but whatever.

I was trying to be casual as I watched the dangerously handsome man admiring me, and I could feel all of my female parts urging me to blow off this gala and take him to bed—currently known as my mattress on the floor.

"Did a bomb go off in here? Your place is a disaster," he finally said.

"You're the one who insisted we go to this Christmas party," I said as his eyes roamed over my body.

"I'm about to call Jim and tell him to find another prodigy of a neurosurgeon to help honor our new pediatric doctor with the prestigious award the company is offering tonight." His lips pursed. "You're so impossibly beautiful." He cocked his head to the side, "But this look you're giving me has me stumped."

The look of wanting to strip you down and ravage your body? I thought, biting my lower lip.

"Are you upset we're going to this thing? I don't want to pressure you. Honest," he said.

That made me smile. Finally, the man couldn't get into my mind with the expressions that always seemed to give me away.

"Of course, I am," I toyed with him. "Let me get my jacket so we can get out of here."

"Jesus Christ, I really should help you clean this place up," I heard him say while I plucked my white, wool dress coat off a hanger.

"We'll be busy tomorrow," I teased. "Let's go. I love this apartment, but having boxes everywhere stresses me out."

"We're going to handle it," he said as I followed him out to his car.

"Holy shit," I said when his metallic gray Lamborghini came into my view. "You're kidding me, right?"

He smiled as the door opened to the passenger side. "I'm not kidding you. This car is my baby. I've had it for less than a year," he said as he closed the door behind me and walked around to get into the driver's seat. "You're the only woman who's ridden in it. So, now it's my favorite of the cars I own, and..." He grinned at me as I checked out the cockpit of this insanely awesome car.

"And?"

"I can most certainly outperform this car since you mentioned last week that I was…" he paused while working with his crazy GPS *computer screen* of a radio.

"Overcompensating for lacking in certain areas?"

"That's it," he said, looking over his shoulder and taking off as the radio started playing where it must've left off when Collin shut off the car.

I smiled at the song and artist. "Lynyrd Skynyrd, eh?"

"You'll find I'm a bit of a classic rock, blues, and soul kind of guy; you name it, I can most likely sing the song and know the artist."

"Oh?" I smiled, seeking comfort in the smells of rich leather, Collin's sweet and sensual cologne, and the seat itself. "You're a music man too? I found it interesting you had Segar playing when you finished up your surgery."

Collin laughed as he casually reclined in his seat, his right hand smoothly shifting gears while the other casually steered. "That song was meant just for you." He smiled ahead as we drove up the onramp to the freeway, merging with traffic.

"Night moves?" I laughed, the music chilling out my nerves as I enjoyed this ride. "Nice."

"Hey, music says what the heart wants."

"Then why the hell do you have Rob Zombie's Living Dead Girl on your playlist?" I asked, pointing at the songs that varied from Arethra Franklin to Sinatra and Led Zepplin to Otis Redding. You name it; this guy had the best hits from soul to classic rock and rhythm and blues.

"It's a badass song. Here." He ran his fingers up the touch screen, and the music titles seemed to scroll on for forever. "Pick a song. There's at least two hundred or a thousand on my playlist," he said with a laugh. "I'm pretty sure you'll enjoy my taste. In fact, I know you'll love it since I'm profoundly in touch with my music and my love for it."

"Okay, then," I said. "I'll pick a song, and you, Mr. Music Guy, have to sing the song to prove just how *in touch* with it you are."

"Go!" He pointed toward the windshield, dropping the hammer on this car and moving at what seemed to be lightspeed to the fast lane, only to slow down and pace with the traffic.

I clicked on the Aerosmith song, Sweet Emotion, to which Collin instantly started to tap his fingers to the rhythm on his steering wheel. The instrumental intro sounded so killer in this car, and it felt like I was in the recording studio. "Want to hear a fun fact about this song?" he asked.

"I'd love to." My mood was lifted as I enjoyed this drive, watching different aspects of Collin's personality emerging. He was a constant, absolutely delightful surprise.

"The band was in the studio with all their shit, ready to record this song." He shifted lanes to move around the guy who wouldn't stop tapping his breaks in front of us. "Anyway," he said as the song moved into the lyrics, "they had everything set to record, but somehow there wasn't any maracas for the intro and the song. Steven Tyler was pissed, but being the genius musician he is, he improvised." Collin smiled over at me.

"What, did he make that sound with his mouth or something?"

Collin softly laughed. "No. He saw a sugar packet on the ground, picked the thing up, told the studio to turn up his mic, and he shook the thing like it was a maraca. You can't even tell, can you?"

"Wow," I said with a laugh. "That's wild. You know your musicians, but you still haven't proved you know their music."

"Turn it to another song, then. Trust me, Alvarez, I *know* my music."

"Okay." I scrolled through, and as I was trying to navigate the sensitive touchscreen, I accidentally chose the wrong song. "Oops. Oh, shit," I said with a laugh.

Collin smirked over at me. "Bad Company?" I exhaled as I watched him fall into the rhythm of this song. "And for the record, this song is dedicated directly to you, Alvarez."

"Feel like making love?" I laughed at the title that Collin started singing—in a perfect voice, I might add.

Instead of being uncomfortable, Collin made me laugh and become highly entertained as he poked my shoulder and pointed to me every time it referred to *making love to you.*

"I need to find a harder one," I said. "I'm making this too easy on you."

Collin chuckled. "Not my fault you absently picked the perfect song for the way I'm feeling by having you in my car."

I scrolled and decided I couldn't find anything to stump him. Then I found one I liked and wasn't surprised that Collin had almost every song from the Allman Brothers Band.

"Soulshine." He smiled and started to change his entire demeanor. "This is one of my favorite songs."

As Collin sang, it was apparent that this was a favorite of his, given how enthusiastically he sang along as if I weren't even in the car. He was so beautiful, sitting there and singing lyrics to a song that'd always been soothing to my soul. Everything he did seemed to make me fall a little deeper for him.

After close to an hour of jukebox driving with Collin, I was thoroughly entertained and almost completely forgot we were heading to this expensive hotel and Christmas gala. Collin was out of the car and buttoning his suit jacket as the valet came over to retrieve his keys. He was quickly at my door, holding out his hand for me to help hoist myself out of his car in my restrictive dress.

Collin pulled my hand into the bend of his arm without skipping a beat and covered my fingers with his other hand.

"Look at what a gentleman you are."

"See." He smiled down at me. "I'm a considerate man, aren't I?"

"I never said you weren't," I said as we walked through the exquisitely decorated hotel lobby to the area where ushers were guiding the Saint John's staff.

"It's time we go ahead and let the hospital gossiping crows discover that they were right about you and me."

"Right about what?"

"You know exactly what. I know you've heard shit flying around the hospital airwaves about you and me."

I laughed. "All I've heard is how Dr. Brooks is obsessed with Dr. Alvarez, and he tried to cover it up by kissing everyone in the cafeteria the other day."

Collin rolled his eyes as I walked into the elite room that'd been set up for all of us. My eyes must've nearly popped out of my head when I saw the insanely rich elegance of the room. I cleared my throat and stopped our progress into the room, being in more shock than I imagined.

"You still with me, Alvarez?" Collin asked, standing next to me as if I hadn't already drawn attention to us as I looked around like a toddler at Disneyland.

There were shimmering, crystal chandeliers, and a stage was backlit like we were at some award ceremony. Velvet red covers were placed over the chairs and tied in the back with white, satin sashes, and everyone was *very formally* dressed—tuxedos and floor-length gowns everywhere. I wasn't dressed for *this*. I wasn't even dressed to work at the front desk of this hotel. As I took in everything, the realization that I shouldn't have expected anything less almost made me feel like an idiot. I mean, the hospital bathrooms at Saint John's looked like they belonged in the Ritz Carlton, so why would I think I could get away with dressing like I was going to a backyard barbecue?

"Wanna go back to my place and have sex on a moving box?" I leaned in and whispered to the tall man standing regally at my side.

"Unequivocally, yes," he answered, then I felt his thumb smooth over my hand that was clenching the inside of his arm. "Just let me rearrange the ceremony really quick and tell Jim that I'm handing out the final award before drinks are served, and the ceremony begins."

"I'm serious."

"I am too," he said, then I looked up into his soft blue and *loving* eyes. "Let's get the hell out of here. I'm only here to give that award, and I don't give a shit when it's given out." He grinned, "Especially after you offered me the one thing I've wanted to hear come out of your mouth since I first met you."

I exhaled. "This is *way* too formal for me," I finally said and stepped off to the side.

"Is the adrenaline junkie afraid of formal affairs?" he challenged with an arch of his eyebrow.

"I'm not appropriately dressed for this, not by a mile. I may as well be wearing flip-flops."

"If you ask me, you're *over*dressed for it." He chuckled, and then his lips came to my ear, his warm breath causing goosebumps to spike all over my neck. "I'll fix all of that later, though. You're already starting to get nasty looks from some of the staff." He pulled back some and smiled down at me. "That means you're doing everything right."

"If it isn't the two doctors of the night," Jake said, walking up to us. "Why the hell are you two standing in the back when you know Jim has our asses planted in the front row?"

"Of course, he does," I groaned, and I smirked at Collin and Jake as they exchanged glances, proving I was behaving like a total chicken shit.

"Fine. Take me to the front row, and let's give everyone something to amuse themselves over."

"What, that you're here with this chump?" Jake laughed and glanced out at the room filled with doctors, nurses, various other staff, and board members—the people who breathed life into Saint John's. "Trust me; there's going to be a lot of pissed-off guys tonight because you're here with this arrogant prick."

I chuckled. "Let's go."

"Where are the ladies?" Collin asked as we followed Jake, weaving through the tables. "If there are any guests in attendance who can keep Dr. Alvarez here until the end of this gala, it's Avery and Ash."

"Avery's already got our food spread at the table." Jake glanced back at me. "You're going to enjoy yourself," he said as he smiled. "The gals looked the same way you did when they entered. I saw your eyes bulge when you and Collin walked in."

"Good to know. And they're sort of used to this, right?" I asked.

"Hell no," Collin said as we rounded a table toward one where I saw Jim, Jake's older brother. "They despise this shit. They're just good women to put up with this nonsense when their men need their beauty and support." He chuckled as we arrived at the table, and Jim stood and smiled. "I think you remember Jim. This is all his idea to keep us feeling *loved* by the company that owns Saint John's," he said, then pointed to the other man I saw in the observation room. "This Johnny Depp wanna-be is Alex; I think you remember him?"

I shook both men's hands and laughed. "Wow, you do resemble a young Johnny Depp," I said while everyone at the table laughed. "That's a pretty great problem to have."

"He hates it, but whatever puts a woman on his arm, he'll take," Jake said, walking over to a beautifully dressed brunette. "This is my wife, Ash." He looked at the bright-eyed young woman. "Ash, this is the woman you've heard about since Collin—"

"It's nice to meet you, Elena," she said, cutting off whatever insult Jake was about to pay his best friend. "Sorry to interrupt my husband, but if we let him and Collin go on a witty word exchange, they'll kick all of us out of here."

"We've got to get out of here somehow," Jake smirked at Ash, then Collin.

"It's nice to see you again, Elena," Jim said, eyeing Collin mischievously as we took our seats at the table. "This is my fiancé, Avery. Collin might've—"

"I haven't said a word about it," Collin cut off Jim as he introduced Avery.

"Very nice to meet you," Avery said, her dark hair making her blue eyes stand out like bright bulbs on a Christmas tree.

"Now that introductions are over," Collin said. "What are you drinking, Alvarez?"

"I'll have a glass of pinot grigio," I said, putting in my order and settling at the table with the most influential people in the room, yet it felt like I was eating with the most casual people in the world.

"Where's Summer?" Collin asked Alex. "Don't tell me, Jim's got her working overtime."

"Quit," Jim eyed Alex. "This dipshit—" He bit his lower lip and glanced over at me. "Sorry about the language."

"Oh, please don't apologize. I haven't been a priest for years," I teased.

"Hallelujah for that," Collin said as he raised his glass.

"Please, continue. What happened?" I asked curiously.

"Nothing more than me breaking things off with Jim's secretary. She then decided to quit her job—working for a great boss and getting paid way more than she deserved, if you ask me," Alex answered. "She was, and you know it."

"I paid her what I thought she was worth. If she wants to walk away from that, so be it. There are plenty of people to promote into her position," Jim added nonchalantly.

"Jim warned you about screwing around with her and that he'd make you pay if she quit on him because you couldn't hold down your fake relationship," Jake added.

"Let's get off the topic." Alex smiled at me. "Sophisticated adults shouldn't be gossiping about such trivial—"

"*Bull*shit," Collin held onto the first part of the word, calling out his friend.

"That's exactly what I said and how I said it," Jake challenged.

"Let's talk about the wedding, shall we?" Jim said, shooting Collin another mysterious glance. "Have you told Elena about your bright idea?"

"Wait," I said, laughing, watching these men poking at each other like grumpy bears. "Collin and I have discussed this, and trust me, we're not getting married anytime soon."

"No," Jim said in a low voice with a laugh like he knew the best part of this conversation was yet to come. "Collin has volunteered a beautiful young woman to stand at his side during mine and Avery's wedding. I'm sure he's brought this—"

"God in heaven, Mitch," Collin said, handing me my glass of wine. "Just chug that one down. I have three more coming right behind it. I forgot to mention you'd be sitting at the table with a bunch of animals dressed in expensive suits."

I sipped the wine and watched Jim smirk at Collin and then wink at me. "You'll get used to us. In fact," he took a sip of his bourbon, "we could be the reason you want nothing to do with Collin, so if you're looking for an out..."

"Don't listen to these guys," Avery said before she eyed Jim. "Why don't we switch it up a little and let all you boneheads sit and ruin each other's nights over on that side of the table? We girls can enjoy our peace with food and drinks while we watch you all act like buffoons."

"Sounds like a plan to me," Ash said.

I glanced at Collin, closing his eyes in utter annoyance, and laughed, "See?" he looked at me helplessly. "I can't even sit next to you at dinner because we all act like we're five."

"Sucks for you." Jake laughed.

"Tell me about your wedding," I said, smiling at Avery and smoothing my hand over Collin's leg and letting it rest there.

After our fun trip here, the gang at the table seemingly fun and more to my taste than the room I was underdressed for, I was enjoying myself thoroughly. Things moved along smoothly as soon the jokes starting flying, and any regret I may have previously had about coming was erased.

CHAPTER FIFTEEN
COLLIN

*A*s I came to expect, Elena and I were separated for most of the evening. I watched her discreetly while I conversed with different colleagues. I wasn't shocked to find that Avery and Ash would—through Elena—become friends with most of this gala's attendees. Elena took them around the room, introducing them to different staff members as if she'd known them all for fifty years. There was something so charming about how people instantly warmed up to Elena, and I loved that she made instantaneous friends with anyone near her, especially my best friends' ladies.

It seemed to me that Avery and Ash were still trying to gain their bearings with the status and perks that came along with being partnered with a world-renowned cardiovascular surgeon and a CEO. Dealing with that on its own might have been easier if the two didn't also happen to be worth billions.

The ladies didn't come from wealth the way the guys and I did, and all I could say was that they navigated the challenges of excess and extravagance gracefully, and they helped keep us all grounded in the meantime. Avery liked to keep things real at all times, and whenever we went to her and Jim's place, Avery's little girl insisted on having Big Macs for dinner, so if that didn't constitute keeping us grounded, I don't know what would.

Ash had a rough start at this life with Jake, and it's a wonder she decided to stick around after the shit some of the nastier Rodeo Drive elitists put her through. Thank God for her resilience because if she'd have run for the hills—something I wouldn't have blamed her for doing—we wouldn't have been blessed with their son last year.

Now, here I was, standing with my glass of Tanqueray, watching Elena fall right into place. I was beginning to wonder if some fairy godmother out there was granting wishes and was, one-by-one, delivering us our soulmates. I had to get this woman to let me into her life. I wasn't the only one besotted by the woman, either. She was a beautiful, dancing flame, and we were all moths, flying wildly to it.

With how nasty hospital gossip could get, people should have hated Elena with all the attention she garnered in the short amount of time she'd been at Saint John's, but I saw none of that. Instead, I was watching Elena blend in with Ash and Avery and about four other women, laughing as if they were friends catching up at a high school reunion. No one could despise the woman even if they wanted to. Her heart, spirit, and vivacity made her one of the most beloved individuals at the hospital, and I wasn't the only one she'd captivated. She had good energy, and it was an energy that was like a breath of fresh air every time she was around, which was why I wasn't surprised when the half-drunk doctors started making their way to her to ask her to dance.

Now, I was fortunate to stand here in this boring conversation and watch her take that perfectly-round ass of hers for a spin around the dance floor.

"I see you brought Elena tonight," one of the doctors next to me said.

I took a sip of my gin and turned to face the group. "And that makes me the luckiest man at the party." I raised my glass to one of my fellow neurologists.

The older man smiled. "She's an anomaly. A huge asset to the group."

"It's why she got the job," I answered.

"Though," Jake walked up next to me after being off somewhere, mingling with God knows who like he always did, "word has it that the only reason she got the job is that the douche chief neurosurgeon handed it to her. His obsession over the woman made that gossip hotline after—"

"Okay, enough." I laughed at Jake's humored grin. "You only wish you had her on your floor to work mental miracles with your patients." I smiled at Dr. Glen. "Turns out the neuro-ward is quite blessed."

"That's the truth," Dr. Glen agreed. "In fact, I might have to steal her for another consult in a week or two. She worked some miracle on my patient who was recently diagnosed with Alzheimer's. In all my experience, I've never seen someone share a brighter way of accepting it."

"Wasn't that Mr. Stone?" I asked, recalling this diagnosis was quite tragic for this particular family—as Alzheimer's diagnoses always are. It's why Elena was first in line when she saw the distress on Dr. Glen's face when he had to meet with them again.

"Yeah," Dr. Glen shook his head. "I don't know how she does it, but she took over when she saw them struggling as I listed statistics for the family. She has a sixth sense, it seems, for knowing what people need to hear."

"There's no easy way to break that to any family, much less the Stone family," I said.

"What did she say?" Jake asked.

"In short, she reminded them not to let the disease define your life. Each day was a gift, and that Alzheimer's, though a devastating diagnosis, wasn't what defined Mr. Stone. Each of us has *something* that can take us and try and ruin us, but fighting for what we love the most is always worth it." He shrugged and looked out toward Elena, being spun around the dance floor, "To live each day as if he was blessed to have a new day. It might not seem like the most earth-moving advice, but it was what they needed to hear."

"It's sort of the motto we all try to live by," Dr. Sharon added, "but when you think about it, we don't."

"We all take life for granted," I confirmed that truth. "Hell, all day, I'm working with aneurysms, strokes, tumors, and shit that comes out of nowhere. You'd think I would personally wake up with that mentality. I know the science, the many complications our bodies can hand us at any given moment, and I still forget to appreciate my health and the fact that I fucking woke up this morning."

"All I know is that what she said got through to them, and a positive outlook means everything with such a diagnosis. She's exceptionally gifted to know just what to say," Dr. Glen added.

"Miguel would definitely be proud," Dr. Sharon said, her beige, painted lips smiling widely. "His daughter seems to be more than just your average psych doctor."

"It seems Miguel instilled good values in his children," Jake said. "He's done a lot of good, nearly sacrificing his health to make a difference for others, and what does he do? Fucking retires to his horse ranch. Now, he's living the good life that his dance-machine out there suggests we all do. Regardless of the rumors about his retirement, he didn't give up. He found a healthier and better way to live when most of us don't know how to let go."

"And he's able to appreciate what his hard work gave him," Dr. Niroshi added. "I miss the hell out of that know-it-all." He nudged me with a smile, "Now, we're stuck with this joker to consult and beg to attend our surgeries."

"Yeah, yeah. We all know there's no replacing Dr. Alvarez," I said. "But I'll do my best to try to live up to his legacy. And, yes, I've noticed Alvarez part two out there on the dance floor. Let's all agree that one can't walk around upset without her somehow sensing it and consulting you to turn lemons into lemonade."

"So original." Jake laughed as the others began talking about something else. "I seriously don't know how you managed your first brain surgery in the room with that woman," Jake added as we slowly distanced ourselves from the rest, moving to where I could have a better view of her on the dancefloor.

"Thank God I know how to compartmentalize shit, or we would have been in that room for twenty-four hours with me trying to focus on what I do best in craniotomies."

"That's what makes you the badass chief on your ward. The ultimate test was seeing if you could handle performing surgery while this woman that you're blindly in love with is in the same room."

"And I managed just fine."

"And how are you managing now with that weasel, Waters, dancing *slowly* with your *soulmate* pulled tightly against his scrawny body."

"It takes dumbfucks like him to make me look good," I smirked at Jake. "Fuck, how did you pull any of this shit off with Ash?"

"You mean me trying to date her after the press crawled up my ass and exposed my playboy and male-slut lifestyle to her and the world?"

I nodded my head. "Precisely. I don't even have my bullshit life experiences on blast, and the woman still keeps turning my sorry ass down." I looked at Jake's grin. "What?"

"Dude, you have her, and you fucking know it," he said. "She's probably playing it smart and keeping your arrogant ass from hurting her."

"No." I narrowed my eyes at her, playfully laughing and dancing with the idiot who brought her onto the dance floor. "I can sense she's not afraid of being *hurt*. She's made it perfectly clear that she doesn't worry about shit like that."

"Then, I'm stumped. Maybe she really *doesn't* like you. Your fancy cars, cheeky grins, and expensive suits..." he laughed and eyed me while sipping his scotch. "Apparently, your ugly looks haven't even helped you land this woman of your dreams."

"We're getting a Christmas tree together tomorrow." I pinched my lips together. "Fuck, did I just say that out loud?"

"Yes," Jake laughed. "A fucking Christmas tree? Shit, you're well on your way to having her cancel all her new patients and pack it up to be in Jim and Avery's wedding. All so you can work your charms on her."

"Well, the tree will be a symbol of our love," I said, trying to defend my acting like this Christmas tree purchase was practically a diamond ring. "You *do know* what the evergreen tree stands for, don't you?" I had to make something up. I'd already blurted this shit out to Jake as if buying Elena's tree was something monumental in starting a relationship. "Trust me, man, this is a sacred—"

"Oh, spare me your bullshit, Coll." Jake looked at me and shook his head with humor. "You might want to let Elena drive you home tonight. You're drunk."

"I'm solid, and that the evergreen tree is the first thing we do togeth—"

"Jesus Christ, you're lucky that Jim and Alex aren't around to hear this," Jake interrupted me. "You know they'd never let you live it down."

He wasn't wrong. I could be corny with Jake, but the other two would never let me hear the end of it.

"True," I smirked. "They just wouldn't understand *why* this evergreen tree was symbolic of mine and Elena's relationship."

"I'm your best friend, who knows you're always full of shit, and I don't even understand what the fuck you're trying to say. So, what is it about the goddamn evergreen tree? What makes it symbolic to your relationship?"

"It's symbolic because of what it represents." I bit my lip wondering how long Jake would play this shit out with me.

"Ah, and what the hell does it represent, immortality?" Jake was humoring me, obviously, so if he was going to drag this out, I was going to impart some deep, ridiculous wisdom about these goddamn trees to shut him up.

"Life," I said, biting back my smile. "And for that reason, it *must* be our first purchase. The evergreen tree will officially represent our love and life together." I tried to remain serious. "Our everlasting love will shine forth from the tree I buy her."

"And once again," Jake shook his head, "you've enlightened me in ways no other can."

"I know," I said. "So, that's why I'm thrilled to have her pick out this monumental purchase tomorrow."

"All this talk about *green* Christmas trees has me thinking," Jake said as he eyed me. "What if she picks a brown and brittle one? What's that say about your *everlasting and evergreen* relationship then?"

"I highly doubt the woman will pick out a brown fucking Christmas tree." I looked over at Jake as we both laughed. "Hell, I've never even been to a Christmas tree lot before, but you and I both know she'll pick out a big-ass, bright green one—like everyone else who goes to buy a fucking tree—and that will be the beginning of an everlasting relationship that was always intended to be," I said, laughing at my ability to come up with the stupidest shit sometimes.

"You're *such* a fucking idiot," Jake said with a laugh as I turned to leave. "Where the hell are you going, *everlasting* lover man?"

"To request a song and kick this relationship into another gear. I'm ready to leave, but Elena needs something to remember this party fondly."

"Another dance?" Jake rolled his eyes. "Didn't help the first time when you did that in Vegas with *Dr. Alvarez*, did it?"

"It's because the song wasn't sexy enough. It's time to cut the bullshit out and get my lady's head in the game."

"Speaking of ladies, I think Ash and Avery are ready to get the hell out of here. Avery was promised milkshakes at some diner, and Ash was all about it if they survived the night of dress-up. You and Elena want to bond and enhance your *everlasting relationship* by sharing a strawberry milkshake?"

"You guys enjoy your night. I'm going to enjoy my woman," I said with a smile. "I plan on using the excuse of sleeping over at her place since I dragged her here, and I owe her my help to unpack boxes."

"You're going to go back to her place to unpack boxes?" Jim asked, walking up to Jake and me.

"Oh shit," Alex said, trailing his best friend. "You *do* like this woman, right? Take her back to your place."

"I would if her place wasn't filled with the boxes that she's delayed unpacking on my account." I smiled. "Unlike you selfish bastards, I am willing to help her move in."

Jake's eyes closed in humor. "Have fun unpacking, and don't get too addicted to popping bubbles in the bubble wrap."

"See you all later," I said, waving them off and moving toward the man who was in charge of this trendy, pop culture music that I would've hated had I not seen Elena dancing so cheerfully to it.

I had to think of a song to set the mood to let her know I wanted to stay with her tonight, and I wanted more with this woman than friendly kisses on my fucking forehead. I made her a promise I'd outperform the car I drove her in tonight, and I planned on keeping that promise if she'd let me.

CHAPTER SIXTEEN
COLLIN

I managed to use the car ride home to convince Elena that if she didn't let me stay to help unpack a few boxes, then she was staying at my place in Malibu. I didn't have to do too much convincing since she was holding onto the fact that she was behind on unpacking because I'd *forced* her to be my date tonight.

Perhaps me stealing her away from her dance partner to dance was also part of why she agreed to let me stay. Thank you, Solomon Burke, for being the original artist to bring your heart and soul into the song *Cry to Me* because Elena and I nailed that dance with sass, sexiness, and style. If anyone questioned our chemistry after our little dance to that song, they were blind. If Elena still questioned it, however, then I was royally screwed in trying to keep pulling things out of my ass to get her to see it too.

I walked into her condo, which was lovely. Still, with my proclivity for having things tidy and being somewhat of a perfectionist, part of me wanted to stay up and unpack these boxes that'd been haphazardly stacked throughout her kitchen and living room. Maybe I'd get lucky, and her room would be in perfect order, and we'd close the door and forget about the rest until morning.

"Damn it!" I heard Elena growl as I started to straighten boxes into an orderly fashion in her living room, where I waited.

"Everything okay?" I asked from the wall away from her large living room window.

"These boxes are going to drive me insane," she said from her room, where she'd disappeared to change into something more comfortable.

There went the bedroom idea, I thought. I couldn't help but smile when things went sideways for me when it came to Elena, which meant I was smiling a whole hell of a lot lately.

"Got a problem," Elena said, prompting me to slide the last box over with the others I'd stacked along her wall to make room for her to walk around her living room. "Wow." She laughed as she walked into the room, "I can see my couch and love seat, but we're still unpacking those boxes, just like you promised me."

I eyed her with a grin of confusion. "Why the hell are you leaning your head back like that?"

Elena's bronze eyes glistened as she laughed and said *ow* at the same time. "My hair is caught on this stupid top button. You're going to have to help me because I'm not cutting it."

"How'd you manage to pull this stunt off?" I questioned as I walked over to where she turned around, showing me that her hair was tangled around her dress's top button.

"As I pulled that clip out of my hair, I tripped over a box. Basically, you're looking at the result of all my clutter."

Fuck. I was looking at the most beautiful tanned skin and a button that, once Elena's hair was free, I was sure would be mine to unfasten. I gently worked to free her hair from the button, and I was no longer in control of what the hell was happening.

"You smell so good," I said as my hands came up and took the thin straps of her dress under my palms while feeling the electric charge of her hot skin under my touch.

She softly moaned, and it was over. I used the palms of my hands to roll the straps of her top off her shoulders, and I couldn't resist tasting the skin of her silky-smooth shoulder. Elena remained perfectly still while I bent to press my lips onto the top of her shoulders. A surge of energy— the energy of me, desiring more than I knew I could handle—took over and urged me on for more. Elena's head fell back against my chest as I continued to massage her shoulder with my lips, my hands guiding the top of her dress off by steadily running them down her arms.

As I kissed over the top of her shoulder toward her neck, I unzipped her dress, allowing it to fall into a pile at her feet. Elena's moans and sighs, and her hand coming up to run through my hair was the permission I needed to be granted to take this where I'd wanted it to go since the night I first met her.

I wanted to see her eyes, but burying my face and lips into her neck was enough to pull me into a trance that I would never fight away. I was completely drunk on this woman's fragrance, tastes, moans, and everything I'd been tortured by in my dreams. They were finally my reality.

My cock felt harder than it had ever been, and to feel Elena press her back against it was enough for me to explode immediately. Instead of worrying about losing my shit early with the woman groaning in response to feeling how hard I was, I let it heighten this moment I'd waited far too long for. I felt like I was sensationally high on this woman, and I loved how it made me feel. I slid my hand around and felt her nipples harden under my touch, compelling me to suck along her jawline and devour the woman I knew I was in love with. I wanted more.

My other hand slid down her flat stomach and toward her pussy. Her groaning and both arms reaching back to grip my hair as I ran my fingers over her clit was increasing my heartrate as if I'd never involved myself in this act before. God, she was perfect.

"I need more," she said in a lower voice than I'd ever heard her use. She arched her ass back against me while our lips finally met, and I closed my eyes to keep from coming then and there.

I was still locked up in this damn suit and had the most beautiful woman in the world moving her pussy against my fingers as I massaged her clit. Her mouth fell open when I had to feel her, hot and wet, and wanting more.

"You're so wet," I said through an exhale. "God, Elena, I want you more than you know."

That's when she broke our electrically-charged moment and the high that my mind never wanted to come down from. She turned, and like usual, the woman had read my mind. I should have been drinking in her naked body, but I was transfixed on her dazzling eyes that held me captive. She helped me out of my jacket while I pulled off my tie, and then her hands moved aggressively faster than I anticipated to unbutton my shirt. As I pulled off my undershirt, Elena already had my pants coming off, freeing my dick that was ready for her.

"Oh, my," she softly laughed, her eyes meeting mine while I licked my parched lips in reaction to her gripping my cock and using my wet tip as a lubricant to start pumping up and down my shaft. "I'm one lucky girl."

I smiled and was able to hold my shit together with her teasing me. "Is this the part where I finally get to call you Elena?" I teased back, only to catch a break to hold my cum back from prematurely ruining everything I wanted with this woman.

"Depends on if you can prove whether or not you can outperform that car."

"That shouldn't be a problem," I said, hoisting her into my arms and stepping around boxes on the way to her room. "Oh, shit. I forgot you don't have a bed. It looks like I'm fucking you against a wall," I said as her mouth latched on to my jaw and moved down my neck.

"There's a mattress on the floor."

"Where?" I asked with a laugh. Was this all part of whatever supernatural joke I'd been cursed with when it came to this black-haired beauty? "Where in the Alvarez fort of boxes in this damn room—" I tripped over a box, nearly sending Elena's and my naked bodies back against the door of her room.

Elena's laugh smoothed over this entire catastrophe. This might not have been how I imagined our first time together going down, but she made everything seem perfect—potentially dangerous or not.

"We're not unpacking boxes," I said, finally seeing the mattress that was hiding behind two wardrobe boxes.

I laid her laughing ass back, and her beautiful breasts transfixed me as they rose and fell to her contagious laugh, her eyes sparkling radiantly with happiness. "Kiss me," she said, becoming more serious than I'd ever seen the woman. "I want you, and I want you now."

Everything switched gears as if we didn't practically climb Mount Everest naked to get to this point. I covered her body with mine and ran my hand over the top of her head as I settled in between her legs that fell open for me.

"I love you, Elena." I meant those words with every fiber of my being. I was lost in this woman, and the way my body and mind reacted to her was something I couldn't control.

"I love you too, Collin." She caressed the sides of my face. "I've known that for a while. It feels good to say it to you finally."

I smiled. "And the whole *Doctor Alvarez* thing?" I needed to know who I was taking to bed.

"It turned me on too much to hear you say my name the way you say it."

My mouth fell open in total shock. "Never in a fucking million years would I have guessed that shit. I knew it had something to do with your—"

I was silenced when she reached between us, captured my cock in her hands, and ran my tip over her slick entrance. My breath caught, and my entire body jolted internally as Elena brought me back to what we *both* had been waiting for.

I took her hands into mine and gripped her wrists while I slowly brought my lips to take hers. I bit at her bottom lip while she moved beneath my body, her arms still caught by hands. She swept her tongue over my upper lip, and this slow-motion way of relishing in our first kiss was the last thing I expected, but goddamn, this was the hottest fucking thing in the world. I was usually more aggressive when I fucked a woman, but I felt the polar opposite with Elena.

She was my treasure, my spark of sunshine, my woman, and she was finally letting me in. Every cell in my body knew this and understood to slow things down. The rhythm we'd fallen into was more erotic than I'd ever imagined it could be with a woman. She was delicious and perfect. This was what it felt like to be with the one who was meant for you —finally.

CHAPTER SEVENTEEN
ELENA

ollin's lips were so soft, firm, and sensually flawless as they purposefully claimed mine. He was perfect inside and out—that was confirmed moments before we decided to blaze a trail into my box-filled bedroom. Our near-collision into the wall as I was growing hungrier to taste his kiss should've put a damper on things. Instead, it was Collin and me, and we laughed our way past that near-catastrophe. I loved the fact that, after what felt like a lifetime of putting off this moment, we were now on my makeshift bed on the floor without a care in the world.

Collin's tongue was as urgent and as possessive as mine, and I whimpered through this kiss as I slid my hand down his firm body, reaching for his hard cock. I was throbbing and aching to feel him inside me. He groaned into our kiss as I steadily ran my hand up and down his hard dick. He was huge, which added to the perfection of his taut and muscular body moving gently over mine.

Without a care in the world, I lined Collin's cock up to my entrance and braced myself not only to feel a man inside me for the first time in too long but to feel the one man I'd been lusting over for too long. Collin pulled away, inhaling smoothly and catching his breath as he gently pressed his cock inside of me. My hands went over his ass, and my legs widened, my body pleading for this.

I kissed along the top of his hard pectoral muscles and whimpered as he stretched me wider than any man I'd ever been with before.

"Fuck." His hands reached for mine and locked them above my head as I went to grip his perfectly tight balls. "Easy, baby," he said in a soft voice before he captured my lips and thrust himself gently into me.

"Yes," I said in a bit of a screech. This felt painfully good. "It's been too long." I loved how his hands grew tighter around my wrists with each movement he made deeper into me. "You feel so fucking incredible."

I was lost in erotic bliss. My eyes met Collin's glassy ones for a brief second before I felt my insides working up toward an orgasm without me using my hand or clit to conjure up any of these sensations. It was Collin, filling me up and me maneuvering my hips as he slowly glided himself in and out of my soaking wet entrance. His hard tip would move right against my G-spot.

"That's it right there, isn't it?" he said, still breathless while his lips sucked along the side of my neck.

I was panting while my legs opened wider, my heels digging into the bed and pushing my body against his. "Right there, Coll—" I stopped when I felt it bubbling down with more force than I expected. "Oh, God," I said, my chest moving up as I rolled with this formidable force, pushing its way out of me and through Collin's dick that continued to press into my G-spot. "Fuck, yes."

"That's right, baby. Ride it," Collin said, his eyes meeting mine as I smiled in absolute pleasure. "Damn, I've walked through hell and back to see this in your eyes."

Collin's mouth captured my breast. The man was perfect; he virtually memorized where my special spot was while I maneuvered myself beneath him, fighting against him restraining my wrist above my head to guide his dick into it.

"Jesus Christ," I panted out while Collin rolled his tongue in circles and sucked on each of my nipples, hardly moving, but his hands locked tighter around my wrists than before. My body shuddered while the orgasm continued, and I clenched my pussy tight to bring in more sensations than ever.

"God-fucking-damn," Collin said, laying his head on my chest, the very last thing I expected him to do in reaction to me coming harder than the first just moments ago. "Squeeze my cock."

I smiled as I licked my lips. "Kiss me, Coll," I begged.

His eyes were wild with hunger, and I swallowed, given the fact I was nearly drooling and pulled harder into this sexual moment than I'd ever been with anyone else. I was fully waiting for Collin to fuck me into another frenzy, but he was doing the opposite. Everything seemed as though he were falling into the same sensual moment I was having. We were riding out this whole experience slowly and loving every charge of electricity. The angst and build-up were just the beginning, and that was *after* having two miracle G-spot orgasms without involving my swollen clit.

"Don't move," Collin said, his tongue gingerly sweeping into my mouth, and his movements slower than ever. "God..." he blew out a breath, pulling his face away, "please don't move a muscle."

I understood Collin was doing everything in his power to hold back. It didn't help his personal restraint since my pussy was fully constricting around his cock in a constant orgasm and pulsating waves of ecstasy.

"It's okay if you come, baby," I said, his hands releasing my wrists and suddenly missing the pleasure of feeling him slightly rough with me like that.

He pulled his face back and tucked his bottom lip between his teeth as his hands came up into my hair. "I don't have a condom on," he said with a half-laugh. "As much as I'd love to trap you into a relationship by getting you pregnant..." He closed his eyes. "Fuck."

"Oh, shit," I laughed at how impulsive we were to forget a condom.

That's all it took to screw Collin's self-control. Collin was cumming inside me before I could react to help him ease out of me. One powerful thrust into me filled me deeper than he'd been since he entered me. I arched my stomach up into him in response to how amazing it felt to have such a large cock buried inside me. Jesus, this was beyond heavenly. Collin's hands fisted my hair as he pumped harder and deeper while groaning in pleasure in a low, husky voice that I found more than attractive.

My body instantly joined the party, and I came as Collin shot his cum deep into me. There was no hating him for this—or even being pissed at this slip-up. We had it coming, and I think we both knew it.

I reached for his shoulders, my eyes filling with tears due to the immense amount of pleasure that radiated through me on round three of my orgasms. His eyes dazzled with a hunger that I would never let leave my mind. I could never again look at him as just a hot piece of ass. Tonight—after dancing seductively with him, listening to his jokes, and him teasing me with the truth of this moment that we'd just uncovered—we were two souls that were destined to be together. I would never see this man as anything but my man, and a man who, even though he'd been holding back this entire time and I didn't know it, was the best fuck I'd ever had.

I used the tip of my tongue to taste his delicious cologne as I ran it up the center of his neck and under his chin, and that's when our mouths fell into a deep and satisfying kiss. I locked my legs around his lower back, keeping him in place as I felt his tight muscles begin to relax.

"You're pretty extraordinary to hold back like that and not say a word," I said to him after he laid his head between my breasts, kissing against the flesh of one. "I'm sorry, I wasn't even thinking."

"I knew I had that effect on you, Elena." He said my name with more humor than usual, prompting me to laugh now that he had the full rights and privileges of referring to me by my first name.

His hand reached for my wrist, and he lifted his head to examine them while pressing his lips into them, "Sorry about the whole *holding you down* thing. I had to have full control of everything with my dick feeling the inside of a woman for the first time and shit." He laughed, "Getting laid for the first time in far too long, coupled with the fact I'd been envisioning this and impatiently waiting for you to come to your senses to share this moment, took extra concentration."

"My wrists are fine." I kissed his chin when he repositioned himself for our gazes to meet again. "I'm shocked you didn't cum all over my hand when I first touched your sexy dick."

He grinned. "That's because, as I just learned myself, I have more self-control than any individual on the planet."

"That you do, and I was so stupid to wait this long for you," I said, squeezing his cock and feeling him still inside me.

"Ah. You're going to work me into another round like this. I'm feeling nothing but the tight and wet pussy of my Elena, and I'm feeling a recovery period rapidly approaching."

"You got another round in you?" I arched an eyebrow at him.

"I've got all night with you, my little fucking goddess."

"I like it pretty wild," I teased him with a bite to my lower lip.

"Is that so?" Collin asked with curiosity in his eyes. "I can go beyond wild and make this the best night of your life. We just had to get my little crippling moment of fucking without a condom on and past the fact that you forced me to wait too long for your tantalizing body."

The night was wild and dangerously fun. The guy definitely knew how to take a woman to heaven, let her enjoy the experience, and bring her back down only to repeat it all again. I made sure he knew I loved watching his biceps flex when his arms held me up against a wall, and he pounded his cock hard and fast into me. While we had sex, his expressions were enough for me to keep my hands off myself and allow for his cock to work my G-spot. This guy was hot without the sex, but add the sweat, all-night sex, the delicious taste of his kiss, and his salty muscular skin while in the middle of a mind-blowing orgasm, and I never wanted the sun to rise. I never wanted our bodies to separate. Hell, I'd never been *this* addicted to sex before. Collin just became a drug that would keep me longing for more of his aggressive sex, his gorgeous eyes, and his stunning face as it twisted into a beautiful expression just before he came.

It didn't take long before we both realized we were still human and needed *some* sleep if we were going to function tomorrow, unpacking boxes and making this place livable.

The next morning, Collin took off to pick up some breakfast after taking a shower with me and changing into a pair of jeans, a simple shirt, and a black leather jacket. His hair was tousled in a messy and trendy way before he slapped on my favorite cologne of his. I shouldn't have been surprised when I spied that it was Tom Ford who'd captured the perfect fragrance of an exotic beach with the undertones of something crisp and light instead of bold and musky. This cologne seemed to capture Collin's personality, and it was delicious to taste as he ravaged my body all night long as well.

I heard my annoying cell phone alarm blaring from the kitchen, prompting me to leave the bathroom after I finished drying my hair. I pulled my favorite soft, red sweater over my tank top and walked out to shut off my damn phone. I had no idea how I'd accidentally set the alarm in the first place.

What the hell? I thought, searching all over my kitchen for my phone that was nowhere to be found. The alarm went off again, and I laughed when I realized it was Collin's phone, and if he and I were going to survive this relationship, he was going to change his ring tone immediately. I couldn't have that ingrained, panic reaction to an alarm every time his phone rang.

I saw *Jakey* was calling in, and I figured I'd leave it for when Collin got back. Glad to see the guy wasn't in a full-blown relationship with his phone, and, like me, he could shut the stupid thing off and put it out of sight when he wasn't working.

The stupid phone went off again. *Jakey obviously needs to get ahold of Collin since he's blowing him up five times in a row.*

"Just because you had the best sex of your life with Collin doesn't mean you're at the *answering each other's phones* stage of the relationship," I softly said to myself, pushing the phone off to the side. The phone instantly rang again.

Fuck my life! What if something is wrong? Jesus Christ, Jake Mitchell, you're forcing me to do this, so this is your fault, I thought before I mustered the courage to answer the phone—something I never would've done if I didn't know the person on the other end of the line.

"Hello? Jake, it's Elena," I announced skeptically. "Is everything okay?"

"Elena? Did you guys get married last night or something? Already taking his calls?" he teased.

"Not quite," I laughed. "He's out getting breakfast, and he left the phone. I wouldn't have answered, but you were blowing it up, and I didn't know if something was wrong, not to mention the fact that his ring tone is the sound of my alarm, so I was psychologically abused for the last few minutes, and it needed to stop."

"Speaking of psychological abuse," Jake said, "you left your clutch at the gala last night. Ash got it, but Collin mentioned something about taking you out to get a Christmas tree today or some shit like that?"

"Yeah. You guys want to meet up or something? Or we can come to get it. I can't believe I left that, and I didn't even notice." I sighed. "Thanks so much to you both for grabbing that for me."

"We'll meet you guys wherever Collin is insisting on getting this tree."

"I have no idea where. It might be out of the way."

"Hey," Jake said, his tone a bit more humored as he cut me off, "as Collin's best friend, it's my duty—to him, of course—"

"Of course," I smiled at the way Jake was talking.

"Well, he takes his love for these *everlasting* trees seriously."

"You mean evergreen trees?"

"Yes, exactly. And that's the problem. I'm telling this to you because I know that Collin would never dare put you in this position, being so young and in love with you."

"Okay," I said, going along with whatever the hell Jake was talking about.

"Well, this is the deal—and seriously, you know how the genius billionaires are always a little quirky, right?"

"Right. Like how some of them like to hunt human beings for sport; that kind of quirky?" I teased.

"Well, he's probably got a good five to ten years before he starts doing that, but we'll cross that bridge when we come to it," he said, laughing and continuing. "As I was saying—"

"Yes, please elaborate," I said.

"Okay, so it shouldn't come as a surprise to you when I tell you Collin is only ensuring you get an everlasting green tree because of love and shit like that. More importantly than even that, Collin has always felt sorry for the poor trees that were cut too soon because—I don't know, they might not make it to see Christmas."

"You're kidding me. Collin has a thing for cut evergreen trees?"

"Has since we were kids. Finds it tragic when they turn brown and won't make it into a home for Christmas because of their ugliness."

I pinched my lips together when Collin walked in the door. "It's Jake. You left your phone here," I cringed.

"Put me on speaker," Jake said.

I did.

"What's up, asshole," Collin said. "You knew I'd be busy today, and now Elena is forced to become my secretary since I forgot my phone, and you were probably blowing the damn thing up."

"Yeah, well, I don't think Elena is complaining since you left her head spinning after that sexy tango last night, making her forget her handbag and phone on the table."

"Oh, shit." Collin looked at me, setting what smelled like a delicious Mexican breakfast on the table. "Thanks for grabbing that. We'll head to your place and grab it after we get the tree...or now?" Collin looked at me.

"We're going to meet him at the Christmas tree farm," I smiled. "Apparently, picking out this tree is a pretty big deal for you at Christmastime."

"Hell yeah, it is," he said, making Jake laugh.

"I was just mentioning to Elena the everlasting tree of love and how much it means to you," Jake said as Collin rolled his eyes and unwrapped a burrito for him and one for me.

"Good. Then she'll know exactly why this is our first shopping experience together."

"Absolutely," Jake said while I was starting to wonder if Collin really *did* feel sorry for the trees going brown too early and not getting chosen to go to a house for Christmas. Both men had their serious doctor voices going too strong for me to discern if this was a joke or not.

"Elena gets to pick the tree," Collin insisted.

"I ensured she knew what it meant to your relationship, man," Jake said. "You can thank me later."

"Great. We'll meet you at..." Collin trailed off, chewing on a bite he took from his burrito and searching up tree farms on his phone.

"Found a place," Jake said. "There's one right in the middle of where we are in Malibu this weekend and where you two are in L.A."

"Where?" Collin asked while I worked to devour my burrito.

"No joke, this place is called Everlasting Holiday Trees. See you there."

"Send me the link, dummy, and we'll see you there." Collin rolled his eyes.

"What's with the whole everlasting tree stuff?" I asked, pouring salsa into the top of my burrito.

"Evergreens?" He shrugged. "They don't last forever, so it's sort of difficult to grab a good one before they toss the poor sucker into a chipper for turning brown."

I covered my smile. I had no idea what the hell to think. Was I still high on this man for the fantastic sex from last night, or was he charming me with his Christmas tree savior syndrome? One thing I knew for sure was that I was in love with the guy.

CHAPTER EIGHTEEN
ELENA

*C*ollin and I unpacked the kitchen in record time. This man was saying that I was his other half, and I couldn't have agreed more. He and I seemed to have this knack for things going in their proper places, and we worked in harmony, getting everything in its place as though we'd lived together forever and knew each other's preferences.

The only thing we couldn't manage to figure out was where the extra shelf that belonged in the pantry had gone. Without skipping a beat—and in man-of-my-dreams, handyman fashion—Collin made a temporary replacement shelf from extra loose boards lying in the hall closet.

It didn't take long for us to get distracted from unpacking and start getting sexy again. As we were washing dishes to put away, my lips were captured in one of Collin's delicious and intense kisses. I breathlessly pulled away and challenged him to a round on my island countertop—a safer bet than trying to navigate the boxes strewn around all the way to my bedroom.

He planted my ass on the counter, pulled off my shirt, and his perfect lips lit the flesh of my shoulder on fire. While I ran my hands through his soft hair, his lips began working the miracles they had done throughout the night and moved up the side of my neck. My moans, his groaning—all of it had us well on our way to fucking on the counter...until he stopped abruptly.

I was left panting, goosebumps still lingering on my skin, and looking at Collin, who snapped into a different mode as if his grandmother had walked in on us.

"I found the shelf! It's next to the fridge." He was so excited about his Eureka moment that I couldn't help but laugh. He was adorable, and I loved everything about him. We inspected the missing shelf, and I helped him put it in place. Our sexy moment was gone almost as soon as it'd surfaced, but I knew we'd have plenty of time later, and with a packed schedule, we needed to stay focused anyway.

"Let's get the bed put together," Collin said with determination.

I glanced over at my phone. "Not only did you miss the window to screw on my island, but we have to meet Jake in thirty minutes."

"Jake can wait. He's taking his little boy to pick out the tree for their beach house. He won't even know we're late."

Collin leaned down and kissed me on my neck, instantly working me up again. I gently held his head and pulled my head off to the side and away from his lips.

"We have to go, you horny man. We've got shit to do," I teased.

Collin sighed and gave me that look of determination that I loved. "They won't know. Let me fix up your bed. We'll fuck, then—"

"We'll leave."

Collin nodded, his eyes glistening and vibrant.

"No. Right now. We're leaving," I said with a grin, grabbing my keys. "My car can handle the tree on top better than yours, I think."

WHEN I BOUGHT my Land Rover in Miami, I insisted upon blacked-out, tinted windows, which wasn't exactly legal in California. I never thought the perk of no one being able to see inside my car would come in handy until Collin started unzipping my pants as I drove. Collin knew precisely what he was doing when he rerouted my GPS to take this alternate, two-lane route through the hills and back down into the city.

He made me laugh at first because I thought there could be no way he could get me off while I drove, but he did. He was not only a miracle worker with his smooth and patient movements in surgery, but these hands were gifts for a multitude of other things as well.

"Fuck." I stretched out my arms while his fingers slid from my clit and found their way into my soaking wet pussy.

"That's it," Collin said with humor and huskiness, kissing me all along my neck. "Let me have that spot, baby."

Thank God for cruise control, guiding us at a solid fifty miles-per-hour. My eyes begged me to close them and enjoy this, but the adrenaline of having to focus while driving as my man got me off was heightened, making this daring adventure one for the books.

I spread my legs and gripped the steering wheel tighter when Collin's fingers glided into my entrance without anything to slow them down.

"You're so fucking beautiful right now," he said, pulling hard against my G-spot with his fingers. "Come hard on me."

"We're..." I stopped, panting and feeling the sparks flying and the throbbing sensation pounding deep inside me. "We're going to crash."

"Eyes on the road. Focus," he teased in a voice he made when he was turned on.

"Damn it." I breathed out hard while I started coming, and Collin's free hand took the wheel from me, his eyes on the road while his other hand drove the intense orgasm. "I'm coming, babe." I blew out another breath of ecstasy.

"Fuck yes, you are," he said, his thumb moving my clit in circles while his fingers dipped in and out of me.

My eyes recovered faster than my body, and my breathing slowed as I took the wheel back. "Holy shit," I said, softly laughing in disbelief that we'd pulled this off.

"You look so hot, and I'm harder than a fucking rock," he said.

"You deserve that," I said, rearranging myself, checking the rearview mirror, and thanking God that my windows were pitch black from the outside. "That was unbelievable, but we could've been pulled over, you horny goofball."

"Your windows are black as night, my sex-goddess," he said. "No way anyone saw that."

"No. I mean, we could get pulled over by a cop for those *black as night* tinted windows. I need to fix them before I get a ticket."

"But would it have been worth it?"

I glanced over at him as he relaxed into his seat. "I hope you have that hard-on all day," I teased. "You realize people would judge us for how irresponsibly you just behaved."

"I wasn't hearing a whole lot of protesting a few minutes ago, and what I did was take care of my woman."

"And if we got into an accident?"

"Not a chance," he confidently said. "I was ready to take that wheel in case you drove over the line or off the side of the road in ecstasy."

"Brakes?"

"The car brakes on its own, just like it accelerated with cruise control on its own. Any other reasons as to why you're going to try and fight me taking this same route home," he reached his hand over and rested it on the back of my neck, "because I'll be driving," he teased, leaning over and kissing my temple.

"Well, I have a rule against drinking and driving," I smirked at him. "That includes bodily fluids from my boyfriend who thinks it's okay to screw around and drive while impaired on the road."

"Fucking finally," Collin said, throwing his hands in the air.

"Did I miss something?"

"You have officially proclaimed that I'm your boyfriend," he said triumphantly, his thumb rubbing the side of my neck where his hand came to rest. "It only took getting you off like this to make you speak the truth of what you've wanted this time." He looked at me with his usual Collin smugness. "You're welcome."

"The fact that you *got me off* while driving to this Christmas song…" I stopped and laughed, hearing Grandma Got Ran Over by a Reindeer playing in the background.

Collin rested his right forearm on his right thigh. "Of all the Christmas songs. What would Grandmother say, young lady?" He feigned shock and laughed, pulling his ringing phone from his pocket.

"You're twisted. Stop ruining Christmas music," I said, unable to hold back my laughter.

"I'm *not* ruining Christmas music," I heard Collin say into the phone, not sure if he was defending himself to the person on the other line or me. "It's Elena. She says my angelic voice is ruining Christmas music."

I rolled my eyes. God only knew who he was bullshitting on the other line.

"Jake wants to know if we should allow me to sing Oh Christmas Tree after you pick out our *everlasting love* tree when we get to the tree farm."

My eyebrows knit together in confusion. "Why do you and Jake seem to be two men who appear to be top doctors, yet act like you're thirteen?"

"Thirteen?" Collin said with a laugh. "At thirteen, I was hornier than fuck, and I surely wouldn't be talking shit like this to my best friend," he defended himself. "Yeah, we're about two miles out." He paused. "Hey, monster," he said in a playful voice. "Oh?" He seemed to be humoring Jake's one-year-old son. "Okay, well, since I'm late, I'll sing Oh Christmas Tree to dedicate Elena's new tree to her. Hey, Johnny-boy," Collin said, "did you pick your tree out with your mom yet?" He paused. "Ah, cute. Well, you look around some more, and we'll be there in a few minutes."

"You *will* sing that song," I laughed. "You owe me."

"Quite the contrary, Laney." He used my nickname and made me love it even more, hearing it come from his mouth. "You owe me," he said, grabbing the wet-wipes I always carried in my car, and he cleaned his dirty, sinful hands on them.

I laughed. "I pick our *everlasting love tree*, and you're singing the dedication for it."

"Might I ask who let you in on the Christmas tree being our everlasting love tree?" he questioned as I pulled into the lot.

I parked next to a black version of my Land Rover and leaned over to kiss Collin's lips. "Doesn't matter. It sounds like something you'd come up with. Let's go find our tree."

THE CHRISTMAS TREE farm kept the Christmas music loud and cheerful. Little houses were everywhere and crafted to give you the feeling of being at the North Pole, and each tree was adorned with a beautiful red bow on it. The white fencing was wrapped with red ribbons to create a candy-cane effect, and I had to admit, the Christmas spirit was alive and well.

"Uncle Collin!" I heard a toddler—a tiny clone of Jake, dressed in Levi's and a black hoodie—manage to say as he ran up to Collin.

I watched in admiration as Collin crouched down, and the next thing I knew, the full force of the toddler's energy was transferred into Collin's arms as the man flipped him over and landed him on his shoulders.

John laughed while Collin greeted Jake's smile. "Sorry we're late, jam on the freeway."

"Hey," Jake held his hands out. "Explain that to the one little boy who *doesn't* like the dude sitting in Santa's chair or the elves who are helping kids up to his lap."

Collin reached up to where John squeezed his hair into fists. "Are you afraid of Santa?" he asked. "We need to fix this immediately."

"He's grumpy," John said in a voice that was very well-articulated for a one-year-old. "So are the mean elves."

"A bad Santa?" I asked when John's vivid blue eyes met mine. "Should we get our tree from another place?"

"We should save them," he said.

Jake snapped his fingers and laughed. "Save them it is." Jake smiled at me. "Good to see you lively and well this morning, Elena. All rested and ready to rescue a tree for Christmas?"

"They all dead, Daddy," John said.

"Wait, what?" Collin pulled John from his shoulders and knelt in front of him. "All right, you listen to your Uncle Collin because God only knows what your dad said about cut Christmas trees." I smiled at Jake's grin. "I surely know your mother would never put it into your innocent mind that we're at a place of death."

"No, you goof." John gave Collin a small punch to his arm. "They dead because they cut."

I pinched my lips. "Well, then we'll make sure we get a good one for its last Christmas."

I watched when Jake winked at his son, who was looking back at him. "That's right. And Uncle Collin will sing a song for the poor dead tree. Unless he's happy that it's dead," Jake said.

"Of course, I'm not happy the trees are cut and dead," Collin said, missing the glances I saw between father and son.

What the hell was Jake up to?

"What if you helped me pick out a tree?" I said to John, only to have Collin and Jake grin at each other in response.

"Yes, but no Santa," John agreed, tugging at my hand.

"I'll hang back and get your stuff from Jake's car," Collin said.

With that, John and I set off to *save* the tree that Collin would want to give a happy send-off after being cut too early for Christmas; and after seeing Jake and John exchange those glances, I knew Jake was up to something.

Collin was oblivious to it all too, which made the adventure of finding a browning Christmas tree that much more fun. I should've gotten it the minute Jake tried to play me as a smitten fool on the phone this morning too. Now I knew. Jake was trying to get Collin to sing Oh Christmas Tree to a brown, reject tree. I wasn't sure why Jake would even give a damn, but Ash and Avery made it clear that all the boys loved pranking each other, so it was best to let this one play out because I knew Collin's reaction would probably be priceless.

"Let's find a very sad tree and make it happy," I said.

"That's what Daddy told me to say to you, Layna," he chirped.

"I'm sure he did," I answered with a smile.

Thank God for this little boy, dressed like a cute little SoCal surfer, because he found the one tree that was heading straight to the burn pile. Its needles were orange and falling off, and it was cast out with others that were starting to brown. This pathetic tree looked like it was dead before it was cut, and here were John and I, getting to rescue it as a declaration of mine and Collin's love.

"It's lighter than a feather," I said, reaching in for it and picking it up.

"Has no water," John said, eyeing it like we were on a safari and rescuing an animal or something. "It's dead, though." He shoved his hands into the pockets of his cuffed little jeans, looked at me, and shrugged. "We gotta get it. Daddy says Uncle Collin saves them."

I covered my smile. "Your dad is a brilliant man."

"He is," he simply stated. "Well, this was fast."

"You seem bummed. We can look for yours next."

"I won't get a brown one," he assured me.

"I won't let you."

"If Uncle Collin makes me?"

I knelt to the little stud of a cutie. "We both know your Uncle Collin won't make you. But," I tugged on his black hoodie, "I think it would be fun to pick one for your dad."

"Mom won't like it very much. Not a ugly tree. Mom paints beautiful things."

"She said that to me last night. Why don't we see how it all goes? If we think Daddy needs a brown tree to match mine and Collins, then I say—"

I paused. "Hey, does Daddy have a favorite room that Mommy doesn't really go to?"

"His office?" His eyes widened.

"At home or the hospital?"

"At home."

"Let's make Daddy get a matching tree for his office at home then."

"I'll get Daddy's tree too. He and Uncle Collin will be happy," he said, and I shook my head at how well this one-year-old spoke and ran around like he was five.

After picking two dead trees, John and I walked back to where Collin and Jake were conversing about a patient, and they were debating about what was best for him. Would it be to have the open-heart surgery before or after Collin worked on the deadly brain tumor? It was buzz through the hospital already, and I was curious about whether the two chief surgeons had come to any conclusions about how the patient's care would be handled. On Monday, we would all sit and consult with neuro teams and cardiac teams, and then in the afternoon, the two chiefs were expected to have decided how they would treat the patient and deliver the news to the family.

"Oh, Daddy," John said with excitement and a bit of mischief in his voice. "Look what me and Layna got."

I pinched my lips and prevented the smile that was the prelude to me, bursting into laughter if I couldn't hold it back, but I held my own. The expressions on both pranksters' faces were priceless and a perfect way of seeing right through them. Collin owed my ass for catching on to Jake doing this to him, and I was playing along with John now. It was this little guy and me up against the two playful and witty doctors. Collin's face was riddled with confusion, while Jake's eyes went straight to mine, understanding I'd caught on.

"Well, well," Jake said, pulling his hands into his pockets. "It looks like Uncle Collin will be wildly grateful that you rescued *two* trees for him today."

"And sing to dedicate them," I added with a wink to John.

"No, Daddy," he frowned. "One is yours, one for Uncle Collin."

"Right." Jake grinned at me. "Of course."

"What the hell is going on here?" Collin asked.

"No bad words," John scowled at Collin's amused grin. "We saved the trees for you and Daddy."

Collin inhaled and bit his lower lip. "I couldn't be more delighted that you and Layna," he arched an eyebrow at me, then looked at Jake, "saved a couple of dead trees for Layna's first Christmas."

"*Everlasting* dead trees, of course," Jake challenged Collin with a grin.

"The interesting piece is one is for Elena and one for your dad. Somehow I don't get one?" Collin asked.

"Nope," John shrugged. "Only two are brown."

"A shame," Collin said. "And now I feel like my voice is too scratchy to sing and dedicate these two shameful trees."

"It's all they have," John said, and I was beginning to think this was getting to the poor little guy.

"You're traumatizing your son," Collin said to Jake.

"No, sitting my kid on Santa's lap was traumatizing my son. This is teaching my son that we appreciate all things ugly, like you, Uncle Collin," Jake grinned. "Or alive and well, like me."

"You're weird, Daddy."

"It's time Collin sings." Jake widened his hand. "Do you want me to hum a low G so you can find your key to sing in?"

"I don't need any further help from you, my dearest friend." I watched Collin challenge Jake.

"Well," I said, pulling John by his shoulder—both of us holding onto our dead trees and facing Collin and Jake. "We're waiting for the official tree song from Uncle Collin." I laughed at Collin's eyes, darting around the crowd we'd caused merely by holding the orange and brittle pine trees.

"Then let's kick off this ceremony of tree dedication," Jake said.

"Wait," I said, still trying not to laugh. "Is this something you guys always do?"

"We do now," Collin smirked at Jake. "It's a new tradition that John helped to start with you, Layna," he said, mimicking the voice John used when he came up with a cute way of saying my name. "Every year, we come to get everlasting trees and rescue a brown one and dedicate one through song."

Jake shook his head. "You realize he's young enough to forget this, right?" I heard him whisper to Collin.

"Not if I don't let him, and especially since you pulled my girl into your crazy schemes. Now, I'm pulling Ash in—but with honesty, unlike you, my friend. So, when Ash learns the truth of what you pulled with Elena?" Collin laughed. "This *will* be a new tradition, and little John will be rescuing brown Christmas trees like Ricky Ranger until he grows out of it."

Jake shook his head. "We'll see, Frank Sinatra," he said. "I believe the crowd that's gathered to figure out what we're doing with brown trees—in an expensive Christmas tree farm—is waiting on you to sing." He let out a breath, "Use your high tenor voice, please. The one that," he waved his hand dramatically in the air, "you know, sounds angelic."

"We're waiting, and it's obvious these trees *do not* have much longer in that department," I urged.

With that, Collin busted out the funkiest and funniest version of *Oh Christmas Tree* I'd ever heard. He sang and danced around, and John giggled uncontrollably. Through Collin's fun way of singing the song, ensuring we were doing good for the poor trees, I was reasonably confident that this moment would stay with John well up until he was a teenager.

CHAPTER NINETEEN
COLLIN

*A*fter our Christmas tree farm experience, all the way up to the time we left to come home, Elena had gotten a good dose of mine and Jake's goofy—yet hilarious, if you ask me—brotherly friendship. The only one who'd missed out on today's shenanigans was Ash, who'd had to work at her gallery.

If Ash knew I would serenade everyone at the Christmas lot with dedication songs for brown Christmas trees, however, I'm sure she would've closed up shop for the day. I have to admit that I never saw that one coming either. God knows what Jake had put in Elena's brain about me and trees, but I was nothing if not a man who always followed through on a gag.

"We've unpacked almost everything," Elena said as she lay curled into my body on the couch. "I have to say this was the most hilarious and productive day since I moved back to California. Except we forgot one thing…" she paused and covered my hand that'd been resting under her shirt and massaging along her stomach.

"Hmm," I said, engrossed by some show she'd put on the television earlier.

"Dear God." She sat up and looked back at me. "You're already a boring man."

"We just finished eating and decorating the tree." I smiled at her and cupped her chin between my hand. I brought her brilliant, smiling face down to mine and captured her lips in a slow kiss that woke up my cock. "And it was your idea to turn on this chick-flick, Christmas movie that I'm now addicted to."

Elena threw her head back and laughed. "Stay right here," she said, popping up and moving through her well-decorated condo. I loved the view from this place. She'd managed to land a second-floor condo in a perfect location, and it even offered her a view of the ocean. The place felt warm and comfortable, and those feelings combined with unwinding on the couch without a care in the world and Elena in my arms—it was perfection. I'd imagined we'd be fucking all over the house until sun up, but instead, we were watching some Christmas movie that was totally predictable, corny, and oddly addictive.

"Gotcha!" she laughed.

I sat up and moved the throw blanket off of me. "What?" I narrowed my eyes and smiled at her as she walked through the living room, holding up her phone. "Are you Facetiming or something?"

"I snatched a few pics of the sexy doctor lying on my couch without his shirt on, staring intently at the Christmas tree."

"You've lost your mind, Laney," I teased with a laugh. "You're not really…"

She nodded with her lips caught between her teeth. "Videoing you for the hell of it. I got you on my live Instagram feed at the tree farm today too." Her laugh escaped as she tried to remain serious, but I could tell she was thinking about my song for the brown trees and the shit I made up for John to hear the toddler squeal with delight.

I sucked in the side of my cheek between my teeth. "Baby, give me the camera—or phone, whatever the hell you're using to blackmail me with later."

"Nope," she teased with the smile that melted every defense I had about wanting not to be captured on film looking like a sap. "You're not getting anything. This part is all mine."

I narrowed my eyes at her. "Okay, then," I said, humoring her and loving this woman more with each passing second. "God only knows what will happen to this poor little rich girl on *your show* and the cowboy who runs the local feed store that her company is trying to shut down."

Her eyes widened as I moved toward her. "God only knows?" Her eyebrows rose playfully.

"What if this Lacy chick decides to take the side of the large firm she works for and closes down the entire town?"

"Her name is Lucy." She arched her eyebrow at me. "And I guess we'll never know if she's going to ruin her fling with Brian by siding with big business."

I glanced over at the television, smirking when I saw the snow starting to fall in the movie, the characters distressed by the decision to be made by the classy businesswoman in the country town. "I say she goes for it with love over money."

"Is that so?" Elena laughed as we stood in somewhat of a silly standoff. "But will he forgive her?"

"For coming back into town, rekindling their childhood sweetheart love, and then having to choose between him and money?"

"Yeah," Elena looked past me to the television. "It sucks to suck sometimes."

"Speaking of sucking," I pulled her into my chest with a laugh. "It's time to delete videos on social media and on that phone of yours. I can't be immortalized in such a pathetic way."

"Hell no." She popped up on her toes and kissed my chin. "It's time for you and me to take a selfie with our new tree."

"A selfie?" I felt like I was on another planet. I was a neuroscience geek who performed surgeries and took on insane challenges in the brain and spinal department. I was not a selfie-taking, social media user.

"Oh, my God," Elena laughed. "We need to get you out of the *hospital world* and into the fun, real world. I have all my friends from Florida on Instagram, and I love sharing pictures of what I'm up to."

"I'm sure the entertainment was riveting today with my *live* performance of a *dead* tree dedication."

"Two dead trees," she chuckled. "Come on. Throw your shirt back on, and put this on." She placed a white fur and red velvet Santa hat on my head. "We're taking a Christmas picture with our tree."

I exhaled. "Where the hell did you get this, you sneaky magician? Pull it out of your ass along with these sudden new things I'm learning about you?"

"You love it, and I know it. I see it in your face."

I pulled on my navy blue, long-sleeved shirt, not missing a second of acting fake annoyed. I'd never given a damn about the holiday season until now. These simple little things that brightened Elena's smile were things I'd never experienced. I grew up around massive Christmas parties, flooded with people of status, and houses that were decorated by interior designers. I'd never even decorated my house before, let alone hang personalized ornaments on a tree. All of those things were seemingly done automatically, in my experience.

This was all new to me. Seeing Elena's excitement about the tree and her new house was worth everything to me—even if it was all going on her social media. Who gave a damn? It was somewhat flattering to know that the woman was bringing me into the private affairs that she shared with others. A significant step in the right direction, I'd say.

I walked with Elena over to the tree that we'd covered in lights, hundreds of colorful glass bulbs, and hanging light icicles. Decorating the thing was fun too. Elena and I were singing along to Christmas music the whole time, and I swear to God, I can honestly say that I've never been so fucking festive in all my life.

Elena fiddled with her camera while I adjusted the Santa hat. "Where did you find this thing?" I asked.

"That drug store where we bought the Christmas lights. You were distracted." She smiled at me. "Now, say hi to *everyone.*"

"What? Are you videoing this again?"

"It's not live, so chill. Oh, wait." She glanced back at our decorated tree. "This isn't the tree I want our picture in front of." She laughed and looked over at her balcony. "It's that tree that deserves the picture."

"The brown one?" I furrowed my brows. "Elena, are you on something?"

"Let's go." She pulled my hand. "I still think we should have decorated it."

"God knows your poor neighborhood *will* be reporting the crazy doctor in the condo with her dead and very brown tree on the porch. This goddamn thing is a fire hazard."

"That's why we're taking our first of *many* Christmases together with it."

"You've lost it, Laney." I glanced down at her phone. "Are you *still* recording this shit?"

"Oh!" She pulled up her phone and giggled. "Whoops. Hold up. I need to switch it to the camera."

"Please do," I humored her as we walked outside to the brown tree I agreed to take home, so long as she picked a *green* one for the inside of her house. Only my best friend would manage to put it into my girl's head that I like to rescue brown fucking trees for Christmas.

We stood in front of it and smiled for her selfie. Fucking weird as shit to do so, I might add.

"That's not going to work," she said, readjusting the white ball of fur on the end of the Santa hat. "There." She pressed her finger into the cleft of my chin. "Now, smile like you love our brown tree."

I smiled and only thought of how I'd get Jake back for this.

"Nope. Collin," she said as she looked at me, "you look like you have some evil smile on your face. Give me your *Collin smile.*"

"My Collin smile? What the hell is that?"

"Just smile like you love me."

I gripped her waist, stood behind her, and kissed the one place I knew she loved—the bend of her neck. I had to end this nonsense.

Elena came down off her Mrs. Claus, North Pole high that second, turning and bringing her lips to mine. The woman was probably a pro at snapping pics as I used my more skillful talents of ensuring this camera shoot would pay off when I took my woman and made her climb the ropes of pleasure as soon as this was over.

She pulled away. "Damn it," she laughed. "My phone was recording that."

"Well, there's another one for your personal library. Perhaps the dead tree doesn't like cameras?"

"I can't focus with you kissing me like that."

"My whole point," I smirked. "Get over here and turn that thing for us to stare at ourselves and pull off a weird-ass smile." I squeezed her, and her smile was brilliant as I laughed. "You realize it's weird to smile at yourself, correct. Then take a picture of it?"

"Then look at me," she ordered. "I'm getting this shot."

"Why don't we act like that chick flick and *gaze lovingly* into each other's eyes."

"Good idea," she said and held the phone out while we tried to pull off my idea.

Elena laughed, I kissed her again, and as far as I could tell, she wasn't going to get shit for her Instagram account if she was trying to pull off some cute picture with a brown and brittle pine tree as the backdrop.

"That's good enough," she said, eying me. "We need to get you used to this."

"Used to taking selfies? That'll be the day. I'm not one for social media."

"Well, I have fun with it. I get to see what my friends are up to and see their kids growing up. And it's all private, so you don't have anything to worry about."

"Is that thing shut off?" I glanced down at my new enemy, Elena's phone.

"Yes. What do you say," she dragged out that last word mysteriously, "we light my first fire in that gas insert, and, well..." Her cheeks warmed to a beautiful pink.

"Fuck under the prettier tree?" I suggested with a smile. "Sounds like a plan."

Elena and I had used last night to get more comfortable with our bodies, moving in ways that we knew would bring us pleasure and ride out intense orgasms that I didn't even know were possible. Hell, I even realized that having sex with a woman for her pleasure was more of a sensual experience than just fucking a chick because you're an asshole who feels he needs to get laid.

I wasted zero time making sure we were both stripped to nothing while Elena grabbed a blanket and a pillow for us to use at our tree. Having my brain controlled a bit better this time, I saved us both the trouble of forgetting a condom as I had throughout the entire night before. She was certainly worth the risk, but we didn't need to keep testing what could easily come of us screwing without protection.

Elena's moans and sighs, and the way she worked my cock by squeezing it tightly while I was deep inside of her had my cock swollen and throbbing for its release. I loved her full breasts and the fact that she told me she loved when I massaged the most tender part of her ass with the wetness from her pussy, working circles around the one entrance I'd never before been tempted to fuck in my life.

When I absently went with the technique of pressure and slow circles around her asshole, Elena became wilder and more aggressive in response. Even now, as I fucked her from behind, I cupped one of her breasts, positioning my body to move my cock in and out of her while giving myself room to touch the other pressure point that made my woman give me her ass in ways I loved.

"Fuck," she said, moving with my hand and now my fingers daringly entering the hole that I'd always considered off-limits.

I watched Elena grip the blanket and ball it up into a fist.

"You like that, baby?"

"God, yes. It feels amazing. Fuck me harder, deeper, Coll," she pleaded, her voice filled with ecstasy.

Elena reached back and gripped my balls as I groaned in response. "Fuck. You have no idea how much I love you doing that," I said as she gently rolled them in her hands.

"Harder, baby," she begged.

I rolled her onto her stomach. "I'm not being gentle. You made me wait all day for this."

She arched her back and buried her face into her pillow, "I need it deep."

I gripped her pelvic bone and pounded the hell out of her, listening to her moans and watching every little movement she made to ensure this was what my girl wanted.

Her cursing, begging, and nearly screaming out her orgasm told me this was another hard climax, and even if I didn't have that, I felt her clamping the hell out of my cock as I moved harder.

We both came and practically collapsed under the wild, chasing lights of her Christmas tree. "Jesus Christ, you're so amazing," I said as I pulled her body in tightly to me. "I may have to quit my job and pursue a full-time career in fucking you in ways that make you climb the walls in ecstasy."

Elena laughed, her pussy clenching harder around my cock and almost forcing me out of her. We moved from our spot under the tree and into her shower. Shower sex was my favorite with this woman. We always used the excuse of soaping each other up, only for me to throw her sexy ass up against the wall, both of us riding the edge while we fucked hard and fast in the steam.

Once we were done, I was starving and headed to get some leftovers from the fridge while Elena dried her hair. When she was done, my little sparkplug walked out in her silk jammies, her nipples tempting my eyes more than the food I'd built up an appetite for.

"I have a question for you, you devious woman," I said, turning around and eating the leftover pasta while offering her a bite from across the counter.

"I'm sure I have an answer," she said with a grin. "By the way, your ass looks hot in those sweats."

"That's the compliment I expected when you walked out here," I teased. "You hungry? There's more, and I'll heat it up."

"We'll share. If we want more, we can reheat or order in."

"Might want to order a pizza," I said with a smile. "I'm just warming up with you."

"What's your question?" She took the fork I offered her to share the bowl of pasta as I grabbed one of my own.

"So, I'm not one to pry," I arched my eyebrow at her, "but as I was putting all your medical books on that shelf in your room today," I took another bite and swallowed, "I noted a book that said *Diary* on it."

Elena walked over to the fridge and pulled out two beers, twisting off the tops and handing me one. "Did you read my deep and dark secrets?" she teased.

"If I knew there was something in there about me, I'd be totally down for you to read me a bedtime story tonight." I took a drink of my beer. "So, selfies, predictable chick flicks, and now a diary? You're a woman who's hard to keep up with."

"I don't think it's a mystery." She leaned her head back and chugged her beer like some sexy woman who could drink any man under the table.

"No?"

"I just do what makes me happy," she smiled. "For example, that diary?"

"Yes, like those vampires?"

"I heard about you making the doctor's lounge turn on that show, by the way."

"I had to know what all the hype was about between you and the patient. I'm hotter than that Damon guy, by the way."

"Debatable," she said with a laugh, twirling noodles around her fork and taking a large bite of pasta.

"Do you do the diary thing because the vampires do?"

Elena covered her mouth as she laughed. "Oh, my God. Really? No." She shook her head and took a drink of her beer to wash down her bite of food. "Journaling has been around a lot longer than the television show, I'll have you know," she said. "I have a method for people who deal with head injuries and wild mood swings. You've probably heard of the technique before. I have them write what frustrates them—things that would've never bothered them before their head injury—then I tell them to rip out the pages and do whatever it takes to destroy them so they can let all of their frustration die with the pages."

"Does that work?"

"Some say it does, and some say it just makes it worse. We work together so I can help them the best way I know possible to move through the injury-related mood swings."

"I don't want to hear about why you make your patients have a diary. I want to know the reason you have your own diary." I insisted as she grinned broadly.

"I have mine because I love to hold onto everything. I love sketching flowers, butterflies, and writing things down that I love and don't want to forget. We all forget the simple, fun things. We get caught up in our crazy lives and forget things that should be treasured. Each day comes with a different experience—a different gift. I like to document those gifts."

"So, what you're trying to say is that book is pretty much filled with stories about me." I smiled at her. "I know I might have to give you a larger book if this is what you do."

"I also take pictures, *selfies*," she gave me that look again, "and I make videos like crazy. Mostly for myself, and some to share with friends. I just love keeping it all if I have time to write it down, film it, or get it in a picture."

"And our amazing sex?"

"Sex tapes," she laughed. "That *scandal* wouldn't be well received."

"Well, it's a good thing that we're so good together that you don't need to throw that in your little *black book* to remember it."

"You never know," she teased.

"All right, another question," I said, knowing this shit had to come up now or never. "Since you're obviously addicted to me, and it just took me getting you into bed to make that happen," I grinned, "I want to ask something crazy of you. I think you'll love videoing this shit and taking pictures too."

"What are you up to?"

"I want to invite you to come with me to Hawaii for Jim and Avery's wedding. It's two weeks and short notice, I know, but we can move things around or not stay as long."

"What?" she laughed her fun laugh. "I can't just leave."

"Jim already approved it since Avery could use a beautiful bridesmaid anyway."

"I hardly know them," she said, her mind reeling behind her eyes.

"You hardly know me, and look at us. We're already acting like a married couple, dead tree adoptions and all."

She eyed me and smiled, "I will regret not going, won't I?"

"Duh. That's a given. I'll help you move your schedule around. We'll do some crazy, adrenaline shit while we're out there too. What do you think?"

"I think as long as we can move my schedule around and we don't stay for too long, I'm not one to turn down a fun time. I don't want to get my ass busted, though. I just started working here." She pursed her lips. "Wait, was this what Jim was talking about last night?"

"Yep, wanting to ensure I got you on board."

She shook her head. "We're insane, you and I."

"I know that. It's why I'm currently ordering pizza and planning on a fantastic night with the woman I'm madly in love with."

"It's a good thing I'm falling pretty hard for you too, eh?"

"I knew you would eventually. Sucks for you that you just wasted a lot of lonely nights teasing my ass about it."

"Order your pizza. I promise I won't tell your best friend, the heart surgeon, about your horrible eating habits."

"I'm enjoying kicking off the holiday season. Jake can kiss my ass."

"You're going to end up like that poor brown tree if you keep up this ordering greasy food while you're around me."

"I'll make sure I order ice cream and cookie dough," I challenged.

"You do that," she said, taking the bowl of pasta with her. "While you're in there, can you pop us some popcorn? I put it next to the fridge. We need to rewind this movie and figure out what happens in the end."

And just like that, Elena and I had fallen in love, were traveling full-speed ahead as if this were our everyday lives, and we finally were united after thirty-six long-ass years of me waiting for a woman like her. Helping her move in had me navigating the place as if we owned it together, and the strange part about that was that it didn't even seem to faze Elena. A few days ago, I expected a lot of nervous progress, and that was *if* I could even manage a kiss with her.

I shouldn't have expected anything less than her and me, colliding as if the universe had been impatiently waiting for it to happen. Now it had, and the full support of everything right in the world was on my side with the woman.

She was worth the wait.

CHAPTER TWENTY
COLLIN

*A*fter a weekend spent with Elena, I felt like a new man coming back to work. I was refreshed, and God, I couldn't possibly be any happier. Being with her through the weekend was enough to make me confident that this was the woman I could happily share the rest of my life with.

Sure, I'd practically shouted that shit from the rooftop before we'd shared alone time, but now it was a concrete fact. This woman was truly put on this earth to be mine, and I would make sure that she enjoyed every single second of being with me. Life just got that much more enjoyable for me, and I couldn't be more thrilled. Anyone could call me a sap, and I'd completely agree with them.

I was the type of guy who would sit here in thought about how she'd cried out my name when she came, the way she practically pulled my hair out while I fucked her hard and deep...all of that. But I wasn't just caught up with how much I loved fucking the woman because there were so many other things that made me wish the weekend would've never ended. The small things—Elena things—like having that damn cell phone in my face.

Half the time, I looked at her phone and still couldn't figure out how to pull off a sincere smile while I felt like I was smiling at myself. All of her pictures must've been of me, looking like a jackass with some weird-ass, fake smile while she kissed my cheek. Who cared? I wasn't on social media, so I would never have to see this shit again. Thank God.

Decorating Elena's place—my idea to help seal the deal in staying with her this weekend—turned out to help me enjoy all things *merry and bright.* Well, all things except that damn brown tree that Jake had to pull his lame prank with, and now I still wondered if Elena thought I was some crazed lunatic who rescued trees every year when in truth, this was the first year I'd ever set foot on a Christmas tree lot. I needed to clear that shit up with her.

"What the heck is Jake doing with a dead Christmas tree in his office?" Dr. Chi asked—the cardio doc who was almost as talented as Jake—sitting across from me at our lunch table. "It's brown. Did you pull another joke on him like you did with that life-sized nutcracker last year?"

I laughed loudly at the memory. "Oh, damn, that was so funny. That was the best, and you know it. And it was *two* nutcrackers that were placed on each side of his door..." I smirked at the prank I'd pulled on Jake's ass last year.

"I forgot what they said when you walked in front of them," Dr. Chi said.

"They said, *'This nut's for you.'* It was perfect," I said, amused with myself all over again.

"So, what's the whole brown tree about, then? Another prank?"

"He seriously has that thing in his office?" I asked, shaking my head.

"Yeah," Dr. Chi said.

"Oh, well, that's all on him." I gulped down a drink of water. "Turns out he screwed with the wrong man this weekend, insisting to Elena that I had this stupid thing for rescuing trees that were cut too soon. Don't ask," I said, looking at his confusion grow. "I'm still trying to figure out how it went from me telling him I was buying Elena a Christmas tree this weekend to me becoming the dead Christmas tree whisperer. Though, I'm pretty sure Jake can give you the details on the tree in his office once he gets out of surgery later." I grinned. "I'm sure he has his own fantastic story as to why it's there."

There was no way I was going to try and explain this to Chi. Hell, I still couldn't figure it out myself.

"Where you headed?" Chi asked, noting I was getting up before finishing my meal.

"Surgery. Waters has one at three," I arched an eyebrow at him, "and I'm going to observe and assist if needed."

Dr. Waters had previously been disciplined due to negligence with his patients. Unfortunately, everyone at the hospital knew it—not exactly the kind of reputation any physician wanted. Dr. Alvarez was chief at the time, so he was the one who dealt with the Waters' discipline, but now, it was my responsibility as the new chief neurosurgeon to be aware of all surgeries this man performed. So, I was doing precisely that, observing this surgery to ensure the doctor was performing his surgical duties properly.

Waters was an impressive doctor, but the negligence on his record from sending his patients home too early, only to have them return with a brain bleed, was not something any doctor at Saint John's took lightly. Even the non-surgical issue in his file of prescribing too high a dose of medication for a patient was enough to have the man called into question. I didn't tolerate anything less than perfection with all of my residents, and that was why I had to ensure that he would perform this surgery in the same skilled manner.

"Have a good day, Brooks," Dr. Chi said.

With that, I took my exit, practically running into Elena as I walked through the doors, distracted by acknowledging two nurses on my way out.

"Shit," Elena giggled. "Sorry I'm late. I had a—"

"If it isn't my *Selfie Queen*," I said as I gripped her shoulders, pressed my lips against hers, pulled away, and smiled. "Listen, I spied an entire selfie crowd in the cafeteria that would love *your* expertise on how to take the perfect picture with an apple." I grinned at her as she rolled her eyes. "Go grab lunch. I need to get up in Dr. Waters' observation room before he starts that surgery."

"Wait," she grabbed my arm and turned back to the group she'd walked in with. "You girls go ahead. I'm going to sit in on this surgery with Dr. Brooks." She smiled at the two neurologists and my new resident neurosurgeon. "Someone has to keep you quiet while the physician performs."

"Ladies," I acknowledged the group Elena walked in with. "Enjoy your lunch, dinner, or breakfast—whatever time of day it is for you." I winked, knowing the group of doctors could be working on-call or could've been here in regular office hours.

"Have you missed me that much?" I asked, readjusting my white lab coat as we walked out of the cafeteria. "You'll starve to death if you keep skipping meals and following me around the hospital like this." I wrapped my arm around her for a quick kiss to the temple.

"Get over yourself." She laughed.

"Never," I smiled at the staff who passed us in the hall.

"Why are you going to surgery?" she asked.

"Because I'm a surgeon," I responded playfully.

Elena nudged my side. "You're in your suit and lab coat."

"Awe," I sighed. "It looks like you caught me following *you* around the hospital like a lost little puppy dog, then. You know, since you're spending Mondays here and standing me up at lunch."

"It's been a crazy day, but I do like the idea of using Mondays to make rounds in the hospital."

"It sucks for me, though," I added. "I have to sit in a lonely office and know my lady is up in the hospital—and the only time I see her would be at lunch? God, whatever shall I do?" I feigned my dramatic response.

"Again, sorry about being late and missing lunch with you."

I wrapped my arm around her, not giving a damn what any doctor, nurse, technician, or janitor thought about it. "As I said to you before, never apologize to me unless you fuck up in my OR."

"Seriously, though. Why are you going into the observation room on Dr. Waters? Why aren't you just attending the surgery?"

I punched the button of the elevator to get us up to the surgical floor. "I called and mentioned to Waters that I wanted to attend the surgery," I glanced around the elevator at some family that was taking the ride up with us, "and let's just say he didn't need me in the room today."

Elena looked at me in confusion. Hopefully, she could deduce that I was overseeing this surgery because the guy already had a record, and that's the only reason I'd clear my Monday afternoon schedule for his craniotomy. I couldn't necessarily blurt out that he had been busted more than once due to negligence, and that shit wouldn't ever happen again so long as I could help it.

It was my duty to ensure my resident surgeons were in their ORs, working for the patient's well-being. When a doctor waved off the Chief Surgeon asking to attend him, that raised a flag for me.

Waters was pissed when he found out the board had selected me to take Elena's dad's position as the new Chief, and his reaction came as no surprise to me. It's most likely the main reason he said I wasn't needed in surgery with him today. I could've pulled rank on his ass and demanded I be in there, but I wasn't that big of an arrogant dick—no matter what the rumors were.

"You should've gotten lunch with the ladies," I finally said. "This might be the dullest surgery we've both had the privilege to attend. In fact, I'll probably have June-bug make me some coffee to keep me awake so I can observe the entire thing."

"Hilarious. I'll get a snack later," she said.

Elena and I walked up into the room and sat down, watching the staff begin prepping the patient and the OR for Dr. Waters.

"Admit it," I whispered to her, "you know you want me to come back to your place tonight."

"I'll admit that." She gave me a sly smile. "But I don't keep surgeon hours, and I don't like to be kept up late at night on a Monday, either."

I smirked. "Good thing I'm clear of surgeries until Thursday when I go on-call this week."

"Then I guess you can sleepover."

Waters walked in, and I watched the room come to life.

"Good damn thing," I teased. "I was hoping this morning when I packed my entire closet that it would be worth my effort."

"You were planning on moving in?" she chuckled while I studied the room.

"Yes," I affirmed, half in this conversation and half watching the group as they rolled in the patient on the gurney.

"What surgery is he doing on this patient?" Elena asked.

"Craniotomy," I answered her, noting the patient was being prepped to remain asleep and leaning forward to observe the images, seeing the tumor located on the right side of the woman's brain.

My attention was then brought to Waters when he walked in and went to work, locking the patient's head in the vice. I brought my folded hands to my chin and studied the images on the screens across the OR from the room I was in, and double-checked to ensure I did, in fact, see the tumor was on the right side of the patient's brain. So, why the hell was Waters marking off the left side of the patient's head for him to make his cuts and then drill into the patient's skull for surgery?

"Did he request you to attend him?" I absently asked Elena after I stood, walked toward the glass, and folded my arms. "Did he request someone to brain map this patient for him to remove the tumor?"

"No. I have no idea why he's marking off the left side either."

"Dr. Brooks," an intern said from behind me as I was studying everything in front of me and discerning if Waters or another resident would stop the doctor from cutting into the wrong side of the patient's skull. "Is he going to do surgery on the—"

"Oh, my God," three people said as I hit the button to communicate with the room.

"Dr. Waters, stop the surgery immediately," I said through the intercom that led into the room.

The fucker had his music blasting and couldn't hear me. This man's head was in the goddamn clouds. He was too busy showing off for the observation room instead of focusing, and he was about to perform surgery on the wrong side of his patient's brain.

The only way to stop this and stop this fast was to bust into that OR before he could drill into the skull. I had to desterilize that fucking work environment, and that would force him to stop. With me not scrubbing in and entering the room, it would do just that.

"Dr. Brooks!" I heard him say, startled and his mouth muffled from practically inhaling his mask after I rushed into the room. "This—"

"This is no longer a sterile environment," I practically growled. "Put the shit down and pray to God that you didn't make a cut."

"This is my OR, and you're in violation of a sterile operating environment. You've lost your mind, Dr. Brooks."

"Turn off the goddamn music!" I shouted, Waters and I, screaming over it like we were both madmen. "Have you made any cuts on this patient?"

I'd never been this pissed off before in my fucking life. He was really and truly about to operate on the wrong side of *his* patient's brain, and no one was paying attention except for the interns in the observation room and me?

"No incisions have been made. I was about to begin my surgery before you ruined my sterile—"

I looked at the anesthesia crew. "Please carefully bring the patient out from under anesthesia. We won't be doing this surgery today." I looked at the residents. "All of you are on administrative leave and will return in a week when you report to training. It is obvious you all did not see the *massive* mistake Dr. Waters has made." They left without arguing, though I did see the horror in their faces when they eyed the CT scans, MRIs, and computer model that showed the tumor wasn't on the side Dr. Waters was seconds away from cutting into. I looked to the rest of the staff in the room while Waters remained silent. "I want this OR clear while the anesthesia team continues to wake the patient safely." Then I looked at Dr. Waters. "You will wait for me in my office. You'd better have a damn good excuse as to why I saw a fucking brain tumor on the right side of the brain from that observation room, and you were prepping to cut into this patient's left side."

"Dr. Brooks—"

"I'll see you in my office after I've assured the family their member will be fine, and the operation will be pushed out."

AFTER THE CHAOS of ending a near-catastrophic event that could've caused crippling effects for the poor patient who was in the care of this surgeon—I left the room and went to speak with the patient's family.

The patient was Betsy Kilmore. She was a female who was thirty-two years of age and the mother of three boys, ages four, two, and ten months. This patient was the wife of Luke Kilmore and daughter of John and Peggy Johnson. I could go on and on with what I'd learned, speaking with her highly-concerned family and informing them that we were forced to cancel surgery until further notice. These names ran through my mind, knowing they were so close to dealing with the worst nightmare a family or patient could suffer from. A botched fucking surgery.

They would have sued the shit out of this hospital for malpractice, and when they won that case and were awarded shitloads of money, none of it would fix anything. If Dr. Waters had gone forward blindly and operated on the wrong side of the patient's brain—as he was intending on doing just moments ago—their lives would be changed forever. There wasn't any amount of money out there that could give Betsy back what this doctor would've taken away.

When I walked into my office, I was calmer and more collected than I'd imagined I would be after what I'd witnessed close to an hour ago.

Dr. Waters turned in the chair he'd been sitting in. "Doctor—" he started but shut his mouth after he looked me in the eye.

"From the brain and from the brain only arise our pleasures, joys, laughter, and jests, as well as our sorrows, pains, griefs, and tears," I said, slapping Dr. Waters' file on my desk and sitting in my seat.

"Hippocrates."

"It seems you know your Greek physicians," I answered Dr. Waters. "It also appeared today as though you must admire the man so greatly that you would treat your OR as if you were living in the same barbaric, surgical times he was *forced* to live through."

"That's not what I was doing, and you know it," he mumbled.

"I'm not getting into what the hell you were *doing* because what you were about to fucking do was ruin someone's life," I said, angrier than before after hearing the man defend himself. He should have been scared as fuck, completely shaken up, after what he'd almost done. Instead, I was listening to an asshole defend himself instead of concern himself with his patient's well-being first.

"Listen," he cleared his throat as he tried to sound more professional. "It was a mistake. I'm glad you caught it."

"Glad." I stared at him with disgust, repeating that word flatly. I watched the man and then let out a breath. "You know the old saying: There are some doctors that make mistakes, and then there are some doctors that are good at *burying* them?" I said through gritted teeth, referring to doctors who've killed their patients, and those fucking mistakes went six feet underground.

"That's not how it was. I'm not one of those dirty and twisted doctors, and you know it."

"I know. It's obvious that you wouldn't have the attention to detail that goes into being a serial killer. So, change my fucking mind. After knowing your record and then the shit I saw today, I would assume that you're a doctor who's good at *burying* mistakes—or at least thinks he could be—

and fuck you for that and everything this hospital should have gotten rid of you over…five fuck-ups ago. But I'm sure those previous errors were all just mistakes."

"Watch your language."

"Excuse me…*fucking* mistakes," I exhaled. "Better?"

"Dr. Brooks."

I ignored the pleading I sensed in his voice. "Because of careless doctors like you, patients and anyone, in general, have a more heightened fear of surgery than they naturally would. Due to horror stories like what I almost witnessed today, they fear doctors. The good doctors who want to help end up having to go through hell and back to gain their trust." I narrowed my eyes at him. "Your careless act is the exact reason I became a neurosurgeon and worked my ass off to get to where I'm at today." I relaxed my clenched fist. "I ensure that when my patients go under my blade, my saw, my drill, even the fucking light in my OR, they are acutely aware that I understand how frightened they are. I know that they made a critical decision to place their delicate lives in my hands, and I don't take one single ounce of that for granted." I watched his knuckles turn white as he held his hands clasped together. "Until now, I valued you as a member of this neuro division. You were a doctor who I believed was just as valuable to Saint John's as any of the other greats who have come before us. Today, you've proven that you're an incompetent snake, and you need to be removed from practice. You will no longer work for Saint John's, and I will ensure this goes directly into your permanent record."

"You can't take my license over an *accident*," he defended himself.

"I'm well aware of that, but after I'm done filing my report on the circus I witnessed, I don't think I'll need to worry about you having a license in the near future."

"You act like you're the be-all, end-all of surgeons, like you've never made a mistake in surgery."

I folded my hands and leaned up on my desk. "Do you know why I will *not* listen to music while I perform surgery, and I only turn it on when I've successfully finished?"

"To celebrate? I don't fucking know."

"I prefer to hear my patient's heartbeat instead. Every time I hear that heartbeat, I'm in tune with the precious life that's in my care. I won't allow my mind to be distracted from each beat of their heart. It's a sacred thing for a patient to trust you with their life, Mike," I said. "It's a dangerous thing when a doctor takes that for granted. Tell me something, how long have you been practicing?"

"Almost twenty years."

"Same," I said, knowing it'd almost been that long for me as well, yet I still treated each patient the same as I did the minute I'd received the *honor and privilege* to practice as a neurosurgeon. "And in all your years, have you lost a patient?"

"Of course, I have."

"Really. Tell me, can you name any of the patients you've lost?"

"Lost? As in deaths? Shit, Brooks, what kind of point are you trying to make?"

"Answer the question," I demanded.

"I think I've lost maybe ten," he answered. "I don't fixate on that stuff."

"You see, I've lost close to fifty in my years as a doctor in the ER and post-op. Mostly gunshot wounds, car accidents, or people placed on life support with the family praying to God that they came out of it. I know every single one of their names, but I won't bore you with that since you don't fixate on such things."

"You would admit to losing patients? Wow, never saw that in you."

"I think we have both seen things today we never saw in each other before, Waters. You know some surgeons won't tell their patients the odds and outcomes of surgery. They aren't honest with them, but I am. I know the odds in this profession, and every day that I recall those statistics, I'm a better surgeon for it." I eyed him as I leaned back in my chair and continued. "Watching you today, even now, I see a doctor with a lack of consideration toward human life, given that you nearly destroyed one today and have the nerve to defend your actions. You've not asked about how her family feels with our pushing out the surgery. You've never once looked apologetic or fearful with the knowledge of what you almost did. You sit here and act like an asshole doctor who got fucking caught. And for the last time, let me assure you."

"I'll find another place to practice."

"When I write my letter to the state board about this, I'll see to it that you won't ever be bringing a surgical blade near a human life again."

"I said it was a fucking accident. I didn't realize I lost my bearings in there and was operating on the wrong side of the brain."

"There's no room for error. Perhaps Betsy Kilmore would have forgiven you if you explained the little mishap you had today as being an accident when she woke up paralyzed," I said in an unwavering tone.

"Fuck you."

"We have no room for negligence in our field. As neurosurgeons, we already have the mystery of the human brain to work with on its own. To walk to the wrong fucking side of a patient's skull to cut into their brain blindly? Would you forgive my *mistake* if I pulled that shit on you?"

"Yes."

"Yeah. I'm sure you would," I said with disgust. "As chief, I will be working on your suspension and calling for a comprehensive review of patients who've been in your care. This will be reported to the hospital board as soon as you leave my office. The state board will be given a descriptive letter, penned by me, to read and determine if you are a safe surgeon, and it will be up to them if they decide you keep your license." I exhaled, "After our interview, what I saw, and what the witnesses saw from the observation gallery, I highly doubt they'll have much faith in you. Get the hell out of my office, pack your shit, and you'll be advised on where you stand while you're on administrative leave and investigations are complete."

"You're overreacting."

"All for the good of that patient, and any future patients that Saint John's would've entrusted to you. I only pray to God that I'm overreacting, and the investigations don't uncover this sick feeling I have about you."

"The board will fire you for this."

"We'll let the board decide that, won't we? Get the hell out of my office."

Dr. Waters was the type of man who made my blood boil. Just by looking into his soulless eyes, I could tell that we'd find negligence with minimal digging. He was one of the doctors who made the respectable doctors look corrupt—a greedy doctor who opted-in for surgery even when the patient didn't need it. I'd been around doctors long enough to separate the good from the bad. I wasn't a fool born into this profession yesterday, and I sure as hell wasn't the chief surgeon around here because I smiled a lot.

You didn't fucking get to make these mistakes in our profession. If doctors gave themselves *passes* like that, who knows what the statistics of patient deaths and recoveries would look like. Hell no. Each life was sacred, and for us to gain a patient's trust—which sometimes was damn near impossible—it meant the world. There were too many noble doctors out there to be in the shadow of dicks like Waters.

CHAPTER TWENTY-ONE
ELENA

*I*t'd been a long day, to say the least, and it would've been exponentially longer if Collin hadn't stopped that surgery. He was quicker to act than the rest of us. He was out of the room and bursting into the OR before all of us observing in the gallery could fully grasp the gravity of what was happening.

For the rest of the day, we all performed our duties as if nothing had happened in that OR. We tried to keep things *business as usual*, but gossip, of course, was flying. Little by little, whispers from the doctors, interns, and nurses started buzzing.

The first rumor I'd heard was that Collin had gone above the hospital board's head and independently fired that asshole doctor. Then, the senior staff started killing those rumors as quickly as they started. It turned out that the doctor was suspended from performing any further surgeries and was placed on administrative leave pending an investigation.

I expected Collin to be done with work by the end of the regular workday, but I saw that his office door was still closed, and Justine, his interim secretary, stated that he'd been on a conference call since he returned to his office.

"Can you let Dr. Brooks know I've gone home for the day?" I asked Justine after pulling on my wool coat.

She gave me the same smile everyone had been giving me since Collin made it perfectly clear we were dating now. Collin preferred to be open about our relationship instead of dealing with gossip that might come out of us spending the weekend together—and future weekends together— and I trusted his judgment even though it made for a few awkward situations. I could've avoided talking to Justine at all, but I didn't want to interrupt him with a text just to tell him to meet me at my place...if he was still in the mood to come over.

LITTLE DID I KNOW, I wouldn't have Collin over at all this week, and by Thursday night, when I learned he was out of his spinal surgery and sleeping in his office before he started his seventy-two-hour on-call tonight, I had to check on the man.

It's not like he was avoiding me. It was just a busy week. Our schedules didn't line us up to see each other, and Collin was spending his after-hours time going over what had happened with Dr. Waters with the board.

I unlocked the back door, knowing that the staff all had left for the day, and turned on a light so Collin wouldn't think some creep was lurking in the office halls. Good God, where was he asleep? At his desk?

I tapped on his door and then opened it, seeing his desk lamp was the only light on in his room. I glanced around. "Collin?" I said, wondering if he was hiding somewhere behind the two doors that led to other areas in his office.

The one to my left opened, and he ran his hand through his messy hair. "Hey," he said. "Where the hell have you been all week?" He crossed the room in fresh scrubs and his million-dollar smile.

"Just walking around offices looking for where my boyfriend's been hiding," I teased as I wholeheartedly welcomed his delicious fragrance and hug that swallowed me up. "God, I've missed you."

"Get in here," he said, pulling me into a room that blew my mind.

"What the hell is this?"

"This is the reason I can live in Malibu on the beach and not stay at a hotel to get some sleep before a long shift."

"You know my place is only twenty minutes from the hospital."

He brought me into an area that was practically a studio apartment.

He had another desk along the wall to my left, a sofa under a window to my right, and a twin-sized bed across the other wall. The curtains were made of blackout material, and it was the perfect little hideout for any doctor if they were pulling long shifts.

"Well, I wouldn't have had time to run to your place, make up for not fucking my lady every night this week, and then get back in time for my damn phone to start blowing up with emergencies."

I took his face in my hands. If the guy had a long week—which I knew he had—you would never know. "You need to get some sleep. I'll see you on Sunday morning if you want to come crash at my place." I stopped, "Wait, I won't be there. I promised Dad I'd head up to his place this weekend. So, I'll have a key made. Seriously, unless I break up with you, just come stay at my place."

He eyed me. "This Sunday, you'll be at the ranch in Malibu?"

"My brother isn't helping worth a damn to organize the house."

"Is this what our relationship is now?" He grinned, taking my hands from his face and kissing my fingers. "You and me, unpacking on weekends?"

"You're sleeping," I said. "I know you're going to be busy as all neurosurgeons are when they're on-call."

"I'm sleeping," he arched an eyebrow at me, then cupped my ass, "with you."

"Listen up. I'm leaving now." I went up on my toes to touch my lips to his. "I miss you like crazy, and we're going to make up for lost time later."

"This isn't going to work for me." Collin eyed me. "Going one day without enjoying your sexy body was bad enough. Now, God only knows what I'll do when I've got you to myself again."

"Selfish man," I teased. "Get some rest. I'm sure you've eaten, but if not, I'll run out and—"

Collin's lips captured mine, cutting me off midsentence. How the hell could I have forgotten the savory taste of masculinity that I devoured when I kissed him? Why did I forget that Collin's kiss was nothing less than intense and always spoke right to the body parts that pleaded for this man to go further? His tongue was forceful and dominant as it met with mine in a way that made my knees buckle.

His hands pressed against my lower back and over my butt to hoist me up into his arms. I moaned and gripped his perfect face as our heads shifted to deepen this sensual kiss. I pulled my lips from his and ran my lips in soft pecks all over his flawless face.

"I love you so much," I said while I assaulted his face with kisses.

"I can't let you leave without giving you something to think about when you drift off to dream tonight, sunshine."

Collin started in on that cute nickname as a joke on Sunday morning, and it had to have been my reaction to the way he said it because he kept using it throughout the day whenever we found ourselves lost in each other like this. Damn, I've missed everything about him.

"It's always been a fantasy to have a hot doctor screw me in his scrubs," I said, pulling my face back and running my hands through his hair.

"I have to wear these damn things while we have sex?" He eyed me with a curious look.

"That came out wrong," I laughed, my head spinning and my body aching now. "Well, are we just going to stand in the middle of your *secret* office bedroom, or are we going to get busy?"

Collin arched an eyebrow at me. "Your sweet ass is mine."

IT DIDN'T TAKE MUCH for Collin and me to have our bodies reunited in hot sex, rekindling the fire of ecstasy we'd shared all day on Sunday before work pulled us away from each other this week.

I loved that I could come hard and fast with him while he managed to hold back and keep going for longer, but I always had an aching need that was about more than my own orgasms. It was seeing his facial expressions and feeling his body react when he came. I watched Collin's face contort into that serious look he always had right before he finally let it go.

His hands went up into my hair and gripped it tightly as he thrust deeper and faster. His vivid blue eyes were wild and hypnotic as they fell into the trance that I had been in since he laid me back on this small bed and kissed my body as if memorizing it. I loved feeling his strong hands holding me firmly in place while I arched into him, selfishly trying to work his cock into my sensitive spot that was deep inside. He made me crawl out of my skin when his cock brought my deep spot to life, and I came so hard that my body always shivered in aftershocks when I slowly came off my *sex with Collin* high.

I watched him lick his lips and clenched my pussy tightly around him, forcing Collin to purse his lips while fucking me harder. I loved the power behind the way he worked my body over. I watched his eyebrows knit together while I reached for his hair, gripping it and holding on for dear life as my man slammed deep inside of me.

"Harder, baby," I begged. "God, I've missed you...this..." I trailed off, absorbing every part of our sex.

"Fuck, your pussy is so goddamn good," he said in his low growl.

Collin and I were both vocal and breathless as we rode this wave of pleasure together. Having nothing left in me after I rode out my orgasm with Collin's, I melted beneath his rigid body. I wished we could do this all night, but I already knew that I was lucky enough to have him want to slide this in before he went on-call tonight in the first place.

"It's been too long," he said, kissing under my chin and down my neck. He licked each of my hard nipples as he slowly moved in and out of me.

I tried to fix his hair that I'd pulled between my fingers in the height of my ecstasy. "Thank God your hairstyle is a natural *just got fucked* look, or we'd both be busted." I kissed the top of his head that smelled as delicious as his cologne, thanks to his hair products.

Collin shifted to where he could lay behind me and pulled my ass into his softening cock. "Can you just stay here and let me selfishly fuck you after I come back from emergency calls all night? Who knows, maybe I never get called up to the hospital at all." His thumb grazed over my ribs from where his hand rested against my stomach. "God knows I deserve a break after this hellish week."

I rubbed his forearm. "We haven't had a chance to talk at all this week. Are you doing okay after that whole incident with Dr. Waters?"

"I'm doing fine." I felt his lips press against my hair. "I've just been in meetings in between seeing my patients. At least the hospital terminated that asshole after this final offense. Thank God he's out of here."

I twisted in his arms to face him. "You did an amazing job stopping that surgery as quickly as you did."

"I just did my job, baby," he kissed my nose.

I traced the sharp lines that defined the features of his face. "So, you're okay?" I asked him, shocked at how well he composed himself through any situation.

"Yes, my little neuro-*shrink*." He smiled. "I'm okay."

"You haven't asked yourself anything like, *what if you weren't there to stop it?*"

"If I let the crippling words of *what if* haunt me, then I would be stuck in the past and completely fucked over by what could have happened that day."

"That's a good and healthy way to process it all." I smiled. "How do you manage to keep such a positive frame of mind, especially with something like that?" I narrowed my eyes at him, "Are you cheating on me with another psychiatrist?"

He laughed. "I am. She's due in this room any second, so you should probably go." He slid his fingertips along my back. "In truth, I learned to not focus on negative shit from the one and only Dr. Miguel Alvarez."

"My dad?" I laughed. "I guess that sounds like something he would do."

"Yes. He taught me that you learn, and you move forward. Everything is something to learn from. The scary-as-shit stuff that has people freaking out at the possibilities of tragic outcomes, well, you can't dwell on that." He shrugged. "They're all lessons, and there are reasons that we're placed in situations at the right place at the right time—or the wrong place and the wrong time. It's all how you process it. If I were to dwell on the *what-ifs*, then I couldn't have helped anyone this week. I wouldn't have finished the rest of that day with patient consultations. It's simple. I was there, I handled the situation, and I learned from it. New and stricter protocols are now being implemented in all surgeries. I will never have this kind of fuck-up happen again in my ward. We're better than this. Waters was already in trouble with a few issues on his record, and that's the main reason I went up to observe him."

"Well, Dr. Collin Brooks, you're a damn fine chief surgeon."

He smirked. "To hear that come from your mouth," he rolled me onto my back, "means we're going another round." His eyes widened in that fun, mischievous, Collin look. "Can you handle another round with me, *my little ray of sunshine?*"

"I can and would, but you need to rest before you go on tonight."

"I will," he assured me, then decided to win this argument by bringing my hand to his hard cock. "But I think I'd rather fuck my girl again."

"You win."

He smiled my favorite smile that highlighted his entire face and creased his forehead, "I always win, my little sex goddess."

We all say we're in love at one point or another, then we *fall in love* with the right person later on in life. I had no explanation for the way Collin made me feel. My thoughts were always with him. Catching a glimpse of his tall and commanding frame while he walked the hospital floors made my heart jump in my chest. His smile made me feel like I was the most important woman in his entire world, and I knew there was no replacing him.

CHAPTER TWENTY-TWO
COLLIN

*L*ast night, I'd finalized our flight to Oahu next week for Jim and Avery's wedding, and I was glad that shit was out of my way. Everyone else in the wedding party was planning to take the private jet, which would've been nice, but Elena could only do so much to move patients around for this to happen. I didn't mind flying commercial if it meant I got to escort my Cuban goddess to a tropical paradise.

As much as I looked forward to attending Jim and Avery's wedding, my real motivation for wanting to take this trip was to spend uninterrupted time with Elena. I couldn't get enough of her, and work had gotten in the way too many times lately.

Today was Christmas morning, and we woke up together at Elena's condo. I laughed at this whole notion of us not wanting to be separated whenever we were fortunate to have time off, and I was grateful she felt the same way I did.

"Merry Christmas!" Elena shouted as she walked out to where I waited for her in the living room. "You ready to do this?"

"First of all, you look smoking-fuckin-hot," I said, planting my hand on her counter. "And second of all, no. Why don't we stay at my place in Malibu and spend the day unwrapping each other and taking fuck-selfies, you know, shit like that?"

"Fuck selfies?" her eyebrows rose in humor. "That's a new one."

"What can I say? I come up with good shit. And trust me, fuck selfies are a must."

"You're full of shit," she played back.

"Let's just stay at my house." I cringed at the idea of heading to my mom's house for Christmas dinner—no matter how much I loved the woman, it was not something I wanted to do. "We can go to your dad's place, and then we can spend the rest of our holiday at my place on the beach."

Her eyes narrowed funnily. "You made it perfectly clear that not only did Jake prank me about you saving brown trees for Christmas, but you've also never even decorated your place before." She smiled, her black strapless dress pushing her cleavage to perfection. "What are you *not* telling me?"

Ring. Ring. Ring. I checked my phone. It was Mom.

"Well, if it isn't my ever-loving mother, calling to make sure I show up to her *festive activities* tonight. You know, Elena doesn't want to go," I announced when I answered my phone, making Elena's eyes nearly bulge out of her head.

"Oh, no!" my mom responded. She knew I was always full of shit, but she probably believed me anyway.

"I know. It's so disappointing," I sighed. "She said it's all too much too fast. You, having all of those elite people over there, she's the odd man out. She hasn't stopped going on and on about this for hours."

"Collin Michael! Stop teasing your mother." My mom laughed, knowing I got most of my crazy personality from her. "For heaven's sake; I hope she knows what she's getting herself into with you."

"Oh, she knows, all right." I held my hand up, knowing Elena had enough personality to rip the phone from my lying hands and set this record straight.

"Listen, honey," she said. "Carey and Max surprised me late last night by showing up unannounced with my three precious grandbabies."

"No kidding," I said with a smile. "Glad I was notified about all of this."

"I'm notifying you now, you impossible son of mine."

"That I am. How long are they going to be here?"

"That's the thing. Not very long, and since the kids woke up to Santa Claus this morning at the house, we're not making the extravagant dinner tonight. I already informed Jim and Jake."

"They found out about this before I did?" I eyed the beautiful, onyx-haired woman who had the most adorable yet perplexed look on her face. "Why am I not surprised? Okay. So, what's the plan, then?"

"Are you and Elena okay with going out to celebrate Christmas night at that adorable village with all of the lit Christmas trees and Santa's village?"

"As much as I love my nieces and nephew, trust me when I say I've had my share of outdoor Christmas tree extravaganzas this year. Why don't we just figure out lunch or something?"

Elena's phone had rung, and she was seemingly having the same conversation with her dad. "There's been a change. Do you think your dad will be cool with us swinging by tonight?" I asked in a soft voice, hearing that she might be getting news of a Christmas change on her end as well.

This is why the holidays were so damn complicated sometimes. Why couldn't we stay back at my place? Hell, I should've swept Elena's ass out of here, and then we wouldn't have had to deal with parents and their confusing plan changes. Elena seemed to thrive on last-minute shit, though, putting us on opposite ends of the spectrum with our personalities.

She nodded and gave me a thumbs-up in response to my question. "All right. A thumbs up from Elena says we're a *go* for a Christmas lunch with my sister, mom, and kiddos."

"And Max."

"Max is a douche," I teased.

"I can't wait to see you," Mom laughed. "I've missed my boy."

"You too, Mom," I said, and then I hung up.

I thought about all of the things I wanted to do with Elena in this strapless dress as she giggled and laughed on the phone. If I could get away with it, which I might—

"Collin!" Elena batted my hands away from running up the sides of her thighs as I kissed along her shoulder. "Don't," she whispered.

Like her teasing laugh was going to kill my hard-on and the desire to fuck my girl right here and now. Unfortunately, it just pushed Elena to pop off the phone much faster and turn back to me. Her eyes looked like the devil—the bad kind—hidden behind some bad joke she was about to deliver.

"I'll go first. My sister and brother-in-law flew in last night with the kids," I said slowly, wary of what the hell Elena was about to tell me. "And so, I'm glad you agreed to Christmas lunch since my mother canceled her usual dinner party where a bunch of assholes get drunk and—" I stopped. "What the hell is it? Your expression is making me nervous."

She bit her bottom lip.

"You're only allowed to give me *that* look when you want me to fuck you senseless," I said.

"Well, the good news is this: Both of our families made us switch our times of visiting them, and so that part works out perfectly."

"Let me quickly emphasize that I'm not a good news-bad news kind of guy—and God help your patients if this is how you deliver news to them. What's the bad news?"

"You're going to meet my older sister, Lydia, but that's not all." She stopped, and I knew an Elena giggle was on its way to bubble out of her merry little heart.

"There's nothing wrong with being prematurely judged," I challenged.

"Then this next part won't be so bad after all."

"Spit. It. Out."

"Lydia has arranged this big ordeal apparently, and all of our friends will be there. She's planned to throw Dad a house-warming party and Christmas party all in one night at the ranch—caterers and everything."

"She realizes that he moved out there to get away from the madness, right?"

"She can be quite the bitch, and that's putting it nicely."

"That's putting it quite harshly, coming from the sweetest woman I've ever met. Should I be concerned about this woman?"

"No." She laughed and grabbed my hand. "Turns out we both have sisters who wanted to surprise our parents this Christmas."

"Well, my sister has made my life easier." I smiled and nuzzled my lips against her neck. "Your sister found a way to complicate it again."

"She sort of goes all out. So much so that I've been known to leave these parties—which are typically reserved for New Year's Eve—and no one noticed my absence."

"That's shocking in and of itself; however, I'm glad about that. This way, they won't notice us slipping out when the night escalates into drunken people, gossiping about their cheating spouses over champagne."

"Oh shit." She covered her laugh. "How do you know that? Have you been spying on these parties my whole life?"

I shook my head. "I grew up with these same lushes, overindulging at parties since I was old enough to remember." I smiled. "That's it. All of our cars have suddenly broken down at my house."

ELENA DANCED around the Malibu place with a cheerfulness I should've expected from her, and I loved the fact that she approved of the place. We were about fifteen minutes down the road from Jake and Ash's house, so we stopped there to give our Christmas wishes and John's gift before going to my mom's place.

Elena and Carrie instantly hit it off, but again, it was Elena, and I would've been shocked if my family disapproved. I knew my dad would've loved this woman without a shadow of a doubt too. The whole day was moving at light speed, and I even got a speeding ticket in my car to prove that theory. Dad designed every last detail of our hidden Hollywood Hills place, and when we pulled up to it, Elena was in awe.

The place was more of a show house than a proper home. However, it was still my childhood home, and I had tons of memories from the hidden passageways to riding our horses with professional trainers when we were young.

We had lunch in the garden room, and without having time for tours of the fifty-thousand square foot mansion, I was stuck explaining how we always congregated in one wing of the house. I could see the confusion on Elena's face when she looked around at this massive place and wondering how my mother could live here alone.

Now, here we were after the entire day had flown past us, and I was enjoying a beer with Miguel. We talked about Waters, and I elaborated more on his being dismissed from the hospital after Elena had explained what had happened that week. It validated me immensely when Miguel agreed with how I went about handling the idiot doctor.

"So," Miguel said as we hid from the party guests, moving out to the patio with beers in our hands, "everything seems to be going well with you and my Laney, huh?"

I smirked at him. "I couldn't agree more."

"She's completely taken by you, Brooks," he said. "I don't say that lightly either." He glanced back through the large windows that showed the guests we ditched, celebrating over eggnog and ham. "I never thought I'd see Laney smile and laugh more than she already did." He looked back at me.

I grew speechless when I saw her moving through the room with a vibrant smile and not a care in the world. Damn, I was speechless. Literally.

"You look at her the way I've seen her look at you." He chuckled. "Better hope she doesn't break *your* heart." His forehead wrinkled the same way Elena's did when she was wholeheartedly humored.

"No kidding."

We walked back into the house, and the woman I deemed the *ice queen*, Elena's sister, Lydia, stopped me.

"I swear I think Elena must've stolen all of the family genetics of cheerfulness," I said when the slender woman with black hair, red lips, and glowing green eyes met me as Miguel left me to fend for myself.

"Now, is that a thing to say to someone you hardly know?"

"Gee," I exhaled, "I was wondering the same when you insulted my best friend and me by mentioning you were pleased your sister brought one of SoCal's most eligible male sluts to your family party."

"Didn't seem to bother Elena." She arched that sharp brow at me. "Tell me, Collin, *does* Elena know about your past with women?"

"I'm sure she watched whatever it appears you watched in that documentary."

"And if she hasn't? I did a little Googling. You're certainly no saint with your little Billionaires' Club joke of a life, and even if my dad thinks you're a good neurosurgeon, it doesn't mean you're good for my sister."

"I think Elena and I have figured out that we're both good for each other," I said with a smile. "In fact, we're in love." I thought I'd taunt the probing older sister who I'd seen talk down to almost everyone tonight.

"In love?" she scoffed. "Something tells me you don't know the meaning of the word. Listen, Mr. Brooks, I love my sister dearly, and I will not stand for her to be played by you."

"Then I'll save you the trouble because I have no plans of playing her."

"We'll see. If you knew what was best for Laney, you'd turn her loose to fall for a man who won't hurt her like my dad hurt our mom. Aside from that, I *do know* Laney comes from money, so it's quite obvious why you, being in that Billionaires' Club, would feel safe using her for yourself. I don't think there's anything you can say that would change my mind about you."

That caught me off guard. "I won't respond to that. I will tell you this: Elena is the love of my life, and I will not hurt her."

"I'm sure you won't," she fake smiled as soon as Elena linked her arm into mine. "Good Evening and Merry Christmas, Dr. Brooks."

I looked at Elena's brilliant smile and was tossed with emotions of anger toward her sister for even considering that I'd hurt this beautiful soul, who'd made this past month of being with her feel like it'd been years together.

"What's wrong?" Laney frowned.

"It's good." I was numb because what if that woman was right—Fuck, no. She wasn't right. She was a goddamn witch or something and got into my head.

Elena pulled me out of the room and into her father's downstairs study. "Collin, what the hell did she say to you? You look like you've seen a ghost."

I smirked. "You know about my past. You know I was a complete asshole who dated chicks for my own selfish reasons. You know I am *not* that man with you, right?"

Elena looked angry and humored all at once. "I know you're the best man I've ever met."

"Laney, I'm serious. Your sister made some great points, and I've been so caught up in making sure I had you for the rest of my life that she brought some things to my attention that I need you to know are not even close to being fucking true."

"Avery and Ash," she readjusted my tie, "well, let's just say we girls talk. I know all about that silly name that your drunk and sexy butt got you and those three guys labeled with. I know there's something more between us. I feel it more and more every time I'm with you. Sheesh," she laughed, "don't let Lydia into your head with her big-shot lawyer stuff."

"I need you to understand. You're the love of my life. Your sister seems to have other plans, though, and I don't want to drive a wedge between you two either. The woman hates my sorry ass."

Elena got that mischievous look on her face and walked over to her father's desk, cut some string, and walked back to me. "Give me a kiss."

I didn't hesitate to rejuvenate my mind and soul with feeling the softness of her lips. "Much better."

"Good." She smiled. "Now, are you ready for something wild and fun?"

"Are we leaving?" I practically begged.

"No, chicken. We're not. We're proving a point. Come on."

I walked with a smile plastered on my face and the comfort of Elena's fingers intertwined with mine as we met with the party guests again.

"Here. Down this shot." Elena laughed as she walked me over to the bar. She clicked her shot glass with mine, widened her eyes, and smiled.

"What the hell are you doing?"

"Can I have everyone's attention, please?" Elena said. She hardly needed to announce herself because the woman grabbed the attention of the entire room without even having to say a word. "There." She smiled at me. "As you all are well aware, Collin and I have been dating for, what, a month?"

"Three weeks." I chuckled.

"Right." She smiled at the room that softly laughed. "We'll round up since it's Christmas." She laughed, and then looked back at me. "Babe." She smiled and fiddled with my hand in hers.

"Babe," I repeated. "What the hell are you doing?"

"A month of being with you, and I'll never forget you telling me how much time I wasted by not admitting that we were meant for each other. You were right." Her radiant, bronze eyes peered up at me through thick lashes. "I can't go another day without telling you that you're the man of my dreams. You're the man I *will*," she gave me a playful smile, "spend the rest of my life with. So, I have to know something. Will you make me the happiest woman in the world by completing what we started and making sure that I'll always be the one you'll love? No other women, just me and you."

The room disappeared, and it was just me and this beautiful ball of Christmas cheer. "Laney, you *know* there will never be anyone but you for me. I'm in love with you. I even serenaded a damn brown tree and brought the stupid thing to my beach house just to see that smile on your face and hear the laugh that speaks more to my heart than anything else has in the world. You're my fucking treasure and my heart," I said when I saw a tear slip from the corner of her eye.

"Marry me, Dr. Collin Brooks. Make me the luckiest woman in the world."

"Laney," I said, biting my lip. "Don't you dare tease me with a prank like this. You've been spending too much time with Jake and me."

I glanced up to find my eyes trapped by the beautiful ice queen who hated my guts and would probably put a hit out on my ass after this. I shook off the woman's evil green eyes and looked back to the safety of my stunning Elena.

"You know I'd get your brother a marriage license online in a flash and have his ass marry us." I winked over at Stevie, who was thrown Elena's phone and had been laughing and videoing this whole episode. "I would marry you here and now if I knew..."

Elena's hands framed my face, and she kissed me in front of God and everyone. I pulled her in tightly, and with a nip to her lips, I smiled. "You've lost your mind," I said. "Let's go home. We'll call your dad and apologize for—"

"Marry me. I don't ever see us living a day apart again for the rest of our lives." She smiled brilliantly. "You promised me already that I had met my future husband the first night we danced together. I didn't believe you until recently, but you were right. When the heart wants, it wants."

"You, Elena Alvarez, are asking *me* to marry you? And you're dead serious? With a bunch of drunk people," I eyed her sister, "and an ice queen as your witness, that you want to spend the rest of your life with me as your husband?"

She did that nod and biting her bottom lip thing that made me want her up against the wall and crying out my name in ecstasy, but God, this was sincere. I think?

I sighed. "Well, I don't have the ring I was hoping for because I didn't realize today would be the day my girl asks me to marry her."

Elena took out that slender piece of rope-string and wrapped it a few times. "You told me once that you don't live in a world of *what-ifs,* and I'm not about to wonder *what if* I never asked him," she said before tying it into a knot around my left finger. "There. We tied the knot and everything."

"What if I said no?" I winked at her playful smile.

"I'd call your bluff with a long, tasty kiss, and then you'd say yes."

I laughed and held her close. "You'll never stop amazing me with your crazy antics," I said. "I love you. And I love my string-ring even more. So, yes, my little ray of constant sunshine, I'll marry you and without a second thought." I wiggled my fingers for her to observe the ring she made and one that I inwardly swore to myself that I would never take off.

"This crafty little ring will stay right here," she announced to her sister's arched brow of judgment. "You can take it off when we both tattoo our *real* rings on our fingers. That way, you'll be married to me for eternity."

Her laugh after that was the only thing that helped me survive the chaos of congratulations. Watching the ice queen melt when the attention of her big shindig had turned into being a celebration for her younger sister—the happiest and most beautiful woman in the room—that was just a bonus. Still, we found a way to give the woman back her night when we left after the guests consumed more alcohol and Elena's brother hit the DJ scene.

"All of that just to prove a point to your sister?" I asked as we flew down the road to get onto the Pacific Coast Highway. "Jesus Christ, I can't imagine how your father handled you two as you grew up."

"I've never done anything in my life to try and prove a point to her. I actually proved a point to myself," she said, taking my hand to her lips and kissing it. "I wasn't joking. I sincerely want to spend the rest of my life with you. I hope you know I wasn't kidding around."

"I just hope you're not drunk, and you'll remember this when I hold you to it tomorrow. That and your brother was videoing the thing, so good luck backing out now."

"I know. I handed Stevie my phone." She laughed. "No, I'm not drunk. I don't get drunk around strangers, especially in my dad's house. I'm dead serious. I want you to marry me. The proposal was probably goofy, but it was fun and livened up a boring party."

I braced the back of her neck and pulled her over to kiss her. "Baby, you're the best thing to ever happen to me. Your sister is probably going to kill me in my sleep, but at least I'd die a happy man, knowing my lady loves me enough to spend the rest of her life with me. And for that," I smiled at her, "yes. I will marry you, and after we get past this next upcoming wedding ceremony—that's now in my way—we'll work on me finding the words to honor you and properly propose to you."

"Hey, my words were perfect!" She playfully punched my arm.

"So, you don't want the ring?" I winked at her.

"No. I want the tattoo rings." She laughed. "But for now, let's enjoy the last of this Christmas together by going home, getting some Chinese Food, and watching Scrooged."

I laughed. "I was going to say turn on some good music and go home and have some crazy sex, but now I'm going to have to go with this method of celebrating a *pop-engagement* that my little sparkplug sprung on me." I brought the back of her hand to my lips. "I was right. That first night we met, you were dancing with your future husband."

"It just took me longer to realize you were right about that too."

"You need to understand that I'm right about a lot of things when it comes to you and me." I licked my lips and shook my head. "We're insane, too."

"And that's why I love us. Merry Christmas, baby."

CHAPTER TWENTY-THREE
ELENA

On our flight, I took the opportunity to tell Collin that I'd lived in Hawaii for a short time after I graduated high school because of a summer fling.

It was an impulsive decision that almost made my parents croak, but it was one of my fonder life memories. Fortunately for my folks, living with a Polynesian fire dancer didn't make for a sustainable life at eighteen years old, so it didn't take long before moving to the mainland again.

The only reason I'd gone into such detail was that Koi, my ex, was still a great friend of mine, and, well, since Collin was now my *fiancé,* he was getting the download of my life history. As I expected, Collin was amused by my admission, and I think, more than anything, he tried his hardest not to make fun of my ex's name.

From the moment we landed in Oahu, the welcoming spirit of *Aloha* was alive and well and wrapping itself around all of us with its different meanings of kindness, compassion, and love, and we'd been enjoying it non-stop for the last two days.

ASH AND AVERY had set up cabanas at the beach with the perfect vantage point to watch the guys in the water with the kids. Listening to the waves crashing as I felt the warm sun on my skin was the perfect way to spend the week after Christmas.

"This sun feels amazing," Ash said. "The kids love the fact that they can be out with the guys and surfing in warm water too."

"The kids are the cutest. Addison is crushing it out there too," I said, holding my hand up like a visor and looking out at the guys as they surfed on longboards with the kids. "She's almost got this sport down to where she doesn't need Jim on that board with her."

Avery's daughter might've been one of the cutest little girls I'd ever seen. It was so sweet to watch her with Jim also. Jim and Avery's story was as sweet as it was remarkable. They'd met on a flight to London and then wound up at Jim's estate in England. One thing led to another, and Avery's vacation to London turned into an extraordinary romantic affair.

Now, here we were, ramping up to a wedding ceremony for the two, and after spending more time with the group for the past two days, I could easily see the softer and less *stiff* side of the handsome, soon-to-be groom. If you'd met Avery and Jim and never heard about their history, you would believe Addison was Jim's biological daughter. I was sad for Addy to hear that her dad was a complete fuck-up of a drug addict, but Jim made up for whatever shortcomings Avery's ex may have had—and it sounded to me like there were a lot of them.

"Addy has been begging to stand up on the front of the board finally," Avery laughed and smiled over at me. "Jim is as bad as Addison sometimes. He's been up my butt about it since he got her out on a board with him a year ago."

"It still surprises me sometimes to see how much Jim has loosened up by having you both in his life. You and Addy really are the best things to ever happen to that guy," Ash said.

"And how exciting that you've got another on the way," I said. "Your wedding night is going to be phenomenal, especially when you tell him about the baby. I can't believe the two of you are both pregnant, and you've managed to hide it from your men for so long." I laughed.

"Tell me about it. It seems like Jim is always offering me a beer these days, and I have to come up with some dumb excuse as to why I don't want to have a drink," Avery said with a laugh. "I have to say that I feel bloated or something. I'm beginning to wonder if he does know and just isn't saying anything. A whole month of trying to hide this from him hasn't been easy, but it'll be worth it in the end."

"Do you think he might know?" I asked, hoping he didn't because this was Avery's special gift for him on their wedding night.

"Well, I know for certain that if Jake had figured out I am six weeks along, Collin would know." She looked at me and smiled. "And I'm quite confident Collin would've blurted something out to you about it."

"I haven't heard a word," I said. "But then again, Collin and I have only been together for a little over a month now."

"God, you both are so cute together, and you're so much fun. I can't imagine him without you anymore. Is that weird? I can't. It's like you've always been there," Avery said.

"It's not weird. I totally agree with you," Ash added. "I never thought I'd see the day when Collin met his match." She pulled her sunglasses down and smiled. "But you are seriously that man's other half."

"Your proposal? Knowing Collin and knowing you better now, I'm not even surprised it happened," Avery added.

Ash laughed and nodded along. "When you two decide to get married, I'll make sure Jake doesn't throw in his two cents and offer up our rowboat as your escape vehicle, or whatever in the hell you'd call leaving your wedding in a rowboat."

I was smiling so widely that my cheeks were burning. I loved hearing these two affirming what I already knew—Collin and I were meant for each other. "Jake's already offered to get a minister's license to marry us." I bit my bottom lip, trying not to laugh when Avery and Ash lost it over that idea. "Guess you two haven't heard about that one?"

"Those two," Ash said, then she looked at me. "I promise I won't let him go through with that. Good God. Those two are too much."

"Back to the wedding at hand," I said. "Mine and Collin's isn't happening for a while. I didn't even want to bring it up because this is your wedding week, Avery. I told Collin to keep it to himself, but I guess that was a tall order for that guy." I arched my eyebrow, sat up in my lounge chair, and turned to face Avery and Ash, "So let's get down to the real business here: your wedding details."

Avery nodded and sat up more in her lounge chair. "Well, we're just doing the beach thing. I searched up a neat gift of Polynesian dancers to do a show for all of us, and then a Hawaiian woman to do the bridal dance, or whatever that's called, for Jim to see."

I'd done my fair share of entertainment with my ex to keep the money coming in so I could spend my entire summer in Hawaii, so I knew that this dance was beautiful and *romantic*, to say the very least. "Okay, I told you guys how I used to do the hula shows for that hotel, right?"

"Yes," Avery's eyes brightened. "Oh, my God. You should do the dance! Have you done it before?"

"Yeah, I have," I said with a laugh. "It's the easiest thing to learn, so what if I teach you the moves, and *you* dance the dance for your husband? You guys are going to get seriously wild in that room when you learn the dance and reveal that he's about to be a father again—all on the happiest day of his life."

Ash laughed. "Thank God he rented out that mansion place with the private beach for you two. I can't even imagine the screams and shrills of ecstasy..." she trailed off while we all laughed together.

"What do you think? It's super easy," I said, hoping she'd take me up on my offer. "I'll help you. Really, you have to do it."

"I can't dance worth a damn." Avery laughed.

"It's your dance for him. All he's going to see is your hips swaying *seductively* and your body calling to him." I smirked.

"Av," Ash said. "I think this is a badass idea."

"At least it adds to my value as your *drop-in* bridesmaid."

"You're most certainly not a drop-in," Avery insisted. "In fact, here you are, being super romantic, and I've meant to ask you for a different kind of favor. Since we've heard all about your adrenaline-junkie adventures, I was hoping you could help me arrange a little payback for the groom and his groomsmen."

"Payback?" I asked.

"It's all in good fun," Avery said with a smile. "But Ash and I can't do jack-shit because we're pregnant."

"Pretty impressive how you both pulled that off at the same time, by the way," I added.

"That certainly wasn't in the plan," Ash laughed. "I was planning to give it another year before we tried again. It turns out that fate always has another idea when it comes to the two of us. Regardless, both brothers knocked their girls up at the same time, and both are completely oblivious."

"Well, I have to know why our future bride wants some form of revenge on her groom and the groomsmen," I said.

"The kayak thing yesterday..." she tucked her bottom lip between her teeth.

"Oh," I laughed. "The whole *this is boring as hell*, and then the guys starting some battleship kayak war with the paddles?"

"Jake and I were the first to get dunked and rolled, thanks to Jake and Collin locking oars," Ash said.

"I have no idea how that didn't knock Collin and me out of the damn kayak," I answered with a laugh. "But Collin managed to *right the ship* all while we looked like insane adults around families who kayaked like *normal* people."

"We should have sat that trip out," Avery said. "We barely survived Alex and Summer's assaults." She grinned mischievously. "So I remember that you mentioned something about you kayaking on some rapids when you lived here on the big island. Is there *any* way you can get the guys over to where you lived and did stuff like that tomorrow? I think it would be a fun gift of *payback*, and if you do it, you have to record it."

"Isn't tomorrow their bachelor day?"

Ash laughed. "What better way to celebrate *that* by kicking it off with a gift from us gals?"

"Okay," I started, "I've done some pretty crazy shit in my life, and kayaking Wailuku River might be one of the craziest. There's Rainbow Falls, and we went over that while navigating through the rapids. I don't want to get the guys killed or anything."

"This is on the Island of Hawai'i, right?" Ash asked.

"Yeah, that's where my ex lives now. He does the tours on that river, but I think Collin will kill me if you two want me to put them in their place in front of Koi."

"Collin prides himself on his confidence," Avery smirked. "Especially when it comes to you and him." Her eyebrow arched. "I think the men deserve a fun kayaking adventure, don't you?"

"Wait, what are we talking about?" I heard Summer—Jim's former secretary and Alex's on-and-off girlfriend—say from behind my lounge chair.

I wasn't the *judgy* type, but something seemed a bit off about Summer. The girl was insecure about her relationship with Alex. Even a person who wasn't trained in psychology, watching behaviors and mannerisms, could determine that. I mean, she was a knockout, but it was plain to see that Alex struggled to settle down with her. I would've dumped Alex's sorry ass by now if it were me.

This girl was arm candy for him, and I wished that she had more self-worth to see that she should kick any man who treated her that way to the curb. Don't get me wrong, Alex was a great guy with a stellar personality, but some people were tougher to crack in the romance department. All I know is that if Collin were using my ass the way Alex seemed to be using Summer, there would be no *Collin and Elena*. What the hell did I know, though? Alex was wealthy, like the rest of these billionaires, and his looks added to all of that. Maybe she was the one who was using him?

"Elena's going to lead the guys out on a more adventurous kayaking trip tomorrow," Avery said with a smile. "It's what they get for the kayak wars they pulled on all of us yesterday."

"You sure they'll be okay with that?" Summer asked.

"If not, they can back out," I answered with a shrug and smile to her confused expression.

"Well, I planned to get a massage with Alex before the wedding," she said.

"If Alex wants to get a massage, then he doesn't have to go," Avery answered with a smile, but I could tell Summer's tone annoyed her.

"Well, I need some sun. They all look so happy out there," Summer said, eying the men with the kids on their surfboards.

"Yeah, ten minutes says sunblock needs to be reapplied on these kids, or my dad and Carmen are going to hate us when they babysit," Ash said.

"So, what do you say?" Avery asked me. "I know Jim will love this. It's the best gift I can think to give him and the guys."

"So long as you let me sneak in a few dance lessons, and you dance for your husband on your wedding night."

"It's a deal." Avery smiled.

. . .

THAT EVENING we all sat around an open fire pit that had been arranged for the wedding party, most likely because Jim had some nice cash on hand to ensure everything was perfect for his bride's big day that was only two days away.

"So," Collin said, his arm around me while he lazily stretched his long legs out toward where the group sat all around us, "what are you ladies going to do while we boys go and show Jim what he's going to miss after he's a married?"

I nudged Collin in his side while Jim laughed, his emerald eyes vibrant while he held Addison. The fun and wild little spark of bouncing energy had just fallen asleep on Jim in the cutest way. She was halfway through telling all of us about singing in her Christmas program when she leaned back into Jim's chest, turned her head to the side, and fell asleep midsentence.

Avery laughed as she brushed Addy's hair out of her face so Jim could readjust her to a more comfortable position to sleep, and then Avery leaned into her man's side.

I'd spent the afternoon teaching Avery the beautiful moves of the song she'd dance for Jim on their wedding day, and I will say, the girl could move her hips. Even Ash played along, but Summer? God help that poor, miserable soul.

Sadly, I didn't think Summer wanted to be here at all. I didn't have enough information to make an informed estimation of her situation, but things were not running smoothly. That much was blatantly obvious. I watched as she tried to talk business with Jim, saying anything she subtly could to convince her former boss to rehire her, but that was *not* happening. Every time she spoke to him, Jim's face became stone-cold. It was just plain awkward, and the poor girl continued to make things uncomfortable for herself more and more. Even now, while Alex and Jake were in some silly conversation, she sat stiffly by Alex's side when it was apparent that he'd given up on enjoying her company an hour ago.

"Mommy, I want Uncle Coll," John grumbled, fighting off falling asleep.

"John, I'll take you back to the room, and you'll go to bed there," Ash said sternly while Jake turned to try and pull his grumpy son into his arms.

"Get over here, Stooge," Collin said, sitting up on the outdoor sofa he and I shared across the fire. I smiled when John was turned loose, glared at his parents, and then walked over to where Collin's arms were stretched out. "Why are you such a little monster tonight?" Collin asked, bringing John into his arms.

John melted against Collin's chest, and I chuckled when he laid his head on Collin's shoulder, and Collin leaned back casually. John smiled at me, and I ran my finger over his little nose.

"Are you fighting off Mr. Sandman?" I asked.

His heavy lids opened and closed slowly. "No." He wrinkled his nose.

"Yeah, you are," Collin said, crossing his legs out in front of him and relaxing back, shifting John into his left arm and draping his right arm around me again. "And you're going to win that fight, aren't you?"

"Mr. Sandman doesn't stand a chance against that boy," Jake said with a laugh.

"You still want to play with your Papa and Tita?" Collin asked, referring to Ash's dad and stepmom, who had gone to a hotel in Maui for the night, enjoying the night off from the kids—the adult ones and the toddlers.

"I heard they want to take you to the zoo to pet the dolphins," Avery said with a smile. "Addy fell asleep so that tomorrow would come faster for her to go."

"You hear that, champ?" Collin asked, then he lowered his voice when John grumbled something, so exhausted that no one could discern his response. "Just *act* like you're asleep, bud. Uncle Collin won't tell anyone."

Jake rolled his eyes. "Fake sleep?" He looked at Ash. "I'll take him up if—"

"No one's taking this boy," Collin interjected with a smile. "He's perfectly comfortable. Now, what the heck were we talking about? Summer," Collin said, and I shook my head, knowing Collin was antagonizing the miserable woman.

"Huh?" she said, pulling her face from her phone. "I have no idea." She glared at Alex as if it were his fault that she had to sit out here with all of us, even though we'd all tried plenty of times to include her. Her misery was self-induced.

"We were talking about the plan Avery has for the four of you tomorrow," I said, saving Summer and Alex the trouble of Collin poking at her. "Remember I told you that I lived here?"

"Yeah, with that goldfish dude?" He smirked at me.

"Koi," I played back with a smile. "Stop calling him that. He's actually going to help Avery by doing this for all of you. I'll be there too," I arched an eyebrow at him, "to video," I added with wide eyes.

Collin chuckled. "This sounds like more of a scheme with ex-boyfriends than a *gift*." He looked over at Avery. "What are you ladies up to, and is this the reason you three took off today after lunch?"

"Part of it," Avery answered. "It's an awesome plan." She looked at Jim's questioning expression. "We need you to get ahold of your luxury helicopter company or rent a helicopter to get to the big island." She smiled back at me while Alex and Jake's eyes darted around the group.

"You four turned our peaceful kayak tour into some water-war because you were *bored*," Ash teased Jake's curious expression. "So, Av arranged for Elena's friend to give you a more advanced and exciting kayak tour."

Collin shifted some to look at me. "So is this Koi friend of yours going to show us *what's up* when it comes to kayaking? Trust me, us four have done some crazy, advanced shit while riding rivers in kayaks."

"That's why I'm Avery's designated video-taking bridesmaid," I teased him.

"Hell, yes," Avery said. "Thanks again for helping me out by asking Elena to be in my wedding."

"God," Alex said, rubbing his forehead. "You all know we're getting our asses kicked by a local tomorrow, right?"

"You're not going to that." Summer snapped out of her phone and eyed Alex. "We're getting massages." She batted her eyes at him while I felt Collin silently laughing at my side.

"We're getting massages?" Alex repeated, looking at her as if she'd lost her mind.

"No, shit?" Collin said while Jim eyed his former secretary as if she'd been smoking crack. Jake was pinching his lips and fighting back a laugh when his eyes met Collin's after my man decided to poke this bear *again*. "Couples massages? You and Alex are pretty heavy these days. I don't even think Jim and Avery have opted in for the romance massage package this week."

Alex exhaled, and the sharp features of his handsome face hardened. "I don't recall us planning anything aside from me being here to support my best friend before his wedding. I hate to disappoint, but I didn't plan on that."

"You said we'd enjoy our stay here," she snapped like a spoiled brat.

"I think we can talk about it later," Alex said.

Summer rose and glared down at Alex. "This was our final chance. If you want this to work, you'll stop putting me last all the time."

"Holy shit," Collin muttered to where I could only hear as Alex stood.

I eyed everyone's response, trying not to be appalled at the scene that was unfolding before all of us. Jim was stoic, Avery and Ash both looked more than a little surprised, and it appeared that Jake and Collin found it somewhat amusing.

"Jesus, Summer," Jim finally said. "If you take issue with Alex being part of my wedding and doing things with his best friend, you might want to rethink a relationship with the man in the first place. I warned you about my best friend a long time ago, and you never listened."

"I'm sorry, Jim," she said pathetically. "I don't want to ruin the wedding, but I just don't understand why Alex treats me like this."

Jim's eyes grew dark, and I was starting to wonder why the man ever trusted the woman as his former personal secretary, given her maturity level.

"You're acting like Jim's a goddamn therapist. This is between you and me. Let's get out of here before you embarrass yourself more than you already have," Alex snapped.

She folded her arms in protest of Alex's words. I couldn't believe I was watching a twenty-something-year-old act like this. I would estimate that a person would have to possess at least an ounce of shame to avoid this exact scenario, and Summer was making it clear that she had none. No shame whatsoever.

"This is damn fine entertainment. She was your fucking secretary?" Jake said to Jim with a laugh after Jake's laughter caused the woman to storm off, with Alex following reluctantly behind.

"She morphed into *that* after Alex crushed her the first time. She quit, and then I really don't know what the hell happened to her."

"She's acting like a bridezilla," Collin laughed. "Poor Alex, man."

"He put himself back in this position," Jake added. "Good God, sex with that woman better be worth it."

Ash nudged Jake in his side. "Really?" she said flatly.

"It's the reason the man is with her," Collin added.

"Good Lord," I said, looking at Collin, thankful Addy and John were snoring to show us they were sleeping through the *guy talk* about Alex and Summer's dire situation. "Let's get back on topic. I'm fairly certain Alex won't be having a couples massage tomorrow and that he'll get to work out all of his frustration while going over Rainbow Falls on our kayak run tomorrow."

"And poor Av and Ash are stuck back here with Bridezilla, no thanks to Alex," Collin returned. "Perhaps we all sit out this wild idea."

"You afraid?" Avery asked, the group instantly refocusing and falling into casual conversation again.

"Is the bride of my best friend challenging us?" Collin shot back.

"I know she is," Jim smirked.

"Well, this should be highly entertaining," Jake laughed. "Wow, Jim, thanks to our fucking around in the kayaks yesterday, your bride has us riding the white in some kayaks while an ex-boyfriend *helps*," Jake eyed me, "guide the way."

"Yeah, we're so fucked," Collin said.

"I'll be going too, dumbass," I said with a laugh.

"Videoing," Jim added while the girls laughed. "Perhaps next time we all don't act like we're teenagers while with the ladies."

"It'll be fun." Avery smiled at Jim. "Do you think you can get the chopper?"

"That's going to be a tough one. They're set to bring back Ash's parents tomorrow." He leaned over and kissed her nose. "It looks like your little scheming won't happen now."

"Bullshit. You own the company," Ash said. "Call them because Koi said he's got all of you prepped to go on an *advanced* course at eight in the morning."

Collin took the beer he'd been nursing and sipped it, then looked at me. "All right," he eyed me, "we're down for this."

"And don't think for a second that if this backfires on us, we won't pay you back," Jake added.

"It's all in good fun. Are you boys afraid of an adrenaline high? I used to race down this river and ride the line all the time," I said.

"So long as Elena believes we'll survive my future wife's gift for all of us, then I'll call the pilot and arrange for a helicopter to bring us to the big island." He leaned over and kissed Avery. "Thank you," he said, then whispered something in her ear that made her laugh and blush all at once.

"Well, then," Collin eyed me, "I hope this Koi guy can handle the fact that I'm pretty damn good looking, and," he sighed dramatically, "I, the man you proposed to spend the rest of your life with, will most likely kick his ass while kayaking in his local river tomorrow."

"Getting a little jealous?" Ash teased.

"This really will be entertaining." Jake chuckled. "And why aren't you and Avery joining us?"

"If you didn't notice in your guys' stupid little kayak water-war yesterday, Avery and I were barely figuring out how to paddle on calm water," Ash said. "Elena's the one who's done this before, and we want it on video, so that's why she's going. That and she knows a local who can make such an exciting kayaking tour happen."

"Aren't we so lucky," Collin said. "God, sometimes I'm more afraid of these women planning shit with ex-boyfriends behind our backs than I am you and your pranks, Jake."

"Nothing to worry about," I said. "We'll have killer footage for everyone to enjoy after we get back."

"Careful," Jim added. "If it looks like it's *too much fun*, then Addy might want to do it too."

"Nice try," Avery said, then started laughing. "You guys are terrified, aren't you?"

"It's easy to see we pissed off you beautiful ladies," Collin assured us with a smile. "We know how this story ends, Av."

"The story ends when we reach the end of the twenty-eight-mile run of thrills, navigation, and excitement."

"Awesome," Jake said.

Now, all eyes were on me, but I didn't care. These guys were a blast, and so long as Koi made sure they were advanced enough through questioning them and giving a quick crash course on safety, I knew they'd love it. They seemed to be aching to do something wild, and Avery coming up with this idea was perfect.

Hopefully, Alex and Summer would work out their kinks. Unfortunately, from the way Summer had behaved and Alex's complete personality change from the laid-back man I'd come to know, I had a pretty good feeling those two were over, and it wouldn't be Alex crying all the way to the airport, either.

CHAPTER TWENTY-FOUR
COLLIN

*W*e all knew we were seriously screwed today after seeing the looks on the ladies' faces last night when Avery revealed her *precious* gift of kayaking for her intended husband and his groomsmen. I shouldn't have been surprised that they'd get us back for being dumbasses when we turned what was supposed to be a *romantic* kayaking trip into a war of flipping boats.

Now, here we were with my little sunbeam of *Aloha love,* who was walking at my side with her chin up and her smile brighter than the Hawaiian sun. Elena held my hand as a vehicle pulled up with numerous kayaks strapped down in the back.

If it isn't the goldfish, ex-lover.

"Is this the ex, and should we be worried?" I whispered after a man who was shredded with muscles and tattoos stepped out of the truck.

"Laney-girl?" he questioned after peering around his opened door. "Get your ass over here."

Elena glanced up at me with a smile. "He's a great friend, and you're going to love him."

"I already do," I smirked as she took off to meet her *guy friend.*

"This guy is going to fuck us up, isn't he?" Alex laughed. "You know, you're half the reason Av could pull this off. All this shit to get some time alone with Laney, and look at us. We're at the mercy of a local and getting ready to kayak down rapids."

"I didn't expect she'd had an ex out here, and I certainly didn't plan on the ladies scheming behind our backs," I answered.

Jim laughed. "If my ass gets kicked today and I can't enjoy my bride on our wedding night, I'm kicking *your* cocky ass for—"

"Hold up," Jake said. He pointed over his shoulder at Elena and her ex. "Poor Collin didn't expect some badass Polynesian local to be his new fiancé's ex-boyfriend? Let's give the guy a break." He arched his eyebrow over his sunglasses.

"It was after she graduated high school," I said, trying to size up the man who could probably kick all our asses and easily hide the bodies in some active volcano on this island. "And they're good friends. I'm confident that my little adrenaline-junky gal will not only show me what she's made of but also that her *great friend* is also excited to show the mainland rich boys a *swell time* in the kayaks heading down *that....*" I paused, trying to size up this river. "We wanted a good adrenaline rush, and I have a feeling that this will beat our original plans of going to Northshore to surf today."

"You're so full of shit," Alex laughed. "All right, Jimmy," he looked at his best friend, "let's get this *bachelor party* started."

"With sweet little Elena guiding, recording, and documenting every last part of it," Jim said with a laugh.

"Yeah, we're about to see how sweet little Elena really is," Jake chuckled.

After introductions to Koi were made, we each took our kayaks, helmets, paddles, and vests, and we prepped to go. Koi was all smiles, laughs, and humor. He had an awesome personality, and the entire group blended in perfectly with the man.

I felt my adrenaline coursing through my veins and my body begging me for a ride down this river after Koi, Elena, the guys, and I talked out the route, the drops, and finished off by saying we were ready to do this thing. The water was rushing well, and the rapids were perfect.

I bent to kiss Elena, looking as adorable as she was beautiful. She had her GoPro camera strapped to her helmet, and her eyes were wild with excitement. "You look as excited as you were last night when we changed up positions," I teased while the guys were in conversation with Koi. "Your ex is pretty cool too."

"I told you he was fun."

"Well, I still have my reservations. We haven't survived the trip yet." I smiled.

"Let's go, or are you concerned?"

"How many times have you done this?" I asked.

"Um," she contemplated my question, looking out at the rapids, "I honestly have no idea. We used to do this all the time—this and hiking to hidden waterfalls to jump off them."

My eyes widened. "A waterfall jumper too? Jesus, I certainly learn something new with you every day, don't I?"

"Let's go." She swung the back of her paddle to connect with my ass.

Once locked in, we each began kayaking down the white, then it smoothed out a little. It was a nice way to get moving, get our bearings, and work through the water.

"You do this a lot, bro?" Koi asked as my kayak caught up with his.

"Only when we piss off the soon-to-be bride, and she uses her witchy ways to find a way to get her man and his best friends jacked up before a wedding." I smiled over at him.

"You'll love this. Laney said that you guys are naturals."

I laughed. "We like to think we're naturals at everything. We're all hoping we're right about that, though, since we're already going down this river blindly."

"Ah," he smiled, "that's why I'm leading the way. Laney told me she's going to trail behind because the ladies who stayed behind want to listen to you scream like girls."

I glanced back at the beaming smile on Elena's face and then to Koi again. "I'm glad they look forward to that." I arched an eyebrow at him. "You know the rapids we kayaked, right?"

"Been there, done that. This course is a bit more challenging, but that's what life should be, right? Challenging and facing it with a fearless heart." He brought his fist to his chest, and that was it for conversation.

The rapids picked up, and I loved every second of the challenge of this run. There were drops, and then our eighty-foot drop at rainbow falls came too soon if you asked me. My heart was racing. The guys and I sounded like we were at a football game, and our favorite team just scored a touchdown. This adventure was right up our alley.

I rode the line, making sure my boat was lined up to go over the falls after Koi disappeared in front of me. Once my kayak was moving a little faster than the flow of the water, I held the bar of my paddle out so the damn thing didn't slap me in the face when I took the drop over the waterfall. I loved the rush as the boat took flight and landed perfectly at the base where the water was calm, and we were set to end the adventure.

The guys and Elena took the drop like it was nothing too. Everyone was all smiles, and excitement radiated through our veins. And, as usual, now we wanted more.

"I'm ready to hike back up and do this shit again," Jake announced.

I looked over at Elena, still laughing and more vibrant than ever. She paddled to me, and I made sure I eyed the camera the ladies were watching. "That was quite dull," I said to it. "We're going to head over and take these boats off the four-hundred-foot falls nearby. Sending our love and last wishes," I said, then put my hand over Elena's camera and managed to bring my arm around her waist and pull her easily from her kayak and onto my lap. Her lips met mine, and the kiss couldn't survive her laughing through it.

"Save it for the hotel. Jesus Christ," Alex said with a laugh. "Hey, Koi, you guys ever jump off that waterfall?"

I pulled back and eyed my laughing beauty. "Have you?"

"All the time," she smirked. "You guys need some more?"

"You're the one who revved up the dark side that lurks inside the four of us," I said.

Elena looked at Jim. "I was only instructed to get you down the rapids. I'm not responsible for you breaking your neck if you jump the falls."

Jim smirked, pulling his sunglasses out of his vest. "My lovely future bride made you and Koi the tour guides." He smiled as Koi laughed. "She placed our lives in your hands; therefore, you're already responsible for anything that happens on this island."

"Let's stop wasting time," Jake said, looking over at Koi. "How do we get back up to the falls?"

"You guys are pretty badass," he responded. "When we're done here, maybe my uncle will give you some tattoos that represent bravery." He raised his hands, showing us the images that told the story of his lineage on his body.

"Don't you dare put them in a position to turn down that high of an honor, Koi," Elena said. "Not fair, you tricky asshole."

"Yeah," I cosigned on Elena's truth, knowing it was pretty heavy to have a Samoan offer you to be tattooed by their family. Their method of tattooing was no joke, either, with the comb dipped in ink and a mallet, beating the hell out of your flesh to blend into your blood. It wasn't the sort of bachelor memento I had in mind when we signed up for this trip.

"Yeah, we'll pass," Jim said, shaking his head. "As honored as we are for your friendship and," I could tell Jim was searching for the right words so as not to offend Koi while I watched my little sunshine cover her smile, "the honor—"

"I'm kidding," Koi finally said with a loud laugh. "You'd have to survive the four-hundred-foot drop at Akaka Falls before we consider you for that."

"Quit teasing them," Elena said with a punch to Koi's arm. "Now, let's go park these things and do some jumping and swimming."

This day was all about Jim having a great time, and it was turning into me being more enthralled and captivated by my lady. It was another exciting day that had my heart rushing with adrenaline, and I was in more awe of her than ever as I watched her fearlessness.

We hiked up the falls to the top, and she leapt off the side of the cliff, did a quick flip, and landed with a scream of joy into the water. Over and over, she did backflips, front flips, and all off the side of an eighty-foot cliff. This woman was as crazy fun as she was beautiful. Even the guys were joining in on the *Elena Party,* and even though Laney was having the time of her life, reliving her days of youth, she made sure she got Jim, Jake, and Alex on video for the girls who didn't make the trip to the main island.

Elena and I swam around like fish, and I finally grabbed my girl to steal a kiss while Koi and the guys were jumping that waterfall. My adrenaline needs shifted to the sensations I felt by holding Elena in her swimsuit, feeling her skin, and most of all, kissing her as if it were the last time I'd have her in my arms like this.

"You're beyond perfect in every way," I said, running my lips along her neck while she locked her legs around my waist. "I love you so damn much."

"So, does this mean you and I will go base jumping when we get back to the mainland?" she teased.

"I think I'm down for anything." I smiled at her. "Is there anything you haven't done?"

She pursed her lips. "I haven't climbed El Capitan in Yosemite yet," she said with a laugh.

"You're shitting me." I shook my head and ran my hand over her slicked-back, wet hair. "You want to do that?"

"I've heard that you sleep on hammocks that are nailed into the face of that rock. It sounds like a fun honeymoon trip."

"There's no way I'm fucking my new bride on some goddamn hammock that's locked into the face of a rock. We'll break the thing with the way we've been going at each other these days."

"True," she chuckled. "We should plan something cool like that, though."

"I was thinking more along the lines of those resorts where the rooms are caves or private huts over the water in the Maldives. Shit like that."

She kissed my nose. "We'll figure it out when it's our time." She draped her arms around my shoulders. "Right now, it's Jim and Avery's turn. We have to respect that."

"Even though you almost killed her groom?"

"Yeah. He sounded scared to death as he tackled those rapids like they were made just for him." She smiled. "Hey, I have to tell you something because it's killing me."

"Go ahead," I said, swimming us over to a place to relax without having to tread water. "What does my beautiful little sunshine have to say?"

"Well, Avery is having a Polynesian fire dance after the wedding tomorrow night. She was going to hire a woman to dance the Hawaiian bridal dance for Jim."

"Hell-fucking-no," I said.

"Exactly," Elena's eyes widened with excitement. "That's what I said. So, I decided—"

"Laney," I eyed her, "I know about your days of doing these shows, and while I'd love to see a video of that, you can't do that dance for Jim."

"Have you lost it?" she laughed and splashed me with water. *"I'm not going to do it."*

"Oh, thank God," I said with relief. "Those assholes would never let me hear the end of it."

"I taught Avery the dance. The people putting on the show will start with a fun act to entertain, then it will end with the fire dancers doing some awesome moves to usher in Avery, and the music will shift to her dancing. She picked up on it fast. I'm so excited for Jim to see this tomorrow, and then when he finds—"

I locked onto Elena's eyes, seeing the fear of almost letting something slip. "Finds what?"

"Nothing." She looked away from me. "Doesn't that sound beautiful?"

"I think it will be nothing less than amazing and only add to the perfect day they've waited too long for." I pulled her face back to look at me with my hand. "What will he find?" I smiled. "Secret's safe with me, sunshine."

"Damn it." She sighed. "I am not ruining this. Please don't ask."

I bit the inside of my cheek. "Baby, what the hell are you girls forever conspiring about behind our backs?"

"Good things," she moved the water in front of her with cupped hands while the guys continued to jump the falls, challenging each other even more. "I talked to Summer, by the way."

"Ah," I smiled at her, running my foot over her smooth legs. "Did you use your psychic-magic powers on her? You realize this is a vacation, right?"

"It was at breakfast this morning when you four were off planning how you were going to deal with my ex-boyfriend leading the fun activities today."

"What you'd say? Trust me; you can't fix those two. Alex isn't settling down anytime soon."

"Well, I just told her that if Alex makes her feel like she's being used, she needs to move on. They're not aligned, Coll," she said, in her serious, neuropsychiatrist voice. "It will be miserable for both of them."

"So, you bought her and Alex a few days of *hanging in there*," I smirked. "Aren't you quite the cupid?"

"I just think it's kind of shitty what's going on. She doesn't seem to be happy around any of us, and it's selfish, but she's only here for Alex, more or less. Then Alex has her here, more or less—"

"Just to fuck," I interjected.

"Right." She sighed.

"You know we were all like that at one time."

"I know," she smirked at me. "My sister made that *perfectly* clear to me."

"The ice queen." I rolled my eyes. "What's her deal besides the fact she doesn't take prisoners?"

"She's always been like that," Elena said. "She's the *know-it-all*, big sister."

"She like that with Stevie?" I asked.

"God, no." Elena pulled her feet through the water. "She's too caught up in trying to make partner at her law firm in Chicago. Stevie sort of fell through the cracks."

"He'll find his way. Give him time." She rolled her eyes slightly. Obviously, this was a topic that concerned her more than she vocalized.

"That might be true. I wanted to be a neurosurgeon at first, but then I heard about the stories of people trying to understand their crippling life changes. It took a while, but Dad told me if that's where my heart was, go after it."

I kissed her cheek. "I love that spirit in you. Don't worry about Stevie," I said, smiling at her returning smile. "We'll kick his butt out of the nest together. For now, what the hell is the big secret?"

"That, lover," she kissed my lips, "is for you to find out. I'll tell you this: it won't be as daring as a kayaking adrenaline rush, but it will be a perfect addition to the wedding day."

I laughed and pulled her down into the water with me. "With *you* at the helm, I'm quite confident good ole Koi is going to be doing the fire dancing, and we're going to be the stars of the show while we try to twirl batons of fucking fire."

She threw her head back and laughed. "I hadn't thought of that one, but *that* would definitely be a perfect addition to Avery doing the bridal dance. She does have Hawaiian roots, you know? We should do our best to give her everything and more since she requested a Hawaiian wedding, knowing that Jim could've taken her to Dubai or Fiji or rented an entire tropical island—"

"Not happening, my little hula-goddess," I said. "Don't get all cultural on our pathetic asses. We'll watch the pros and the men who won't insult the heritage of the islands."

She sighed dramatically. "Fine." She looked around and then eyed me. "Those guys seem pretty occupied, and there's a secret cave behind that waterfall."

My cock, which was in full vacation mode, decided it was time to be completely aware of the woman who called to it. "You up for a quickie, sunshine?" I smirked, teasing her.

"Aching for more of last night. Let's convince the guys to take the kayaks up the river in Koi's truck, and you can fill the aching need I've had since seeing you dressed in these boardshorts."

"You need only say the word, and I'll clear the place right now."

"Let's do it. It's always been a fantasy of mine."

"So, you and goldfish boy didn't do crazy shit like this in waterfall paradise?"

"No," she laughed. "He wasn't as creative and fun as you. It's why I dumped his ass." She grinned. "And now, I have the perfect man to start fulfilling my wild and crazy fantasies."

"That's damn good to know, and yes, we're fucking in that waterfall cave."

CHAPTER TWENTY-FIVE
ELENA

*J*im and Avery had the most breathtakingly beautiful wedding ceremony, and it wasn't because he was a billionaire with endless amounts of money to make it all happen, either. Everything about the ceremony was lovely, from the exquisite décor to the glistening ocean that shimmered as their backdrop.

I had to give high props to Clay and Joe, the fun couple who happened to be Ash's two best friends. They'd coordinated this entire affair, and not only was every last detail perfect, but everything went off without a hitch as well.

If I had to choose a favorite part of the ceremony, it would've been when Jim turned to Addison and knelt to read the vows he'd written to her. He started by calling her the other love of his life, and he promised to love and protect her for as long as he lived. I don't think there was a dry eye in the place after that. It was so sweet to see how much all of them were absolutely in love with each other.

I had to say that standing as one of Avery's bridesmaids was an immense honor. I loved looking across the way to see my handsome fiancé, wearing his simple button-down shirt, khaki shorts, and his ti-leaf lei. It wasn't easy to focus when the man I was utterly in love with was distracting me. It was so damn hard to keep my eyes off him, especially during the quiet times while the musician played the ukulele for the bride and groom.

I couldn't help my heart from pounding in my chest with all this lovely romance and when Collin's smile went from staring in adoration of the bride and groom to when his eyes drifted to mine and held them. It was a goddamn miracle the two of us *smitten in love* fools survived standing up with the bride and groom at all. Who knows how many times we were pulled into this loving trance, caught in the moment and seeing the love we felt for each other in our stare and smiles.

As the fire dancers entertained us after the sunset, our laughs, cheers, and giddiness for the couple were elevated to extreme levels. I knew the moment Avery's dance for Jim was coming and couldn't be more thrilled. We sat in the front row of an audience of friends and family that had flown in yesterday afternoon. Even though I didn't know any of them and hardly had a minute with Ash's dad and stepmom, it didn't matter. Love was in the air and bringing all of us in perfect unity to celebrate Jim, Avery, and Addison.

"I can do that shit too, you know?" Collin said, pulling me to lean closer against him as we watched the magnificent ceremony.

"Just because Jim asked Koi to replace the other fire dancers, that doesn't mean you need to get all competitive again," I teased him.

"True," he said.

That's when Koi came out and did a fantastic finale with multiple fire sticks. He spun them swiftly, creating a beautiful visual effect that enhanced the change from drums beating into the beautiful, slow music shift into the song: *Ke Kali Nei Au*. It was perfect, and my God, was Avery ever more elegant and beautiful when the lights turned toward her, and her song began.

I was beaming like a child, and I couldn't imagine what Jim's face looked like while his wife danced this song to perfection for him. I felt tears of joy for the couple while I watched Avery fearlessly perform for Jim, and I laughed when the words *forever mine* prompted her to rotate her hips in a lovely way, all while teasing her husband with a smile and pointing toward him.

I watched Addison smile and watch her mom with a look of wonder on her face as Avery danced like an angel up on stage. As the bridal song was concluding, the music shifted while women in beautiful dressage

came out, and the lights enhanced their outfits as they danced and
serenaded Jim, coming up to accept his bride's dance and honoring their
love.

"I would've paid countless amounts of money to have you in this part
of the wedding," Collin said as the beautiful, half-dressed women moved
their hips gracefully.

"Later." I smiled at him. "I'll dance for you, as I promised."

Collin glanced over his shoulder. "We can leave now, and those two
wouldn't even notice."

"Calm down," I laughed at him. "We still have to cut the cake, and that
secret I've managed to keep from you no matter how hard you've tried to
get me to say something?"

"Yeah," Collin smiled, "you're coming clean on that tonight."

"Avery's about to fill you in on it. So, shh," I finished with a smile.

"Did you just *shush me?*" Collin challenged.

"Seriously." I pointed to where Avery had taken a microphone in one
hand while continuing to hold Jim's hand with her other. "You have to
listen."

Collin kissed my temple and relaxed further in his chair.

"Today was the most beautiful day of my entire life," Avery started as
Jim smiled and waited patiently while she spoke. "And I have another
special gift to add to this day for my husband."

I watched Jim's expression turn to that of confused happiness.

"You've given Addy and me more than anyone in this life could have
ever asked for," she started to say, choking back tears as Jim drew closer
to her. "And in saying that," she exhaled with a laugh, "Jim, I am so excited
to announce that you're going to be a father...again."

Jim's eyes widened with love, excitement, and shock—all at once. He
instantly pulled Avery into his arms, his tall and large frame hiding the
slender bride in his arms.

"Holy shit. Yes!" Collin said as he and Jake simultaneously stood and
clapped, prompting a standing ovation for the happy family.

Jim and Avery met an overly-thrilled Addison as she rushed on stage.
They knelt to her level, and the three hugged and held each other in this
beautiful moment.

It all worked out perfectly.

.   .   .

THE FESTIVITIES of the night played on in such a fun way. We all danced, I taught Collin a little hula, and when the kids had fallen asleep with Ash's parents, the helicopter fired up and swept the beautiful couple off to the location Jim had arranged for their honeymoon. From what Ash had said, they would spend a few days on the island, and then Jim would bring Avery to relive their earlier days of when they first met in London at their estate in the countryside. They had plans laid out for Addison to meet them there, and that's where they'd officially begin their lives as a family before returning to the states.

"So, Jake knocked Ash up the same time Jim worked his magic on Avery, eh?" Collin asked after we arrived late back in our room.

"I think it's so cool. Jim's going to find out about Ash being pregnant tomorrow," I said, wrapping my arms around his waist. "Jake's going to call him and fill him in on the fact that Dr. Allen will be pretty busy when these babies are ready to make their appearance in the world."

Collin kissed my forehead. "Those two Mitchells have got to be the happiest men on the planet right now." He smirked down at me from where he'd leaned back against the wall in our room.

"And you?" I asked. "Are you the happiest man on the planet?"

He eyed me with that devious smile of his. "It depends. Is a man who can twirl a fire baton more badass than a man who can perform brain surgery?"

I started unbuttoning his shirt, having special plans of my own for Collin. I kissed the center of his tanned chest. "You jealous?"

"Never," he said, running his hand over my head. "I've got you in my room; he doesn't."

"Then why ask the question?" I said, my voice lower as I moved down hearing Collin's breath hitch at me as I knelt in front of him and unbuttoning his shorts.

"Well, if I was a tad bit jealous of that man's talents..." he stopped when I freed his hard cock and licked beneath the tip, "it's all out the window now and gone with the island winds." He sucked in a breath as I began to work all of my energy into taking his large cock as deep as I could. In the numerous times that I'd enjoyed having my mouth around Collin's large cock, hearing the sounds of him enjoying it and swallowing every last ounce of him, I had never been able to deep-throat my man.

I managed to relax all the muscles in my throat and allow Collin to push his cock further down my throat than I'd ever let him in. "I can't hold this back," he said as I pulled off his cock and licked from his balls, the base, and back to his dripping tip.

"I don't want you to," I said. "I have a long night planned for us, and you need to come, baby. That way, you can enjoy the rest of the night with me."

"Fuck, you're beautiful," he said through panting breaths while his hand gripped the back of my hair, and he allowed me to take him deeply again.

When my hair was tightly fisted by Collin's hand, he rocked his head back and moved his tip further down my throat, his warm cum shooting into me as I swallowed every last drop of my man's orgasm that rocked his ass back into the wall as he continued coming down my throat.

When we finished, Collin's arms pulled me up, and I was lost in his deep kiss of gratitude. He gently pulled away and smiled at me. "You never cease to fucking amaze me. You took almost all of my cock."

"I know." I bit my bottom lip and smiled triumphantly. "Feel good?"

"And why the sudden need to get me off so quickly?" He set me back down and unzipped the silk dress I had on. "I had plans for you, sunshine."

"Trust me, we'll be making good on any and all plans tonight, but first," I pressed my hand into his chest, "I owe you a naked hula dance."

"That you do." He arched an eyebrow at me. My already soaking entrance and throbbing clit needed to feel this man, but I could wait. I had to wait if I wanted to *really* go through with this particular fantasy with Collin.

Collin's eyes were beautiful as I turned on a Hawaiian song and began dancing seductively for him. I loved the brightness in his face as I enhanced each move I'd learned years ago. I was grateful I had remembered this dance, given the current look on my man's face, because this night was going to be as special as Collin had made me feel since I popped that proposal on him.

I never thought that dancing seductively for him would heighten my sexual desire, but it did, and it didn't take long before we were on our bed, and Collin's perfect lips and tongue were devouring my body. I loved this more than words could explain, and I was more than ready for him now.

"Baby," I said as he reached for the box of condoms, "I want—"

"You can have anything you want," he answered, his eyes glimmering with a hunger in them that I loved.

"I want you in a way I've never had a man before." I chewed on the corner of my lip.

Collin's hands framed my face as he shifted his hard cock away from my entrance and repositioned himself. "What do you want. You know I'll take my girl anyway she wants me."

"Well, I brought lube..." I trailed off, knowing he would understand where I was going with this.

His eyes narrowed. "Oh, yeah?" he said with a spark of desire and a smile. "And from how wet your tight little pussy is, I'm assuming it wasn't for that."

I shook my head against the pillows. "I want you to take all of me if you're down for that sort of thing?"

Collin licked his lips, and I swear I saw a light in his eyes I'd never seen before. "Fuck me," he answered. "You know I'm down for claiming and filling every part of your body with my cock. The sounds you make when I move my fingers over your ass..." He let out a breath, "Shit. The only thing I'm not down for is hurting you, Laney."

"I've read up on it. You know, because it was really heightening my orgasms when you did that." I smiled. "God, I love that we can casually talk about this like we've been together for years."

"Hell, if you trust me with this most delicate and," he arched an eyebrow at me, "most taboo way of having sex, then yes, we have to talk it out some. I've never fucked a woman like this before."

"Which will make it that much more intimate between you and me. I read where women feel more intense orgasms while her lover's cock rubs behind her G-spot."

Collin smiled. "Goddamn, I love you. You have to guide me, though. I might get overzealous and fuck you too hard."

I shook my head and leaned up to kiss his lips. "I know you won't. You've always been about me and my pleasure. Let's do this, baby."

I reached over and grabbed the lube, then grabbed my vibrator.

"Oh, if it isn't the reason you were able to hold me off longer than a week when you knew I was your man," he teased. "What's this for? I can loosen you up better than this device could ever do."

"It's for you."

"You're not shoving that thing up my ass," he laughed.

"You'll see," I said, taking a condom out of the box, leaning up and kissing Collin.

His hands held my neck as we kissed hard and desperately, knowing we were embarking on a level of intimacy we'd never shared with anyone but each other. I rolled the condom onto his cock that always reacted to my touch, and then Collin laid me back and kissed my stomach as he warmed the lube in his hands and worked it over my virgin entrance. He applied pressure to my tight area while his thumb moved my clit in a circle, dancing the two areas into one perfect, harmonic rhythm. I reached up into the pillows, fully trusting Collin, wanting him, and needing this more than my fantasies allowed me to imagine.

Once I was loosened up, I lay on my back, and I began pleading with him to give me what I wanted from him. Collin was gentle and perfect, and once he was in, we both froze in amazement at the sensations.

"Fucking unreal," Collin nearly growled. "Goddamn, this is too fucking much."

My body was so loose, relaxed, and desperate for this feeling of completeness of sexuality with the man I loved beyond explanation.

"Fuck me," I begged him, his lips sucking my nipples through his cursing.

I slid the small vibrator I had brought into my soaking wet pussy, and Collin growled and grunted, feeling the vibration as he began thrusting his cock in my ass.

"Jesus Christ," he panted out while I ran my hands over his ass. "This is beyond fucking unreal. This is a high, baby, shit I'm never going to want this to end."

Collin was panting, grunting, and pumping himself in and out of me, and the thousands of sensitive nerves that were right where Collin was thrusting gently in and out of me were firing up sensations I'd never felt before.

It was everything. It was Collin's wild eyes, the way he moved, moaned, licked his lips, and bit at my hard nipples—this shit was euphoric. I spread my legs wider and grabbed his ass while my vibrator danced inside of my pussy.

"Harder, Coll," I said in a hoarse voice. "Jesus, this feels better than I ever thought."

Collin didn't respond vocally. He just answered my pleas as his cock moved deeper in me. I felt like we were floating in the air, and I was in such bliss that all I could do was enjoy this ride of the man I loved fucking me in such a delicate way. Some people might've been appalled to do this —I'd certainly never considered it, not until recently anyway. Collin was innovative with everything sexually that we did, and if his fingers had never teased my ass entrance as they'd done, I was sure it would've never really been something I thought about.

I felt energy move through me, unlike a regular orgasm, as Collin and I kissed, and he continued fucking me like this. It was a build-up of sensations I knew I would've never felt if we weren't in this position. It spiked beneath my skin like electricity needing to ground itself, but instead, it flowed through each living nerve in my body. I was moaning out sounds that I didn't even know I could make as I rode this wave of rolling energy in my body out, and that's when, for the first time ever, I came so hard that I actually ejaculated.

"Holy Fuck!" Collin practically shouted loud enough for all of the islands to hear. "Goddamn, you just fucking came all over my cock, baby. Fucking hell," his eyes met mine in the same shock and elation that I felt. "You're so sexy. I'll never get enough of this, sunshine. Can you do it again for me, baby? That must've felt so fucking awesome for you."

I was still moaning in pleasure, satisfaction, and most of all, my triumph at not just feeling the most insanely intense orgasm I'd ever experienced in my life, but also the fact that my pussy had done the one thing I never believed I could pull off.

"I want it from behind," I said. I was on a complete high, and I wasn't about to end these feelings anytime soon. "You think you can fuck me in the ass like that and hold back, baby?"

"Jesus, I almost just came right now." He smiled as I gently rolled over, rendering him speechless at whatever he felt in that movement while still being inside me.

Once in position, I decided to play with his cock after pulling the vibrator out of my pussy to help give him a better chance of fucking me and holding back. His hands gripped my hips, and he began thrusting, his groans telling me how much he loved this position.

Collin and I spent the night fucking in our new intimate position. We decided that since our flight was a six a.m., and we had to be up at four, that we'd just fuck until it was time to leave.

We bravely and boldly went into this act with love and lust. When we were on the plane the next morning, it was almost hard to sit still. Damn, if only we had that luxurious company jet all to ourselves. Having him all night without sleeping should've been enough, but all it did was make me more addicted to the man than I already was. With Collin and I having to work tomorrow, we had to find a way to make up for not sleeping all night. Lucky for Collin, he was no stranger to going two to three days with little to no sleep while being on call, but I wasn't quite so resilient.

Once we'd landed, we went straight to the house closest to the airport —my condo—and managed to have a fun-filled day, which included napping, driving to Long Beach for tacos, and then ending our night, watching some action film before falling asleep on the couch together.

It wasn't until we were driving to work in the morning that the first *major* issue we were to face as an engaged couple reared its ugly head— the string ring. He was serious as hell about never taking the thing off until I reminded him that he eventually would have to scrub-in for surgery. Thank God I came up with a technique to slide the thing off because he was beginning to act like this raggedy string was the Hope Diamond.

I fiddled around with the thing while we sat in traffic, and Collin was able to take it off and hide it in his scrubs so we could keep the world-renowned neurosurgeon in business and saving lives. This man was the silliest, sexiest, and best guy I'd ever met, and the memories we'd created since day one were going to be epic stories for our grandchildren one day —well, leaving the intimate parts out, of course.

CHAPTER TWENTY-SIX
ELENA

*C*ollin and I had officially made it to February as the couple everyone in the hospital loved to tease. We were very much in love and weren't afraid to show it. I loved working with him, and I loved spending time off with him. I couldn't even imagine my life without him in it anymore. He was my joy, my laughter, and the very core of my happiness in this world.

We spent most of our time at my condo since it was close to the hospital, and when we got a weekend off, or at least a day to escape together, that's when we found ourselves wrapped in each other's arms at his insanely beautiful beach house.

The office was quiet, as it always was on Wednesdays, which lent me some extra time to spend with my new patient. Victoria was a fifty-eight-year-old woman who had suffered a traumatic brain injury in a roll-over car accident last week, and Collin initially treated her since he was on-call when she came in.

Collin sat quietly next to me as Victoria cycled through various emotions, learning about the long road of recovery that lay ahead. Collin had laid out the facts as he'd always done when we consulted together, and now it was my turn to help my patient cope.

"I see that you were a very active woman before your accident," I said.

Tears formed in her eyes as her sister, Nancy, reached for her hand. "I was. My life was perfect. Now, I'm using a walker."

I leaned forward and smiled. "The fact that you're walking with that walker has even shocked the surgeon," I said, looking at Collin as he nodded and smiled, her eyes going directly to him. "You need to focus on the fact that you're one lucky woman."

I watched her scowl at me. "This isn't fair," she truthfully stated. "I don't deserve this. My mind, it blanks—" She looked at her sister. "How am I supposed to continue with my life when everything tells me I should be fine, but then I'm slowed down by these crippling issues?"

"You need to focus," I said in a firmer voice, knowing I wouldn't be able to get through to her if I didn't get a bit more severe. "No, it's *not* fair that this happened to you. I will tell you that I've met with my fair share of patients who've had horrific experiences after they've woken from a traumatic brain injury. Some cannot speak or walk or are forced into a wheelchair after months in the hospital. But this isn't about them; this is about you. In injuries such as yours, neurons have died, and it's your job to learn to cope and work with those facts. You must force yourself to have hope, even if you don't see immediate results."

"Will I ever be able to do my tax consulting business again?"

"In your case," I answered, both ladies' eyes on me, "that's solely up to you. You will be working with a rehabilitation center and me, and together we will fight for you to get your life back. But you are the core reason you'll either get it back or lose hope. I won't allow the latter. You're a young, healthy woman." I smiled at her sister. "Your family will play a huge supporting role in ensuring that you fight for your life again. You will not let these natural feelings of defeat to destroy any of your ability to fight back."

"I just feel so hopeless. To have to concentrate so hard just to move my legs—it's so difficult. I was jogging last week..." She trailed off in tears.

"You will suffer through different stages of grief," I said, "and we'll all be here for you as it happens. The denial is already present, and that's natural. You have woken up, are being discharged from a hospital, and are struggling to accept that life is different now. Every time you feel this way, I need you to allow the feelings to come in, and then you must move on. Whether it's making something and completing that task to feel a sense of accomplishment or taking your walker and knowing that, with each step you take, you're getting closer to getting rid of it. Dr. Brooks has looked at your current MRIs and determined a full recovery is possible for you through rehabilitation."

"That recovery, Ms. Parsons, will not come easily, but it will come, as Dr. Alvarez has mentioned, by you battling your way through it. Your brain will learn and adapt to this new way of walking, and I guarantee you'll be singing and dancing through our office hallways in a month or two," Collin added with a smile.

Victoria smiled back. Collin's smile seemed to help all of my patients. He sounded so confident. The tone he used was soothing for our patients, and they responded well to him.

"Talking and even the way I try to think—it is a struggle sometimes."

"I will be candid with you," I said. "It could take up to four years or so of you using the constant activity of challenging your brain to move past the last part of your injury."

"God, why me?" she looked up as her sister took her into her arms. "I'll get a second opinion." She trailed off again in tears.

"I completely understand your feelings. It's not something I wish to tell you, but I would be a horrible doctor if I lied to you and said it would happen faster than I know. You suffered a severe brain injury, and I need you to accept that. I need you to accept that there is more to life with you, Victoria. I want you to know that everything comes from your heart; your ability to prove me wrong on this diagnosis will come from sheer determination and will power. If you choose to find another neuropsychiatrist, I will gladly step away and allow you to find one."

"I won't," she softly said. "I'm just so scared."

"Then let's work together." I smiled. "I want you to leave my office today, and before you go into that rehab center, I want you to find small things to appreciate. The small things that we always seem to miss in life, and you know," I shrugged with a smile, "sometimes things happen to slow us down a little so that we can appreciate them when our lives are so busy."

"True," she answered.

"Do you have any questions for me before we conclude today and you're discharged to the rehab center?"

"I think my only question was answered."

"How long," I smiled again, my heart swelling with sympathy for her.

She nodded.

"I see nothing but a beautiful woman who has a lot of life left to live," Collin added. "There's a reason you survived that accident, Ms. Parsons. Don't let this bump in the road of life stop you from coping and moving forward. Some people give up, some fight back, and Dr. Alvarez has shown her full support in helping you on your road to recovery, as well as the staff at Saint John's rehab center, who will be nothing less than amazing with you. As your doctor, I will have you visiting me in the office after brain scans to explain where I see the brain healing as we discussed before this consultation. I expect that in a week, you're going to walk into this hospital, showing us all signs of improvement and possibly not needing that walker."

I watched Collin nod toward the device that seemed to trigger my patient's devastation, but the way he treated it in conversation was like it was so temporary she would never need it again. I hoped he was right, and after all that I'd learned in working with Collin and our patients, he certainly didn't bullshit them. He'd said that Victoria's brain was injured severely, but she was fortunate not to suffer trauma in more complicated areas.

I loved that we complemented one another so well in consultations. If I were getting a little too harsh while trying to help the patient to move forward with their new life, Collin would slow it down with his knowledge of what he saw in images and his experience with patients recovering. If Collin seemed stiff and somewhat cold toward a devastating outcome that I knew he wasn't happy with, I offset that with my methods of striving to help the patients in the best possible ways I could. That was rare, though. I don't think I'd ever really witnessed Collin in that cold doctor mode except for with a paralyzed patient who'd broken his neck and suffered a severe spinal injury after diving into a shallow pool of water. Besides that, Collin was never shaken.

After we'd concluded our consultation, I was relieved when Victoria and her sister hugged me goodbye. My only goal was to help, and even though she apologized for her outburst, it was completely unnecessary. The hard part of my job was delivering brutal truths, but the rewarding part of helping them triumph was worth it.

"So," Collin said, leaning in the door frame as I went back to gather the patient's file, "we're going to stay in Malibu tomorrow. I want you in a wetsuit and out riding some waves with mine and Jake's friend, Flex."

"We can do Malibu, but I'm not surfing," I said with a smug grin as I tilted my head up when he bent to kiss me. "I love to watch you surf, but you and I already talked about me not surfing in freezing-cold water."

"Oh, come on. You're already losing your edge?" He shook his head. "Is this where it all ends for you and me?"

"I was thinking about doing a little redecorating of your beach house," I said, ignoring him. "What do you think we add some color to the place? I mean, no offense because it's pristinely decorated, but it's a little…" I bit my lip, which always made Collin smile.

"Plain?" he said. "You can do whatever you want to add your flavor to the house. As far as I'm concerned, it's yours too."

"Stop." I rolled my eyes, walking out of the door and back to my office with him following me. "It's not my place until we're married."

"I disagree. I can't imagine living in that home without your smile brightening it anymore anyway. Do whatever you want to make it yours." He smiled, sitting across from my desk. "And I take no offense at your suggestion, by the way. I hired an interior designer to decorate the place while I was busy doing a million other things."

"You hired a decorator? Spoiled little rich boy," I teased, knowing he hated being referred to as such. "Well, your decorator sucked."

"Apparently so," he said, flipping through a medical journal that was on the edge of my desk. "Hey," he looked up, shut the magazine, and grinned. "Let's get Clay and Joe to spice the place up. I'm pretty sure you miss your South Beach lifestyle in Miami. We'll have Clay and Joe bring all of that in. You already know I love what you love."

"That's an awesome idea. Let me pay for some of it, though."

"Ah, ah, ah." He waved a finger in front of me. "It's my place, as you've stated, and I'm paying for the designers and all the stuff they do to paint the plain, white canvas of the beach house."

"Fine. It's my place too." I smiled.

"Nope." He pinched his lips together, texting on his phone with a smile. "There, done. Clay and Joe are stopping by, and those two will turn the place into your beach dream home."

"I'm excited," I said with a smile.

"I'm—" His eyes darted back to my open door, then over to me again.

"Well, you know what I always am, and you started it with that bottom-lip biting thing."

"Relax, Dr. Brooks. We're out of here in an hour, and then we'll go get dinner and chill out on my couch tonight."

"Chill?" he arched an eyebrow at me and grinned. "Okay."

"Dr. Brooks," the intercom pager went off, pulling us back into doctor mode.

"Right here," he said, answering the button to the line that the trauma center used to contact doctors in our office.

"This is Dr. Gilmore," he said. "We're sending a patient to your trauma center. The patient is a sixty-seven-year-old woman. All tests show she's in a coma after a ruptured aneurysm. Your trauma unit can save her life. Dr. Brooks, her family is in distress and knows she may not survive this."

"Understood." Collin stood up; his entire demeanor changed. "Have you sent over any brain imaging for me?"

"Yes. The family should be there already, and chopper has an ETA of three more minutes until arrival."

"Got it," Collin said. "I'll check out the images and prepare the surgical team."

"Thanks, Brooks. Good luck."

"Got it, Gilmore. Have a good evening."

Collin looked at me. "I want you on this surgery with me," he said in chief-surgeon mode. "I'll see you in the trauma unit after you're changed. All good?"

"I'll change into my scrubs and meet you there."

I changed and had caught up with Collin, already in his scrubs and briskly walking down the hall to the trauma center. His head was down as he studied images from his touchscreen pad.

"What are we looking at?" I asked, practically skipping to keep up with him.

"We're looking at an intracranial hemorrhage. The patient's Glasgow numbers are on a scale of four, still unresponsive. She was found on her front lawn, face down, by a neighbor."

"Good God," I said, peeking at the brain image he had shown me. "That's an enormous rupture. Can you save this woman?"

"There's no answer to that until I get into her brain and see the cerebral aneurism with my own eyes. The fucking thing ruptured, and, honestly," Collin looked at me, "this woman shouldn't be alive."

"Let's get in there and let you do your magic, Dr. Brooks."

Collin slightly smirked, and then we were met with the trauma unit and the medical staff from the hospital that'd transferred the woman to Saint John's. Collin nodded through conversation; the outlook seemingly grim if you studied the faces in the room.

Collin's face wasn't grim, though. He showed determination while each person read vitals to him, and he glanced at the most current images coming in from our MRI machines. Collin was right: this woman should be dead. Fortunately for her, she was alive and had the best possible surgeon as her advocate.

"I'll speak with the family while all of you prep the patient for the craniotomy. Let's get to work and save her life," he ordered, and the room dispersed, each person given their task while Collin requested me to follow him to the ICU waiting area.

He punched the doors and walked into the room that had been reserved for the family. "Mrs. Yi's family?" he questioned the concerned room filled with people our ages.

"Yes, I'm her oldest son. She was found on the lawn."

"She was perfectly fine yesterday, doctor," a young woman said as she walked up to Collin and me. "How did this happen? It's not possible."

"I need all of you to try to calm down and listen to me. My name is Dr. Brooks, and I'm the surgeon called on to operate on Mrs. Yi. She's suffered a rupture of a brain aneurysm and is quite lucky to be alive. I've studied her brain scans, and her EEG is telling me that she has not suffered brain death. She has given all signs of a coma, but once I operate and relieve the pressure from her brain and find the cause of the bleed and stop it, her brain should recover, and she *should* wake up. I need all of you to understand that, even though I've operated on multiple issues like this, there is still only a fifty-percent-chance of survival. My duty is to save her life, but I won't stand here and mislead any of you into believing that I will. I need full consent to operate, and once that is done, I will work to save her."

"I'm her power of attorney," her oldest son said. "We gave all of our consent as soon as we got here."

"Great," Collin said. "It'll be a while in surgery, but I'll be in that room doing everything in my power to ensure that Mrs. Yi survives."

"Thank you, doctor."

With that, we left, and Collin stayed in full surgeon mode. The surgeon, who was unsure if he'd save a patient's life tonight or not, and who had an enormous challenge in front of him. This surgery required a skilled physician, and I knew Collin's mind was keenly aware of the challenge that faced him.

"The patient is in a coma," Collin said. "Her brain waves are not active, but I want you in that room while I perform the surgery."

"To talk to her," I guessed, knowing that it was still quite the mystery of whether or not patients were aware of their surroundings while in a comatose state. When Collin nodded to the intriguing idea he had of having me there to speak with the woman, whether or not she heard me, I found it endearing that he would consider it. There was no time to question his method, but knowing Collin and seeing how he worked, his passion for his patients, and the unknown, was intriguing.

Collin was three hours into the surgery while I read the book *Little Women* to Mrs. Yi after calling out to her family to ask what kind of stories she liked. It turns out she enjoyed this story immensely, and so I downloaded it onto my phone and read to her while Collin worked to save her life.

While I read, Collin started drilling the interns in the room to answer questions as he worked and then started hitting them with questions completely unrelated to the issues at hand. I watched as he worked, smiled, and challenged the interns in the room with us.

"There's our culprit," Collin said, and I exhaled, knowing that once he used the clamps to clamp off the bleed, this woman would have a fighting chance. "Clamping four areas should end the bleed."

"Swelling is down seventy-five percent," Dr. Nathan, Collin's attending surgeon, advised him. "We're well on our way to saving this woman's life."

"We are," Collin said, his eyes glued to the magnifying device that gave him the perfect vision of the microscopic problem area.

It was five hours in, and Collin worked to close the skull and prepare the patient for ICU and recovery. There we would hope she would wake soon from this comatose state. Collin did the needed job, and each of us in that OR smiled with pride that Dr. Brooks had successfully saved this woman's life.

Two hours after we met with the family, Collin snatched my hand, his mind calm again, and his smile was beaming.

"You were amazing in there," I said to him.

"Does Beth die of scarlet fever?" he asked, relating to the book and how far I'd read in before we were able to end the surgery.

I laughed. "How in the heck do you pay attention to that all while going after an angry brain?"

"Angry brain?" Collin draped his arm around me and laughed. "That's a new one. I like it. The brain that wants to fight the doctor at every angle. Now," he kissed my temple, "I have to know what happens to Beth?"

"Why don't we finish the story tonight while we eat our tacos on the beach?"

"That sounds like an awesome idea. You still up for Long Beach, or do you want to grab something and head to Malibu? I'd love to spend our night on my private beach and rekindle that evening that you and I...you know." He eyed me.

"We're supposed to be reading Little Women, not violating beach laws by having sex on the beach again. We're lucky we didn't get caught that night."

"That night was awesome." His lips twisted up into that sexy grin. "I'm going to get that ending out of you on the drive to my place, and then," he leaned down and brought his lips to my ear, his warm breath tickling my skin, "I'm going to fuck you on the beach while you fight back your screams of ecstasy."

"Oh," I teased back. "If that's the case, then I say we get some tacos by the beach house and make out like kids on the beach and see if we can pull off that highly illegal stunt."

"It's *my* damn beach. Though the public can walk the shore in front of it, of course." He laughed as we reached our offices. "Good thing that it's eleven at night, and no one will be out. I'm fucking you on that beach tonight."

"We'll see. Let's change and go home, you horny, crazy man."

"Hey," he stopped me. "Thanks for following me into surgery. It was an excellent idea to read to her."

"Do you think comatose patients can hear what's going on?"

"Some can remember being in their coma, and some can't. I don't like the idea of them in my ER, especially in brain surgery, if they could hear what's going on. I want that patient's mind soothed, comforted, and me working to heal it."

"So, before me?"

"I would have an assistant do the same," he confirmed.

"You are so sweet. You really are the greatest." I smiled at him.

"I know," he smiled. "Let's get dressed, go eat, and go home. We have decorators coming tomorrow to turn the place into Casa Elena." He waved his hand dramatically in the air.

That was it. I had to nail a date down and marry this man.

"A spring ceremony," I said when we both changed into regular clothes again in his office.

"What the hell are you talking about?" Collin looked at me with confusion.

"Let's get married this April."

"Three months? Damn." He laughed. "I hope it's a small affair."

"Yeah, we both know my family is going to make a big deal out of it. It's going to be big and marvelous." I walked over to him and held him. "It will be our day."

He kissed my lips. "Finally, she can confirm a date to spend the rest of her life with me," he teased. "You know I'll marry you any day, time, or season."

And that was it. I would take my annual snowboarding trip to Big Bear in March, and then in April, Collin would be stuck with me for the rest of his life.

CHAPTER TWENTY-SEVEN
COLLIN

"Oh, God." I hung onto my ragged breath after I came so hard that I was the one claiming to see stars this time. "I'm going to miss you."

Elena was in one of my favorite positions to take her: up against the wall after one round of sex wasn't enough for us. She'd stopped by the office tonight to bring me Chinese takeout before I started my on-call shift this weekend, and she took off for Big Bear.

Her eyes were dazzling and lit up with humor, and I loved it. I gently set her feet back on the ground after pulling my cock out. It was always certainly a welcomed surprise when Elena showed up two hours before I started the long weekend ahead of me, living at the hospital. Since she got here, we managed to catch up on binge-watching some series Elena had gotten me hooked on, we ate our food, and then, we fell into our usual routine of saying *fuck it* and ended up having sex in my on-call bedroom.

We were still catching our breath as we rushed to clean up and get our clothes on again.

"I'll only be gone for three days. We're both off on Monday, so I'll head to Malibu when I come back," she said with a smile, tying my scrub pants at my waist.

I took her hands and brought them to my lips. "You might as well sell the condo. We practically live at the beach house now." I smiled at her as she pulled her hair into the ponytail it was in before our sexual escapade.

"That's because the beach house is beautiful," she said. "Clay and Joe worked a miracle on that place, and now it's some tropical, Miami Beach resort."

"I have to admit that in the two months we gave them, they knocked that shit right out of the park. Well, everything except for those stupid pink flamingos." I arched an eyebrow at her.

"They're the focal point, and they pop," she flashed her hand at me dramatically, "when you walk in."

"They pop, all right. Well, I say we get rid of the condo and make Malibu your real address when you come home."

"That comes next month after our wedding," she said. "Okay, I seriously have to get out of here. I'm leaving late, and the roads can get icy up there."

"I'll never forgive myself for allowing your sexy ass to pay me a visit this late, knowing you should've headed up to the ski resort hours ago."

"It was my idea." She smirked and pointed at my flat screen that was playing the show we'd been watching. "Turn that off. No watching it without me. In fact," she grabbed the remote and hit the rewind button, "there." She smiled at me, kissing my nose while I sat on the edge of my couch and tied my shoelaces. "It's back where we left off."

"Wow. We were fast if we managed two rounds in less than one full episode of whatever in the hell this show is," I said.

"It's called *The Crown*," she reminded me, "and you said you loved it."

"I love you, so that's why I love it." I rose and brought my hands to her face. "Now, get your ass out of here and drive carefully." I sighed. "Shit. I can't believe I'm turning into this, but do me a favor and call me when you get in."

"Oh, God," she rolled her eyes.

"Icy roads, babe," I said. "And you're driving late and alone."

"Don't worry about me, but I'll call or text when I get there." She smiled.

"Take plenty of videos and selfies," I smiled, taking her hand, walking out with pagers, hospital phones, and all the other communication devices I needed while working the trauma unit. "*You* didn't build me that stalker Instagram account last month for nothing," I teased her.

"I still think you're funny enough and intelligent enough to be as fantastic of a social media influencer as those doctors on Facebook, Insta, and YouTube."

"Yeah, not happening. I don't talk to cameras unless Jim has my ass planted in front of one for some university."

"Or they're in your surgical room."

"Still trying to adjust to that." I smiled and kissed her forehead. "I have to get up to the hospital. Drive carefully. Only one more fucking month until your ass is officially mine."

"Any idea on that honeymoon location yet?"

"All booked, and no, I'm not telling you where." I smiled.

Elena wrapped her arms around me tightly. "I think I'm going to miss you most," she softly said with a laugh.

"That's because I intentionally worked over your sexy body in ways that will make you want to rush down that mountain and skip out on your friends to get back to me sooner than later."

She laughed, and I pulled her in for one more quick kiss before she turned to leave.

TWENTY-FOUR HOURS into my on-call shift, and thank God Jake was working on-call in the trauma unit this weekend, or I'd be out of my mind with boredom. It was a slower than usual shift, and these shifts tended to make the fucking clock stop. As a neurosurgeon, our shifts mainly consisted of treating head traumas due to car accidents, gunshot wounds, busting our asses to get a nonresponsive patient's life saved, or—in all too often worst-case scenarios—calling the time of death. I was used to the constant rush of emergencies, and so this particular weekend was driving me nuts because it could've been much better spent with my girl, hitting the slopes instead of waiting around the hospital for some action.

Outside of Jake and I fucking off to help pass the time, Elena had texted me pictures of her dressed in her snowboard gear and videos of her boarding down the mountain. I loved that she was enjoying herself, but I ached to have my woman in my arms again.

Things started moving forward after I was called down to the ER for a consult. Dr. Robertson needed my opinion on a patient who'd been involved in a car accident, resulting in a possible severe head injury. After perusing the scans, I confirmed the patient was not a candidate for surgery, which was a good thing for the family who'd been going out of their minds with worry since he was brought in. Going over CTs, I found nothing that would call for a brain-related injury.

"Looks like he's lucky," I said. "Taking a fall like that should've called for bruising, but nothing is showing up. Keeping him for another day, to be sure, would be a call you'd have to make. I don't see any bleeding or swelling, and all his vitals look good."

"Thanks, Dr. Brooks," he said and then relayed the info to the charge nurse, who took down everything I added to the conversation.

"Saint John's dispatch, this is AirMed transport five," Dr. Robertson's ER phone announced from his desk.

"Dr. Robertson here, AirMed. Go ahead."

Being a Level I trauma center in Southern California, it was common to have hospitals divert helicopter transport patients to us when they didn't have the proper equipment or surgical teams on staff. Nearly all traumatic injuries coming in by medical choppers were typically the result of an accident, and they were usually patients who ended up with my trauma team. Knowing this, I stayed back to listen as the call came through. This call was coming in from the flight nurse instead of a doctor from another hospital, so I instinctively knew the patient was likely headed directly to my team, and we needed to be ready to save a life tonight.

"We have a thirty-two-year-old female patient, involved in a snowboarding accident whereby patient collided with a tree. Patient presents with an obvious head injury, patient is unconscious, and Glasgow scale currently at four."

My eyes zeroed in on the phone, knowing this patient was heading to my unit from the Glasgow level alone.

"Patient was in cardiac arrest and has since been resituated to normal sinus rhythm. Bilateral AC IVs are in place. Patient presenting with shallow respirations."

I took my phone out and called up to my trauma unit. "I've got a patient coming in on AirMed. I need Dr. Mitchell and his cardiac team called into OR-Five and our team ready to receive the patient," I ordered, needing to hang back because this call was coming straight to Jake and me.

"Vitals are reading a pulse-rate of forty-eight and dropping, respirations twenty-four and rising. BP is one-eighty over one-ten, pupils bilateral and not dilating. ETA eight minutes on route to you."

"Stop the IV and place the patient in the reverse Trendelenburg position," I said. "My team will receive the patient."

I rushed out of the ER, knowing that with the call I made for the patient, who was in bad shape, all of these vitals were pointing to extreme cranial pressure, and I didn't want to exasperate that with more fluids from the IV. I needed the patient's head up to decrease the cranial pressure and, at least with this patient's condition, get the patient to my surgical team alive.

Goddamn accidents like this were horrible, but they were something that we dealt with too often during skiing and snowboarding season. I'd seen three head injuries in the last two months: one who didn't survive after skiing without a helmet and colliding with a tree, and another snowboarding accident who was fortunate to walk out of here the next morning. This one sounded like the snowboarder was moving down the slope at a high velocity, and they got rocked after colliding with a tree. I hated this shit. They were always young and wild on the slopes, and then a fun run turns into a potential nightmare for the victim and their family.

Jake met me at my trauma unit, everyone flooding into the room as I read off what dispatch told Robertson and me in his emergency room. With the patient's heart having stopped and being resuscitated, and this particular trauma and a Glasgow reading of four, it told me this one might not survive. At best, they would probably be in a coma until I found a way to heal this brain, hopefully.

Jake and his team were there to monitor the patient's cardiac trauma while I worked with my team to prep the portable CT machine. I had to save this patient's life before I could bring them into a full CT to see exactly what damage had been done to render those vitals.

With the commotion of a gurney and people shouting off more vitals outside of our OR, we all knew the task at hand, the patient whose life we would work to save, and were all hands on deck and ready to do our job.

The patient was rushed in, vitals being read to Jake and me as the CT scan was rolled up to the patient's head. "I need to get that fluid and pressure off the brain," I said to Jake, the flight nurse, who happened to be an ex-fling of mine, standing in front of us. "I need you to keep an eye on that heart." I looked at Kaci, "Any other info we need?"

"No," she affirmed.

"Nice work bringing her in alive," I said, then turned back to check the pupil dilation of the patient.

"Oh, God!" I shouted when I saw Elena's face pinned in a neck brace, looking next to lifeless. "Oh, Laney. No, no, no." I scrambled, desperately trying to compartmentalize my emotions. I wanted to grab her from the gurney and cradle her in my arms. I wanted to follow all of my core instincts and hold her or try to shake her awake. My human instincts and my training as a neurosurgeon were colliding, and I stood there, frozen, trying to process what was happening.

"Dr. Brooks." I heard Jake's voice like an echo inside my ringing ears, and his voice was grim as he understood the nightmare that had been shoved into my face. I stood there, shocked, with a thousand things running through my mind. My brain knew I needed to keep it together, but I felt like my heart had been ripped from my chest, and I'd never been more confused and frightened in my life. "Collin!" Jake shouted, snapping my attention to him. "What does the CT show?"

I locked eyes with my best friend, and that was all it took for me to pull myself together. Elena needed me to be focused. If I lost it and crumbled to the floor like I wanted to at this very moment, she was going to die.

I took a deep breath and cleared my throat. "I've got intracranial pressure that I need to release from the brain to get these vitals stable. Dr. Mitchell, please inform me if there is any issue with the patient's cardiac condition."

I went through all the necessary motions, and my neuro-trauma team had been given their duties to work together so I could drill into Elena's head and get the fluid drained from her swelling brain.

"I need a nurse to call Dr. Miguel Alvarez and inform him immediately that his daughter has been in an accident and is in our care," I said. "Allow him back as soon as he arrives."

Draining the fluid on her brain was the most urgent task at hand. I had always prided myself on being unshakable in my OR, but nothing could have prepared me for this. All I knew was that there wasn't a moment to lose, and there was no way in hell I would fall apart when she needed me most.

CHAPTER TWENTY-EIGHT
COLLIN

I studied the CT scans, showing me that what I thought was a pool of blood was actually a mass. I could see that the brain had suffered a contrecoup, seeing the brain had contacted the skull on the front and the back when Elena's head hit the tree in her snowboarding accident. The bruising was apparent in the scans, but what made me more concerned was that the tumor was actively bleeding, putting me in a significant bind for time.

"When the brain hit the back, that's when her heart stopped," Jake said, standing next to me in the darkroom, studying alongside me. "Thank God they managed to restart it."

"Yes," I said, holding a hand to my chin, desperately wishing Elena would wake up before I was forced to remove this tumor with a craniotomy. The tumor was in her frontal lobe area, where the area for higher mental function was located. I needed her awake and talking.

"Doctors," I heard the voice of Dr. Allen and turned back to acknowledge him as he entered the consultation room.

"Dr. Allen. We're getting ready to consult on Dr. Alverez's CT scans," I said, studying the doctor with concern.

"I have an update after being called up to the ICU for Dr. Alvarez." He inhaled while I stared at the man, confused that he was here. "Elena suffered a miscarriage just now. There is no additional bleeding, but I wanted you to be aware of this situation in moving forward with your surgery."

As he delivered news that struck me like a blow to the gut, Trey, one of our medical assistants, rushed in with Elena's bloodwork. I numbly took the labs I'd called for, and I sucked in another breath, desperately forcing myself to treat this like it was any other patient and not the love of my life who was comatose and who'd lost our child—a child I didn't even know about yet.

"I'm so sorry, Collin," Trey said, being friends with both Elena and me, knowing this was a devastating report to receive and not one that anyone wanted to deliver.

I nodded to Trey as he dismissed himself, and then Miguel rushed into the room with my resident neurosurgeon, Dr. Nathan, neurologist, Dr. Shannon, and two more nurses.

"Dr. Alvarez," I greeted Elena's dad. He was my mentor and the most experienced neurosurgeon I'd ever met, but first and foremost, he was Elena's father, and no one understood what I was dealing with in every way more than he. "Thank you for joining us in the consultation. I need—"

"I see an active bleed," he interrupted, looking past me with the eyes of the surgeon I admired more than any other.

"Yes, it's why we're consulting."

"She has hours, Dr. Brooks," he said.

"I understand that." I turned and addressed the top surgeons, the neurologist, and the anesthetists I'd called into this meeting. "The patient was stabilized with two shunts through a craniectomy to relieve fluid and pressure from her brain. If I do not do an emergency craniotomy, we will lose this patient." I turned to the scans and pointed to the mass. "I believed this to be a pool of blood from the first scans. These current CT scans show that this mass is a tumor with an active bleed. It must be removed to stabilize Dr. Alvarez and save her life." I looked at Jake. "Dr. Mitchell has been monitoring vitals and will be joining us in this emergency surgery with his team to monitor all of Dr. Alvarez's cardiac vitals. Dr. Mitchell?"

"With what Dr. Brooks and I have seen, our patient has suffered a contrecoup, resulting in the frontal lobe making contact with the front of her skull. It is easily seen that the patient's heart stopped when the brain was jarred and the occipital lobe and cerebellum made contact with the back and base of her skull. My team and I will ensure that Dr. Alvarez's heart condition will remain stable during this surgery since she has already suffered cardiac arrest at the scene of her accident." Jake looked at me. "Dr. Brooks."

"This is intricate brain surgery, given I will be going in and operating on areas that may or may not do damage to the brain tissue I will be working around to remove the life-threatening tumor. These areas are extremely delicate, and I will be working with precision and all of my extreme effort not to bring my suction device anywhere near this tissue," I said, looking at the doctors in the room. "All of you have thoroughly studied her scans, and so I welcome any and all input at this time."

"Dr. Brooks, we are ready to assist when the patient is prepped," Dr. Shannon said. "Are there any updates on her condition?"

"Dr. Allen just informed me that Dr. Alvarez suffered a miscarriage, but her bleeding has stopped," I said. "All of Elena's vitals are stable, her Glasgow score is at four, her pupils still fixed, and therefore, all tests are confirming she is in a coma. I have no further details from the accident at the scene from any witnesses."

We went through our exact plan for this surgery, and I was mentally holding firm by pushing my emotions down. If I let the slightest emotion in, I could fuck all of this up, and God only knew how Elena would pull out of this if I did.

I hadn't seen a brain injury this extreme in months, and that injury—with no tumor—had a high probability of leaving the patient unable to speak or walk. Severe brain injuries were no fucking joke, and right now, I was facing a goddamn tumor that was bleeding and threatening to kill this patient on top of all that.

I stood in the room as everyone filtered out, heading to the surgical room, and as they left, Miguel stood steadfast in his spot, studying me.

My eyes met his severe gaze. "You didn't add anything," I said.

"Nothing to add, Dr. Brooks," he answered. "I appreciate your bringing me into the consultation for my daughter, but now that the room has cleared and it's just you and me, I will say one thing: I need to know your state of mind."

"I will save her life, Dr. Alvarez," I answered.

"Yes, you will. My Laney couldn't be in better hands," he said, his words tugging at the emotions that wanted to burst out of me like water through a broken dam. "You have also learned that you lost your child."

I pinched my lips together. I knew what he was doing. He was pulling these thoughts to the front of my mind, ensuring I wouldn't break while performing surgery. He wasn't an asshole for his tactic. He was protecting his baby and saving her life by making sure I didn't lose my shit in that room while trying to save her life. Emotions have a weird way of creeping up on you, and he wasn't about to run the risk of that happening while I had her skull open.

"I did, sir." I stayed stoic and detached from the weakness of emotion I was trained long ago to detach myself from in challenging situations. "I will save her life."

"You're the best there is, Brooks," he said. "Thank God your mind is in this as it should be. I wouldn't trust another surgeon—including myself— to operate on my little girl. Go save her life."

THREE HOURS into surgery and I was steady-handed, looking through my microscope with the neurologists. At the same time, my resident surgeon watched the computer models that my sucker tool showed the room as I worked to get safely around the tumor.

The pathology lab came back twenty minutes after I'd sent off a sample, telling me the highly-vascularized, gold, ball-sized tumor was benign. Since then, I had been working to break up the tumor, gently cut away the sides of it, and I was grateful to everyone and everything that this was what could be referred to as a *kind* or *nice* tumor. It was a tumor that wasn't fingered into the brain with hundreds of blood vessels that needed to be clamped off or cauterized. This was growing with a few blood vessels and was mainly pushing out into the brain's soft tissue areas. Elena never showed any signs of having this, but many people lived long lives with benign brain tumors, not ever knowing they had one.

This son of a bitch was not only something she had no idea she had, but it was also the only reason I was in her brain, working as hard as I could to ensure I did no damage to her brain tissue after the fucker decided to pop a goddamn bleed.

Elena's heart was all I listened to as I worked for hours to ensure this active-bleed tumor was removed. My hands were steadier than any other surgery I'd ever performed as I focused solely on the one thing that was trying to steal my Elena away from me.

Toward the beginning of surgery, I almost lost my shit that the room was too silent, and, coma or not, Elena's mind could be with all of us. I needed someone talking to her. Thank God Jake was here and knew her well enough to bullshit like he always did, so he and Dr. Kim, the anesthesiologist, began bullshitting about something.

For the first time in all of my surgical career, I couldn't speak a fucking word unless I called for my nurse to give me a scalpel or suction. I called for vitals and relayed information of the tumor be broken up and suctioned out by my device, and that was it. I watched Elena's brainwaves, and they were still showing signs of life since we hooked her up to the EEG machine. Jake and Kim's bullshitting, I'd hoped, would have shown more activity with the lines on the computer, but there was nothing. Elena was in a deep coma, and I knew she wouldn't be waking up any time soon.

"That's the last of the tumor I can safely remove," I said, pulling back and nodding to my attending resident. "Let's get Dr. Alvarez stitched up and back to the ICU."

"Well done, Dr. Brooks," he said.

"Nice work, doctor," Jake added.

The room went to work while I closed Elena's skull, and from here, she would remain in the ICU to be with one nurse and doctor, watching her closely for any activity that may call for a surgical answer or even Jake's cardio team to step in.

"Brooks," Dr. Nathan said, stopping Jake and me from our pursuit to the waiting room.

"Thank you for coming in and assisting, Dr. Nathan," I said.

"Why don't you turn the last of your shift over to me?" he asked. "Allow me to take the calls so you can work through this."

"I will remain at this hospital as long as Elena is in that ICU unit," I said.

"Coll," Jake said my name, and I looked over at my best friend, "let him take the calls. Let's handle the family."

"Thank you, Nathan," I answered. "I'll go speak with the family and update them. I appreciate the help tonight and taking my shift."

"Talk to me, Collin," Jake said. "You've got to let this shit in."

"I will once I handle the family," I answered.

Jake's hand went up to my back. "I'm not leaving your fucking side," he said.

"Thank you for talking in there."

"Well, I had to do something," he softened up, knowing I was as stiff as a corpse right now. "I had to take a fucking leak, and you were taking forever. Jesus Christ, you're the slowest surgeon I've ever been forced to work with."

With that, I smiled, "I did that shit to you on purpose."

"Wouldn't surprise me," he said as we hit the elevator button that led us into the consulting room with the family.

Jake and I walked in, and Miguel was the first to stand and greet us. "They're caught up on everything except for the outcome of the surgery."

I glanced around, seeing Elena's sister, brother, and mother, and then I saw a group of about seven girls, still in snowboarding gear. Those were the ones I really needed to speak with. I'm sure they'd already worked with staff and offered more insight and details into Elena's accident. These were the girls she met up with and enjoyed a fun weekend with until this accident fucked everything up for her. Goddamn it, what the fuck happened?

Jake spoke first as I went into a mental block for a minute, then he turned to me.

I looked at Miguel, Steve standing to his right, and his ex-wife standing on his left side next to Elena's sister. "We were able to remove most of the tumor. We have no reason to believe it will grow back at this time, but with Elena still in a coma, I didn't want to get further around her brain tissue than needed." Miguel nodded as he rubbed his hand over Steve's back. All of them looked like they'd been crying non-stop—Stevie especially. "Elena is in ICU and will remain there until we are assured she is stable and able to be transferred."

"When will she wake up?" Lydia asked.

"That I don't know," I said. "It could be tonight, but with this severe of an injury, it could take days, weeks, or months." I almost choked on that last word of truth I knew.

Fucking keep it together, Collin.

"Everything went as well as we could hope," I said and looked at

Miguel, who nodded in some mutual understanding, knowing I needed to get the fuck out of here.

"Thank you, both of you, for saving Elena's life," Miguel said. "We'll wait for the nurse to give us instructions about when we can visit Elena."

"When you do see Elena, I ask all of you to speak to her as if she can hear you," I said. "Give her a reason to wake up and come back to us."

I knew I was cracking, so I quickly turned, and Jake and I left the room. I had to get fresh air and fucking quick. The gravity of the situation was starting to suffocate me. Elena had been pregnant? Did she know? She had to know because she must've been three months along or so. Why didn't she tell me?

Oh, my God. We lost our baby.

The walls of my life were caving in around me, and I was powerless to stop it. The love of my life was fighting for her life, her body in a coma to heal itself and do what I couldn't do in surgery. Yesterday, she was in my arms, and today, I held her skull in my hands. How could any of this be real?

I threw open a back door and was thankful that the only person to follow me was Jake. I turned, and when I saw the sadness cross his features, I lost it. My knees buckled underneath me, and Jake grabbed my arm to steady me from falling.

I doubled over, stabilizing myself with my hands on my knees while tears streamed down my face. I tried to swallow my grief for so long that it made me gasp for air, sobbing between breaths.

"It's okay. You need to let it out," Jake said, his arm on my back.

"How—how did this happen to her?" I stood slowly, looking at him as if he had some magical answer.

"I don't know, Coll. I wish I could tell you," Jake said.

"What if I did something wrong? What if that tumor—"

"No. You did everything you could as well as you could," Jake comforted me as I ran my hands through my hair.

"Our baby—" I stopped, choking on my tears. "We were going to have a baby."

I saw the saddest expression I'd ever seen cross my best friend's face. "I'm so, so sorry, Collin. I'm sorry you lost your baby, and Laney is in there fighting for her life."

"We were going to be parents, Jake. I was going to be a dad, and I had no idea," I said in shock, happiness, and grief.

"You were. She was three months along, close to Ash and Avery. I can't tell you how sorry I am." Jake had tears in his eyes when he brought me into a tight embrace. "She is tenacious, and she's a fighter. You have to have faith. I'll be here as long as you need me. Both of you."

How the hell was I going to get through this? I wasn't a stranger to severe brain injuries. I knew the results and outcomes and statistics. I knew it all; this was my profession. It would take time and tests. Right now, all I knew was that she was alive and in a coma. Once she woke up, would she be paralyzed? Would it be months before she could retrain her brain to speak again? Only time would tell.

CHAPTER TWENTY-NINE
COLLIN

I'd dozed off in a chair in some vacant on-call bedroom on the trauma ward, if you could call it dozing off, anyway. I felt like I was more in a trance, floating outside my body. My new reality seemed to be somewhere between a nightmare and hell, and once I had let the gravity of the situation sink in, it swallowed me up.

I bent over in the chair and ran my hands through my hair, letting them rest where I gripped the back of my neck. I closed my eyes, and all I could see was Elena, strapped to that gurney, her face bruised and swollen, eyes closed and non-responsive. She was helpless and dying right before me.

I'd seen cases similar to hers many times before, but this time, it was my Laney. I don't know how I'd managed to rein in my feelings and perform surgery because from where I sat now, it seemed impossible to focus on anything, but I knew I needed to try.

I rubbed my face and gathered myself, knowing I needed to see her again, and I rose from the chair and left the room. I left my cellphone, hospital cell, and pagers back in that room, and I didn't care if I never saw them again. I walked past doctors, nurses, and all kinds of other medical personnel, avoiding eye contact with all of them. I couldn't bring myself to have a conversation or accept any sympathy. I had one mission, and it was to be with my love.

I walked into the intensive care unit and was met by Kelly, the usually chipper RN. She looked weary with concern for Elena, but she quickly pulled it together the moment she saw me.

"Dr. Brooks, I'm the nurse assigned to Elena. She's in ICU room three. She only had family members visit, and Dr. Mitchell and his team monitored her cardiac vitals. There's still no change."

"Thanks, Kell," I said, turning toward Elena's room.

"Dr. Sharon," I said when I saw Denise outside of Elena's room, studying the charts she held.

Denise's head snapped up when she heard me approach. "All her vitals are good, Dr. Brooks. I've sent for another MRI as you requested. The team will be up in about forty-five minutes."

"Thank you."

"I'm so sorry, Collin. I can't tell you how sorry I am."

I nodded. "Just make sure she's well taken care of," I answered.

"You know she will be," she said. "I was finishing up here. Her brain activity hasn't changed, but it looks okay and is showing that she is still in the coma."

"I see that," I said.

"I've got to answer a page from the ER. I'm here for anything you need." She patted my arm as she walked by me and headed down the hall.

I looked at the doorway to Elena's room, realizing that, for the first time, I felt like a stranger in my hospital. I felt utterly helpless in the place where I was usually *always* in control, and it was terrifying and humbling in the most horrible way. I'd spent almost every day in these rooms, checking on my patients, but this was the first time that someone I loved —the person I loved most in this world—was fighting for her life inside.

I went numb when I walked through the door, and I froze in place, staring at her beautiful face. Her head was neatly wrapped in the bandages and gauze from when I completed her surgery hours ago. I rubbed my clammy hand over my forehead, and that's when the tears pushed their way to my burning and aching eyes.

I'd worked the trauma unit long enough to know every possible fucking outcome of Elena's scenario. Her life hung in the balance after I worked to save it, and it was all up to her now. She had to fight to come back to me.

I collapsed into the chair someone had pulled up next to her before I'd arrived, and I took her hand into mine. I stared at her full lips, thinking about how many times I had woken before her and watched her sleeping peacefully like this.

I let the tears stream down my cheeks as I held her hand, wishing to feel life in her grip, but there was nothing. I rose, unable to resist pressing my lips against hers, and even though I felt nothing from her in return, I needed to feel her lips on mine.

I wanted to climb into bed next to her and hold her until her bronze eyes reopened and met mine again. I wanted to hear her laugh at me as if this were some silly prank she'd pulled just to scare the living shit out of me. I gently brought my lips to her nose, chin, and each cheek before I sniffed and settled into the chair again. I propped my elbows on the bed, held her hand in mine, and allowed the tears of grief to flow as I rested the side of my face against her hand.

I had no idea how long I sat crying, feeling Elena's limp and warm hand against mine.

"I always tell people to talk to their loved ones when they're in your condition," I said in a hoarse voice. "I always say that talking will help them, that they'll hear what's being said. I like to believe that's true. How funny that I sit here now, but I have no words, Laney." I rubbed along her arm. "This was your part, remember?" I smiled. "You always have the right words. That's why you're so good at what you do. And look at you; you've left it all up to me now? You know better than that." I blinked through tears and kissed her palm, listening to the beeping of the machines that were monitoring her. "How am I to find the words when I'm the boring scientist?" I kissed her fingertips.

"She mentioned it was the sound of your *sexy and assertive voice* that woke up Mrs. Yi from her coma. Those are her words, of course," Kelly said with a half-smile, coming in to check vitals as they always did every fifteen minutes for patients in one-on-one care in this unit.

"She gave me too much credit, Kell," I said to the RN. "You and I and everyone else in this place know she always did."

"Well, if I hadn't seen Mrs. Yi move her fingers after you told her she needed to wake up, then I wouldn't have felt compelled to agree with Elena when we both saw it," she teased.

"You and Elena were always trouble when left alone up here, you know?" I said, thinking about how much fun the two used to have at work.

"You know what you need to do, Coll," she said to me. "We all know she needs to hear you speaking to her. Just keep talking."

"I was going to be a dad, Kell," I said, my mind running all over the place. "I had no idea."

"I'm so very sorry, Collin," she said. "I wish I knew what to say, but I don't. I'm in shock that this has happened. Everyone is."

I looked at Elena, "I've done nothing but brag about the perfect way to handle the patients who are in Laney's condition, and now, I've got nothing."

Kelly finished her vitals and looked at me. "You've got everything, Collin Brooks," she said, and the redhead stared at me with fire in her eyes. "I won't allow you in this ICU if you want to talk like this around my patient. You need to pull it together for her while you're in here and let the negative emotions go somewhere else."

"Wow," I smiled at her. "I don't think I've ever heard you talk like that before, especially to me."

She inhaled and smiled sympathetically in return. "Well, you've never stayed in this ward for long enough for me to yell at you, so now you know how my husband and kids feel." She let out a laugh and then arched an eyebrow at me. "The only thing you need to do is to be the man she fell in love with. She's in there, and we both know that. She's probably listening to this and laughing at us inside. Don't lose hope, Coll. If there's any man I know who could find *the words* to say to me if I was knocked out, it would be you."

"You say *knocked out* like she's in some—"

"I say it to pull you out of this grief so you can help her," she cut me off. "I understand the gravity of it all, and I've also seen some pretty astonishing miracles happen up here. You know what Elena would say about this."

"Just the fact that she's breathing on her own is a goddamn miracle."

"And it is. Elena's whole motto in life was to appreciate each breath you take and each day you're fortunate enough to have—if you have a full enough heart to appreciate life in such a simple way, you can meet any challenge."

"You're right. You're speaking one of the many speeches she's delivered about how there's always a reason to *have hope that you'll get better and get through any difficulty.* I must have heard her say that to a hundred patients by now."

"Dr. Brooks finally admits I'm *right* about something?" Kelly mocked with a wink. "Hang in there, tough guy. You know what she would tell you. Now, what would you tell her?"

I managed to regain some composure after Kelly left the room, knowing I needed to talk to my girl.

"What would I tell you?" I said, my thumbs running over Elena's hand. "Well, you owe me an apology, Alvarez. You fucked up in my OR tonight. You were supposed to be awake while I did that craniotomy. You were supposed to guide me, and you slept right through all of it." I stopped when I heard her heart rate slightly change, and I looked up at her EEG, watching her brain waves respond. "That's what it takes, baby?" I asked, eying her and watching her brain waves subtly move on the screen. "You need me to tell you that you fucked up in my OR?" I laughed through more tears. "I need you back, Laney. I need you to open your eyes and look at me. Open your eyes," I pleaded, hearing nothing but silence beyond the beeping of machines.

Elena's heart and brain waves had settled into their previous pattern again. I prided myself on being a patient man, but this would be where patience would be my greatest challenge in life.

"Laney, wake up," I demanded. "I can't fucking live without you. I don't want to. You need to come back to me, baby. I know you can hear me. God, please, open your eyes. Fight back, and come back to me."

I had no idea how long I sat next to her. I didn't want to leave her side, but I knew I had to. I had to get up and allow her family to come in and sit with her. Elena needed to hear them too, and I felt like I was starting to become absolutely worthless to her.

I knew I would have to face people soon, and they were going to want to make me talk about this shit. I'd have to listen to their sadness and sympathies for Elena and me, and that's the last thing I wanted to hear. I wanted the love of my life back, and I wasn't getting that.

I told Elena I would be back after her family came to see her, and I left the room and headed toward the restroom to splash water on my face and refocus. I knew if I were left to my thoughts, I would go mad.

As soon as I walked out of the restroom, I nearly ran directly into Jake. He'd come to find me and take me to a room where all of my best friends and my mother had gathered to support me. Now, it was up to me to see if I could make it through when all I wanted to do was lay in bed with Laney—alone—and not move until she woke up.

CHAPTER THIRTY
COLLIN

I held my mom the same as I did the night that we lost my dad on Jake's table. She'd fallen in love with Elena as quickly as the rest of us had, and I knew she was heartbroken for both of us. If anyone could relate to my current emotions, it was my mom. She'd grieved the loss of her life-long love not so long ago. The only difference between us was that I was in this state of limbo, not knowing if Elena would live or die, and if she did live, what deficits might she have? I had no idea whatsoever was waiting for her—or us.

Mom released me after imparting all the right, motherly words, all the words that one needs to hear when faced with an impossible situation. The problem was, I was too numb to be receptive. I felt like I was in a dream and everyone's voice was an echo, and I was outside of myself, watching and listening, but not really engaging.

I was a fucking wreck, and I couldn't hide that shit if I tried. It didn't help to stand in the room, seeing Ash and Avery's puffy eyes, and my three best friends showing nothing but concern on their faces.

I looked at Jake first. "Have you found out how the accident happened? I saw a group of girls in snowboarding outfits in the family room with Elena's family. Were they with Elena? Did you speak to them?"

"No, I didn't," Jake responded, eyeing me carefully.

"How are the cardiac reads? What are you seeing?"

"I know you saw all the monitors while you were in her room, but I'll say what you already know," Jake said. "Even after suffering cardiac arrest due to the immediate trauma and jarring of her brain, she was resuscitated before any brain death or heart death could occur. She's got a strong heart beating in there; however, we will continue to keep her monitored due to the severity of the accident."

"Good. And thank you." I kept my eyes on the only man I could connect with on a surgeon's level. "I don't want her out of that intensive care unit until I release her. She's vulnerable to that tumor growing back rapidly since it was exposed to oxygen as I worked to try and get the damn thing out. If it grows back, she needs to undergo another surgery."

"You know that isn't necessary right now unless it's life-threatening, Coll," Jake answered.

"I'll learn more with the scans," I countered.

"Collin," Jim walked up to me, Ash and Avery showing their remorse but hanging back with any words of concern, given I wasn't in a mood to hear sympathies and sadness. I wanted Elena fixed and awake. That's it.

"What, Jim?" I answered.

"I know that telling you I'm sorry doesn't begin to cover the words you need or want to hear right now, but you need to be in a normal mindset before—"

"Don't even tell me I'm fucking taking time off," I snapped. "I'm not leaving her, and I'm not going home—to *our* home. Being there without her will only drive me off the goddamn rails, and I'm not leaving her in the care of anyone else."

"We understand that," Jim said. "We need your head straight, Collin. You know this better than any of us."

"I know I have to get Elena through this, and I'm not stopping until that woman wakes up from this," I seethed.

"Coll." Alex stepped up, the man who held nothing back when it came to shooting shit straight with any of us. I turned to him, ready for the man to sit me on my ass.

"Please, Alex, say something I don't know."

"How the hell do you plan on helping Elena when you're in an unstable state of mind?"

"I'll find a way," I said, not backing down to Alex's somber expression.

I gripped the back of my neck. "I'll get my head straight and find a fucking way."

"And what would Elena tell you?"

"That's a low fucking shot, and you know it," I said, my voice cracking.

"What would she say?" Alex pressed.

"I don't know, damn it!" I shouted. "Why don't you wake her up and make her fucking tell you herself? Make her wake up." I must've sounded like a madman, screaming at my well-meaning friend for trying to make sure I was okay.

"You need time off, bud," he said, diffusing my mood. "There are therapists and neuropsychiatrists who deal with people in your position. You need to start speaking with them before anyone is comfortable with you continuing to practice. You know that better than anyone."

"The only goddamn neuropsychiatrist I want to speak to can't talk back, asshole. She's the only one who would know what to say."

"Elena has enhanced this hospital with her outlook on situations like this. The hospital board is regularly receiving reports from Elena's colleagues about how Elena has given them more insight into how to do their jobs better. Let them talk to you. You know Elena wouldn't stand in this room and allow you to self-destruct over her like this."

Alex was somewhat getting through the rage inside me that made me reactive to everyone and everything. That rage was why I knew I needed more time alone. It's why I didn't want to leave Elena's side.

"She'd kick my ass for this," I finally said.

"Thank God you see it that way," Alex said with the hint of a smile, "because Jim, Jake, and I were hoping Elena would permit us to kick your ass back into shape. You're the best neurosurgeon in this hospital, but you have to accept that you're going to have to take a step back and let the next in line take this one until you're mentally prepared to go back to work."

"But will I ever be?" I finally admitted. "That woman is the other half of my soul. I knew that from the first moment I saw her, and now—" I choked on my words. I didn't even know if I could say it out loud. "Now, I don't even know if she's going to live or die."

"You know her better than any of us," Alex said. "We all know the vibrant, daring, ball of energy our best friend fell in love with, and none of us can see her giving up. You know everything else about her. You consulted with her on multiple issues. You understand how she saw them, felt about them, and advised her patients and their families in these situations. Right now, your job is to mentally stop and listen to what you know she would say to you about this. You know the answer, Coll."

Everyone in the room watched Alex and me silently. It was as if they all knew what needed to be said, and they knew Alex would be the best one to lay down the facts. They weren't wrong. Jake and I were too emotionally connected for him to set me straight. He would ride with me until the bitter end, over a fucking cliff, no matter the consequences. Jim —despite how much of a hard ass businessman he was—had a huge, empathetic heart. As much as Jim might crack the whip on everyone else, when it came to the people he loved, he wasn't one to say no. But Alex? Alex was as steadfast as they came, and no matter how much the situation might tug at his heart, he had a brilliant gift for prioritizing and organizing in chaos. He could always see the bigger picture, and he would never let any of us make an emotional decision that could ruin our lives. Not on his fucking watch.

"I don't know," I lied. I knew precisely what Laney would say. I just didn't want to admit it because it wasn't what I wanted to do.

"Elena would advise you to take the time you needed to get your head straight. She told me that she dealt with these traumatic situations as if they were a death, and she said that she would insist the families process them as if they were going through the different stages of grief. If *I* managed to have that conversation with her on a random beach in Hawaii, then I sure as hell know that you've heard her say it inside the hospital walls at least a thousand times. You have to get to the acceptance part before I'm comfortable with you practicing again."

"Alex is right," Jake added. "You have to drill down and start to process. You can't float around this place with that look on your face. I know you, and I know when you're mentally checked out. You have every reason to be, but you also need to listen to the people who love you. You have to start by clearing your head and getting your mind right."

"If anyone is going to bring Elena back to you and the rest of us, it's you," Ash spoke up with a smile as she walked up to me and hugged me. "Don't worry about anything else."

Avery stood at Jim's side quietly with a sadness on her face that mirrored how I felt inside. "Get your ass over here, Av," I said and hugged

Jim's wife after Ash stepped next to Jake. "I know you'd probably go in there and cuss her out for doing this to me." I felt Avery laugh through her tears before she pulled back.

"And risk her remembering that and kicking my ass when she woke up? I don't think so." She sighed, and her eyes filled with tears. "She just asked me to be in your wedding the other day."

"And you will when she's recovered," I smiled.

"Collin," my mom said, "be the man I raised to stand solid against such tragedies. It will take time, and during this time, you will be with her and be the voice she needs to hear."

I nodded in understanding.

"I'm sure that, by now, you are all aware Elena and I had a child on the way," I said. "Were any of you aware of this?"

"None of us knew," Ash answered. "Did *she* know? She's so petite that I would've never guessed it."

"I spoke with Dr. Allen, who'd been called up because of the miscarriage. He needed to deal with the situation and ensure there was no additional trauma that would prevent the emergency surgery," Jake said. "Dr. Allen said that Elena had visited him two weeks ago and was rendered speechless when he confirmed she was three months pregnant."

"Fuck," I said. Being a doctor, I knew mine and Elena's baby would have been fully formed, tinier than a lemon, and that the gender of our child would've been noticeable to Dr. Allen when he handled the miscarriage. "I have to call Dr. Allen."

"Are you sure, Collin?" Jim asked. Everyone exchanged glances, probably wondering if it was a good idea to let me go down this road at the present moment.

"I have to know what Elena thought about this, and he would know," I responded. "I need to know."

I dialed Dr. Allen, not allowing anyone to interject their feelings about it.

"Dr. Brooks?"

"Yes. I'm sorry to bother you. I know you're on-call. There's information I need about mine and Elena's child."

"Were you aware of the pregnancy?" he asked.

"No."

"Ah. I'm sorry, Collin," he said. "All I can tell you is that she was in my office after missing a cycle last month. After a blood test and ultrasound, I confirmed she was fourteen weeks along."

"And she just found out?"

"Two weeks ago, yes," he answered. "This is such a—"

"Allen," I interrupted, "I need to know how Elena felt about it to move forward with what I believe she would want after suffering a miscarriage. I have to act on her behalf for her and our child."

"Collin." Dr. Allen must've thought I was an asshole lunatic, but I didn't care.

"It may sound like I'm out of my fucking mind, and I probably am, but I lost a child tonight. I need to know how Elena felt. I need to know how to handle this."

"I understand, Dr. Brooks. Elena had great remorse about consuming alcohol before finding out she was pregnant, but I assured her the baby would be fine with her minimal alcohol consumption. She raised concerns about snowboarding as well. She was concerned she would somehow injure the baby if she took a fall..." he paused, knowing the actual outcome. "In a normal situation, if she took a *fall,* the baby would be fine. She agreed not to go wild on the slopes. Her concern was for the baby first. She was excited to tell you about the pregnancy and mentioned she would."

"The gender?"

"She wanted to wait until you were with her to find out."

"But you saw the gender when you dealt with her miscarriage, right?"

"Collin, you and Elena were expecting a girl," he said.

"What has been done with our child, the fetus?"

"Placed in the same location as all miscarried babies. The child is marked with Alvarez in the unit it's been placed inside. If you wish to take any further action with the miscarried fetus, the morgue will help you."

I rubbed my forehead. "Elena was excited to find out about the baby?"

"Extremely. She had an appointment with me on Monday to do an ultrasound, and she said something about wanting to surprise you."

"Is it normal for..." I paused. "Do you think some burial—"

"Normal is not a word I like to use in reference to people's choices when dealing with a loss. What is normal to one might not be considered normal for another," he started. "I have had a few patients request cremains for fetuses at this stage of development, but not many. I say this not to insinuate that a baby is unimportant at this early stage; however, it is usually the stillborn babies whose parents have more formal funerals."

"I want to do what I know Elena would've done."

"I cannot tell you what Elena would have done, unfortunately. I can only say that she was delighted to share the good news with you, and I am deeply grieved to have to relay the bad news."

"Dr. Allen, will you please ensure that our child is placed in the hospital infant burial grounds. It will be up to Elena when she wakes if she wishes to go forward with anything else."

"I'll make the arrangements for both of you. Again, I am truly sorry, Collin."

"Thank you, and thank you for this information. You know it is all very foreign to me, and I want to do what's best for Elena while she is unable."

With that, I hung up. Avery and Ash were crying, and my mother was comforting them, and Jim, Jake, and Alex were still studying me if I needed a psych eval.

"So, you'll bury the baby?" Jim asked.

"What would you do?" I asked him.

"That's the hardest question to have to answer," Jim said, glancing at Avery, knowing there was no right answer.

"The love of my life doesn't even know she lost the child she was thrilled about, and I have no idea what the fuck to do to help her grieve the loss of it after she wakes and learns about it," I said. "On top of everything else, she has to find out that too."

"Going through the hospital protocols in how they care for miscarried children is an excellent idea," Alex spoke up. "We've created that method for situations like these. A plaque will be put in the gardens for her once you and Elena have decided on a name."

"Now that we've handled that," I saw Jake's expression and heard his tone change. If there was anyone in this room who would get my ass back in the game, it was him. "Let's get you squared away with Elena. Go sit with her and talk to her. You have been given privileges over the immediate family, and you can thank Miguel for that." He pulled me into an expected hug. "We're going to get through this, man. All of us."

CHAPTER THIRTY-ONE
COLLIN

*I*t was day five of Elena's coma, and I couldn't say if I were doing better or worse. What I could say was everything in my life revolved around Elena being in that intensive care unit.

The decision was made to keep her in the ICU and in the one-on-one care of a nurse because of the severity of Elena's brain trauma. This fell in line with protocol, and I expected nothing less. Elena's brain was staying in this coma to keep activity at a minimum and any additional swelling down. The swelling could easily cause the brain to suffer death in areas, leaving patients disabled for life. Yesterday, a feeding tube was inserted, and that was another cold reminder of where we were.

As a neurosurgeon and scientist, what was happening to Elena wasn't new to me. Still, I was a complete stranger to the gamut of emotions that came with all of this—even after having consulted families and dealing with this for all of my career. The bottom line was this: the surgeon in me understood, but the emotional side of me fucking hated every part of it and wanted this nightmare to be over.

I wanted Elena under my care and my care alone, but I'd let my feelings about this overwhelm me. I felt a bizarre sense of loss and helplessness, being in this frame of mind. I felt like I was failing her. I wasn't mentally capable of being the doctor she deserved, caring for her better than any doctor at Saint John's could. It pissed me the fuck off to realize that and try and cope with that fact alone.

"Collin," a soft voice called my name as I sipped my coffee and paced these hospital floors as its victim and not its chief surgeon.

I turned to see the sad blue eyes of a blonde woman close to Elena's age. "I'm Stef," she said, extending her hand to me.

I forced a smile, confused, and shook her hand. "Can I help you with something?"

"I'm one of Elena's friends. I was with her when we were snowboarding," she said. "I met you the night Elena was brought in. Dr. Mitchell asked us some questions about that night a few days ago."

"You'll have to forgive me. Certain pieces of that night are somewhat of a blur for me," I answered truthfully. "Dr. Mitchell told me that it was a snowboarder who cut her off, and..." I trailed off and rubbed my forehead. "I'm sorry. As I said, my recollection isn't what it usually is."

"Shit. I'm so sorry. Maybe I should—"

"Please don't apologize." I looked past her and gathered myself through a deep breath before looking back at her. "Can you tell me what the hell happened on that mountain?" I asked, pulling her toward the wall for a more private conversation. "Was she boarding unsafely? I just need to know something, anything."

"Quite the opposite," the young woman smiled. "She was playing it so safe that we were teasing her for wanting to take the easy slopes. It was so unlike her not to hit the black diamonds and do crazy flips and stuff, you know?" she looked at me half-humored and distressed. "It was after we heard about the miscarriage in the waiting room, we understood why Elena wasn't her usual *dare-devil* self."

"Then how the hell did she wind up crashing into a fucking tree, of all things? The velocity that was calculated must've been nearly thirty miles an hour," I said. "None of that adds up."

She let out a breath again. Damn it, I was harsh, and I didn't mean to be. I was running on bits and pieces of information I recalled from conversations.

"That's what is so upsetting for all of us too," she said. "Everything was fine at first, but since hitting the slopes, there were these guys who'd been flirting with us since we got up there. They were just a bunch of idiots, really," she shrugged. "It was when we decided to go night skiing..." she paused, and I saw tears fill her eyes.

"Night skiing? Boarding?" I knew that Big Bear had a cool way of lighting up the mountain at night, safely allowing skiing or snowboarding.

"We only decided to do it because Elena said she was leaving a day early. She wanted to get home because she had to tell you something that couldn't wait any longer. When she said she was bailing on us early over a *guy*, we all teased her," she said with a half-laugh. "We seriously couldn't believe that any man could tame our feisty Elena enough to make her consider leaving our annual trip." Tears pooled in her eyes. "I think she was coming back early to tell you about the baby."

I felt a lump stick in my throat. The idea that Elena was leaving her trip early to tell me about the baby had added up. I even managed to smile at the idea of Elena coming into the hospital while I was working on-call, walking into the trauma unit, and knowing her well, she would have blurted it all out right then and there.

"Perhaps that's why she was coming home early," I said. "She wasn't one to leave a good time because she missed me."

"Well, with her leaving a day early, we convinced her to do a fun night run with us. We said that we'd do our last runs together at night if she were going to leave. She was down for it, of course, and that's when it all went bad. I feel like this is all our fault."

"You know that Elena wouldn't want any of her friends to feel that way," I said as I looked into her puffy eyes. "I'm sorry. I've forgotten your name."

"Stef," she smiled.

"It wasn't your or Elena's fault, Stef. I am just at a loss as to what exactly happened to send her into a tree." I tried to smile and not look like an asshole.

"Right. It was one of those jerks who'd been up Elena's butt the entire trip." She exhaled in annoyance. "The guy came out of nowhere while we were on the steepest part of the mountain and almost lost it when he clipped his board on bad snow, trying to carve an edge in front of her. Elena swerved to miss him, and that's when ski patrol told us he saw her go over toward the packed ice, and she went off of the groomed area she was on.

She overcorrected to slow the board down, and it only increased her speed more because of the ice. Ski patrol said it put her on a collision course with that tree. She couldn't carve or turn out of it fast enough to avoid it."

"The ski patrol? This is the man who showed up here the next morning and reported to Dr. Mitchell that he was the one who did CPR and restarted her heart?"

"He called 911 with all of us there and kept talking to her. We knew it was bad, especially after we saw Laney's helmet was split. We didn't think she'd survive," Stef said. Her bloodshot eyes searched mine.

"Thank God for that man. Thank you for telling me this. I'm sorry you all are going through this. I wish she would have stayed as planned," I said with a heartfelt smile.

"There was no keeping her there." Stef softly laughed. "She talked about you nonstop, like a schoolgirl in love with some crush. Laney was never like *that* with boyfriends. We teased her persistently about it too." She pressed her lips together. "Anyway, I just wanted to say that I'm sorry and thank you personally for saving her life. She's been my friend since kindergarten." I watched as she folded her arms, dropped her chin into her chest, and began crying.

I touched her elbow. "I'm still trying to process this," I said. "The man she bragged about to you up there would naturally have the right words, but I'm sorry that I don't. I will tell you that I'm glad you told me all of this, and I'm sorry for your pain."

"Will she wake up?"

"She's breathing on her own and has been since being in the coma. With brain injuries this severe, we can never know when our patients will wake up from a coma, or if they will." I ignored the truth of the fact I'd just delivered. "But I will tell you that it seems we all know and love that woman for the feisty and strong spirit she has. I don't doubt she'll pull off one of the many miracles our ICU trauma staff has witnessed."

"It's nice to meet the man—I'm sorry, the *fiancé* that she told us about," she said. "I'll let you go see her now. There was no one waiting after I left."

She spun around and walked toward the elevator, and I made my way over to ICU.

"Hey, baby," I said when I walked into Elena's room. I reached for her limp hand, staring at her monitors and seeing all vitals were strong and good. I kissed her forehead and rechecked her new bandages. "Whoever wrapped your beautiful head after changing your gauze totally sucks, and once I get my head back in the game, I think I'll hold a class on how to wrap bandages around our patient's heads."

I kissed her forehead, nose, and lips. "So, day five of this, huh, Laney?" I said as I kissed her hand. "Well, since you're not telling me how life is going inside the quiet mind of my sleeping beauty, then it's up to me to fill you in on my thrill of a week. You know, the week you decided to ruin?" There was more humor in my voice than I imagined I could muster. "I'm such a fucking mess. You should probably wake up to kick my ass on that fact alone, babe. I have to tell you that Jake is officially pissed at you now because you aren't here to keep me in line and stop me from doing stupid shit." I smiled, and it felt good to feel my face lighten some. "I have to confess that I might've made a rash decision, but once you hear why, I'm sure you'll understand."

I rubbed her hand as I talked, pretending—hoping—that she was listening to me. "No one has ever accused me of being an overly sentimental person, as you well know, but throughout the course of a day, I'm confronted with things that remind me of you and me being together, and yesterday morning, I think I finally lost it. After I left you to rest, I walked to my car, and it hit me like a ton of bricks that you weren't getting in the car with me." I kissed her fingertips, my eyes not once leaving her peaceful face. "After I sat in my car, my radio came on, and all I could think of was you changing the music and forcing me to sing the song. The goofy radio DJ shit you always did whenever we were in the car. Then, as if all of that wasn't enough for my fragile ass, it was as if I saw the ghost of you in my passenger seat. I saw you smiling at me and teasing me, and then I blinked, and you left me." I had learned to accept the tears when they came, instead of fighting them, and they flowed down my cheeks.

I sniffed and gathered myself. "So, after that, I just freaked. I went and bought a new car as soon as the dealership opened because, you know, you've been in all of my cars, and I can't go near those now." I laughed, knowing how ridiculous it was. "Maybe I temporarily lost my mind, but at the time, it seemed like the best solution. Jake, however, is not pleased because I took the liberty of doing something that made me feel a little more like myself by pranking him. We have a rule that none of us buys a car that *matches* another's, so naturally, I went and bought the same car that Jake drives, and he's furious. So, now I'm driving a fucking Bugatti." I kissed her palm. "How's *that* for being born with that silver spoon, eh, Alvarez?"

Elena's brain waves reacted to that more than anything I'd said thus far. Her heart rate was picking up some, and while I watched her brainwaves reacting, I swear to God, I saw her mouth twitch out of the corner of my eye.

"Dr. Brooks," Nancy, Elena's nurse, said as she walked in, "I have no idea what you're saying in here, but this is the best activity I've seen on my monitor since Elena has been in here."

"I was giving her credit for her always saying I was born with a silver spoon in my mouth. She knows I hate to hear that shit," I said to the RN as she watched vitals with me.

"Well, we all know that, Doctor," she chuckled. "That and your arrogant butt roaming the halls like you know everything."

Nancy's specific brand of humor was always lost on me, and though we connected well on a doctor and nurse level, we never found ourselves naturally joking around.

"That's because I *do*, Nancy." I decided to banter with the nurse, hoping to get Elena's brain waves more active. "You just had too much pride to accept that."

Nancy smiled at me. "Me? Too much pride and ego?"

"You heard me. Even Elena said you run around up here, talking crap behind my back." I smiled at her.

Nancy laughed, and I watched the woman's forehead wrinkle in humor. "She wasn't supposed to tell you."

I was thrilled about the uptick in Elena's brain activity. It was the most promising thing I'd seen yet.

"Is she in Dr. Nathan's care?" I asked, wanting my next-in-line to be in here to see this.

"She's currently under Dr. Singh," Nancy said. "Collin, this is looking good. You jarred her quiet brain past something. I'm going to get the doctor."

"Thanks."

"Good God, woman." I looked at Elena. "I'm learning more and more about what cracks you up about my sorry ass," I said truthfully. "Would you also give me more activity on that screen if I told you that I have to stay at Alex's house now? Yeah, imagine that shit. I guess we can agree that it's better than buying a new house. I stopped at the car, so that's got to count for something. Alex is going to kick me out if I don't stop watching chick flicks and eating ice cream to get through all of this, though."

"Looking very nice," Dr. Howard said, walking in with Dr. Singh. "This is excellent activity. What are you saying to her?"

"Just telling her stories of what a jackass I am. Apparently, she loves it," I said.

Both doctors laughed. "Well, you are one of the biggest assholes we know," Singh's eyes crinkled in humor. "Who would've thought that's what Elena fell in love with?"

"I'm shocked her eyes didn't snap open at that one, Singh," I said.

"Keep talking to her; whatever you're doing is working," Dr. Howard added.

"Is Miguel here yet? Any of her family?"

"Miguel called in about forty minutes ago saying they were going to continue coming down in shifts of two. I told him you were on your way in, and he said he and his son would head here."

"How are they doing?"

"They're going be doing much better once Miguel sees these brain graphs. I'll let you fill him in on what got our lovely Elena's mind sparking some neurons today."

"My sorry and pathetic bullshit? God, give me half a chance with her dad," I teased.

"When have you cut corners on anything, Brooks? You pride yourself in challenges, remember?"

"You two can leave once you're done taking the info down," I smiled.

"You're not the acting chief, partner," Dr. Howard teased. "So, no bossing us around and telling us what to do."

"Well, I'm glad stupid crap like this gets some activity going with Elena," I said. "If only those sleepy little eyes would open."

"Any progress is excellent progress up here," Singh said. "You know that all too well, Brooks."

The doctors left me with Elena, and I swear I could sit here and stare at her beautiful face for however long it took her to wake up again.

"I know you're in there trying to come back to me, baby. I need you to try harder," I pleaded.

"Dr. Brooks, Alex is here to see you," Nancy said when she peeked her head into the door. "He's waiting just outside."

I looked over at Nancy. "Tell him to give me a minute. There's something I need to say to her," I said, and she nodded in understanding.

I rose from my chair and kissed Elena's lips, letting my lips linger longer than usual, then reached back and took her limp hand and clasped both of mine around it.

"Baby, I need to tell you about our child—our daughter," I said, my tears flowing freely again. "Saint John's has gone through the proper measures of laying her to rest for you and me. I didn't know what to do in this situation." I kissed the hand that I held. "I've been so lost. You, our daughter, everything. I know women grieve a miscarriage in so many different ways, and I didn't know how you would grieve the loss of your little girl when you woke up." I licked my lips and bit down on my lower lip. In a profound effort to pull it together, I sniffed and gathered myself. "So, the hospital ensured our daughter was laid to rest, and a plaque with her name was placed in the butterfly gardens where families gather and visit in the children's wing. I know you would love it and approve of that part, at least.

"When I was at our home in Malibu, I saw the diary you wrote in. You know, the one I gave you for Christmas that you allowed me to read? Remember that one?" I looked up at her brain waves, and I didn't seem to cause any difference, but I knew she had to be listening to this. "Well, after I completely lost my shit, I decided I needed to pack my things and go to Alex's house. Being home felt overwhelming because all I saw was *you* fucking everywhere. I took a break and sat on the outdoor sofa, and I found your journal had fallen behind the cushions." I kissed her again.

"I hope you won't be mad at me for going through your journal, but I wanted to know if you wrote anything after finding out that you were pregnant. I know it might sound strange, but I felt like I needed to hear you tell me about it, and that's the only way I could. Anyway, I saw where you wrote that you cried when you found out. Babe, I wish you would have told me for that reason alone, to share your joy and fears and everything that happens when you find out something life-changing has happened. You drew the most beautiful butterfly after that entry, and I assume that was when your thoughts must've been running wild with questions, concerns, and how to process it all. I have no idea. Maybe it's because you were happy," I said, rubbing my thumb over the back of her hand.

"I won't know until you wake up and tell me. Either way, then I turned the page, and I see you had already started picking out names without me!" I chuckled. "I should have known you loved that story, Little Women, so much when you read it to Mrs. Yi in surgery. However, I didn't expect that you'd want to name our child after one of the characters. Josephine March Brooks has a lovely ring to it; Joe March Brooks, on the other hand, isn't my first choice for a boy, I've got to tell you." I smiled at the fact that she'd want to name our child after a book character. "I never told you this, but I always imagined that character, Jo, to be you when you read it to Mrs. Yi. Jo was wild and free and headstrong, but she's also passionate and full of life. So much like my Laney. No wonder you attached to her.

"So, baby, Josephine March Brooks is the name I had the hospital inscribe on the plaque in the garden, and I also had them etch the butterfly that you drew on the pages before you named our daughter. I think it's perfect, and I think you will love it."

I stared at her unresponsive reaction and the nasal cannula that was delivering her oxygen through her nostrils. "Whatever you hear in that beautiful mind of yours, I hope you're mentally smiling that smile I miss and love so much that it hurts." I kissed her forehead. "I love you, sweetheart. Alex and I are going down to find the perfect place for our daughter's plaque. When you wake up, we'll go there together. If you could wake up now, I wouldn't have to do this without you, you know? If you could open your eyes, Laney," my voice became stern. "Open them and be with me in all of this, Elena."

I sat with her quietly before I knew it was time to go. As I always did when I left my Laney, I kissed each of her closed lids and left her in the care of the ICU staff. Walking out and leaving Elena in that room would forever be the hardest thing in my life until she woke up and came back to me.

CHAPTER THIRTY-TWO
COLLIN

*I*t was week two of Elena in her non-responsive coma. She remained in ICU after Dr. Nathan, the one working the ward of Saint John's in my place, determined she wasn't to be moved yet. He was still watching her scans, and even though the tumor I couldn't completely get out showed no signs of growth, they were monitoring for swelling.

I still didn't want to go to places that jarred my memory of happier times spent with Laney, which was a wholly unexpected abnormality occurring within my personality. As of now, I just stayed the fuck away from our place in Malibu, and the car thing? Well, I'm sure I could've gotten behind the wheel of one of my cars again, but it was fun parking next to Jake's Bugatti at the hospital just to watch him cringe.

Little by little, I felt myself pulling through this disaster—stabilizing, anyway—and I was starting to feel the aching need to go to work again. I was no longer the zombie who walked the hospital halls, even though I was there all of the time. It wasn't until this week that I'd pushed back a little and spent a few hours at Alex's place, bugging the hell out of him to make sure he knew I appreciated the hospitality of his badass Beverly Hills bachelor pad.

If I wasn't working aggression out of my system through swimming vigorous laps in his pool, I was doing what I was doing right now: chilling on the couch with his black cat, curled up on my lap, finally catching up with the vampire show Elena had begged me a million times to watch. Something about this shit drew both Alex and me in, and even though we'd skipped ahead a few seasons, we were officially sucked in.

"Hello, lover," Alex said as he walked in from work. He shook his head as he looked at me, my legs crossed and stretched out, and feet propped up on his marble table in front of the couch. "I swear, Zeus," he said to the cat he'd rescued out of some dumpster. "I'm never gonna be able to bring another chick home because of your new pal, here."

"Thank God for that, eh." I scratched the top of Zeus's head. "Zeus thinks it's all bullshit anyway. Take the chicks somewhere else, so he doesn't have to hear them say how much you suck in bed," I teased.

"I brought takeout." He eyed where I'd already eaten a salad, a fruit bowl, and a chicken caesar wrap. "I see Jake's chewed your ass out for not eating."

"That was last week, my friend. But what's in the bag?" I said, smelling the Mexican food from here.

"La Mariada's," he answered. "I got your favorite burrito from that place."

"This is why you're my man." I smirked and held my hands up to catch the burrito he tossed at me. "The thing is worth the fifty dollars you paid for it too."

"Whatever you say. Want a beer?" he asked.

"Sure, I ate all my healthy food like a good boy. I'll take the beer as a reward for that."

"Anything I can get you?" Alex asked his cat as he scratched his head.

"Zeus could use his litter box cleaned out," I smiled.

"That was your job since he's turned into your therapy cat. And since I'm pretty much your bitch now, you can at least clean out the litter box when my cleaners don't meet your or Zeus's needs."

Alex came out with two beers, gave me one, and sat on the opposite end of the couch I was on. Zeus eyed his owner and stretched a paw out over my leg. "What the fuck? When did Bonnie get out of that prison world?" he asked about the show I was watching.

"Well, I got bored, so I skipped a few episodes." I shrugged and sipped my beer. "It was sort of depressing, watching the poor witch-girl in there all by herself."

"I thought we were past this?" he smiled at me as I bit into my burrito and offered Zeus a piece of shredded beef. "No fucking human food, man."

"Too late. Zeus loves this." I looked at Alex. "Speaking of my buddy here, it's obvious you have a thing for that hot chick who grooms him."

"Jen?" he chuckled.

"Yeah, she's fucking hot, and I saw the way you two looked at each other when she came over last night."

"First of all, we were making fun of your stupid ass, and secondly, she's hot, but she's not into guys."

"Oh, damn." I laughed. "Sucks for you."

"Ain't that the truth," he agreed, holding up his beer.

"How was work?"

"Hit pause," he said, trying to watch the show I'd been half-watching and half-spaced out while it ran in the background. "Now that we're *husband and wife*," he started, "allow me to give you a run-down of my day. I'm not telling you shit about your dad's company—that he *so generously* left to you—or its lovely vice president, Tatum."

"Hang on a second. First and foremost, let's not pretend my dad deciding to drop that into my lap in his will *had* to be a joke. We all know it was certainly something to make him laugh beyond the grave," I said with a laugh. My dad knew I wanted nothing to do with his architectural firm—which I made clear by becoming a neurosurgeon instead of an architect. "So, about Tatum. Is the devil in stilettos still giving you hell after Jim and I agreed I wanted Mitchell and Associates running the company?"

"She's manageable." He rolled his eyes.

"The hell she is. Glad she's your and Jim's problem, not mine. I told you both to fire her ass."

"Like I said, not talking about your dad's company. Instead, my day over at Mitchell and Associates was delightful," he said with sarcasm. "I managed to acquire two companies today, fire the VP of our media department, and break someone's heart after they tried to pitch some insane idea about balloon farms."

I choked on the beer I was swallowing. "Is *that* the shit Jim pranks your ass with? God, I thought Jake and I were bad."

Alex smiled. "I'll get his sorry ass back for it. Trust me," he said. "Anything else, or are we going to talk our feelings out tonight also?"

"I just asked how my *husband's* day was at work?"

"That's why we need *you* back and working again," he said.

"That's a damn fact," I answered, hitting play on the remote.

"Alright, catch me up on this show since you've gone rogue and started skipping episodes," he said. "Wait, I'm lost *again*. A wedding is taking place now? What the hell? This has to end bad, man."

"No shit, that's why I jumped ahead. That sociopath, Kai, is on the loose."

"Oh, fuck," Alex said.

"And Elena's human again," I said, catching him up on the episode I was watching. "I can't remember where or when that shit happened, but the five-hundred-year-old vamp dude? The one with my eye color?"

"Damon?" Alex laughed. "You don't have that man's eye color, by the way."

We were turning into a couple of chicks, watching *my Elena's* vampire show. We must've looked hilarious.

"Well, I know that shit. My eyes are so much more enticing," I teased as Jake walked in.

"If it isn't the happy couple. Come here, Zeus," he said, walking in like he owned the place.

"Hands off, bro," I said. "Zeus is my boy, and he's not moving. Besides, you probably smell like your doctor's office and need a shower anyway."

"I just finished rounds and checked on your lovely lady," he added, sitting in the leather chair to Alex's right.

"Is she alone?" I asked, practically standing up and ready to bounce.

It was hard enough leaving Elena's side, and also the hospital...let alone trusting everyone understood that I wouldn't allow her to be left alone in that room.

"Sit your ass down." Jake rolled his eyes. "I thought the emotional-support cat was working?" he said, looking at Alex.

"Well, we're ramping up to a *thrilling* event in this show, and then you waltz into my place like you own it and drop an *Elena-bomb* on Collin's sorry ass; what'd you expect? Zeus doesn't have *that much* therapy in his paws."

"She's not alone, dumb-fuck," Jake rose. "Everyone working ICU was practically besties with her before the accident, and she has family rotating non-stop. I'm getting a beer."

"You know where the kitchen is." Alex pointed to the room behind him.

"What are her monitors reading?" I asked.

"All good," he said from the kitchen. "Fuck, I hate this goddamn kitchen. Where's the fucking fridge, Alex?"

"Next to the cabinet, asshole," he said. Alex and I zoned into the show again after my stupid knee-jerk reaction about Jake seeing Elena.

"Your entire fucking kitchen is designed to look like cabinets, dick," he grumbled. "Got it. Shit, that needs to be changed. Why the hell does your kitchen look like some massive-ass cupboard?"

"It's called being fancy," Alex said, trying to ignore him.

"Gets him laid too. That's what he told me anyway." I laughed.

"That's true," Alex arched an eyebrow at me. "Until you and Zeus decided to take over the place."

"You've got like ten thousand square feet and three stories of space to fuck outside of this loser moving in with you," Jake said, then practically choked on his beer when he looked up at the flat screen. "Why the hell are you watching this show?"

"Because it takes my mind off of the noise," I answered.

"It's sort of addicting," Alex admitted with a laugh. "Even when this dipshit fast-forwards through seasons and episodes, and you have no idea what the hell is going on."

"Nope," Jake said, snatching the remote and shutting off the television.

"What the hell? We were about to find out what this Kai joker was about to do," I insisted.

"He's going to fuck that wedding up. I have to see if my prediction is correct," Alex said.

"Yeah, you two look like a bad episode of the Odd Couple. Now, put on some sports or something. Remember those days of watching football and basketball...shit like that?"

I eyed Jake, thinking his reaction to us watching this show was a bit much. "I don't give a fuck about sports right now." I pet Zeus, who responded by purring. "I want to watch the wedding of the century. You know, since I'm obviously not getting mine anytime soon."

"Nice play, asshole," Jake said. "You're not watching this particular episode."

I smiled. "Ah-ha. So, you've watched this too, eh? Little rerun, chick-flick closet freak."

"I…" He looked at Alex for help, and Alex only laughed, apparently not picking up on some cue Jake was trying to give him.

"You what?" I pried. "What happens that we already can't predict?"

"Nothing, I'm just not watching vampire shows," Jake said, his eyes narrowing at me.

"Shame. Because you're sort of missing out," I said. "And so am I, now turn on the damn show."

"Not happening."

"Give it up, man," Alex said. "Blame it on Ash, unless you sneak out and watch this shit by yourself?" he laughed.

"All right, it's one of Ash's favorite shows to binge-watch. After I made fun of her for watching a show that isn't on anymore, she insisted I watch it with her."

"And just like that, you were hooked, right?"

"Well, I was more hooked on laying my head in her lap after a long day at work and having her run her hands through my hair. Then it was like something came over me, and when I came home, it just became part of our routine."

"Right," I answered. "Elena roped my ass the same way. Well, not the laying my head in her lap and acting like a bitch when I got off work like you are with Ash part anyway."

"It doesn't matter. I know how this storyline ends, and I'm not about to let you watch *television Elena* go down and then compare that shit to *your Elena.*"

"Why the fuck would I do something that ridiculous?"

"You went out and bought the matching car to mine, dumbass. Should we go over the reasons you went out to buy the car in the first place?"

"I was in a dark place. I'm doing better, though. I'm actually planning on getting my ass back to work." I looked over at Alex. "I'm sure you and Jim heard about that today too?"

"Yes, and I've been feeling you out all night. I haven't heard you sound this good in a while," Alex said.

"Cheers to that truth," Jake raised his beer to me.

"Anyway, the board and I are sitting down in two days, and after I can show my head is back in the game, which it is, I'm going back."

"You think you can handle surgeries?" Jake asked.

"I know I can," I answered. "But I'm going to recommend I take a week back at work before I start in on the surgical part of my job again."

"Good call," Alex said.

"I know," I smirked. "I'm probably going to start staying at my house again starting tomorrow too. I want to be closer to the hospital."

"Elena made it clear that her condo was yours too. She'd give you hell for making that long of a drive to Malibu from the hospital just to crash for a few hours," Jake added.

"True." I rubbed my forehead. "I guess Malibu seems more like her place than the condo itself does." I laughed.

"So, stay at the condo," Alex said. "You know you can keep crashing at my place too. Zeus is going to miss the hell out of you when you leave."

"More like the other way around," I said.

"Adopt your own damn cat. Don't even think about taking mine." Alex laughed. "So that's it then? Our big, bad chief is coming back?"

"Thank God," Jake said.

I rubbed the cat's back. "Thank Zeus," I laughed. "This guy gave me some good therapy—cat style."

I'D BEEN BACK to work for four days, and it was going more easily than I'd anticipated. I should've had my ass shoved back into work a week ago. I managed to do well, seeing Elena for about thirty minutes before I started my morning rounds, then during my lunch and patient cancellations, and after work. I spent the majority of my time with her. My mind was functioning at a healthy level, though, and I didn't even freak out as I'd imagined I would, seeing her office door closed and even peeking in to find it empty.

All-in-all, I was getting through this week smoothly, and my surgeries were set to start taking place next week. Being back in routine made all the difference in the world, and I was feeling lighter.

This shroud of darkness that had clouded over me for the last three weeks was all but gone, but like any normal person, I had my moments. There were moments of grief, disbelief, and frustration with Elena's situation, but I took time alone to let tears flow if need be or take a jog on the beach. Whatever it took to keep the bad energy away from me.

"Dr. Brooks," Anna, the RN working in ICU, said as I made my rounds in the post-surgery ICU floor where Elena remained, unconscious. "Your patient, Bethany Keen, the car accident victim?"

"Yes? Her glucose levels, have they come down? I was checking her first," I replied.

"They have. Her family wishes to visit her," she said, following me into my patient's room.

"Beth?" I'd put her in a medically-induced coma to save her life, and her family insisted I use the name Beth when trying to rouse her. "Beth, it's Dr. Brooks. You need to wake up now. Your family wants to visit you."

"You think she will?" Anna asked.

"Beth," I said, reaching for her hand as I'd always done with my patients. "It's Dr. Brooks, and it's time to wake up." I used a more assertive tone.

Beth's fingers flicked against my palm.

"Here you come." I looked at Anna. "Call the family in. She's waking up, and she needs to hear them and see them if she wakes within the next hour or so."

"Yes, doctor."

I went through the floor, always saving Elena for last, so I could stay with her until I changed and went home. When I got to Elena's room, her sister was sitting in the chair next to her bed, and I ignored her as always, looking at Elena's charts instead. I didn't like the ice queen one fucking bit before Elena's accident, and time hadn't changed my opinion.

"All of her vitals and readouts are looking fantastic," I muttered to myself, studying Elena's charts. "Elena, you can wake up any time now."

"Dr. Brooks," Lydia said.

"Yes, Lydia?" I said, eyeing the chair she sat in, knowing I'd be taking it once Lydia's green-eyed ass was out of here. Thank God for her she was positive when she was with Elena, or my ICU nurses would've thrown her out.

"Will they be moving her as Papi said?"

"Elena's swelling is no longer a threat. Her brain is healing quicker than we anticipated, so she'll be transported to our rehab location."

"I don't want her leaving the hospital," she insisted.

"Neither do I. It's why I'm paying outside of Elena's insurance for her treatment and care from that state-of-the-art coma facility to send a fantastic rehab unit over to Saint John's to work with her."

"But will they wake her up?" Lydia asked.

Why the sudden questions?

"Elena will wake up when her brain is ready. I'm in here countless times throughout the day to ensure she wakes."

"I can't do this anymore," she wailed, bringing my ICU nurse into the room.

"Okay," I said. "I understand. Perhaps it's time for a break, Lydia."

"I'll leave on my own," she snapped at me.

While I frowned, Anna stepped up. "It's time for you to leave, Ms. Alvarez," she said directly. "I will not tolerate you arguing with the doctor in front of his patient. We have other coma patients who can hear this too."

I remained silent because the words that would fall from my mouth would get my ass kicked out of here too.

Lydia stormed out of the room, crying, and I shook my head. "Call for Miguel, please," I said to Anna. "He's been showing up with her, and I believe this is why. Perhaps Lydia is cracking at home."

"It's not the first time I've asked her to leave this ICU unit," Anna said. "She's starting to yell at the staff, and I overheard her saying that you put Elena in this position."

"In grief, it's always easy to blame the doctor. I've blamed myself numerous times before I moved forward. The woman needs to be kept away from the patient until we can determine she remains positive when she's in here. I need to finish these reports," I said. "Inform Lydia, in Miguel's presence, why she was asked to leave tonight."

"Yes, doctor."

I rolled my eyes at Lydia's dramatics. "You hear that, Laney?" I said, walking over and getting vitals with my stethoscope, sneaking a kiss to her lips. "Your sister needs you awake so you can keep her in line." I rose back up and met the other nurse working the ICU at the foot of the bed.

"Doctor, I need to go over a lab," Nancy said.

"Let me finish with this patient and—" I looked at her paperwork. "Why isn't Singh up here?"

"Sorry, I didn't think to call him up."

"I need to understand why he has his patient on this dose before I advise on the lab work. It looks like we're trying to keep the blood thin? Call him in, and we'll—"

"Oh, my God, Elena!" Nancy practically shrieked. "You're awake."

My knees almost buckled when I looked and saw two wide eyes were staring up at the ceiling as if looking for answers from it.

"Elena?" I said. We approached her slowly, knowing that patients coming out of comas usually were disorientated.

Those beautiful bronze eyes met mine, and my breath caught in my chest. I smiled through the fact that I impulsively wanted to kiss her beautiful face and hug her again. I followed my usual protocol and stood next to her.

I slipped my hand into hers and licked my lips as her eyes were searching mine.

"Can you squeeze my hand?" I asked, level-headed and with my usual steadiness. "Elena, it's Dr. Brooks. Can you please squeeze my hand?"

She did, and my smile widened so much my cheeks burned.

"How about mine?" Nancy asked on the other side. "Give mine a good squeeze, Elena."

I was watching intently. Could she smile? I was close to those motor skills while removing that tumor. God, I could easily see she was completely disorientated.

"Elena, do you know where you're at?" I asked.

"No," her voice was hoarse but angelic and soothing to my soul that had been raked over coals for three weeks.

"Elena, you're in the hospital," I said.

"Did my parachute not open?" she asked me.

Fuck.

"Elena, you suffered an injury while snowboarding with your friends," I said. "Do you remember any of that?"

"No, doctor," she said.

"Elena, do you know who I am?" *Please, God. Please. Please.*

"A doctor." She smiled. "A really, really, good-looking doctor."

I held my smile and my tears all at once. Where was Elena in her head? It was normal to be completely out of it after waking from a coma. It was also usual to know and have heard everything going on while in a coma.

Nancy pulled Elena's attention from me and took over with exercises that showed her fine motor skills were working, and I didn't fucking damage anything. The contrecoup jarring of her brain did, though—Elena didn't know who the hell I was. She was waking up from what she believed was a skydiving injury.

Oh, my God. Did I lose her? I was terrified to think the thought. I had to pull my shit together. Sometimes memory loss would last, sometimes not. It was time for evaluations, and since she wasn't reaching for me to hold her and be *her Collin*, I stayed in *her doctor* mode because that's what she knew me as, and I had to respect that for her.

"I'll notify her family she's awake," I said to Nancy. "I'll have a team come to work with her, and we'll keep running tests." I smiled at Elena when she looked at me. "There's a lot to catch you up on. We'll get your family in to see you first."

"My Papi. I know he's upset. He didn't want me to go," she instantly said.

I smiled at her. God, I loved this woman more than words. "Your Papi is far from upset, and when you see him, I promise that he will never have been happier."

"You know him?" She eyed me with those probing, beautiful bronze eyes of hers. "Dr. Brooks?"

"I worked under him for many years," I said. "He's a mentor of mine. One of the best surgeons I've ever known."

"That's neat." She smiled. "He's the best. But he won't be happy about this." She raised her hands with IVs in them.

"A lot of people are grateful you're back with us, Elena," I said. "Trust me on that."

I winked out of habit, and when I saw her lips tint pink, it was a beautiful reminder of when she loved me before I knew. All I could do was pray that this was temporary.

CHAPTER THIRTY-THREE
ELENA

I was so confused. I had no idea what the hell was going on or why I was in a hospital—in California. I kept looking at the doctor's bright blue eyes, eyes that were so striking and more captivating than any other shade of blue I'd ever seen. He seemed upset about something, though.

I became agitated almost instantly. "Don't!" I snatched my arm away from him when it looked like he was going to rest his hand on me. "Don't touch me. Go get my Papi like you told the nurse you would," I demanded, aggravated by being in this bed with these plastic tubes up my nose and IVs in my arms.

"Elena," he said in a softer response than I expected a doctor would have with my sudden outburst. "You need to try your best to remain calm."

I couldn't help but start crying. I was so lost and scared.

His warm hand returned to mine, and my eyes went slowly to where the IV was that he ran his thumb over. "Get me out of here," I told him, desperate and knowing he was the only man keeping me here.

"Elena," the nurse said, my head snapping over to her as if she and Dr. Brooks were suddenly holding me prisoner in this small room. "Your mother is on her way."

"I want my Papi," I shouted back. "I want out of this room."

"I'll call for the therapist. Her BP is rising, and we need her calm," Dr. Brooks said.

"I don't need a fucking therapist. I need to go home."

I didn't know what I was saying, thinking, or doing—everything was instinctual. All I knew was that I was scared out of my mind. These people, calming blue eyes or not, weren't listening to my pleas to leave this room.

"Laney! My baby girl," my mom said as she rushed to my side. Dr. Brooks stood back. He was probably trying to kill me in this room, and that's why he wouldn't let me go.

"I don't want to see you," I barked. "I want to see my Papi."

"He's on his way to the hospital, Laney." She ran her hands on my cheeks, aggravating me even more.

"Why isn't he here? He left me with this doctor and nurse." I eyed her with the fear I felt. "Mom, you have to get me out of here. Papi would've knocked that man out for keeping me in this bed." I leaned my head up and whispered, "I think he's trying to kill me. He won't let me go!"

Mom's expression shifted from careful concern to worry as she looked at the doctor. "Is this normal?" she questioned him.

"Are you fucking joking?" I shrieked. "You're in on this with them too?" I glared at her and shifted away when mom went to rub my arm.

"Elena Marie Alvarez," she said in that stone-cold voice I hated. "You will watch your mouth and calm down."

A switch flipped in my head, and I started gasping for air, trying to tear the tubes out of my nostrils. Tears erupted as I started sobbing, scared out of my mind.

"This is normal. She's disorientated, and it's part of the post-traumatic amnesia. Get a therapist in here, STAT," the doctor ordered. Then I watched in fear as he pulled his phone up to his ear. "Miguel, yes," he paused, his eyes watching my monitors. "Hold on. Her BP is going up again." He looked over at the nurse. "I want an extremely mild dose—"

I closed my eyes and tried to block everything out, feeling my heart racing faster than my confusion. "I'm going to have a heart attack," I cried after who knows how long I held my eyes tightly closed. "Oh, my God. I'm going to die. I'm going to die."

That's when my sobbing mom turned to Dr. Brooks and held onto him for dear life. What the hell was going on? Did I go skydiving and land in some other world where my mom was cheating with this handsome doctor? She realized he was in here to kill me, right?

"Elena," he said after he shifted my mom to the nurse that'd walked in. "I need you to listen to me, okay?" He finished that last word soft enough that it seemed to calm every reactive nerve in my body. "Okay?"

"Okay. Please, God, don't kill me," I said to him, pleading with his eyes that were locked on mine.

The smile that was present on his face allowed me to take a deep breath. "The very last thing I want to do is kill you." He smiled that lovely smile that made his eyes lighter. "My other patients, however," he said, eying the hospital staff that was in my room, "they might want to if you keep screaming like this." He gently sat on the side of my bed, took my hand, which was trying to pull the IV out of my other hand, and held it. "Luckily for you," that smile that was keeping me focused only on him, "I won't allow that to happen, and neither will my staff. We want to keep those patients out of your room. Your family has been waiting for you to open your beautiful eyes, and they will be very grateful to learn you're able to speak after your little accident." His eyes widened, and his humor made me smile back at him. "Not quite sure your Papi is going to be thrilled to walk in and find his daughter is cursing like a sailor in my ICU, though."

"He'll blame you," I challenged. "You started it all."

His dark and light blond hair was messy, short, and so youthful. He was a dreamy guy, which made all the more sense of why I was lured here to be killed by him and his nurses.

"Your eyes are going wild on me again," he said, studying me. He looked up at the monitors when that machine started beeping loudly to tell him I knew all about this man and his plans.

"You're trying to kill me, but I'm not afraid of you, asshole," I said, letting this handsome demon-doctor know I was onto him.

"Why would I want to do that when all I've done is work my ass off to keep you alive, Elena?" he became sterner, and that made his answer feel like the truth to me.

"Then why do I feel like I've been kidnapped?" I asked.

"Because this is normal. Things are a bit disorientating for you. Can I ask you a question? You don't have to answer it," he said.

His warm hand holding mine felt nice. I curled my fingertips up some to keep us like this. "It depends on what you want to ask," I answered.

"How old are you?" he asked.

"Too young for you," I smiled at him.

I watched him bite down on his bottom lip, and my heart felt like it flip-flopped in my chest. I loved that feeling but didn't know why him doing that made me feel that way.

"You think thirty-four is too old for you, eh?" he smirked.

My heart did that thing again.

"Well, I'm only twenty-two, doctor. I don't think my Papi will approve."

His lips pinched together, and I watched his face grow serious again. That look scared the hell out of me, but I felt an intense wave of calm wash over me. I felt warm, like I was wrapped in relaxation.

"Oh, wow. Um, yeah. Anyway." I think I was mumbling, but I remembered what we were talking about, and I forced a smile. "This feels nice. You feel nice," I said to the doctor, but his eyes were looking above my head. "Doctor, look at me."

"A little more. I don't want her completely asleep, but I want her fully relaxed," he said to whoever he was looking at.

"I don't care anymore," I giggled. "You can kill me if you want."

He smiled at me. "If you don't stop insisting that I'm trying to murder you, I might have to kiss you just to make sure you know I have no intention of that."

"No way," I said. "My dad won't let me date you. I can date anyone except a doctor. Papi made me promise him that when I was little."

"Is that so?" he asked. "I think I could change his mind."

"He doesn't even know you."

"Apparently, you don't know me, either," he said, his voice calm. "But you must've forgotten already that I know your father." His eyes searched mine in the way that scared me before, and then he looked away. "Miguel should be here at any time. Where's the therapist?" His voice was stern about the therapist part.

"Are they not following your orders, doc?" I asked.

His eyes shifted to mine. "No, they're not, Elena."

"Getting mad?" I tried to flirt with him because I wanted to see him smile again.

"I rarely get angry," he confirmed.

"Your eyes are gorgeous," I said.

His face turned to mine, and I got that doctor smile again.

"I've been told on more than one occasion that they resemble the eyes of a character named Damon on some vampire television show. I wonder if you remember that you've watched it. I think my eyes are sexier, and I think you might agree."

"Flirting with me, doctor?"

"Stating facts is all," he said.

"I bet everyone in this hospital is in love with you," I said, so loopy on whatever the doctor had the nurse give me.

He smiled that smile. "I bet they are too," he said with a wink.

"Laney," I heard Papi's voice as he entered the room. "My God, Brooks. She's awake." He studied the doctor and me and stayed back.

"You can go now. My Papi is here. I won't tell him that you like me." I thought I was teasing, but Dad wasn't happy at all.

"Laney, baby, how are you feeling?" Dad asked as the doctor and nurses walked out of the area to give me the time I wanted with my dad. The only person I trusted around me.

"I was scared. I thought the doctor kidnapped me, I think?" I couldn't remember why I was scared anymore. "I don't know why I'm here, Papi."

"You were in an accident, Laney. You're waking up from that. It's okay. We're all here."

"But why am I in California?"

"Because you moved back home to live with Stevie and me," he said.

I looked at him in confusion. "That's impossible. I would never graduate college and not go to med school."

"Laney," Dad said as he sat carefully next to me on my bed, "I want you to listen to me, okay?"

"Don't scare me, Dad."

"I won't, baby girl. Do you remember asking me why I was sad when I came home from work one time? It was the only time you saw me sad."

"Yes, I remember that. You cried. I was in middle school."

"Right," he smiled. "I had a patient who I'd been working on long and hard, trying to help her after she was in an accident. She woke up scared, like you, from her coma. It made my heart sad to see her so frightened. I knew that, with time, she would get through it, but she had a very long road ahead of her."

"It's why I'm going to go to med school to do what you do, Dad. Or do what that doctor guy does, the one I thought was trying to kill me. What does he do?"

"Quiet your thoughts." He kissed my forehead. "You will become frightened again. I want you to focus on small things. Little things."

Great, now my dad was acting weird. "What is that supposed to do?" I demanded.

Dad's face hardened some. "I understand what you're feeling right now. We're going to take small steps and gradually allow your mind to absorb things. You live here now, and you were involved in an accident that made it difficult for you to remember things and process them. Dr. Brooks isn't trying to kill you." He smiled as if the thought amused him. "He's going to help you, and you need to follow his guidelines like my patient who lost all of her memories followed mine. Do you understand me, young lady?"

"I knew you would bust me for this." I smiled at him. My head felt fuzzy. As happy as I was that my dad was here, I didn't really know what we were talking about anymore.

"So, why won't you be my doctor?"

Dad looked like he wanted to say something but tightened his lips. "Because Dr. Brooks is your doctor. Now, your brother and sister want to see you. I need to tell you that they might look different to you—maybe about ten years older—but you and I already know they're weird anyway." He chuckled.

"Can it just be you and me for a while, Papi? I don't want to see anyone but you. Tell me what happened, please."

"As I said, little-by-little. Too much stimulation will make you feel the way you did before Dr. Brooks calmed you down."

"He took care of me," I said. "But I thought he wanted to kill me."

Dad's face was worn, tired, and filled with sadness, but he wouldn't let it surface. I'd seen this look before on his face so many times because of his work. It frustrated my mom, my brother was too little to understand, and my sister was too worried about her grades to care. Not me, though. I would hug him and not say a word. I knew he needed to feel love, and I loved him more than anything in the world.

My dad was the best man for saving lives, and that's why I was going to go to med school. I wanted to grow up and work with him one day. I wanted to be his attending physician and learn from him. I wanted to be just like him.

I felt so strange. Part of me felt like a little girl who wanted her Papi, but I knew I wasn't little anymore. So why was I feeling this way? I just wanted my dad to help my sadness go away and smell the familiar fragrance of his Old Spice aftershave.

I just wanted—I didn't remember. What was I doing in here again?

CHAPTER THIRTY-FOUR
COLLIN

I was so thankful Elena was awake. Thank God that I'd managed to pull myself together in the last week or so because if I hadn't, I shudder at the thought of what my reaction would've been to her amnesia. She woke up disorientated, scared, and confused, having no clue who I was except for assuming I was trying to murder her, and in my previously fragile mental state, I don't know how I would've handled it. I can guaran-fucking-tee that I wouldn't have been able to keep it together as I did, though.

All of the medical staff in the room had seen our fair share of comatose patients, waking up as Elena had. Behind my surgeon's exterior was the heart of a man, watching the woman he loved suffering through Post Traumatic Amnesia.

By the next morning, we had a therapist and neurologist working with the family to prepare them for how to communicate with Elena. Another therapist worked alongside Miguel—who she wouldn't let out of her sight —trying to help Elena start to grasp what was happening and how to cope with visits from her family. Elena had lost ten years of her life, and seeing appearances changed wasn't the easiest thing to accept, amongst other issues she was trying to process.

I made my rounds early, and Elena was asleep when I checked on her. She was so beautiful, but I thanked God I was stacked in with surgeries today. My mind was in *doctor-mode*, and it was easier for me to cope with the fact that she'd forgotten us when I was in that mind frame, and I needed to be efficient, as her doctor, to ensure she was cleared to be moved to the recovery unit and out of ICU today.

I'd just walked out of my first surgery. I'd performed a spinal fusion that would work to stabilize my patient's spine after I removed a herniated disk. All went perfectly well, and I looked forward to seeing my patient when she woke and was ready to move forward with her life again.

After everything was settled, I scheduled a meeting between surgeries to meet with the neurologist who would be monitoring and working with Elena now that she was awake.

Dr. Marshall and I sat in the darkroom, studying Elena's most recent brain scans and comparing them with the first scans of her brain that were taken.

"Right here." I pointed to the hippocampus and temporal lobe areas of Elena's scans. "This is where the contrecoup took place, and the back of her brain hit her skull."

"That also caused the heart attack," he added. "This bruising—"

"It's likely the cause of her retrograde amnesia," I finished his sentence.

"From my assessment of her, she's showing signs of mild semantic memory loss."

"Yes. A bit episodic at times, too," I confirmed, having been in and out of her room all night, monitoring her condition. "She thought the nurses and I were there to kill her."

"A normal reaction after waking and dealing with this PTI she has," he added. "Did you calm her with medication?"

"An extremely low dose," I answered. "When she tried more than once to rip out her IVs, seeing her blood pressure on the rise, I didn't want to risk her stroking out."

"Very good. We'll keep her stabilized on that while we get her to start coming through this." He looked at me. "I know that you understand the situation you face with your fiancé; am I correct?"

I eyed him. I was the Chief of Neuro. Of course, I knew what I was fucking dealing with. I couldn't fault him for asking, though. I'd trudged around this place like the walking dead for a month. He was doing his job, and I would've done the same.

"I know that this will be an extremely long and hard process for both of us, but I am willing to do whatever it takes to help her retrieve her memories."

"Elena believed her brother to be a—"

"She had hallucinations, I'm aware," I said. "Stevie and I talked, and Miguel is doing a phenomenal job of informing the family about her current mindset."

"I also can see where the outbursts, agitations, and also the child-like behavior is present."

"Yes," I said. "I've heard of situations like this lasting anywhere from days to months; maybe the patient never recovers their memories."

"We need to continue to monitor, but I don't see where we'll need to administer medications or electrical stimulations currently."

"I'm glad that's your conclusion," I said, my arms folded. "I believe that if this is as severe as we think, her neurons will map around this damage if it's long term."

"We'll continue to monitor it, Dr. Brooks."

"Don't forget I have a goddamn brain tumor in there that I'm monitoring as well. It's not life-threatening, but I won't allow her recovery to be spent in this hospital under medications and knives if it's not necessary."

"That's not what I was saying."

"You didn't have to, Dr. Marshall. I'm informing you. We both know that she'll most likely spend time in rehab, and we will ensure that Elena is receiving proper care and that she works on her own to recover."

"This isn't as bad as the initial assessments led us to believe." He turned to face me after I flipped the lights on in the room again. "I'm going to tell you something, knowing your relationship with Elena." He eyed my stern expression. "You being a neuro chief or not, you will experience this all much differently than you might imagine. You, Dr. Brooks, must know that this will be a long, tiring road for her and those around her."

"I understand that. My only desire is that she remains comfortable and moving forward, Dr. Marshall. Thank you for your concern for me, but I'll manage."

"Then you'll be patient with her as she works through unnecessary outbursts, sudden rage fits, happy one minute—"

"Cussing me out the next? Acting like a teenager who's flirting with some doctor? Completely *not* the woman I fell in love with?" I said in response. "No, I'm wildly aware of the situation. When the woman I love woke up after three weeks of me begging her to, she woke up thinking I'd kidnapped her and wanted to kill her. I think I understand fully the road that is ahead of Elena and me at present."

"That there *is no* Elena and you at present?"

I smirked, pissed-off, but I got it. "Jesus Christ, are we this brutal with our patients?"

"We have to be, Collin," he said. "I'm so sorry she woke in this state, but I know you're strong, and I only hope that you're willing to continue to support her..." he stopped himself.

"Even if she hates me?" I finished his sentence.

"Well, she does ask where the sexy surgeon is." He chuckled. "So, there's that."

"Right," I smiled, "That's where it will be difficult, I assume. She'll enjoy my company for one minute and hate it for no reason the next."

"We have the support, even for you, for family members in situations with patients who are dealing with this PTI. It's not easy; trust me. You *will want* the support."

"I understand that," I said truthfully, rubbing the back of my neck. "Thanks for going over the scans with me."

Dr. Marshall and I went separate ways after we revisited everything. Miguel was saving mine and the staff's asses with Elena, who was altogether *not* herself, and the family needed to understand she may not be herself for a while.

So these would be three disastrous occurrences that I was forced to stomach in less than a month. Elena's accident, the loss of our child she knew nothing about, and now this. She was all over the map with her emotions—all while not remembering anything about our love or relationship.

"Jake," I said, seeing my best friend on the floor, checking on a patient who'd come in overnight after suffering a cardiac arrest and a stroke. The patient would be pronounced brain dead this afternoon, and Dr. Sharon would be the one to deliver the news for the family to pull Mr. Weston off life support when they were ready.

"Coll," he said, glancing up from his charts. He stopped and turned back to me, "You looked like hell ran you over again last night. Good thing you didn't let that shit get to you."

He was in chief surgeon mode, and it worked for me. I wasn't in the mood for emotions. I had to check Elena's vitals and release her from ICU and into the recovery room that'd been set up for her. I needed to have my head on straight.

"You realize she referred to me as demon-doctor, right?"

Jake sighed, and his lips twisted up. "Demon-doctor, huh? Last I heard you were the sexy surgeon."

"She'll be like this for a while. It's something, but it's a fucking life change for her." I ran my hand through my hair. "She won't be the same person we all remember."

"Miguel caught me up while you were in surgery first thing this morning," Jake said. "We've seen some crazy shit with brain injuries, and I've heard your stories, but I don't recall you ever dealing with a patient waking with memory loss like this."

"Elena will be my first one," I answered. "Miguel has dealt with his fair share of them, but the way she woke, that's what I typically see. Not this long term memory loss shit and certainly not with the woman I love."

"Can you swallow this?" he asked as if anything else was an option.

"What choice do I have?"

"True," he answered. "What about you and her? Does she know?"

"No. In speaking a bit with the therapist, I've decided it's probably not the best idea to drop the bomb on her that we were about to get married. She's got too much to process, and that's massive."

"Shit," Jake's hardened post-surgery face softened some. "I can't even imagine. You're not going through any of this alone, do you hear me?"

"We need to be there for her. The therapist said to do things that might stimulate her memories, but expect she may not respond to any of it." I chewed on the inside corner of my mouth. "Miguel says she's been asking to go home to their Beverly Hills place, and she threw a raging fit when she learned he'd rented the place out."

"Didn't you say something about the first time you went to their ranch? The way she loved that place?"

"You'd think she would've been all in, but it stacks up on all the changes she has to face. We're letting her in little-by-little, but fuck, even the little things are overwhelming to her."

"This is awful, man."

"More than." I glanced at his charts. "Sorry about the patient. Are you doing okay?" Jake hated losing patients more than anything in this world, but this was a hopeless case as soon they called Jake into the surgical room.

"You know me," he smirked. "I feel for the family when I know they're about to receive the worst news of their life."

"Yeah, I know." I clapped his arm. "Well, this conversation has been completely depressing. I guess I'll let you head down to your office and start your day now."

"I figured we might as well hang with Dr. Temple in the morgue and maybe do some autopsies after this fun run-in," Jake said with a grin.

"See you later, man."

"Hey, are you going to meet up with us tonight? It's Wednesday."

"Kinder's? I just might."

"I'll text you or catch up later. We'll talk this shit out when we're out of these fucking lab coats."

Jake and I parted ways, and I headed to the room of my unpredictable Elena. Once I walked in, the ice queen shot me a nasty glare, and Elena matched her sister's expression.

Here we go.

"Good morning, Elena," I said, glancing up at the monitors and seeing the feeding tube had been taken out, and she was good to go to the recovery room. "I see you've eaten some this morning."

"I see you're doing the job I was going to school to do," she said, her sister looking at me for a response.

I had no clue how Lydia could be such a bitch to me after all this, knowing the hell I was going through. Did she have a lump of coal for a heart inside that statuesque body of hers?

"I am?" I answered. "I remember you being thrilled to be hired on as the neuropsychiatrist here at Saint John's."

"Is that so?" she answered with animosity.

"That is so," I said, bringing my stethoscope to her chest.

"What are you doing?" she sighed in agitation.

"Quiet." I smiled at her, listening to the rhythm of her heart and checking the beats per minute. "There." I grinned and loved the hope I felt when I saw her cheeks turn that pink color when I smiled at her.

"There, what?" she gave me her flirty and feisty look.

"You *do* have a heart after all."

"Don't you think that's a little harsh?" Lydia said, rolling her eyes toward Elena, who laughed at my teasing.

"I think it's the truth. For all I know, Elena here hates me for—" I looked at her. "Why am I the bad guy this time?"

"You stole my job, asshole," she said, trying to be funny, but it was off-putting since Elena had never talked to me like this, and the tone she was using was one I wasn't familiar with.

"Ah," I maintained my composure. "I don't think I did. You didn't pursue neurosurgery as you once wanted to."

"Why's that? I always wanted to work with my dad. Now, he's *your* chief surgeon, and you get to work with him while I sit in this bed and go out of my mind."

"Well," I answered, prepping to leave, "I know you're learning, and you're still dealing with some confusion with all of this, but your dad retired to the ranch. Now, I'm the chief surgeon. So, I'm pretty sure you'd hate your job, knowing now that you'd be working for—"

"The demon-doctor," she laughed. "Listen, Dr. Brooks," she said in more of the voice that I cherished. "I'm sorry I said that about you, and I'm sorry for being mean. I'm just struggling."

"Elena, don't apologize. He knows," Lydia said, interrupting the first time I'd heard Elena speaking to me, sounding like *my Laney,* since her accident.

"You can apologize to me all day long, and I will never grow tired of it." I winked at her as she shrank down in her sister's domineering presence. "In fact, I might just ask your dad if I can make good on my idea of kissing you to make sure you know I'm not Dr. Death."

"I said that too?" she shook her head.

"It humored everyone in the room, trust me," I said. "All right, you are well on your way to recovery on the lower floor. Congratulations, Alvarez."

I said it out of habit. It was the first time her eyes locked with mine, and I swear, not even the ice queen herself could've interrupted our locked gazes.

"The way you said my name just now," she mused, her breath somewhat light with relief. "That sounds so familiar to me."

"It's because you wouldn't let me call you Elena when you first started working here."

"Why not?" she was curious, and I was walking a fine line.

"Well, because you were the most beautiful woman I'd ever met, and you knew I had a thing for you," I said. I stayed locked on her eyes that seemed to be begging me for more. "So, I called you Alvarez. Do you remember anything about that?"

"You liked me then?" she asked while ice queen glared at me.

"Does that frighten you?" I asked her.

"I just wish I could remember. You seem like you would be fun." She smiled so sweetly, and it took everything I could not to bring her close to me and hold her.

"We had fun times. We'll get back there again." I smiled. "You look just as beautiful today as the first time you insisted that I could only call you Dr. Alvarez."

She licked her lips and shrugged innocently in response to her sister's glare, and I could only laugh in response.

"Is that all, doctor? Little stimulation, remember?"

"Yes, ice queen," I said.

"Ice queen?" Elena laughed spontaneously with so much amusement, and it was music to my heartbroken soul.

"He loves calling me that as if I care what he thinks," Lydia said snidely. "Because I knew what was best for you with this one. As usual, you never listened to me."

I stood in silence, wondering what Elena's response would be.

"And what if I wanted him to kiss me?" Elena reverted to a more immature—fighting with her sister—demeanor.

"You see what you started?" Lydia snapped.

"I see that Elena's happy," I returned. "And that's the entire point in moving her rapidly on her road to recovery."

"When do we move her?"

"I'm going to call down to the floor now." I smiled at Elena as she watched me with a look of confusion on her face. "Elena, enjoy your ride down. I ensured you had the corner suite that overlooks the fountains. It's quite lovely."

"You'll still visit me there?"

"You're my patient. I'll make my rounds and discuss the therapy that is planned for you."

I turned to leave.

"Were we friends?" she asked before I drew back the privacy curtain.

My eyes closed. There was no way I was leaving the ice queen to answer this question. If Lydia had it her way, she'd probably influence every thought in Elena's head since she was at her most vulnerable point. I didn't necessarily think Lydia was evil, but her Type-A, control-freak personality preferred things to go the way she wanted them—and she made it clear months ago that she didn't like me. Lydia didn't graduate top of her Harvard Law class because she was an idiot. The woman knew exactly what she was doing, but as far as I was concerned, she could save all that shit for her law firm.

"You were one of the best friends I've ever had," I answered.

"Did we date?" she asked. The immaturity in her voice was gone, and a hint of the Elena I loved—albeit very confused—was present.

"We did." I nodded.

Her cheeks blushed, and I watched her inhale deeply.

Elena, we were in love. Why couldn't I just drop that on her?

"I'm happy you don't hate me for acting so weird, Dr. Brooks."

"You also used to call me Collin."

"Do you want me to call you that?"

"I want you to call me whatever you're comfortable with."

"Why can't anyone give me a straight, fucking answer?" Elena snapped.

The normal mood swings that I was prepared to deal with.

"What question do you want to be answered, Elena?" ice queen interjected, her voice livid.

"I don't know," she growled. "I don't fucking know."

"Keep your voice down, sweetie," Lydia said. "What do you want him to tell you?"

"I want to know why—"

"Why are you feeling something more with him?"

"Lydia," I said, stopping her. This truth bomb about Elena and me was mine to drop, not the bitch-sister's. Elena was already agitated; why toy with that nerve?"

"Why are you stopping her?" Elena seethed.

"Elena, little stimulation is best for you, especially now," I said, watching her carefully.

"You want to know if you had a relationship with this doctor, don't you?" Lydia pressed.

"Yes," Elena said, exasperated.

"Then, the answer is yes. You were in a relationship with him." Lydia smiled at me as if she'd claimed a victory. "You were going to get married, and all within three weeks of being together."

"Married?" Elena said, daggers in her eyes as she glared at me.

"It's probably something that you could have waited to find out. Your sister hasn't approved of me since—"

"You're both liars," Elena snapped, irrational and in a mood that I saw coming but didn't want to escalate by telling her bitch sister to shut the fuck up. "I would never date a doctor. I promised my dad."

"Lydia," I interjected before she could respond to Elena, "I need to speak with you, please."

"I'll sit with my sister as long as she wants me to and tell her whatever she wants to know."

"My God," Elena said. "Papi must've hated me."

I wanted to strangle Lydia for putting her disdain for me above Elena's well-being. Didn't she understand her sister had reverted to her twenty-year-old mindset and that all of us were slowly trying to catch her up to fucking speed that she was thirty-two years old now? That, of course, was a rhetorical question. She knew. The bitch just didn't care.

I had to stop this and scrub-in for surgery in thirty minutes.

"Miguel," I said, seeing the man outside the ICU room, talking with a group of physicians. "Jesus, you're a sight for sore eyes."

"Dr. Brooks," he pulled away from the group, "I was heading in to visit Elena."

"Yeah, well, Lydia is doing a great job of dropping bombs about mine and Elena's relationship. Bombs that I know she isn't prepared to find out about yet. God only knows what else is going on in that room. Elena has been released to recovery, and I have to get into surgery."

Miguel gripped my arm. "How did Elena respond to what Lydia told her?"

"She's acting as though she's on her way to spring break, college-style, with her responses. She wasn't ready to hear it. She already had some swift mood changes, and I couldn't settle Lydia down fast enough."

Miguel rubbed his forehead. "We're all going to get through this, son."

"We're going to have a shit-ton of work to get through if you don't stop your hot-shot lawyer in there from messing with Elena's mind. I get the woman hates my guts, but—"

Miguel smiled and nodded. "Go do your surgery," he said. "Are you okay after all that?"

"Just a little pissed."

"And you can work past that?"

"Yes."

He gripped my left hand. "This needs to come off before you scrub in," he said, pointing to the string-ring Elena had made for me when she proposed. "She may be off right now, Collin, but she's still with you. Don't worry about that." He smiled. "Now let me go unwind the disaster my eldest daughter is in there creating."

I knew it would be an even longer process now, and Elena's walls would be up at every turn. I had no idea what my next visit with her would bring, but I wasn't giving up or losing hope. Fuck that. She was my Elena. I was in this for the long run. Precisely one week from today, we were supposed to be reciting our vows. I didn't need those vows to know what *for better or for worse, in sickness and health* meant to me. I felt more love for her than ever before, and I would never abandon her.

CHAPTER THIRTY-FIVE
ELENA

I hated this damn walker, and I was about to throw the thing at my physical therapist if he kept encouraging me to accept it and treat it like it was my fucking *buddy*.

"I'm ready to do this without the stupid walker, Brian," I seethed with as much anger as I felt.

"So, three days of being out of bed, Miss Alvarez, and you think you've got this thing down to a science, eh?" he smirked at me.

I hated being mean to Brian. He was young and so super optimistic, which was the only way he could put up with me, fighting him since he introduced himself as my therapy guy. I felt bad for him too. He tore his ACL in college and lost his opportunity to be drafted by the NFL. Instead of stopping his life, he turned to help people in the same unfortunate and life-altering positions. I couldn't relate as much. I didn't feel like I'd lost out on my future with my head injury; I'd just lost out on whatever in the hell happened in the last ten years of my life.

The most frustrating part was hearing things about my life that made zero sense; the things I did and decisions I'd made that didn't seem anything like me. Number one on that list was moving back to Southern California to work at Saint John's as a neuropsychiatrist and not the surgeon I'd planned to be since I was a little girl. I didn't care how anyone tried to explain it to me. I couldn't comprehend that abrupt decision change. It was always a dream of mine to grow up and work with my dad.

"Son of a bitch," I said, my right toe tripping on the carpet.

"Lift that leg, girlfriend," Brian said, and I glared at him in response.

"Easy for you to say, asshole," I snapped.

"I see that's your favorite name for anyone who is trying to encourage you," Brian said, his hand on my back as I steadied myself with this stupid walker.

"Please, don't touch me," I tried to say as nicely as I could.

"Hey," Brian became sterner like he always was when my mood was nasty. "You're the one who said you want to get out of this hospital and stop smelling all those beautiful flowers in your room. This is how we get you out."

"By using this fucking walker?" I grumbled.

"Well, if it isn't the resident foul-mouth of the recovery unit," the sexy voice of Dr. Brooks said.

I looked up and loved being caught like this, lost in his eyes and smile. This man was rehab bottled up in one beautiful body. Though, since I was brought down here and he'd visited me, I sometimes cussed him out for no reason too. I hated that because I really loved it when he was around me.

Apparently, I'd always liked him around, but the accident stripped me of those memories, another frustration about my past that didn't make sense, but I was okay with that one. He was the finest man I'd ever seen, and he and I were an item. Too bad I couldn't remember any of it.

"She's just mad at me because we're doing exercises with her favorite buddy here." Brian smiled at Dr. Brooks.

"How many times do I have to tell you that this thing isn't my *buddy*," I snapped.

"What would you like to call it, Elena? Yesterday, you were fine with it," Brian said patiently.

"I don't want to call it anything. I want it gone," I said.

"Then let's get those legs walking. Care to take a walk with us, Dr. Brooks?"

He looked at Brian. "If you think it might help, why don't we try it without the walker? I think Elena will do great holding onto my arm."

"Stop talking about me like I'm not here, goddamn it."

Jesus. Why couldn't I turn off my frustration as fast as it turned on?

"Give it a try. Careful, though, Dr. Brooks. This patient bites," Brian teased.

I rolled my eyes and reached out to Collin's hands. "I'm stronger with my left side. I'll hold onto to your right arm," I informed him.

He slid a hand behind my back and took my left wrist in his. Shivers shot through me like an electric current, having him touching me like this.

"Let's get you steady," he said as I stared at his perfect hands.

"You have beautiful hands," I told him.

"We've got this, Brian. When is her curfew?" he said in that teasing voice I was attracted to.

"She's in the surgeon's care," Brian smiled. "If she gets tired, then page me, and I'll get the wheelchair down here."

"Oh, God," I sighed. "I just—"

"I'll get her back to the room, even if I carry her myself," Dr. Brooks said, and his eyes seemed to be doing that searching thing with mine again.

"Thanks, Brian," I managed.

"You two enjoy your walk, and try not to cuss out the others on the floor." Brian winked at me and left me in the care of the man who always made me excited when he came to visit me.

"So," I said as he walked carefully, allowing me to move for the first time without the walker. "You would carry me..."

Left leg, right leg, I thought, feeling a bit stronger with this hot doctor holding onto me.

"Without hesitation," he said. "Looking good." He praised me as I managed to get one foot—very slowly—in front of the other.

"But what about wrinkling your nice suit?" I said, focusing on putting one foot in front of the other. God, my legs felt so weak.

Don't get pissed, I thought, knowing I'd finally calmed myself down.

"Well, I'm off for the day, and that's why I have them pressed," he answered.

I looked up at him and smiled. "So, you and me, huh?"

That's when I saw the most beautiful features soften on his perfect face. "You and me. The couple everyone envied," he said with a wink.

"Come on. We only knew each other for three weeks, though."

"Hey, man. You fell hard for me, what can I say? I can hardly blame you." He laughed.

"Is that true? It was all me, acting dumb?"

Sort of like I was acting now when I drooled over the man.

"Don't worry. Do you recall me saying that you wouldn't let me call you by your first name? I was the one in hot pursuit of the beautiful Elena Alvarez." He chuckled.

"Oh, right," I laughed. "I don't understand why I would be mean like that to you. I'm sorry about that. I guess I still don't understand a lot of things about my last ten years, either."

"I don't blame you for being confused about what's happened in the last ten years. Our experiences shape us and lead us in different directions, and you can't remember those, so where you ended up seems strange. You'll get there, though." He steadied me as I tripped. "At least now you allow me to call you Elena."

"Did we have sex?" I asked when he had me stop to rest and let me hold onto him after I tripped.

Shit, why do I keep blurting out these fucking things? I hate this.

Dr. Brooks didn't seem to let it affect him. In fact, his face was more beautiful now than I'd ever seen it, and it almost seemed like he was holding onto *me,* so he didn't trip the second I asked that incredibly personal question.

"Um," he pinched his lips together.

I laughed, which made him laugh, and I loved it.

"So, Dr. Brooks," I said. "Did I enjoy it?"

"Elena," he tried to maintain his composure and then turn to help me start walking again. "Perhaps, this is a conversation that should wait."

That pissed me the fuck off.

"I hate nothing more than when I ask about things I've forgotten, and everyone tells me I need to wait." I glared at him.

"Okay, then," he said, lifting his chin, with his arm around my back and gripping my waist. "Did we have sex?"

"Did we?"

"The best sex ever," he answered while he gave me a teasing look. "You, Elena Alvarez, couldn't get enough of me."

"So, I enjoyed it." I blushed and laughed. "Do you think we'll have all that back?"

"It's my greatest hope," he answered. "So, now that you know we had sex, and you loved every single second of it," he eyed me, and I knew the look—he was feeling out my emotions again, "what else would you like to know?"

"People knew about us?"

"I made sure of it. You were hesitant to let everyone know at first, but I knew how gossip ran in this hospital and didn't want to give them shit to say about us."

"Was I the only girl you had here?"

He frowned. "What do you mean? Did I cheat on you?"

"No," I smiled. "Like, were there other girls before me? I see the way they all look at you."

"Remember being upset because you promised your dad that you wouldn't date a doctor?" he asked.

"So much for keeping that promise."

"Well, I made a promise to myself not to have anything to do with doctors or hospital staff too," he said. His thumb rubbed my wrist, and I liked it—all of my body that had been numb since waking up after a three-week coma liked it. "I broke my own rules the second I laid eyes on you."

I was getting tired and was no longer in the mood to hear about something I forgot. *The other Elena*—I started referring to the Elena I used to be and knew nothing about now. That bitch had ten years of making decisions and living life—and having this man to herself. My therapist said these feelings were normal, though they felt far from that. Who would split their personality like this on their own?

"Are you still with me?" he asked. "The answer is no, Elena, there was no other woman for me but you."

It was beautiful coming out of his mouth, but my brain felt overloaded and wasn't accepting it. "Quit talking about *her*. I'm not *her* anymore, Dr. Brooks." I started crying, which I did a lot since I'd woken up. Crying, cussing, and acting horribly to people, and I couldn't control it. We stopped, and he turned me to face him. "I know that I may never be that Elena you loved again. She's not here."

His piercing blue eyes swallowed me up, and I was swimming in them. "I will be here, and I will wait for you to remember us for eternity if I have to," he said in the sincerest voice that I'd ever heard him use. "I will wait, and we will go through this together. Hell," he smiled, "we are going through this together as we speak."

"What if I'm never *her* again? You fell in love with a woman that I don't know. She makes no sense to me," I said.

He touched my face, and I felt like I was going to pass out. "I fell in love with *you*, Alvarez, every part of you, even if you like to be a little rougher around the edges with people these days. You have to understand that I will do everything to help you fight to get your life back."

"I love to hear you say that," I said. "But I'm not sure…"

"Why don't we talk about something else?" he said. This guy must've been a genius doctor with superhero hearing because my heart was racing, and my head was spinning. All of the good feelings I was having were being twisted into everything negative.

"Good afternoon, Dr. Brooks. It's great to see you," a beautiful woman my age said.

She wore scrubs, and I watched her blush when Collin smiled at her.

"How's it going, Dr. Solano?" he asked her. "Your patient looks great."

"You did an amazing job with the fusion of her spine. We're all in awe of your work," Dr. Solano said while Collin readjusted me to hold me into position. He must've felt me coming off balance as my rage built from this woman and him talking.

"I'm glad the surgery went as we all expected."

"How are you, Elena?" she asked me with a smile that seemed fake.

I forced a smile. "I'm fine," I said.

Her eyes met Collin's, and it showed me that the woman acted as though I'd cussed her out. I looked at Collin, and his expression was the concerned, thinking one he made when I said something that seemed to upset him.

"Have a good day, doctor," she said to Collin first, and then she looked at me. "Have a good day, Elena."

"What the fuck was that?" I asked Collin as the woman walked away.

"That was me conversing with a neurologist," he said. "I performed surgery on her patient. She's checking on them after they were cleared for recovery over here."

"Did you have sex with her too?" I lashed out.

"Elena," he looked at me, and it appeared the perfect and happy doctor was caught. "You need to try and think of other things. We had a beautiful—"

"No," I said, trying to walk toward the wall. "Let me go, and I'll walk back to my room. You're a liar."

"Elena," he said, working on getting me to the wall safely. "I understand a lot of this is frustrating, but there is one thing I will *not* do, and that is lie to you. That woman is a co-worker, a doctor, and a professional."

"I saw the way she looked at you."

"I saw it too," he said, his voice leveling my behavior. "She was behaving naturally for a doctor who is grateful that their patient is recovering well."

"You both looked at each other weird, and I didn't like it."

"I have no idea what you saw in that exchange," he said. "But you'll find that most of these professionals knew you and know what you're going through. They also know that you're the love of my life. That's it."

"I want to go back to my room," I said.

"Then let's walk," he was stern and using that doctor's voice on me. This time it wasn't working.

As we turned back, there she was again. "I think I hate her," I said.

"You don't mean that, Elena. Please relax."

"Don't tell me what to fucking do," I said to him. "Don't touch me."

"I will be holding you until I get you back into your room, Laney," he said, and I heard the sorrow in his voice. "Let's go."

"Dr. Mitchell," I called out to my heart doctor—and the man I heard was Collin's best friend—when I saw him down the hall. "He can walk me back."

"You know what the therapist says about this behavior," Dr. Brooks said.

"It's irrational, and I don't care," I said. "Dr. Mitchell!"

"Laney, Coll," he said with a bright smile as he approached. The dark-haired man was as handsome as Collin. Both men wore short and messy haircuts that were so attractive. I had to stop thinking like this. Dr. Mitchell was married, and apparently, his wife was supposed to be in my wedding. I wanted to make Collin feel jealous, the way I felt about that woman just now, and nothing was changing my mind.

Oh my God, I hated myself right now. I started crying again and crumbled into Collin, who was there to catch me. "Why am I like this?" I sobbed into his suit.

"Because you were injured," he said.

"Is everything okay?" I heard Dr. Mitchell say. "Ash is here with John, but maybe it's not a good time."

I sobbed more, knowing I'd ruined my chance to meet Dr. Mitchell's wife and son, who I was told I adored. I couldn't do anything but repeat the words *I'm sorry* over and over again.

"Don't apologize," Jake said. "We all are working through this. You can meet Ash and John tomorrow."

"Please don't send them away because I'm like this," I said, trying to dry my tears.

"No one is sending anyone away. Ash was fully aware that it might not be an ideal time, and that's okay. No one wants you to feel rushed. I'm going to go and tell her," Jake said reassuringly while he smiled at me and Collin in understanding before heading down the hall.

"Don't worry about anything. You did well with your walking. A lot of stimulation can cause this, babe—I mean, Elena," Collin stumbled over his words.

He'd called me babe before. I don't recall exactly when, but I cussed him out for it. This time it was soothing, and I loved it. I loved being in his arms.

"I love to hear you call me that."

I felt him chuckle. "Yeah, you were condemning me to hell for it slipping out of my mouth last night."

"I hate this."

"Stop talking like that, Laney," he said. "Stop fighting your emotions. It would be best if you let them in. I'm prepared for it all as best I can be."

"I love the way you smell." I inhaled deeply of his crisp cologne that made the hair stand up on my skin in a good way. It was a masculine scent with a hint of the tropics.

"You always have," he said. "And I love the way you smell."

"I want you to stay with me tonight," I said, oddly feeling secure with him for the first time.

"You had the chair that I fell asleep in last night taken away." He laughed. "I can have someone try to find it."

"Wow, I'm horrible."

"You're a survivor, Elena," he said. "You've survived a horrific traumatic head injury. You're dealing with that outcome now."

"I don't feel like a survivor," I said.

"Of course, you don't, but that's natural. You must try to fight the feeling of being defeated, and if you can't fight it, you need to accept it, conquer it, and move forward.

"Stay with me," I said when we'd reached my room, and he laid me in my bed.

"I have to visit another patient. Your sister is on her way." I looked at the clock. "You know you love her visits."

"When the hospital is quiet, I'm scared," I said strangely, almost in the voice of a five-year-old.

"Baby," he instantly reacted and took my hand, "have you told anyone you feel this way?" It didn't bother me to hear him call me baby.

"No," I said. "I just want to go home to the ranch now."

"Then," he smiled at me, his eyes glistening, "let's bust ass to get you moving and out of here. I'll get you home. Do you trust I'll help you?"

"I think I do."

He smiled. "I'll let everyone know that it's time we get you home. I'll stay with you, or at least close by, when the hospital gets quiet. I don't want you to be scared."

"Okay," I said, feeling sleepy like I did after I worked my mind up.

"Close your eyes. Think about how much you love flamingos," he said, and I smiled.

"I love dancing," I said, remembering that was my favorite thing about Florida.

"Then think about dancing," he said. "Just let your mind be calm."

"Don't let them give me that medicine."

I felt his hand on my wrist. "Your heart rate doesn't require it. You're doing fine, and I will stay after it gets dark and quiet."

I felt like I'd been drugged, but Collin was so peaceful and serene, and my mind was in love with these feelings. I felt him kiss my hand before I drifted off to sleep to the images of me, salsa dancing on the beach with my friends in Miami.

It was so crazy how my mind could get fired up into a frenzy, and then I would crash hard, and I was so tired I could hardly move. Thank God that Collin agreed to stay with me. He would be my comfort in these storms, but what if I woke up to hate him again? I wanted these mood swings gone so bad that it hurt, and it made me suddenly frightened of the dark and quiet nights.

CHAPTER THIRTY-SIX
COLLIN

*E*lena worked her ass off in the recovery unit, and I was pleased to see her physically progressing at the rate she was. Her mental state and recovery were not as advanced as her physical progression, though.

On numerous occasions, I had sat in with Elena and her family as the therapist worked to help everyone understand that we had to be patient with her as she dealt with the fallout of a brain injury. It was surreal for me, a neurosurgeon and neuroscientist, to be on this side of the fence. It was usually Elena and me, sitting on the other side of the table and consulting families in this situation.

I'd had a pretty immense amount of guilt since I'd been on the receiving end of this amount of trauma. As a neurosurgeon, my job was to fix the injury and move the family forward with a neuropsychiatrist at my side to help them cope with the outcomes. I know for a fact that I wasn't an asshole of a surgeon, and I cared about my patients deeply, but I also had to detach from patients as well. It's why I had the therapists and neuropsychiatrists. This is where they filled that gap so I could take on my next surgery. Now that the shoe was on the other foot, I realized how much more painful this experience was, and it made me wish I'd handled a few people a bit more carefully.

"I heard Elena is being released to go home tomorrow?" Jim asked after he and Avery had shown up to visit Laney.

Elena was more mentally stable but was still uncensored at times. Still, she wanted to meet the people who she'd been told were *our friends*. She wanted to meet their children and hear the stories of them clinging to her like she was Minnie Mouse.

Knowing Elena's brazen mood swings were still an issue, I asked her therapist to be present when the kids were around her because the kids didn't quite grasp the severity of Elena's injuries.

Ash was pretty much a therapist on her own. That woman managed to bring zen into the room when she visited, and little John made Laney laugh nonstop when they showed up for a couple of visits this week.

Addison, Jim and Avery's daughter, being only five years old, was hesitant at first, but once Laney started asking her questions about surfing with Jim, Addison opened up. Avery acted very casually, and once the conversations started rolling, Elena was fully engrossed. She was especially interested in learning about Avery and Jim's wedding once Avery told her about the hula dancing.

Jim and I stood outside of the room as Jim informed me about a deal for my dad's company that needed my final approval. I didn't give a shit about what the company took on, and Jim knew it. So long as Alex was in control, I was all-in. Ever since I allowed Mitchell and Associates to take over, I trusted Alex's decision-making entirely.

"Hey," Jim chuckled, "you with me?"

"Sorry," I looked away from where I watched the sweet sight of Addison, sitting on the bed, showing Elena something from her mom's phone. "Miguel confirmed the ranch is set up and ready for her."

"Are you planning on bringing her to your place in Malibu? What's the deal with her condo?" Jim asked.

"Well, you know I've been staying there. Before the accident, Elena and I were living out of both houses together," I answered and looked back to Jim. "I've told her a little about our living arrangements, and she didn't seem to want to hear about it, so I let the conversation die. The therapist said she'd ask when she was ready. So, I just sort of go with the flow now," I said as Jake walked up.

"Hey, Jim," Jake said as he approached. "You need to see this shit. It's bugging the hell out of me, but the whole remodel of this wing is going to hell."

"Can it wait?" Jim half-laughed.

"No," Jake smirked. "While I have you here, I want you to see it with your own eyes."

"What the hell is going on?" I asked.

"Let's just say they're overdoing my cardiac floor, and pink and gold aren't going to fly," Jake said with an eye roll. "I'm not approving this princess remodel."

"You're way too damn picky," I laughed.

Jake looked at Jim. "Just come look at this shit, and give me your opinion. If you were recovering in the new heart facility, would you like to feel as though you were moved into a cartoon version of a princess castle?"

"Go," I said. "That heart center opens up next month, and we can't have the chief heart surgeon spiraling out of control before his *baby* opens up."

"*Fuck you, too*," Jake mouthed, making me smile.

The guys walked off, and as I turned back to walk into Elena's room, I heard Addison crying. Elena was sobbing and saying she was sorry over and over again—as she always did when something slipped out, and she immediately felt remorse for it.

What the hell happened? I thought, walking briskly up the hall toward the open door of her room. Addison met me first, crying for Jim but settling for me. I knelt and brought the five-year-old into my arms, looking up to see Avery crying with Elena and trying to calm her down.

"Uncle Collin," she said, her voice muffled in the scrubs I was wearing.

"What's wrong, munchkin?" I said, using the nickname I always called Addy.

"I'm so scared. I'm so sorry."

I held her tight. "Why are you sorry and scared?"

"Your baby is dead. Mommy's baby can die too." She pulled away, and tears streamed down her face that I instinctively brought my hands up to hold. "Laney said she killed your baby."

My mind was reeling. Thank God Avery was holding it together with Elena while I had Addy out here. Where was the goddamn therapist who usually sat in there in case Elena switched gears and blurted out something like this? Dear God, who told her about the miscarriage? She wasn't ready for that yet, and even the therapist confirmed it.

"Addy," I brushed her tears from her cheeks with my thumbs and held her face for her sad blue eyes to look at mine. "Your mommy's baby won't die. That baby is nice and safe in your mommy's tummy, just like you were before you were born."

"Why did Laney say mommy's baby can die?" she said through quivering lips. It ripped my heart out to see this naturally vibrant child so broken. "Your baby died, uncle Collin."

"Listen, sweetheart," I said, trying to comfort her, "remember how we talked that Laney was hurt in a bad accident?"

She nodded, and I nodded with her. "We also talked about her not being able to remember a lot of things and about how sometimes she says things that she doesn't mean."

"Are you sad?" she asked.

I would've naturally been angry that someone would say such things to upset a little girl, but Laney had no ability to restrain herself. It was messed up on every level.

"I understand that it wasn't time for me and Laney to have a baby yet," I said. "You shouldn't worry yourself over these things, sweet Addy."

She sniffed. "Laney said your daughter died."

Good God, I thought.

"Yes, our baby daughter died in Laney's accident, but she has angel wings now, and that makes me *very happy*," I said. "I don't think of her as dead; I think she is an angel who watches over all of us now."

Addison smiled, thank God. "She protects us and her mommy, who is hurt."

"Exactly."

"And mommy's baby won't die?" She eyed me as I heard Jim and Jake's approach behind me.

"Nope," I said in a voice I always used with Addy. "That baby is nice and safe in your mommy's tummy. I think Laney might have said something that she didn't mean, just like we talked about before. Don't you?"

"Yeah," Addison said, then she looked up and saw Jim. "Dad, Uncle Collin's baby is an angel."

I rose when Jim gathered Addison up in his arms and held her. I looked at Jake and Jim, and all I could do was shake my head.

"I need to get in there with Elena," I said. I bit my lip, my anger growing that the therapist in that room allowed this to happen. "She must've found out about the miscarriage and said something in there. Addison is now aware that mine and Laney's daughter is an angel who watches over all of us." I eyed both men's confused expressions.

"Yes." Addison looked at me as if to inform me of that being a fact.

"Let me get in there. Avery looks pretty shaken up, and I don't want all of us to rush the room."

"You got this?" Jake asked while Jim nodded.

"Yeah," I turned and walked toward the door.

When I made it to the doorway, Holly, the therapist—who was supposed to be in the room for Elena's support—rushed past me into the room again, slipping her phone into her pocket.

"Come here, Av." I held an arm out to my friend's sobbing wife, who met me at the doorway while Elena—who was upset and crying—reached out for Holly, who she'd grown attached to recently.

All I knew was that Holly had better have a good fucking reason to have been out of this room while Avery and Addison were visiting. If she were taking a personal call, I would lose my shit.

"You okay?" I asked Avery, who'd hugged me, pulled back, and wiped her tears away. She and I looked into the room, watching Holly comfort Elena. "I had no idea she knew about the miscarriage, or I wouldn't have let Addison talk about her having a surprise baby brother or sister coming. We went from talking about the wedding, dancing, and laughing, to Addy saying I surprised Jim and her about the baby…" Avery started crying again. "Then Addy just went off about the baby, and poor Laney started crying and then told Addy that her baby died, and if I wasn't careful…" she trailed off.

"Jesus Christ," I said, pulling Avery back in for a hug. "I'm so sorry about this."

"No," Avery stepped back, "I am. I didn't know Elena knew."

"I didn't either. We all agreed she wasn't ready to know yet." I said. "I talked to Addy, and I think she'll be okay."

"We're all good here," Jim said as he approached with Addy in his arms.

"Thank God." Avery looked into the room again. Elena was sobbing, and the therapist who'd bailed on her ass was rubbing her back, trying to soothe her. "What about Laney?" She looked at me. "Coll, I'm serious. I'm so sorry about this."

"So long as you're okay and understand Laney is still struggling, that's all I need from you, Avery," I said.

"No, I get it," she said. "This whole fucking thing breaks my heart for you both. I can tell she's just wading through the darkness, trying so hard to find herself again. I can't imagine the suffering that comes along with it."

"We're going to get through it, sis," I said.

"Love you, Coll, both of you."

"Go, make sure Addy is okay," I said. "Let me see if I can talk to Laney."

I walked slowly into the room.

Holly's guilt-ridden eyes met mine. "Collin," she said.

"I hope that was an emergency call you were taking while this happened," I said, looking at the panic in her eyes. "While I appreciate all of your help in Elena's recovery, there was only ever *one* specific request, and that was not to leave her when the kids were visiting."

"I understand," she said, and then she looked to my crying and broken Elena. "Dr. Brooks is here, Elena. He always puts that smile on your face that we love so much."

"No," she growled. "I can't. I don't want to see anyone. I'm awful."

"Elena," I said, rubbing her back. "Baby, look at me."

The babe and baby thing seemed to work magic on her about fifty percent of the time, but when she went into hysterics, it was over.

"I can't," she said. "I'm sorry."

"I'll calm her down," Holly said. "I'll give her some medication to help her relax."

"We're tapering off of that," I said as calmly as I could. "Half the dose. It's what she requests, and her family approved."

"I understand."

"Call me when she's calm. Someone took it upon themselves to deliver information that we all know Elena wasn't ready to hear."

"I'm sorry, Dr. Brooks. I'll make sure she's okay."

I walked out of the room, closing the door behind me to give Elena privacy. I wanted to speak to the person in charge of these therapists immediately because this was bullshit, but I knew I was angry. I had to trust that the therapist—who Elena loved—would calm her and make this right in Elena's mind in my absence.

I ran both hands through my hair and closed my eyes, letting a large breath of air out and calming my mind.

"Coll," I heard Jake. "What the hell happened?"

"Someone told Elena about the miscarriage. You were standing there when I told Jim," I said, so pissed about this that I was taking it out on Jake when he was only trying to start the conversation.

"Fucking unreal."

"How's Addison?" I asked.

"Sitting over there with Jim and Av. We thought we'd go grab dinner, and we thought it might be a good idea if you came along." He shrugged.

"If I find out it was Lydia who told Elena, I might strangle that woman," I said, surer of that than anything else in this world.

"Collin," Lydia's voice said.

"Wow. It's as if I summoned the ice queen myself," I said, eyes wide and turning to her.

"It was Steve," Lydia said, quieting the anger in me with the sorrow I heard in her voice. "Dr. Mitchell, do you mind if I speak with Collin alone?"

"Good to see you, Lydia," he said in his professional voice.

"Why?" I snapped.

I narrowed my eyes at her sad ones. This was *not* the Lydia I knew. She was actually showing emotion and not shooting daggers out of her eyes.

"What happened in there? All I heard was that she's inconsolable right now," Lydia asked.

"The therapist took off while that sweet little girl was visiting Elena." I pointed back to where Jim, Avery, and Jake waited for me. "Elena unloaded on her about our *dead baby*, unfiltered-style."

"Dear God," Lydia said, rubbing her hands together. "Collin, I have to apologize to you. For everything."

"Come again?" I couldn't believe my ears. What fucking episode of the Twilight Zone was I in now?

"I'm sorry for the way I've been treating you." She sighed. "And I'm sorry my brother told Laney something critical that was between you and her. All of it. I've watched you care for my sister so beautifully since her accident. You've proven that you don't deserve my scrutiny." It was evident that I was looking into the eyes of a woman who *rarely* apologized for anything. If she weren't so genuine and vulnerable because of her sister, the words would've probably made her uncomfortable. "I am a big enough person to admit when I am wrong—which isn't often, by the way, I assure you," she said with a confident arch of her eyebrow. "However, I will admit that I was wrong about my assumptions."

"Well, Lydia," I said, pretty fucking astonished that this exchange was taking place. "Thank you for that."

"I'm serious. You're a remarkable man, and you've been with us every step of the way. To deal with all of this...I'm so sorry. I love my sister more than anyone in the world, and I don't want to be your enemy," she said.

"Well, who am I supposed to take out my frustration on if you and I start getting along?" I subtly smiled at her, still utterly baffled *this* was even happening.

She reached out and ran her hand on my arm in a careful yet earnest way. "I want you to know I'm here for you—just like you've been here for us. In all of this. I'm here for you and Laney."

"I do appreciate that," I said.

"You can still call me the ice queen if you'd like. Nothing wrong with being a queen." She flashed me a humorous smile—one that I wasn't even sure she had the capability of mustering until now. "Can I talk to the girl?"

"I handled her the best I could after Laney told her that her mom's baby might die too."

Lydia looked past me and closed her eyes. "All of this is so unbearable at times. To hear things like that—it's so unlike Elena. It's a brutal reminder of the loss of personality that we're struggling with." She started to tear up.

"I know. If anyone gets that brutal reminder, it's me, but she's got tremendous support from all of you," I said. "I have to say that I don't understand why Stevie would let that slip. Why would he tell her that?"

"He's not handling this well at all, Collin. Laney was Stevie's lifeline— his anchor. She always has been," she said. "I'm sure you've noticed that she's the only one he listens to. Papi lets the kid walk all over him, and I— well, let's agree that I don't have the patience for his frivolousness."

"You don't say?" I teased, having the first open and honest discussion with this woman.

She raised her eyebrows to confirm that she wasn't sorry about the facts she'd laid down. "We're all very different. Laney was always the perfect balance to all of our personalities. Where I'm driven to be in control, following the rules and the letter of the law, she's wild and free and goes jumping from planes and waterfalls. Where Steve is lazy and unmotivated, she knows exactly what she wants and has goals to get there. It's hard for us to fit without her, and we're trying, but it takes its toll on our family dynamic as well, as strange as that sounds."

"It doesn't sound strange at all," I said. Lydia was right. The family needed to learn how to function with Elena's personality change too. Elena had been the glue that kept them all together—she was the magnet they were all attracted to the way she'd attracted everyone else who knew her. And now, she was different, and that left a void in their lives and relationships with one another.

"Papi won't allow Stevie around her again until he can figure out how to work with all of this. When Stevie came home crying and telling us he accidentally told Elena about the miscarriage, I came straight here, and Papi lost it on him."

"It's hard on all of us and in different ways. I'll talk to the kid," I said.

"You don't have to do that. He's not your responsibility," Lydia said.

"Yeah," I ran my bottom lip between my teeth, "but I made a promise to Elena that we'd get him on the right path. He's part of my promise to help her."

"After what he did, you're willing to do that?" she questioned me.

"I love Elena, and although she's forgotten our history, I haven't. Steve was part of that. I can't help but be sorry for him. We'll repair the damage that's been done with Laney losing the baby."

"Uncle Collin," I heard Addison say from behind me, "why is Laney's sister so sad?"

Lydia took over for this abrupt subject change as my friends came up after Addison had most likely broken loose and rushed over to me. Now, here we all were—the dysfunctional unit of people outside of Elena's room.

"Hey, there." Lydia knelt, and I watched in admiration as Elena's oldest sister spoke to Addison. "I want to make sure you're happy, little blue eyes."

"I'm sad for Uncle Collin," Addy said. "Laney is very sad too. Their baby died but has angel wings now."

"That's right," Lydia smiled, flashing a look that resembled one of Elena's expressions. "And what a beautiful and wonderful thing to learn today. I didn't know she had angel wings until you just told me."

"Yes," Addison said. I choked back my emotions, knowing that my Laney was in that room without me, dealing with the loss of her child after not even knowing she'd been pregnant. "She flies with the butterflies in the children's garden."

"I heard about that," Lydia said. "I will go to visit it soon. I want you to know everything will be perfectly fine, and Laney will be happy to know her baby has angel wings now too."

Jim was studying Lydia with his no-bullshit, CEO face, Avery wiped away her pooling tears, and Jake most likely had the same shocked into silence expression I had.

"Laney is tired," Addison informed Lydia. "Do you want me to take you to the butterflies?"

"Addy," Avery interjected as she looked at Lydia, "I'm sorry. She's sort of processing it right now."

Lydia smiled up at Avery warmly, looking like an entirely different woman from the one I'd grown to loathe. "Would you all mind if I went with her to see the butterflies?"

"Collin," Lydia smiled at me, "have you been there?"

"Only to ensure the plaque faced the fountains."

"Why don't we go together?" she rose and placed her hand on my back, and I had to rewire my brain not to shiver at the gesture.

"We'll meet you guys down there," Jake said.

Lydia pulled back. "I know this has got to be painful for you, losing Laney as you have. What you've done for your baby is a lovely thing, and I *know* if she'd woken up with her memories, she would have loved what you did."

"I'm happy to know that," I said, still a bit indifferent to the loss of our child and knowing it was a subject I had to bury until Elena got her bearings again.

She smiled at me, "Let's go see her together."

"Did your dad kick your ass or something?" I smirked at her while we started walking toward the pediatric area of the hospital. "This is completely unexpected."

"I've still got my eyes on you, Dr. Brooks," she smiled at me. "Don't let me catch you slippin' because you know big sister is always watching."

"Oh, I don't doubt that." I smiled. "Well, this has been the most eventful visit of them all."

She laughed. "She's put you through hell, and most guys would've taken off on that fact alone. But you stayed, and you won't give up. I admire that tenacity."

"I love that woman more than life itself," I said.

"And if she doesn't return to the woman you fell in love with?"

"Then, I will fall in love with her all over again." I looked over at Lydia. "Nothing wrong with falling in love over and over again, is there?"

"Even if you're the *asshole* who cheated on her?"

"You heard about that one, eh?" I smiled. "God, I think I've officially *cheated on her* with everyone, including the gardeners."

Lydia laughed and nudged me playfully. "You're all right, Collin Brooks. I'll take you as my brother any day."

"Well, outside of me thinking you're high," I eyed her with a smile, "I'll gladly accept the gesture."

"We're all going to get through this. Papi already said that you're part of our family, and we want you to know that."

"Thanks, Lydia."

"That does sound weird, doesn't it?" she chuckled.

"You prefer ice queen?" I looked over at her as we walked into the elevators behind Jake, Avery, Jim, and Addison. "It does suit you, being a hot-shot lawyer and all."

She laughed. "Damn right."

I was grateful that Lydia was on my side but torn by the fact that I was leaving Elena in the arms of Holly when she needed me most—but she didn't want me for this, and that hurt like a mother fucker. She needed things to happen at her pace.

If I was honest, coming down to the gardens to see the plaque was not something I'd planned on doing unless Elena wanted me to go with her. Addison seemed to love all of the serenity and beauty that Saint John's had created in this lovely garden. They'd managed to create a whimsical world that felt enchanting. I'd expected I would be a bit traumatized by facing this whole thing, but I wasn't. However, I felt my lungs constrict when I saw the etching of the butterfly on the plaque. It was a reminder of something Elena had drawn, and I would never know what her thoughts were that day she went home and cried when she first learned she was pregnant.

She was crying now as I left her room and came down here with everyone. I couldn't hold her. When she went into these fits, it always seemed to take a therapist to calm her down. It tore my soul in half to know that she was hurting, and I couldn't be there for her.

Addison gleefully played with Jim and Jake as Lydia and Avery started to open up to each other, and I started to feel like I was suffocating. I had to get the fuck out of here. It was all finally starting to hit me, even though nothing had really happened to set it off.

"I'm going to take off," I said, my voice unexpectedly hoarse. "Lydia, I'll stop by the ranch tomorrow after work." I couldn't control how weird I sounded.

"Are you okay?" she asked, her and Avery looking at me as if I'd suddenly turned into the madman I felt I was.

"I need to get out of here for a while," I said truthfully.

"I was just inviting—"

"Seriously," I cut off Avery. "I have to bounce."

With that, I took off out of there like demons were chasing me.

"Collin!" Jake shouted after me by the time I'd gone into a sprint after the front doors of the hospital had turned me loose. "Fuck, man," he said, on my heels.

"Stop, Jake, I have to get the hell out of here."

Jake grabbed my shoulder, slowing me as we reached our parking structure. "Talk to me, goddammit."

"I'm done *talking to people*," I snapped. "Fuck, I don't know what's happening to me."

"You're flipping the hell out. Take a breath. Was it Lydia? The baby?"

"It's everything. I miss the hell out of her so much it fucking hurts worse than any pain I've ever felt. She's right in front of me every day, but it's not her. She doesn't want me. I can't help her or do anything to ease her suffering. I can't play *nice guy* right now. I can't be fucking soft and vulnerable. I have to get the hell away. I'm off until tomorrow, and I'm getting the hell out of here."

"You're not taking off like this," he said.

"Jake, if you know what's best for me, you'll let me get the fuck out of here."

"All right. It looks like you and I were both blessed to be off at the same time." He glanced up. "Let's get the bikes and turn those things loose up the coast. You and me."

"Ash ain't going for that shit. You know that."

"Just sent the text, prick." He smirked. "Let's see who can get to Malibu and suit up first. You know I always kick your ass when it comes to a good night ride."

I smiled and inhaled. "A ride is just what I need."

"Then we're wasting good fucking time."

On the bikes was where we had always found our solace. Once I was on the bike, I hit the radio and turned on the music I always played, encouraging a good, adrenaline-filled ride up the coast. This was my therapy, and, holy shit, did I ever need it.

CHAPTER THIRTY-SEVEN
ELENA

I had been at the ranch for three days now, and I hadn't seen Collin since I blurted out those horrible things about killing his baby to sweet little Addy, terrifying her. I insisted that I didn't want to see him so many times, and now, I had no idea what he thought of me.

Thinking about seeing him again brought up the horrible things I'd said and done to that poor little girl, and it made me feel wretched. Holly would visit in the mornings, and even with her help and encouragement, I wasn't ready to face Collin or any of his friends yet. It made me cry and go into hysterics—which I despised—when I even thought about seeing them again. I had no control over myself, and it was scary and frustrating and making it feel impossible to move forward.

I was told that this was the week Collin and I had planned to take our two-week honeymoon. The first two weeks of June were supposed to be for us to enjoy each other after our wedding, and he'd planned a trip that was intended to be a surprise for me. I only knew any of this because of what my family had relayed to me.

Lydia, Mom, and Dad worked overtime to help bring me to accept being around Collin again, but nothing helped. All it did was send me off in another direction, making me hate the *other Elena* again. I just wanted to start over from where I was now. Nothing my family was doing jarred any of my memories, and it was starting to make me angry. It felt like they were trying to push me to be someone else instead of accepting *me*. Maybe it sounded ridiculous given my situation, but that aspect of it hurt my feelings. They didn't want me: they wanted her. *That* is what made me hate her.

Even if my memories came back, my therapist told me my erratic behavior—the mood swings, the uncensored cussing, and everything else that was uncharacteristic no matter what stage of my life—may or may not go away. I was told not to dwell on that, though, and that everyone understood.

"Stevie." I caught my brother before he left the kitchen to hide in his apartment above the garage. "How's my baby brother?"

He smiled and wrapped his arm around me as I walked with him. "Good, Laney," he said, kissing the top of my head. "How's my crazy sister?"

"I'm good. On top of you being much taller than me now, I love being with you the most, you know," I said. "You don't treat me like I'm some fragile person, and you shoot me straight."

"Yeah, well, because of that and my own mistakes," he said, "you refuse to see Collin, the only guy you've ever dated who is actually cool and who I liked."

"Stop blaming yourself for that, Stevie," I said. "None of that was your fault. If Collin weren't always so scared to talk to me about stuff, then he would've done what was right and told me himself. It's more his fault than anything."

Steve stopped. "You can't mean that." He glared at me. "Laney, you need to stop doing this. I know you're having a hard time, but the nicer people are to you, the meaner you are to them. Then you go into these fits and look at where it's all at now?"

"If I don't want to see Collin Brooks," I leveled Stevie with a glare of my own, "that's up to me. Now," I looped my arm through Steve's, "let's sneak out Cookie and Oscar and go ride them up to the lake."

Steve gave me a look that I hated. Everyone gave me the same look whenever I forgot that something had changed in the last ten years or when no one had told me yet. I know I hadn't asked to ride my horse, and I know for a fact I hadn't been out to the stables, so this was something I hadn't been told.

"Spill it," I said.

"You sold Cookie when you started med school," he said. "You didn't want him locked up in the stables."

"Sounds like something I would say or do," I smiled at him. "See, I do well when people actually answer me. So, let's get on the other horses and ride then."

"You're not cleared to ride yet," Steve said. "That's a doctor's order for now."

"God," I rolled my eyes. "Cookie would've never thrown me. He would've been gentle. I should've never sold him. I would have him here, and we would ride."

"Hey, I have to run." He used his usual avoidance tactic with me.

"You're afraid to be around me," I said, my voice more elevated than before.

"I'm afraid of hurting you, sis. After accidentally saying I was sorry that you were in the hospital and that you had a miscarriage, I don't trust myself anymore."

"Fine," I folded my arms. "Maybe you should sit in on these stupid family therapy sessions then."

"Elena, I love you." He kissed my forehead. "I'm job hunting today. Something I promised you I'd start doing. That and going back to College."

"Well, this is good news." I smiled at him. "Can I go with you? I need to get out of here."

"I'm afraid the interviewer wouldn't appreciate my sister cussing them out if they don't hire me." He chuckled, and I punched his arm.

"Good luck," I said.

AFTER A DAY of roaming around the house, I spent the afternoon outside, watching a little girl jump one of the horses she had boarded here. What a cool thing my dad did to allow kids to board and train their horses after we all had grown up moved away.

"Laney," Lydia said, making me roll my eyes. "You've been out here for hours."

"Well, it's the only place where I can get any peace." I looked at her as I stood from my chair. I walked up to the split rail fence, stepped a boot onto a rail, and watched the girl jumping.

"I see that," she said, joining me at my side. "You know you've got to stop hiding from all of us."

"I'm not *hiding*, Lydia," I said, looking at her. "I'm avoiding all of you."

"Why?" she smiled.

"Because of that stupid look on your face. I'm sick of it," I growled and looked up in annoyance. "I'm so sick of everyone treating me like damaged goods."

"Is that why you won't see Collin?"

"Part of it, yes. No one answers me when I ask questions, and the only person who ever did runs around this place sad now because I did such a god-awful thing to Avery and her daughter." I sighed. "Collin is the worst of all of you. He hid that from me. Why would he hide that from me?"

"Because he knows this is all a process, Laney. He planned on telling you, and time and again, the therapists—you know, the people you trust like we do?—they told him you weren't ready to find out that you and he were going to have a baby."

"Well, it's all in the past now," I said. "I'm done talking about it."

"You need to knock this off," she said. "This is childish, and you know better. You shared a pretty awesome life with Collin, and you're refusing all of it now. It's stupid."

"How can I *not* act childish when all that you guys ever do is treat me like a child?" I said. "And I want my horse back, but the *other Elena* sold him."

"Stop referring to your memory loss as the *other Elena*," Lydia said.

"How can I not?" I laughed in disbelief. "That part of my brain doesn't seem to want to fill in the missing ten years of my life. That Elena was who I used to be, and I can't get her back. The more I try, the angrier I get."

I started crying again, and Lydia wrapped her arms around me. This was usually where my days ended. It was so difficult to come out of these fits when I let it all in.

"Laney," she tried to calm me, "don't do this again."

"I can't help it!" I sobbed. "I want to see Collin," I finally admitted.

"Then let's call him," she said. "I know for a fact that man would be here in seconds."

"No." I sniffed and stepped back. "He might think he still loves me, but

I'm telling you, I don't even *like* myself anymore. He's wasting his time if he thinks he's in love with this bitch, standing in front of you."

"A man who sticks by your side *after* he saves your life," she paused. "You truly believe he would stick around after all you have forgotten about him and all the hateful things you've said to his face?"

"It would get old, and I don't want to fight. I know this will only frustrate him as it does me. God, I can't even live with myself. Why should I allow him to try and live with someone he didn't fall in love with?" I started crying again. "I want to ride again. That's all I want right now. It was always soothing to just ride."

THE PREVIOUS DAY ended with me avoiding everyone, holed up in the attic, and looking at pictures of when I rode Cookie in competitions. In one picture, I was standing in Cookie's saddle and getting busted for trying to turn an expensive show-jumping horse into a trick horse. Instead of crying at the memories, I smiled, knowing I *could* remember them. It was so comforting to see things I remembered, and part of me wished I'd taken that early flight with my mom this morning to go back to the life I remembered in Miami.

Thinking of going back to Miami made me think of yet another thing I couldn't manage to do anymore: dance. It was like that part of my brain wouldn't allow me to remember. I busted my ass to learn salsa, tango, and even hula when I lived in Hawaii, and now, all of it was gone. Well, my mind understood it, but my legs didn't want to do what my brain tried to tell them to do.

After getting it out of Papi, I found out my surprise brain tumor was still in there, and scans would most likely show that the tumor was jarred in my brain, possibly pushing on that part of my brain and causing me to struggle with something as simple as making my legs move to music. It was so crazy how the brain worked. If Collin Brooks wanted to do anything for me, he could take out the last of the tumor and let me dance again.

"The door is for you, Laney," Dad said when I walked out from doing the dishes. "Get out here." He had a smile in his voice that I liked.

"I'm not seeing anyone," I said, eyeing him.

"Too bad." He hit me straight with a smile and his usual *no bullshit* look.

I covered my mouth when I saw a magnificent horse trailer and Collin, holding the most stunning, tall Chestnut mare. They both were so beautiful.

"Care to take a walk with me?" Collin asked with a dazzling smile that could only make me say yes.

"Are you boarding a horse here?" I asked, leaving my dad laughing in the doorway when I walked out to where Collin held onto black leather reins.

"No," he answered as the horse remained perfectly calm.

I ran my hands over her mane and the nameplate on her fancy black bridle. "Grace," I said, and the horse seemed to tug at the reins Collin held. "What a beautiful name." I smiled at Collin. "Why are you and Grace here if you're not boarding her?"

"She's yours," he said, his eyes shimmering.

"I can't accept this. Did Lydia call you?" I glared at him.

He ignored that, and I diffused immediately. "Come with me."

He turned the horse and led her as we walked. I loved hearing the sounds of her hooves clicking on the cobblestone walkway.

"Where are we going?"

"Well," he looked at me, "Lydia called yesterday."

"She needs to knock that shit off."

"It's a good thing she did," he said, "because I wouldn't have known it was finally time to give you the gift I'd planned on giving you as a wedding gift."

I stopped and swallowed hard. "Why would you think to buy me this beautiful horse?"

"Lydia mentioned you wished to be cleared to ride?" he ignored my question.

"Yes."

He stopped once we reached the grass. "Obviously, we're not going to allow you just to take off and let your healing brain bounce around in that skull of yours." He pulled the reins up over Grace's head. "So, if you'll allow me," he reached for my waist, and I shivered and smiled at his face being so close to mine right before he effortlessly lifted me and placed me on her back. "You still enjoy bareback riding, correct? She has all new tack that was delivered with her today as well. We can saddle her too."

I narrowed my eyes at him. "How did you know I like to ride bareback the most?"

His expression made butterflies swarm in my stomach. "We had a few *fun* conversations about that." He arched an eyebrow at me and laughed. "All right, Alvarez." I loved when he called me that; I just didn't know why. "Here's the deal. You're only allowed to go as fast as a walk with Grace. No trotting or galloping, am I clear?"

"Listen to you, Dr. Collin Brooks," I said in a low, silly way of mocking him.

He grinned. "As *your doctor*—and the man who loves you more than you care to learn about—you'll follow my orders if you wish to ride again." He looked up at me, and this horse was so calm and well-trained that I could feel her serenity rushing into me by being on her back.

"Are you going to let go of the reins?" I asked.

"Nope," he answered. "The Elena we all know from *before* I even met you might just give this horse a kick, stand on her back, and take off."

"You knew how I was?"

"I would be a foolish man to fall only for the woman and not want to know about her history too," he said, holding the horse at her mouthpiece and letting us walk.

"This feels amazing," I said with a smile of freedom. "Tell me why you bought her for me."

"We had a discussion when you wouldn't let me date you. You showed me a picture of Cookie, and you told me your *real dream* was to have your very own rehab center, knowing that equine therapy was a beautiful way for patients to accept their altered lives."

"Wow," I said, feeling in complete agreement with that statement at the moment. "So, you bought me the horse after Lydia called you yesterday, I'm assuming."

"Lydia informed me that she'd seen you out here, and your family knew about Grace after she came in two weeks before your injury."

"Where have you been hiding her? That beach house?"

He laughed. "No," he looked up at me, "at a place I can officially say would've been a surprise after my mom informed me about her plans for the future this week."

Suddenly I felt terrible instead of upset by the tone of disappointment or sadness in his voice. "What do you mean?"

I couldn't focus being on the horse, and everything inside me told me I needed to be able to talk and listen to Collin.

"It's nothing. The horse was at my childhood home. I had the stables renovated, knowing that I was bringing the mare in."

"Collin, help me down," I said sternly.

He turned back to me. "This is nothing to get worked up about. I'm sorry if I seemed annoyed."

"Help me down," I insisted.

He did, and I took his hands in the middle of the field we were in and smiled at him. "Sit with me," I said, loving the confusion in his eyes and our closeness. Something felt warm and beautiful about it.

Collin sat crossed legged in front of me, and we both laughed. "Now it's time for your therapy session, not mine."

He covered my hand that held his cheek, and I felt so many burning emotions inside of me. I could hardly handle it. Now that I was seeing him again, I was reminded that I *actually* dated this gorgeous man. Not just that, but he and I made a dreamy life together, and instead of being jealous of the *Elena* who shared that with him, I stayed right here, solid in this moment.

He dropped his hands, and his eyes met mine. "Well, then," he smiled. "I'm all ears, Dr. Alvarez."

"You say that like I'm still that doctor."

"I see it in your eyes and hear it in your tone, and officially, I declare you my doctor. I have to warn you, though," he laughed when I reached forward to hold his hands, "I might intermittently cuss you out."

"Shut up," I said, knowing how erratically I behaved. "Now, Collin, tell me what's bothering you."

"Well, the woman I love more than life itself seems to hate me." He stared at me, and I nodded with a laugh. "I should be on my honeymoon with her, but alas, I'm not."

"A horrible woman to do that to you. We can agree on that."

"She was tolerable, I guess." He chuckled. "Then," his eyes widened, "with all of that going on, and while I'm in the middle of planning to hire plumbers to replumb my mother's house, my mom drops the bomb on me that she's selling it."

"What did you say?" I asked, knowing that this was what was bothering him.

He shrugged. "I told her that I wouldn't allow her to sell the place I grew up in, the house that my dad designed and built for us. She was happy about that, at least."

"Why does she want to sell it? Because of that bad plumbing?" I asked.

Collin chuckled, and his face was so beautiful when it was lit up with humor. "No. She wants to live closer to my sister in Maine. She misses her grandkids, and I get it. They're all growing up too fast, and my mom needs something more than being in that massive house alone."

"So, why are you upset?"

"It's news I wasn't expecting. It seriously didn't call for a therapy session with my new doctor," he teased.

I took his large hands and traced my fingertips over the top of them. Something was very familiar about this, and Collin sighing seemed to alert me to it being something I must've done before. Weird.

"Why does this feel familiar? Or why do I like this so much?" I looked up at his striking eyes.

He smiled. "You always seemed fascinated by my hands. I still have no idea why."

"They are beautiful, and I'm glad to hear there's something you don't know about us. Welcome to this shitty club I'm in." We laughed together. "Tell me what I would do. You changed just now. Like you remember something that I don't know."

"Well, after you and I had amazing sex..." he chuckled and shook his head.

"Good God," I laughed and gripped his hands. "What happened to being reserved?"

"Stevie told me you're sick of that shit, so I'm breaking the rules now."

"I like that."

"I'm sure you do. Anyway," his eyes widened and smiled beamed, "it was either after our wild sex or lying on the sofa together and doing nothing after a long-ass day that you'd run your hands over mine when I held you close."

"And you miss it?"

"I never thought I'd have it again. Thank God that after all of this, she still loves my hands." He laughed.

"And your smile and eyes."

"Of course." He was a little cockier than I'd ever heard, but it was charming. "I believe I loved your smile more, though," he said, reaching for my face.

I closed my eyes and held very still, letting in the rush of tingling sensations that followed his fingertips as they ran on my skin. "You're so beautiful, Laney."

"I'm not her anymore, Collin," I said, feeling a sincere tear slip down my cheek for the first time. Typically, my tears were rushing and hysterical, but this was genuine sadness.

"I will wait, babe," he said. "I love you more than anything in this world."

My eyes reopened when he brushed the tear away. "Even after I blurted out those horrible things about killing your baby to that little girl?"

"Even after that." This time, he took my hands into his. "Look at me, Elena," he said. My heart was pounding after I'd brought this up, and I looked into his eyes.

"We lost our child, and I should have told you earlier. I knew you didn't remember the baby, so I didn't press the issue."

"You should have told me what we had and lost, but it doesn't make up for what I did."

"Bringing up something you couldn't remember, only for you to have mixed emotions of grief or anger that you possibly didn't feel grief over it, all of it seemed pointless at the time."

"I'm sorry," I said. "I'm sorry I lost your baby. I named her Jo?"

"Our daughter was named before you even told me about her." He smirked. "How about that for keeping a secret?"

"I didn't tell you I was pregnant?"

"No. I had no idea. You were coming back early from your snowboarding trip to tell me, at least that's what your friends and I think." He kissed the back of my hand, and the air was stolen from my lungs at how lovely that felt. "I learned about the gender after you miscarried and had no idea what I should do."

"God," I said, sad—but not irrationally sad. This was okay. I wanted to hear about this. "I heard you had a plaque put up, but how did you know about the name?"

"Long story short? You wrote it down."

"I loved Jo from the book Little Women," I smiled. "I loved everything about that character."

"That's why I went down the road I did with the plaque and naming her. I still don't know if it's what you wanted."

"I know I love it now," I said. "I don't know what the other Elena would've wanted, though."

He gave me a stare that was both loving yet admonishing. "No more referring to your memory loss as the *other Elena*, you got that? I'm talking to the Elena I fell in love with right now, and I now want to know, did I do the right thing for our daughter?"

"You did a beautiful thing for her," I said with all the sincerity I felt. "All while I was in a coma."

"All while I didn't know if you would survive it. I just went into some weird gear and called to find out what you felt about it all."

"Was I upset?" I asked. "I haven't asked that before."

"You cried. You drew a butterfly after you named the baby. Dr. Allen said you were extremely excited when you found out. I just don't know why you cried and then drew the butterfly."

He was so perplexed, but I knew the reason I loved butterflies, and I also knew how I was feeling right now with him saying we didn't plan on a child.

"I might know why I cried," I said.

"Do you remember, or are you having feelings about it?" he asked, his eyes searching mine.

"I know why I love butterflies," I said. "Maybe I drew that because my Papi always told me to *dance with the butterflies* when I left for Miami. He knew I loved to dance, and he told me that butterflies meant embracing change and a new life. I didn't want to leave him when Mom left for Miami." I smiled and then tried to mock Dad. *"Dance with the Butterflies!"* I sang out in my best Miguel Alvarez impersonation.

Collin smiled. "I guess you were embracing the change that would happen then?" He still seemed to want to know more, and I didn't blame him.

"I might have been feeling the way I do now."

"How's that?" he asked.

"Well, you said we didn't plan on the baby. What if I were scared it would upset you? A child changes everything. Even I know that with ten years of my life stripped away."

He smiled. "You're the most amazing human being I know," he said. "Perhaps that is what it was, then."

"Would you have been upset?"

He grinned. "Well, I did the math on the gestational growth of the fetus. It would place us in the earlier days when we just said *fuck it* and had sex with or without a condom."

"God," I coughed out a laugh, imagining what it would be like to have sex with him. "I was that wild?"

"We both were," he said, laughing. "You certainly couldn't resist my sexy ass, and that is the reason you got yourself pregnant." He winked at me.

"So, it's all my fault?"

He licked his lips. "We couldn't resist each other. We barely managed to survive watching one movie, and then we were..." His eyes grew distant.

"You miss us as badly as I wish I knew about us."

His eyebrows knit together. "That couldn't be a more accurate statement. All in good time," he smiled. "We'll get there."

"Until then," I said. "About your mom leaving, are you okay?"

"Well, it seems I'm buying the place from my mom now. So, I'm fixing the plumbing myself since I've already taken these two weeks off, and I'm doing exactly what you dreamed."

"What's that?"

"There are at least fifty hidden acres with that place. I'm turning it into the equestrian rehab center you said you once wanted. Perhaps I'll move there. It's not too far from the office, and I found out you're selling the condo."

"Sorry about that," I said. "I heard we shared that place."

"We did, but that's not your home anymore. I hardly visit the place anyway. On our honeymoon, I wanted to propose that we buy something like my childhood home. Now, here we are talking about it, and my mom is allowing me to buy it from her—after twisting her arm a little." He laughed. "I think it would be the perfect for an equine therapy center. That's if it's still your dream."

"I want to know more about why I never became a surgeon."

His lips twisted some. "I saw how your dad fixed people but didn't help them like you're being helped—like we're all being helped—after the fallout. You toured a hospital, and you said it just hit you one day. You wanted to be the one to fix them mentally while your dad fixed them physically."

"That's quite beautiful," I said, finally getting why I changed career paths. "Do you mind if I help you this week? I mean, we were *supposed* to be on our honeymoon."

"You want to help fix the plumbing?" His forehead creased in humor. "I wouldn't have it any other way."

"Did I name this rehab center you want to build?"

"No. I'm sure I said something stupid."

"Well, let's come up with something together."

"Well, I'll be damned. That equine therapy really does work," he laughed. "If I'd known that Grace would put all of these smiles back on your face and we could manage to get through a conversation for this long, I would have walked that mare right through the hospital and handled shit immediately."

I laughed and felt happier than I had since I woke up to this life. Collin stayed for dinner, and I watched how he blended so beautifully with my family. I wanted to know more about us now, but I wanted to be stable in my head.

We opted for a day together, and he would take me to the beach house where we lived. We would go from there, and I would try to gather the missing pieces of our relationship.

CHAPTER THIRTY-EIGHT
COLLIN

To say it had been a long fucking week would be a vast understatement. Elena not wanting to see me from the moment she'd cracked after telling Addy our baby died wasn't what I'd expected. I was pissed it had come to this, but what the hell was I going to do, bust down Miguel's front door and demand she see me? I was powerless in the situation.

I'd been trying to keep myself occupied since Elena had gone to the ranch, refusing to see me, but nothing was working. Surfing wasn't even working. Just when I thought I couldn't take on anything more, my mom dropped the bomb about moving to Maine.

It shouldn't have come as a surprise to me. Mom and Dad had a summer house in Maine, and being close to my sister and her kids made it all the more enticing to Mom. Who wanted to live in a mansion alone? I could hardly be at home since Elena's accident, so what made me think my mom enjoyed being in the big-ass house that my dad built for her— without him?

It didn't take much convincing to insist that I buy the house instead of my mom putting it on the market. It's not like she needed the money, and this way, the house stayed in the family instead of sitting vacant.

After Mom knew Elena was healthy and I was going to survive this, she confirmed her usual summer trip to Maine, giving me the idea to try and take on the old plumbing of the massive-ass house myself. I had plumbers on standby to fix anything I fucked up—since, you know, I was a surgeon and not a plumber. It was a fun challenge and one that kept my mind occupied up until I got the call I'd been anxiously awaiting.

When Lydia called yesterday, I knew it was time to change the game. My mind had already been made up that I wasn't going to sidestep shit with Elena anymore. I just needed a nudge. That nudge came with Lydia suggesting I could introduce Elena to Grace, the mare I'd boarded at the stables at Mom's place—all set to surprise her for our wedding that never happened.

I wasn't off my rocker. I wanted her back and would do whatever it took, even if it meant showing up with the horse uninvited. I wasn't having Grace delivered. Elena was getting both of us, whether she fought me on that or not.

From what Stevie had told me—after I took him out for a heart to heart and got his head back in the game—Laney was sick of the secrets and us being guarded around her. Holly even agreed it was time to stop holding back, and with her brain healing, it was time to start moving forward. We needed to continue to be cautious and remain unoffended if Laney lost her shit on things. I was prepared, and from what Lydia had told me, so was Laney.

After Laney and I shared the best day since her accident, being together at the ranch and introducing her to Grace, she asked to see the beach house and spend the day with me. I couldn't put my joy into words, but I knew I needed to stay cautious.

"You ready, sunshine?" I asked, seeing if she would react to one of the many nicknames I called her. Working to get her to access her memories was part of our job now too.

She blushed. "I like that," she said, walking to my car. "Wow, this car is so badass."

"I know," I smiled at her, "that's why I bought it. It was your favorite one."

"You have more?"

"Sort of a hobby," I said, helping her into my Lamborghini. "So, to the Malibu place, right?"

"Let's do this, sexy," she played back.

I smiled. "I like you calling me that."

"Did I used to call you that?" she asked.

She frowned when my music came on—way too loud—and I instantly shut it off. "Sorry about that. I love loud music, fast cars, and pretty Cuban girls." I smiled at her. "You loved it too."

"Ah," she laughed. "Then punch it and get me out of here."

I probably could've left the music on, but I didn't want to blast Elena with sensory overload. I would see if the beach house jarred any memories of our time there, and we'd go from there.

When we rolled into the garage, Elena was quiet. "Don't let the cars intimidate you. You always made fun of me for having them."

"I did?" she said softly. "You're seriously rich. These cars alone are worth—"

"You always said I was born with a silver spoon in my mouth," I said with a smile. "Let's go inside. This house misses you."

We walked in, and Elena was greeted by all of the vibrant colors of Miami. I stood back as she moved into the living room area that led out and overlooked the infinity pool. Seeing her here again was the most beautiful sight in the world, and it felt like a dream to have her here again. She continued to wear a crocheted beanie to cover the shaved areas of her scalp, but I wished she was comfortable enough around me to take it off if she wanted to. I didn't care if she was completely bald. I had the love of my life back, and she was in the one place I'd felt the most immense void —our Malibu home.

The pool dumped over the side and appeared to fall into the surf beyond the beach that spread across the back of the house. The decorators had been called off, for now, so she had to deal with my *plain* décor, which was exquisite but not what she liked before the accident.

She was quiet, so I decided to follow her lead and sit next to her on our blue sofas. "What do you think?" I asked.

"I think I just landed in Miami," she laughed. "All this wicker, the flamingos, palms—and to think I almost booked a flight back to the life I remembered there when you have it all bottled up in this living room."

"You designed it," I smiled at her bewildered expression. "No shit. You and Ash's best guy friends designed all this. They're crazy talented."

"Those flamingos, the water behind them looks like it's moving." She pointed at the large portrait that Clay and Joe had designed to be the room's focal point.

"Ash painted that for us. I think that woman sprinkles fairy dust in her paintings, and they magically come to life."

"This place is beautiful. I love your home."

"Well, it's *your* home," I said with a laugh. "The pool and cabanas in the back are the remainders of what was mine in this house."

"Before I took over the place?" she laughed, and it made me smile. "I was pretty damn bold to do that."

"You were the same person you are now." I looked out at the pool area. "This was your next big project, and since you just scared the shit out of me by saying you wanted to move back to Miami, what would you change out here to make this home for you?"

"I think moving in with you is a pretty big step," she shrugged. "I can't even dance anymore. If I can't mentally move my legs in big steps—" she stopped herself and frowned. "I don't know what I'm talking about." She half-laughed. "It sounded right until I started talking."

"Your dad told me about that." My heart broke, seeing the sadness in her eyes, but even if this tumor was pressing on this particular motor skill in her brain, it didn't warrant emergency surgery.

I heard she threw a raging fit with Miguel, saying she wanted the tumor removed, but thank God that man was a brilliant neurosurgeon himself, and he explained to her why I wouldn't do the craniotomy. I watched her, curious if this would turn into a sudden nightmare because she wanted the tumor removed, and I didn't know if this would wind up being a conversation of her trying to convince me to do that.

"And I'm sure he told you I want you to get the rest of this tumor out of my head," she said in a stiffer tone than before.

"He did."

"Why won't you?"

"Because I know you can fix this on your own," I answered. "Come with me."

She looked at me with confusion, but I only smiled and prayed I could help her understand that she could live her life without the surgery.

We walked out to what used to be our favorite place, next to the outdoor bar and under a pre-lit pergola. I called for the outdoor music to turn on. My rhythm and blues playlist came on, playing the last song we'd listened to before her accident when Elena and I had turned a night of dancing by the pool into a night of hot sex. I knew how much this woman loved dancing. Hell, it was how we met, and we loved doing it when we were home.

Setting aside my memories of the last time Otis Redding played for Elena and me, I cleared those thoughts and appreciated the perfect tempo to lead the woman I loved.

"I seriously can't dance anymore," she laughed as I slid a hand around her waist. "I can do it in my head, but my feet won't do it. I swear to God that this is a waste of time."

"Bullshit," I smiled at her. "Follow my lead." I stepped back. "Step forward to follow my foot."

She stepped forward and laughed. "Wow," her forehead wrinkled in humor. "And now I step back..." she followed my simple steps.

I stepped my other foot forward, watching her follow perfectly. "Yep, you got it," I said as we slowly moved our feet in with the beat of the song. "Now," I pulled my hand from hers and took her chin between my fingers, "look into my eyes and allow the beat of the song to guide you."

She tripped and laughed. "Um, not a good idea to look into your eyes."

"Eyes on mine and listen to the music," I said with a smile.

"This feels nice," she said, gently swaying her hips to where I couldn't resist both of my hands holding her waist and guiding her. Her eyes widened, "Are you trying to distract me?"

"Trying to get these sexy hips moving again," I said. "Can you squat down on one leg and up to your toes before moving the other side the same way?"

She did, and I smiled. "It's like shaking these hips can't be stopped by anything."

"Oh, my God, I'm doing it."

It was a matter of retraining her brain with a little bit of a confidence boost. I was thrilled to see her cheerfulness by conquering something she thought she'd lost. She wasn't at full speed yet, but the song's tempo didn't lend to that anyway. I was pulling her into me and bringing her closer to my cock that was hard and dreaming this was my Elena—before her injury.

Shit, I had to be careful. The last thing I needed was her taking off down the beach because I turned this into a *too much, too fast* sexual situation, but this felt amazing. She molded herself against me, and it felt like the world of disaster and chaos left us both, and it was my Laney and me, dancing with a second chance we deserved more than anything else in this world.

She held onto me tightly, and I knew she could feel I was harder than a rock. Thank God she didn't let my issues bother her. Instead, we danced as if the accident had never happened, and we'd reversed time and let it stand still.

"You're an amazing dancer," she softly said.

"And thank God you think so because that's how we first met," I said. She pulled away, tearing me from this moment of peace I'd been begging for since I lost her.

"Can we walk on the beach?" she asked. "I feel so good right now, and I just want to talk."

I nodded and knelt to slide off her sandals. "Let's get these feet back in the sand," I said after rising back up. "Everything cool?"

"It just seems like we must've had a lot of fun together out here."

"We did," I said. "We took walks together all the time when we got off work. We ate taco truck food like crazy." She started laughing at that statement, and it made me laugh with her.

"Oh, God," she said. "Was it me or you who was about the taco trucks?"

"You," I said. "My best friend's a cardiovascular surgeon, remember? We both had fun lying to him about how *healthy* we ate, though."

"That's so weird. I'm not a huge fan of them. I never really was," she said as we hit the beach and started walking, people passing us as they walked their dogs or were jogging.

"Well, you said you missed the hell out of them after living in Florida and going to med school."

We walked, and I filled her in on every detail she questioned me on. She wanted to know about our first meeting in Vegas up until now. This time she wasn't as brazen with her questions and asking about *sex* with me. That was my curse this time.

"So this is your beach," she said.

"Our beach, I'll add," I smiled at her when we came to a stop in front of the private part of the beach I owned below my house.

"Our beach?"

"Yeah, we pretty much ensured we *owned* it." I smiled.

She arched her eyebrow in that playful Elena way, and I felt myself staring at her in awe. It felt like I was getting a damn good second chance with her, and I wasn't going to blow it.

"How exactly did we own it?"

"How do you think?" I thought I'd play with her.

"Well, from the stories you've told, I'm pretty sure we violated some laws." Her cheeks tinted pink.

"We unquestionably had sex on the beach, and you wanted to hate me for it too." I laughed.

"I highly doubt I would've hated to have sex with you, ever."

"You despised me pulling crazy shit when it came to *illegal sex*," I smirked. "Like when we had sex in the car."

"We did not."

"We most certainly did." I eyed her with a grin. "You didn't believe I could pull that shit off. So I proved to you I could, driving up to Big Sur on the two-lane highway."

"In your tiny little car?" she laughed and rubbed her forehead.

"No. The blacked-out windows on your Land Rover made it pretty easy for me," I said.

"How in the hell did we pull off *sex while driving*?" She was laughing and her face so beautiful while her bronze eyes dazzled.

"Cruise control, my awesome driving, and you climbing on my lap. You loved every single second of it too." I chuckled.

I was getting hard just thinking about that wild ride. That was near the top of the list of the hottest sex I'd ever had with Elena.

"Well, for being a neurosurgeon, you sure do take a lot of risks." She grinned. "You're going to laugh when I say this, but I'm craving a taco-truck taco now."

"Glad we're changing the subject," I exhaled with a laugh of my own. "And also, I'm truly grateful you want your usual taco truck fix because we practically own the damn trucks down here." I took her hand to guide her up the steps to the house. "What do you say we grab some tacos, head to Jim's place, and then I'll show you where I grew up?"

"You're sure they're okay with me coming around? I still don't trust myself and get a little anxious sometimes." She sighed and stopped. "I really couldn't handle it if that poor little girl thinks I'm some crazy woman who says horrible things."

"Everyone understands, Laney," I said. "The kids are cool too. Trust me, if there is closure you need with all of that, *our* best friends will allow you to see that you didn't damage anyone or anything by saying what you said. We all know we're in this together, all of us, and that includes you with our friends."

"I don't get it."

"You don't have to," I said, leading her up to the house. "Just know that we're all tight, and if Ash or Avery were in your shoes, you'd be leading the pack on forgiveness, understanding, hope, and moving forward. They all love and adore you."

"Okay," she smiled at me. "You'll be with me the entire time?"

"I'll smother you so much that you'll be pushing me off of you so that you can enjoy some girl talk with Av and Ash." I smiled at her. "Let's go get your life back."

CHAPTER THIRTY-NINE
ELENA

The taco truck was more delicious than I thought it would be. It tasted so familiar, and even though I knew I'd apparently been eating these like crazy for the past ten years, it was still strange to have such a familiar reaction to something completely foreign to me. I felt the same every time Collin touched me. It was like I subconsciously craved him, but I had no experiences to back up my feelings. It was so unfair.

I remained positive, though, and after we ate our tacos, we reached Jim's place in Hollywood Hills. All I could say was that Collin and all his friends were seriously loaded. Growing up in Beverly Hills, I had my share of *wealthy* acquaintances, but this was insanity.

"My dad designed this house with a buddy of his," Collin said, probably because I got quiet as I stared at the imposing house, built beautifully into the mountains that overlooked all of downtown Los Angeles. "We got lucky he convinced Jim to buy it and more or less keep it in the family."

"You guys blow me away," she laughed. "Was I surprised by this place before?"

"Shit, who isn't? My dad was a goddamn genius, and his skills are seen throughout the home. I'm sure Addy would love to give you the tour." He winked, and I settled down.

When we walked in, I was awestricken again—all the walls were windows. I couldn't believe such a marvel of a home existed. I could easily understand why Collin would be proud of his dad, seeing what he'd done in this house.

The group of us settled into conversation, and I felt at ease and happy. Another one of those familiar feelings washed over me. My brain knew this was a meaningful environment, but it wouldn't reveal why. I ignored the frustration I felt as soon as Jake and Ash's little boy came running in with Addison. They made a bee-line toward Collin, screeching with delight.

"Oh, no." Little John's bright blue eyes widened, and he made a perfectly round O with his mouth when he giggled out the word *no*.

"It's him." Addy rushed to John and ducked behind the cute little boy. "It's the *mad scientist*," she said in a funny voice.

Collin released my hand and rose from the couch where we sat when the kids rushed in. He hunched over and started growling at the two laughing kids. John balled up his fists while I laughed at him, pursing his lips and frowning at Collin. John's spikey and messy hair was like his dad's and Collin's and made him look so cute.

"No, you crazy, mad doctor," he said as Collin crept toward where he and Addison laughed and giggled. "No Frankenstein today, bud."

Collin held this crazy doctor pursuit while we all laughed at John, who was protecting a giggling Addison. "No!" Addison shrieked when Collin swiped at John's feet.

"I feel like..." Collin said in a funny voice, "like putting..." he grabbed John and held his arms up, "this rib..." he began tickling the laughing boy, "in Addy..." Addison laughed while John tried to get serious again. "And this femur..." he gripped John's leg and made the boy laugh, "in Addy too."

"Get him, Addy," John screamed. "Layna, save us!" I felt everyone's eyes on me, but that didn't stop me. I joined in and rushed to help John and Addison, who were now in Collin's grips.

"She can't help you, little boy," Collin said. "I'm the mad scientist."

"Tell him he's the *sad* scientist," Addison said to me. "It makes him sad. That's what you say." She smiled and laughed while Collin acted like a gorilla, swinging the kids back and forth.

"You're the *sad scientist*," I said in the best authoritative voice I could use.

"No!" Collin released Addy. "It's the only woman in the world I can listen to."

"And she's here to stop you!" John shrieked, still held by Collin.

"Tell him, *don't touch my John and Addy*, you crazy sad man!" Addy laughed, sitting with her mom.

I repeated Addison's words and laughed at Collin, acting like I was the cure to his mad scientist rampage.

"Now, the only way I won't operate..." Collin said to the giggling boy he held.

"Is if the beautiful woman saves you!" Addison squealed.

"Saves him?" I laughed and looked at Addison.

"You have to do the grossest part," Addison said, then ran up to me. I knelt for her to whisper in my ear. "You have to kiss him, and then he's our prisoner."

Collin's eyes dazzled while John squirmed in his arms.

"Hurry, Laney, hurry!"

I walked up to Collin, and before I could do the one thing I'd been curious about doing, Addison called out orders to me. "Kiss his brain. His forehead!" she laughed. "It's what makes him mad!"

"I always thought it was the lips?" Collin said in a voice that made me laugh. "The slimy kiss is all that stops me now."

I laughed when Addison looked at Collin like he was ruining this game. "That's just gross."

"So gross. Poor Laney," John said.

I walked up and kissed Collin's forehead. "There, mad scientist, now you're cured."

The kids broke loose as soon as Avery walked in with pudding and fruit for them to eat out by the pool.

"Damn," Collin sighed. "So close."

We all laughed and then followed the kids out to the pool. The day was light and breezy, and Jim and Avery's badass pool made it even better. I fell effortlessly into a conversation with the ladies, and it felt right. I wished I knew how it seemed like we'd all been close friends for all our lives.

Instead of going back to Collin's place, I felt great and was in high spirits, and I gladly told Collin that I'd love for us to accept the invite to go out to dinner tonight. Maybe, if one thing led to another, I'd be able to kiss this most incredible man on his lips later on.

It was no wonder I'd fallen in love with him so quickly before my accident. He was brilliant with kids, he was an all-around happy guy, he showed remarkable patience with me through everything, and he was still here with me even though I couldn't remember him or act like myself anymore. Regardless of all of those attributes, he was also, hands-down, the most beautiful man I'd ever met in my life.

THAT EVENING, Collin was transformed from the sexy way he looked in jeans and a simple blue tee into a crisp, button-down shirt and one of his perfectly-tailored navy suits. This restaurant was supposed to be quite fancy, but when I looked in my closet, I seemed to have plenty of nice gowns to show it wouldn't have been my first rodeo with this group and their lavish styles.

It was hard to believe the wealth that filled the air when I was around Collin and his friends. They didn't talk or act like the snobs I remembered from the extravagant parties and events my parents threw at the Beverly Hills house. These people acted normal and fun, but I guessed they also appreciated a fine-dining experience now and again.

I wore a black, strapless dress and flats. My balance was a disaster, and there was no way I was quite ready for heels. Collin was waiting for me downstairs, and it was somewhat odd to see Lydia thrilled to pieces that I was back up and on my feet again. From what she'd told me, she changed quite a bit after she almost lost me in the accident. I guess that was *one* upside to me losing ten years of my life, my career, and accepting every single day that I wasn't twenty-two years old anymore.

"You look radiant. Smile," Lydia said, and I did. She dusted some blush onto the apples of my cheeks and touched the brush playfully to my nose. "There."

I laughed. "Why so nice? What the hell is wrong with you?"

"Just making sure my baby sister shines like the light she is."

"We never acted like this before. It's kind of weird."

"I almost lost my little sister, and a situation like that tends to change one's outlook on life."

"So, we weren't close before the accident?"

She leaned against the vanity and smiled. "I moved away, and all I cared about was being successful, and I was. I was successful at making it on track to be a partner at my law firm, and I was successful at running off the love of my life because of my ambitions."

"Wait," I smiled at her. "The love of your life?"

"Allan Hall." She smiled, and her eyes became dreamy. "He and I lived together. He was great, but I found out he cheated on me." She shrugged her shoulders and rolled her eyes.

"Oh, my God," I said. "What an asshole!"

"I had it coming. I didn't make any time for him," she said. "We went from having a dreamy love-affair to this mundane and distant relationship. Maybe that's why I was harder on Collin than I should've been."

"You saw me on the same course."

"I did, and I knew a lot about him. Being a world-renowned neurosurgeon, totally gorgeous," she winked at me, "and his face plastered all over the health magazines with some broad on his arm, I guess I figured he'd crush your heart."

"What makes you think he still won't? What changed your mind about him?"

"My eyes were opened after your accident. Papi even said Collin was the strongest man he'd ever met even to attempt to perform your surgery while faced with the impossible idea of it being you."

"When I woke up, you seemed to hate him as much as I did when I fought with him."

"At the time, I wasn't overly convinced he would stick with you as your family would. Instead, he proved me completely wrong. I saw a man in love with my little sister, a man who lost a child he didn't know about and grieved for both of you." Her eyes suddenly filled with tears. "It broke my heart to see the man so broken. He felt every bit as lost without you as we did—the way only people who love unconditionally do."

I hugged her. "I was so horrible to him. I still don't know if he'll ever really fall in love with the woman I am now, Lydia. I'm not the woman he shared a life with before that accident. If I were her, I'd be on a honeymoon, married, and with—"

"Stop that," she sniffed. "He wouldn't be waiting downstairs to take you out for a wonderful dinner if he didn't love you still."

"He told me he would wait. That doesn't mean he loves me." I felt tears pooling in my eyes.

"Laney," she said with a smile, "then make him fall in love with who you are now if you're so worried about that. You've lost your mind completely if you can't see it in his eyes. I see it. He loves you. The question is, do *you* love him?" She cocked her head to the side. "I don't think any of us have asked you that."

"I don't know him," I said truthfully. "I've seen the funny videos of us on my Instagram page—after Stevie showed me what it was and how to use it—and I've seen videos and pictures on my phone, but all I see is my face with this beautiful man who made me smile. It's like I went out, got black-out drunk, and had the time of my life, and then I'm looking at videos of it the next day, and I have no idea who any of the people are." I sat back down, a bit defeated. "I feel like I'm this other woman with *her* face."

"Just give him the time he asked for with you. I was there at the dinner table when he said he'd make you fall in love with him again. He's genuine, and I don't think that man's going anywhere."

"There were so many videos, but there was one that stood out to me. He was singing this silly song and dancing for little John and me as he held two dead Christmas trees." I shook my head and laughed.

"Tell me you watched the video of *you* proposing to him."

"I haven't watched that one yet. I'm afraid to."

"There's nothing to be afraid of. It shows who you both were. I saw it all as foolish and reckless. You always seemed to live this wild life, not caring about the fallout, but I know now that Collin was put on this earth to be your other half."

My eyebrows rose. "If only I were still that wild-life living, carefree person."

"You are," she said. "Now, go fall in love with the man who wants to steal your heart again."

I WALKED DOWNSTAIRS, and Collin was laughing about something with Stevie and Dad. His hands were casually slipped into his pockets like he wasn't wearing a thousand-dollar suit. He was tall, beautiful, and I wished I could see beyond his exterior sometimes. It was okay to be smitten by a man's flawless and handsome looks, but I had seen more of his personality, and I needed to hold onto that.

I saw the mad scientist games he played with the kids, the way he looked at me with confidence when he worked to teach me how to dance, and the tender way he held my hands when we talked in the meadows yesterday. So, why wasn't I feeling more? Was I being difficult, or did my brain know I loved him, but my heart couldn't understand? Just like my brain knew I could dance, but my feet couldn't do the job.

Stop thinking, Elena. It's been a beautiful day. Just go with the flow.

"Wow," Collin said when he saw me. "You look beyond ravishing, and I see you picked out my favorite dress of yours."

"Your favorite dress?" I smiled back at his perfect smile.

"I almost didn't send it with all your clothes when you moved back home," he said, taking my hand when I hit the last step.

"But I threatened to kick his ass," Papi smirked and chuckled at Collin. "Take care of my little girl tonight."

"Have fun, sis," Stevie said.

"Bye, guys. See you tonight."

My dad laughed, and Stevie followed in suit. I didn't understand it, but Collin whisked me out of the house and into his car before I could start asking a million questions.

"So, this is your favorite dress?" I asked, smiling at him as he got in his car and started it.

"Yep," he smiled at me, putting the car in gear and taking off. "I think that *might be*—" He squinted over at me and grinned, his eyes fell to my cleavage, and then he nodded while looking out at the road. "Yeah. That's definitely the dress that got you knocked up, Alvarez." He chuckled, and the way he said it made me laugh.

"You keep saying I'm the one that *got myself* pregnant," I teased back, "but I think it was probably more *your* fault than mine."

"You're probably right." He smiled at me. "But I do blame you and your hotness for luring me into doing...well, being impulsive with you."

"Impulsive?" I questioned.

"Yeah, usually I have a good head on my shoulders until you walked into my life. You, Elena Alvarez, are my greatest weakness and my strongest desire."

"Well, that's quite flattering," I said. "I'm no fool. I see that I am pretty lucky to have you feel this way about me."

He glanced over at me and gave me a look I couldn't discern. "You give me too much credit."

"I landed the hottest doctor at that hospital." I laughed.

"No. *I* landed the hottest doctor at that hospital." He nodded and then turned on his music. "Let's get our night started with some high speeds and good tunes."

With that, Collin and I settled into the car, and I let the music playing on his radio soothe my nerves and set the mood for a fun and fancy night with Collin and his fun friends.

"THIS IS my first time being in public," I whispered to Avery and Ash while the men stood in conversation together. "What if I say or do something…" I paused at the idea of embarrassing everyone. Shit. We didn't go over this part. Elena's first night out and at the fanciest place around.

"You won't, and if you do," Avery smirked at me, her black hair putting such a beautiful spark in her blue eyes, "Ash and I have your back."

"Hell yes," Ash agreed. "Nothing to worry about." She glanced over at the group of handsome men. "If anyone is going to embarrass us at this extravagant place, it'll be those four."

I laughed. "You two are so kind to me. Thank you."

"Elena," Ash said, her brown eyes twinkling with excitement, "you have no idea the kindness you've shown to all of us. Like we talked about earlier, we got close and fast. You're still the spark of energy that we love. Now, let's go have fun and watch the guys banter over something stupid and get us kicked out of this place."

COLLIN WAS at my side as soon as the group was called to our table. The restaurant's fancy atmosphere should have calmed my nerves, but it made me feel a bit intimidated. Maybe I wasn't ready for this. I should've kept the eating-out thing exclusively to taco trucks.

I tried to laugh along with the group, but the anxiety I was feeling was something I was working to keep at bay. Jim's presence exuded power, and Alex, who sat at my right, was the same. I hardly knew these men, and suddenly, I felt like I didn't want to ruin their expensive dinner.

Jake and Collin were in some funny conversation, but I couldn't keep up. I focused on simple things like Collin's thumb rubbing along the bare skin of my upper back and wondering why I didn't feel sparks like I did before when he touched me.

I swallowed my water and wished I was clear to drink alcohol. Maybe that would loosen me up, but I had my brain surgeon sitting right by me, saying I needed more time before alcohol consumption would be safe because it wouldn't agree with my medication, among other things.

Shit. Calm down and breathe. I'm okay. It's all fine.

"Hey, Laney," Ash said, most likely seeing me fade. "I would love it if you'd come to the gallery tomorrow. After Collin said that you liked the flamingo painting today, I wanted to show you more pieces that go with it."

"It's interesting how your paintings come to life when you look at the picture," I said.

"It's all in the way I paint the canvas. I do black at first, and then I sprinkle in colors as I go. It was Jake who noticed it under certain lighting."

"Yeah," Jake smiled at me. "After she dumped my ass for being an idiot back in the early days, I found out she was going to trash the things."

"Instead," Collin chimed in, "Jake realized the black magic that drew him in to love Ash must've been the same black magic she used in her paintings too."

"No shit," Jake said as Ash laughed.

We silenced as two waiters came and placed our plates in front of us. My food was arranged so beautifully that I was afraid to cut into it and ruin it. Damn, no wonder I had a million pictures of food on my Instagram page. This is how we ate.

I cut into my Poulet de Bresse with cream that I'd ordered and took a bite. It was so flavorful and delicious. A bit chewy for chicken, but who knew, maybe that's what the world's most expensive chicken was supposed to taste like.

"Oh, fuck!" I shrieked. For no reason, all of my panicked nerves that I'd been pushing down surfaced like a bomb. "It's not cooked all the way through."

Please, God, don't be louder than you think you're being, Elena, I inwardly hoped while my breathing picked up, and I rose from the table like it was on fire.

Collin was at my side. Goddamn it, I'd fucking blown it. All this work and I was shouting in fear and fighting off Collin's hands like I did when I threw the tantrums I hated. I couldn't stop it and trying to made it worse. The waiter was at the table, but I couldn't hear him.

I don't know how long it took or how he did it, but Collin sat me down, and I was facing him. Me, the lunatic who ruined dinner for everyone in this restaurant, embarrassing myself and everyone at my table.

"Eyes on me, Laney," Collin's voice finally cut through my internal freak-out. "Baby," his hands held mine like they did when we sat in the meadow.

I started crying.

"I'm so sorry," I said, my body shaking. "I'm so sorry."

"Breathe with me, Laney," he said. "It's okay. I'm right here, and so is everyone else. We're all with you."

"That chicken." I eyed my plate. "It's going to make me sick." I looked back at him as I spoke in that stupid fucking whiney voice of a five-year-old. "Shit," I growled that baby voice away. "The food isn't cooked," I said, my rage growing.

"We'll handle it." He smiled and brought me into his chest. "Relax, Laney."

"It was a five-hundred-dollar plate, and I ruined dinner." I started crying.

I hate myself more than anything in this world. I hate this. It's not fair that I can't stop doing this, even after doing so well.

I heard the waiter ask us to leave, and my attention was brought to apologies directed toward the man.

"Listen," Alex, the handsome, billion-dollar-suit man who sat to my right, said in an authoritative voice. "We're not leaving." He spoke as if he owned the place.

Collin held me as I watched Alex's sharp features level the waiter. Why, though? To protect his lunatic friend's outburst?

"Sir," the waiter said, "our guests have been disturbed—"

"I wasn't done, *sir*," Alex shot back. "I want the plate taken back, and the chef brought to our table immediately."

"As per our—"

"No," Alex said. "As the customer and the man who had papers drawn up for the executives who own this restaurant today, I want the chef brought out, and I demand to speak with Gabriel LeFevre."

"Mr. LeFevre is the owner, sir. I can assure you—"

I cowered into Collin's side as the restaurant grew so quiet you could hear a pin drop.

"I can assure you, Alberto," Alex said, a bit more aggressively, "that if you don't get the head chef out here and tell the owner that Mr. Alex Grayson is seated and most unhappy, we might have a bigger problem than my friend getting salmonella poisoning from undercooked food."

"I believe she is overreacting."

I shot up from Collin, only to see Jim look at me and his stare alone settled me down. "I demand the owner to be notified that James Mitchell and Alex Grayson are patrons at his restaurant this instant," Jim said to the angry waiter.

"Que lest le problème?" the head chef said, storming into the dining room.

Alex responded to the man in perfect French, and they went into some French conversation—Jim chiming in—and I had no idea what the hell was happening.

"What are they saying?" I whispered to Collin.

"That the food sucks," he had a smile in his voice, "that it is criminal to charge more than five-hundred-dollars a plate for undercooked food, and that they are going to terminate the contract of Jim's company that is investing in this unique French restaurant business."

"What?" I pulled up while Alex continued to speak French in some demanding voice.

"Alex was acquiring this business, and we were here tonight to celebrate on an exclusive invitation from the owners," Collin said. "Turns out the chef sucks, and he's not too bright to be arguing with the two most powerful men in Southern California right now. This is all bad for the owners if the asshole doesn't get on the phone with Jim or Alex fast."

"I feel horrible I started this."

"You didn't cook the plate of food, Laney," Jake said from across the table with a smile. "The chef, who is continuing to argue with Alex and my brother, allowed a disaster of a meal to be served. He won't apologize and is remaining firm that he did nothing wrong."

"I've seen three plates go back now," Ash said. "You're not the only one who would've been thrown in the hospital with food poisoning from undercooked chicken."

Jim was on his phone, and I wanted to leave.

"Laney," Alex said.

I looked over at him. "I'm sorry."

Alex smiled. "Don't apologize for saving Mitchell and Associates from a horrible investment. I'm truly sorry your dinner was unsafe and unfit to eat," he said as he placed his hand on my shoulder reassuringly. "Jim is handling the owners after such horrendous customer service. Perhaps the owner will hire a new chef and regain our trust. Nothing to worry over."

"I didn't have to make a scene," I said to Alex.

He shrugged and handsomely pursed his lips. "I probably would've thrown my plate back against the chef's wall." He smirked. "Acted like that show..."

"Hell's Kitchen?" I laughed. "Yes, Gordon would *not* have approved of what was served."

"Uh, not likely," Alex said. "It's all good, love." He winked and then returned his attention to Jim, who was speaking in French to a man who seemed scared to death of him.

"Let's get out of here," Collin said. "You've stopped shivering, and I think you might enjoy a taco from the taco trucks."

"That sounds delicious," I said.

"No shit," Jake said and stood, prompting the others to stand as well.

"Jim and I will be out once we've finished up here," Alex said. "We heading to Malibu?"

"Yeah. The taco trucks practically moved there because Elena and I funded them being out by Venice," Collin said.

"Tacos and sitting on the beach is just what this doctor ordered," Jake said, putting his arm around Ash.

"Wow," Collin raised his eyebrows at Jake as we walked out, "the cardio doc is approving this?"

"Eating tacos on the beach while watching the surf roll in is just the trick for good health," Avery added. "It's all good, Laney."

I felt a bit better, but now, I had a new insecurity—freaking out in public over something minor. There was no excuse for my behavior, and I knew that. I didn't mean to react when I did, but I couldn't stop myself. Whether or not I was justified, and regardless of how everyone was trying to calm me, I needed to find a way to stop this.

CHAPTER FORTY
COLLIN

*E*ating tacos at the beach with the gang was a perfect way to help ease Elena out of her embarrassment. Her outburst was certainly unexpected, given how well she'd been doing; however, it was also something the neuropsychiatrist and therapist had repeatedly told us could happen. It was all part of the unfortunate package that came along with Elena's brain injury, that and the anxiety she told me she'd been suffering from when we were on the way back to her house.

As much as I wished it would all go away, I also knew Elena was more exhausted than anyone else from dealing with this, and this wasn't about what I wanted. My heart was crushed when she told me she was scared to go into public after what'd happened tonight, and I'd be damned if I wouldn't help her regain confidence. The last thing I was going to allow Elena to do was isolate herself because she was dealing with the expected outcomes from surviving a traumatic brain injury. She survived that accident *and* the tumor, and she was a walking miracle. The only issue was getting her to understand that.

"Home?" she said when I pulled up to the ranch house. "I figured we'd stay at the Malibu house tonight."

"As much as I'd love that," I smiled over at her, "it's probably best we take it slow as you wanted."

"Collin," she sighed and ran her hand over her forehead, "I'm so confused. I thought we were trying to get *us* back."

"We are," I said, taking her hand into mine.

"Then why am I home and not staying with you tonight?"

She looked away, and I softly gripped her chin and turned her face back to mine. "Because it's the right thing to do."

She sat in my passenger seat, and I was fully prepared for her to lose her shit again.

"I want to be with you. I want to kiss you, at least." She stared at me with some anger.

"You have *no idea* how badly I want that myself," I said. "Laney, I want you to be ready."

"What makes you think I'm not?"

"I've dated enough women to know when love isn't present between us. I know you're not there yet."

She stared at me, and tears filled her eyes. "What if that will help me remember us?"

I couldn't help but smile. "Sex?" I softly laughed. "If that were the cure, I would have had my way with you the first second I had you alone."

"I just want it all back. I've seen videos of us, and I see a woman in those videos and photos that I'm not. I hate her, Collin."

"You hate that you can't remember us in those videos and photos, you mean. That woman is *you*, Laney. It's the same person that I'm looking at right now."

She let out a breath of frustration. "Well, I don't, and no matter how hard I try, I *can't* see it that way."

"That's why we're moving slowly."

"You aren't attracted to me anymore. After the outburst tonight, I wouldn't blame you for taking off."

"I'm not going anywhere, Elena," I said. "I already told you that."

"And if I don't come back? If you don't get the woman back who you fell in love with? You just said it yourself, you dated women like me, and there was nothing."

Goddammit, that came out wrong.

"Fair enough. Allow me to put it to you this way, then. You, Elena Alvarez, are the love of my life. I'm not abandoning you over memory loss and outcomes you're dealing with due to your injury. However, I will make you *this* promise: I will make you fall in love with me again. Like you did before. I wasn't going to stop pursuing you when I first fell for you, and I don't plan on stopping that pursuit even if I'm forced to have to relive those days of you turning me down all over again."

"You say that like it will happen."

"I say that because I *know* you'll fall for me again. Through all of this bullshit, you'll be in my arms soon enough." I smiled at her.

"Then take me back to your house."

"I won't allow you to ever suffer regrets from being with me. While I am seriously fighting the urge to take you up on this offer, I just—I don't know. Call me selfish or whatever, but I want you to love it, to love me, to wake up in my arms and not feel anything but how amazing it was."

"And you don't think I'll feel that way now? You have no idea how I'll react."

"I know that too," I said. "But if I brought tears to your eyes after we were together, I would never forgive myself for it. Aside from that—to be perfectly honest with you—I'm not sure I'm solid enough these days to handle that kind of rejection."

Unexpectedly, she smiled, "Fine," she opened her door. "We'll wait, but when it does happen…"

"Best sex of your life," I finished her sentence.

She blushed, and I loved it. "You held me off before, trust me. I think you even liked making me bust my ass to get you in bed."

"I was different from all your other girlfriends, then?"

I laughed. "You have no idea. It's almost as if that part of my life never existed after you waltzed in and staked your claim on me."

"Did I now?" She licked her lips like she always did, making me hunger for her kiss. "Well, I promise you this, I have plans for you and me. I'll work through all of these issues that make you think I don't love you, and then I'm tearing your ass up."

I laughed out loud. "Now that could get you taken right to the beach house without another word."

"Good, I hope you sleep well, knowing you could have taken your favorite dress off me, but you decided to play it safe."

"Trust me," I arched an eyebrow at her, "I'll get to the *fuck it* part soon enough if you keep this up."

"Don't make promises you can't keep."

"I'll be back early tomorrow. I'm plumbing my mom's house, and you said you wanted to help, remember?"

"I'll have my overalls on. I hope you won't mind those."

"Like most of your clothes, I wanted to rip those things off you the first time I saw you wearing them." I laughed and got out to help Elena to the front door.

Stevie was walking out as we were walking in, so the small kiss goodbye I was hoping for was put on hold. I'd eventually have her, but I knew it was all a matter of patience. The *old Collin* wouldn't have given a damn, but the man I was since this goddess bounced into my life? Hell no. I treasured this woman, and there was no fucking way I would have sex with her and then wonder if she regretted it. Fuck no. I couldn't handle that.

Elena

COLLIN WAS at the house bright and early like he said he would be. I had to admit, longing to be with him, just hanging out, was overshadowed by these raging flames of wanting him sexually. The guy was gorgeous, and that wasn't helping these feelings either. Rejecting me only made me want him that much more, and because of all of that, I hardly slept last night— tossing and turning and aching for his touch, wondering what it would all be like.

Hopefully, getting busy with this plumbing today would curb my sexual appetite for the man.

"I still can't believe you're doing this," I laughed, sitting across from him in the massive house's basement.

Collin glanced up, smirked, and continued to work on connecting the new pipes he was installing for the kitchen.

"Well, who knows. If I can perform brain surgery, I can certainly plumb a house, right?" He laughed. "Though, if the plumbers were here, they'd laugh at me for that statement again, and rightfully so."

"So what are you doing now?" I asked. My feet hung down from the concrete I sat on and into the dirt that was dug up to get to these particular pipes.

Collin was tweaked and bent over, and I was trying to ignore how perfectly defined his biceps were and the way they flexed while he worked. He was using some tool to smear blue stuff around the pipe. "I'm gluing this so I can attach these two." He grabbed the final piece of PVC pipe to finish his current job.

I watched with humor. "I can see you as a sexy handyman, you know?"

He laughed. "You haven't seen me in my surgical room." He glanced up at me with his beautiful smile and winked. "All right." He looked back at the pipes he'd just glued together. "Your turn. Twist that valve on, and let's see my magic unfold."

Collin was inside of this manhole that'd been dug, and I was closest to the main valve he'd instructed me to turn. I twisted the valve, and we waited.

"Looks like you did it," I said.

Collin stood there, inspecting a small leak when suddenly, the thing exploded with water, breaking loose the pipe Collin had just glued into the other piece.

I shrieked and laughed while water shot out of the hole, hosing down Collin and reaching up to spray water all over me.

"Shit! Turn it off." It was all I heard him say as I laughed so hard it made tears stream from my eyes.

I cranked on the main valve, shutting it off.

"Well, hell," I said with another laugh.

Collin ran a hand through his wet hair, and his once steely eyes turned humorous. "That's one way of putting it. The other way would be, well, I suck at this." He laughed, and I couldn't help but laugh along.

"Tell me this is clean water," I said, "not sewer?"

"Yeah, and straight from the well from hell." He smiled at me and pulled himself out of the manhole he'd been working in for the last hour.

I rose with him and picked up the can he was using for the glue. "I thought you said you were a patient man." I arched an eyebrow at him, both of us dripping wet.

"The most patient man you'll ever meet," he said with a smug grin.

"Then why didn't you let the glue actually dry?" I laughed again. "It says here, at least an hour…"

"Give me that," he said as he took the can and studied it. "Damn it. I thought I bought the quick cement shit. Well, fuck."

He made the funniest expression of defeat, and the water dripping from his spikey hair and down his face made him so desperately gorgeous. I couldn't resist closing the gap between us and wiping the water from his face.

"God, I'm one lucky woman," I said.

Collin didn't respond. Our eyes locked, and my heart started to fall out of rhythm in my chest. "Other way around," he finally said.

I watched his beautiful face twist into an expression I'd never seen before, and then his hands were holding onto my face.

I reached for his forearms, mainly to brace myself when he let out a breath, and his lips were finally on mine. My mind was fuzzy but focused. I was frozen in place while I felt his warm, soft lips cover my bottom one, then gently kiss each corner of my mouth until it dropped open, wanting more.

"Damn," he said in a ragged breath, his lips firmer as they captured my bottom lip again.

I swept my tongue into his mouth, on my toes, and reaching back to grip his waist and pull him against me. He groaned as his tongue met mine, and he held me closer as his kiss became so wild, aggressive, and hot that I could hardly take in how this made me feel.

I moaned, tasting his delicious kiss and yearning for more. Both of us were caught up in this hungry kiss, and I felt how hard he was. I felt energy rushing through my body on another level, and it was enough to make me feel dizzy and powerful all at once.

Collin pulled away and sighed when he kissed my forehead.

"Hell, Laney," he said, "we need to go take a walk or something. Jesus Christ, I'm—"

I stepped back and pulled off my overall straps. "You're what?" I interrupted, my new hunger for him urging me on.

"Listen, no one wants this more than I do," he said as he reached for my face and then tightened his lips, his eyes deep in their blue color, "but, I swear to God, if we do this, I won't be able to stop. My mind is already struggling to manage to keep my shit together, and that was just a kiss."

"I'm not afraid of you, Collin," I smiled at him.

"You should be," he laughed. "Baby, I swear I..."

"What?" I smiled at his struggle. "Stop fighting what you and I both want."

"I won't be gentle. I don't trust myself."

That shot a spasm of aching between my legs. "I didn't ask you to be gentle."

"You're sure?"

"I haven't been more sure of wanting something since I woke up in that hospital bed."

"Well, if there's one thing I know," he swept me up in his arms, "it's that since we're both drenched in ice-cold, well water, I'm certainly not doing this down in an old basement."

Collin must've had the entire house memorized because I had no idea where we were or where he was taking me after he finished that sentence, and we resumed his delicious kiss.

My feet were set on the ground in a room with a balcony to the right of the bed where Collin stood. I ignored the stylish room and focused on the only thing I wanted, and that was for Collin's clothes to be off.

He stood as still as a statue while I pulled his shirt off and examined the defined ridges of his pecs and ab muscles. "Wow, you're beautiful," I said, kissing the center of his warm, tanned chest.

I stepped back and wanted to see Collin's expression when I stripped down to nothing for him. I hadn't been *this* daring since—well, never. Collin's sharp blue eyes grew darker, and I loved seeing them fall to my exposed breasts while he licked his lips, watching as I pulled off my lace panties.

"How did I ever forget the body I always worshipped?" He smiled a devilish smile.

"I know I forgot yours," I said, stepping up to him.

I unbuckled his leather belt and worked fast to give myself the pleasure of seeing this outrageously handsome man entirely. My eyes followed the V-shaped muscle that was cuttingly defined, and then my eyes took in the perfection of this man's enormously large and hard cock.

"You're perfect," I said, looking up while I instinctively reached for his hard cock.

His eyes closed while I felt his wet tip and then tightly ran my lubricated hand from the top of his shaft to the base and then back. "Holy Christ," he said in an exhale. His eyes reopened and met mine. "Elena."

"Stop." I smiled and looked into his dazed eyes. "How in the world did I ever forget about this?" I squeezed his tip while twisting its moist surface in my hands.

Collin grinned. "A question I've asked myself since you forgot about me."

That's when the man had me back against the wall and took my breast in his mouth. I groaned in satisfaction, my nipple being tugged and toyed with by his teeth and lips. I ran my hands through his hair, loving its soft, wet texture.

"I need more," I begged through a choked up and hoarse voice. "Fuck me, Collin. Please don't make me wait."

That's when the patient, funny, witty, and kind Dr. Collin Brooks turned into the sexiest man I'd ever been with. I could only remember having sex with two boyfriends before this, but I knew that most men fucked hard and couldn't last long. I'd only hoped I could keep up with this man.

Collin had me on the bed, my body writhing beneath his as he kissed and bit along my neck, then he did something I wasn't expecting. He dipped his fingers into my soaking wet entrance and licked up the center of my chest. "I need to taste you," he said, his eyes demanding and possessive. "Are you comfortable with that?"

"Fuck," I arched my waist up, his fingers pressing into a spot that made me feel like I was electrocuted as his thumb moved my clit into circles. "Oh, God," I said, and my eyes met Collin's brilliant ones.

"Come on me," he said with a triumphant smile that only made me want more.

"I don't want it to end," I said, feeling the rolling sensation of this orgasm spinning deep inside me.

"We can go all night, Laney," he said.

Feeling more ecstasy than I'd ever remembered having, I did the one thing I'd never done and shoved his perfect face down, begging him to taste me.

"I'm coming, Collin," I arched up my pussy, and he caught it with his mouth.

His hands covered my hips while his long fingers gripped around my ass.

Oh...My...God... I thought when his tongue ran in and out of my pussy.

His grunts told me how much he loved this, and then as I screamed again that I was coming hard, his mouth covered my pussy, and his moans made this orgasm rip through me with so much more power and ecstasy than I knew was possible.

"Fucking hard," I called out again, coming in his mouth.

Once I started coming down, I felt my body working back up again. He was right about being able to go all night. It was perfect, and my pussy was desperate and needing that massive cock of his inside me.

"You're so fucking beautiful when you come," he said, kissing the inside of each of my thighs. "You want more, baby?"

"So much more," I panted out. "Kiss me. I need to taste myself on your lips."

I was stoned on this man. I had the most intense orgasm ever. Usually, I was pretty much done after I came, but now, I was just getting started. After tasting myself on Collin's lips, running my hands through his messy hair, and feeling his tip teasing my entrance, I had no earthly idea how my brain could let me forget this man.

CHAPTER FORTY-ONE
ELENA

I have no idea what'd washed over me, but I wasn't stopping it. This was the best sex I'd ever remembered having. Not just that, but it was with the man I'd been secretly wanting it from, wondering what it would be like to have him all over me.

I knew there was more to it than the way he held himself so confidently with his tall, robust frame or the way his eyes sparkled like jewels when they seemed to recall our sexual past the few times I'd asked about it. It was even more than just that smile of his that took me under his spell, but that's exactly where I was now, and I never wanted to leave this bliss.

I couldn't bear not having him inside me anymore, and my thoughts were wild and extreme when his daring eyes met mine. His kiss was delicious, especially when mixed with the taste of myself and Collin's flavors combined into one. He was a man who every chick seemed to pine over, but he was mine, and I loved it.

I reached down while his tongue moved aggressively with mine, and I grabbed his dripping wet cock. Collin pulled away that second, and his eyes met mine.

"Fuck, baby," he said, exhaling and bringing his cheek to mine. He sighed in the most beautiful way that told me he was following me into this world of bliss that had shrouded me.

I spread my legs where I lay beneath him, feeling his hard abs against my flesh. "I want it."

Collin's bottom lips went between his teeth. "Once I start, I could be rough."

"I want you, baby," I whimpered, kissing his hair that I'd destroyed while he swallowed my orgasm. "Now."

"Fuck it," he growled with a smile so dangerously beautiful I felt my stomach coil up in response.

Collin's eyes closed as he pushed through my entrance, spreading me so wide that I gasped in pleasure and some pain. "Oh, fuck," I said, my chin lifting while he kissed it and thrust deeper inside me.

"Open your legs for me, Laney," he said in a low voice. His eyes met mine, and his face was so serious that it nearly pulled me out of my exquisite bliss. "Goddamn, I've missed this tight pussy." He pushed in, and I watched his eyes go into a trance while his mouth fell open.

My own eyes rolled back behind closed lids the deeper he filled me. It was slow and so sexy that I could crawl out of my skin. I reopened my eyes and saw Collin's head turned to the side; his eyes closed as he moved in and out.

My pussy throbbed against the sensation of his huge cock, moving deep and pressing against an area that sent a shiver up my spine. I fell back into my daze, pushing my tits up into his chest while his lips went to my forehead. I licked from the base of his neck and under his chin, feeling so powerful that my body was creating this feeling for the sexiest man I'd ever met. His grunts and groans were so erotic, and I could only whimper in response.

Everything felt like it was moving in slow motion when Collin's fingers twisted into my hair and his lips forcefully met mine. He began moving harder and faster, and my body welcomed his cock in a way that had me wondering how I could have another orgasm without using my clit to set it off.

"Oh, fucking God," I cried out. "Oh, God, Collin, just like that."

"That's my girl," he said in a low voice, his lips and tongue on my neck. "You taste so delicious and feel so fucking good." He let out a breath and started thrusting harder.

Collin and I whimpered and moaned together while I gripped each of his biceps and further opened my legs. My body coiled up deep inside as if Collin's cock was pushing this orgasm through me like he knew exactly how to do it. This was heaven.

"Harder?" he asked, our eyes meeting.

"Fuck yes," I smiled at him.

"Baby, I've missed this."

We both used voices I'd never heard before, and our eyes locked onto each other and wouldn't let go as I felt Collin's body flex. Then, with a hard thrust and his head falling back, eyes closed, we both cried out in orgasm together. I went wild into shivers beneath him and loved him moving himself to complement the way my pussy contracted around the one thing it had wanted from this man for too long.

"I love this goddamn part so much," Collin said, his tongue circling my hardened nipple, and then he moaned, taking my breast in his mouth, sucking and moaning while moving in and out.

"You feel so good," I said.

He moaned in response, and I could sense he was having his own moment of pleasure while coming off his high. I wasn't done with him, though. Not even close.

When Collin rolled off of me, my eyes took in the dreamy sight of his perfect body while he panted out the last of his pleasure. I traced my fingers over the rigid lines of his abdomen when his hands went up behind his head.

"You're so beautiful," I said, my fingers moving to that sexy V-shaped muscle. "And sexy."

He smiled, his eyes remaining close. Then he reopened them and eyed me. "Thank God, you approve."

"More than, Collin Brooks." I smiled.

"You used to call me baby or Coll," he ran a hand through his hair. "Never this *Collin Brooks* BS," he chuckled.

"I'm not who I used to be, remember?" I peered up at him as I repositioned myself between his legs.

"You're my girl," he said, eyes studying me. "That's all that matters." His lips twisted up into a smile.

"We used to go all night, eh?" I said, grabbing his soft cock and moving it through my hands. "How'd we manage that?"

"By doing what you're doing now," he arched an eyebrow at me. "You want more, my little goddess?"

"You're the sex god," I teased. "I've never had sex with anyone like I just had with you."

Collin's head shifted against his pillow. "Well, I'm happy to hear that. You never brought that topic up before, nor did I care to ask."

"Why wouldn't you ask?" I asked, feeling his dick grow hard and sparks ignite between my legs, knowing I was blessed to be with a man who didn't pass out the moment he was done having sex.

"Two reasons: the first is that everyone has a past, and it's in the past for a reason, and the second is that I *knew* I was the best you ever had." He grinned.

"I want to swallow all of your cum, baby." I dipped my head and covered his hardening tip.

I watched Collin's legs fall slack and give me all access to his perfect cock, his balls, and his beautiful body. He grinned and let out a breath when I used the fact that he wasn't fully erect to take all of him in my mouth. "Jesus," Collin whimpered.

I took his balls and ran my tongue around them. This man was beautifully and meticulously groomed for a woman to devour him. I couldn't resist sucking on his balls and seeing his heels dig into the bed.

"You may not remember any of this, but you could've fooled me," he said in a beautifully tranced voice. "I'm all yours, sunshine."

I watched him close his eyes while I licked up and down his shaft and took his tip into my mouth. I closed my eyes and worked Collin's cock like a hungry sex addict. That's when Collin moaned again.

"The way you get me hard again blows my goddamn mind. Take me deeper, sunshine," he said, me seeing his muscles flex and stiffen while I worked him harder and harder.

It wasn't long before I watched Collin writhing and groaning, his severe-like eyes watching me as I took him as deep down my throat as I could. "You want me, baby?" I groaned out sexily.

"God, I'm going to..."

I inwardly smiled, watching his hands fist the sheets, and then his cum shot deep into my mouth. The savory flavor of Collin was fully welcomed, and I swallowed his cum like it was the best thing I'd ever had.

"Damn," I said, licking his tip for the last of him. "I've never swallowed before." I smiled at his eyes, snapping open and looking at me.

"You're fucking kidding. Well, that's another new one for me. Aren't you full of confessions in bed today?" He smiled. "Well, hopefully, you're not thoroughly disgusted."

I ran my tongue around his leaking tip. "No." I smiled. "Not at all. It was pretty amazing."

I COULDN'T SAY how long we continued our sexual escapade. It was all about crazy positions, groaning in pleasure, being on some crazy high, and Collin being so rough sometimes that I had an orgasm by that alone. The man sent me into some crazy sex frenzy, and it wasn't until I woke up and saw it was dark outside that I realized we'd been at it nonstop until we had actually passed out.

There was a soft light filtering into the bedroom from the living room, giving me the view of Collin's perfect body with a sheet that was draped slightly over his legs. We'd stopped for food at one point, walking around the house naked, and me, acting like a drunk weirdo, smearing peanut butter over my breasts to see that look in Collin's eyes and feel him lick it off my flesh. It was wild, and it was passionate…and it was self-indulgent and hedonistic, and right now, as I looked around—not under the love spell anymore—I felt dirtier than hell.

Fuck, I have to get out of here, I thought, feeling like the whore I'd acted like with him. I slipped out of bed and gathered my half-dried clothes, and went to leave the room. I grabbed my cell and called Lydia, but there was no answer.

Shit! Why did I feel so disgusted with myself…and him?

I tried to call Stevie, but no answer. *Okay, fine. Get some fresh air.* I went outside, trying to rid myself of the disgusting way I felt. I sniffed, knowing I couldn't do this again. I was repulsed with myself.

With my mind reeling, I decided to see if Lydia was right about Collin Brooks. I decided to search up a hashtag on Instagram to see if he really was some guy who always had a hot chick on his arm. I had no idea why I was doing this, but it's the way I felt after being with him— cheap and replaceable. Our sex was hot and amazing, and there was a reason he was a natural, knowing how my body would want to be pleased. He let me do things to him that showed this man was probably a male slut himself.

Why are you thinking this way? I pleaded with myself. I knew where it was going, and this wasn't going to be good at all. I felt my spiral, and I couldn't stop it.

That's when I saw some beautiful brunette when a video started rolling, and Collin appeared and ran his tongue up her cheek.

They were on a boat, and Collin's hand slid over her waist while someone videoed them. "We're celebrating my birthday," she squealed when Collin's mouth covered her neck.

"Get the fucking camera out of here," Collin said. I could see he was drunk and delighted to be *all over* this woman.

"I love you, Collin Brooks!" she screamed as he hoisted her up in his arms, and she waved off the person videoing them.

My stomach knotted up. I checked the date of the video and saw it was three years ago.

On some crazy witch hunt, I kept going. It seemed Dr. Collin Brooks was quite the playboy and the male slut that Lydia was right about all along. No one is that good in bed without a good reason. I watched more videos with different girls, and mostly on that boat. All the others were uploaded with a younger Collin and even Jake, probably six years ago or longer. It must've been when they were interns, but it didn't matter to me. I couldn't separate it in my brain. I was repulsed because I was one of *those* women too.

"What are you watching?" Collin asked. I should have felt like shit or something, but I didn't.

"Videos of the man I just slept with," I said, standing up and turning back to where he stood, confused and staring at me without his shirt on. "You're quite the hot item; you know that?"

His face darkened some by the accusation in my voice. "What are you trying to say?"

"Was this who I was to you?" I asked, turning my phone and shoving a picture of a woman in his face. "I thought you didn't cross lines with medical staff, yet here you are up in a helicopter with the same nurse who checked on me after I woke up."

"Kaci came to see you?" he questioned.

"Doesn't matter. She's a nurse, and you said I was the only medical professional who made you break your stupid little rule of dating medical colleagues."

There was something inside me that knew I was making something out of nothing. It's like I should've known better, but that voice inside me wasn't loud enough to drown out what was urging me on.

He ran a hand through his hair, looking almost terrified. "We're not doing this, Laney. There's no fucking way I'm going to allow you to act this way. Not after everything we just—"

"We both acted like nymphos, Collin." I glared at him. "I'm sure Kaci, who has a million pictures of you and her, was the same as I was in bed with you too."

Collin's expression was dark, and I shivered under it. "Those videos and pictures are from another fucked-up life I had before you. Ever since I met you, it's like I never had that life, Laney," he said in a sad voice.

"I bet your patients love seeing this," I said.

"I haven't lost patients over ex-girlfriends and their social media posts, no," he snapped back. "Laney, I'm telling you that's from a life I hardly remember. You're my entire world. Fuck."

"Did I know about all of these women?"

"If you did, you never accused me of being an asshole for it."

I smirked in disgust. "An asshole? Try a male whore." I glared at him.

"Jesus Christ," he said. "Is *that* what you're thinking? Good fucking God. I knew this was a bad idea. Goddammit!" His eyes leveled me. "Now what?" He lifted his chin, and this was the first time I could see that Collin was furious and not playing the *Elena has a brain injury* game.

"I want to go home."

"God, Elena, over my past? You'll judge me for that shit, but not for being the man who loves you more than anything?"

"Thank God, I'm on the birth control pill," I said, strangely hardened against him. "God only knows who else you knocked up the way you selfishly fuck women without protection." I stared at his stoic expression with disdain of my own. "Is that how it would have been, a girl from your past, walking into our lives with some kid she had you didn't know about?"

He ran a hand through his hair, looked to the side, and closed his eyes.

"Answer me, goddammit!" I yelled. "You have a history that's obvious you just want women sexually and don't give a shit whether…"

"Stop it!" he growled. "I fucked up by once again, losing myself in you and fucking you without protection. No, I've never had unprotected sex with any other chick I fucked." He paused, and his eyes widened, glossy with tears like he just had a revelation. "Oh, my God. What did I do? What the fuck are you doing to me?" he asked in a soft voice.

"Realizing you weren't the man they all say you are," I responded coldly. I could sense him pulling into himself. It was like an animal who'd been struck by its owner one time too many.

His lips tightened, and he coughed out a laugh of disbelief. "My fucking God, I can't—I've done everything under the sun to work with you, and you're just not going to let me in, are you?"

"I wish that I could."

"No, you don't." His voice wasn't filled with accusation or malice; he was heartbroken. "I knew better. Having sex with you was the worst thing I could've ever done. I see that perfectly now. God, I wish I had you back." His eyes filled with tears, and my heart broke, seeing that this man was torn.

"That's the thing. You see, every day, I'm reminded that I'm not twenty-two anymore. I have to force myself to imagine I'm thirty-two. I guess this ruins everything because I'll never be the Elena you fell in love with." I walked up to him, but he stepped away from me as if I were the devil I was behaving like. "I'll never have my career back, my life back, my life with *you* back, and I'm sick of fucking trying." I waved the phone in front of his somber expression. "I am pretty sure the *other Elena* wouldn't have stalked you out like I just did, and if she did, maybe she'd be more forgiving than I am. I'm not the woman you fell in love with, and I'm glad the sex we had made me see we're both wasting our time trying to get back something I know I don't want. I'm sick of trying to be who everyone wants me to be."

He pulled a fist up to cover his mouth. "It's over," he said to himself. "Fuck me. I can't believe this." He looked over at me with a tear slipping out of his eye. "Okay, then. It's easy to see people fall in love when the time is right. We met at the right time before, and it was all beyond perfect."

"You see what I mean? I can't even tell you how sick I am of being compared to someone I don't remember without you immediately bringing her up. Everyone is clinging on to some hope that I'll one day *come to my senses*. I don't want to be her! Fuck her!" I couldn't help but shout. But I wasn't out of control. I didn't need to be calmed down. I was angry, and I was finally speaking my mind, and I didn't give a fuck how it made him, or anyone else, feel. "I've heard you talk about me regressing, and maybe this is what that is, but I don't care. Nothing I do changes anything, and I think it's time you leave me alone for good. I have no interest in being the woman you loved. That's not me anymore."

I was tired of trying with him and with everything. I was tired of all of this period. I wasn't getting my life back, no matter how hard I tried. I didn't wake up from a night of passion, feeling in love like I'd hoped would be the case. There were no bells or memories flooding back— nothing. It was just me and the man who'd been relentless at trying to make me someone else again.

I was hurting him, but my instinct for self-protection felt so much bigger than any of this. Maybe I blew the video thing out of proportion to have an excuse to get out of this. My subconscious had been sabotaging me for months, so I didn't know anymore, and I didn't care. I was done.

CHAPTER FORTY-TWO
COLLIN

I was numb. Elena had sat quietly in the car for the entire way back to her home, and she didn't say a word as she got out and went inside. Yesterday, I wouldn't have let her leave that way, but I couldn't do this anymore. I fucked it up, and I knew it. She wasn't ready, and yet, I still impulsively jumped off the deep end and destroyed any progress I could've made with her and her goddamn memory loss.

I felt like a piece of shit, worse than the man she recalled from my past: the player, Collin Brooks, who didn't give a shit. I was all about enjoying hot women, booze, and good times when I wasn't studying. Fuck that life, and fuck me now for putting Elena in a position to have regrets about being with me and make her think I would fuck her like any other piece of ass I had in the past.

Regardless of the videos she'd seen sending her off the deep end, she made it clear that she was moving on and accepting life as the person she was now. She had no interest in trying to get her memories back, and pushing her to keep trying was only making her regress farther into herself. I'd fucked up on so many levels, and I knew there was no putting this genie back in its bottle. Maybe I'd been fooling myself that she was farther along than she was because I wanted it to be true so badly. That mistake cost me my happiness—my entire life.

Ring! Ring!

I was headed to Malibu after dropping Elena off, and low and behold, at seven in the morning, Alex was calling me. I would've ditched the call, but the man never called this early.

"What's up?" I answered through the car phone.

"We're going to need you at the firm today."

"Not a good time, man," I said, driving faster than usual.

"Yeah, well, unless you turn the entire company over to Jim, I need your ass here for an issue that came up yesterday with Tatum."

"You're fucking kidding me. She's the last goddamn witch I want to see right now."

"We need you present, or she'll fucking sue your ass after we fire her."

"Fire her?"

"Yes. That's the only thing that you're needed for. After multiple complaints about Tatum abusing her position as VP and accusation of sexual misconduct, we hired an outside and non-biased investigation on her," he said. "We have two individuals who've come forward with her on video—setting her up—and it turns out that she'd mislead them into believing they'd be promoted in return for sexual favors."

I steered the car to head toward the freeway that would bring me to downtown Los Angeles.

"You still there? I was notified of her immediate termination by the board and Jim. I'm five minutes out from the firm myself."

"Don't sick and twisted men in power pull this vile shit?" I questioned, in shock that Tatum was sick enough to consider such a thing.

"*Anyone* can pull this shit," Alex said, "but Tatum will fucking try to sue. She's that ruthless. You need to be present, sign papers, and we'll handle the rest from there. She's requesting a meeting with you and me first."

"I don't want to be anywhere alone with a woman as demented as she is," I answered. "What about the complaints? Is this shit going to put the firm on blast and shed my dad's company in a bad light?"

"Not if we terminate her. We've had our lawyers speak with the lawyers of the victims. A healthy settlement has been reached, and there won't be any media involved. Jim's a genius when it comes to this shit."

"I'll be there in about thirty," I said.

. . .

I PULLED my car up to the valet and tossed him my keys. "Park it in the VP parking place, please."

"Sir, that is Ms. Adams' usual spot. Her car is parked there currently." He smirked at me in confusion and humor. "I'll park your car in your—"

"Tow the Mercedes that belongs to Ms. Adams, and then park my car in her spot. She's terminated." I glanced down at my Rolex. "She'll be packed up, and that car will be considered illegally parked in about half an hour. A towing company should be here by then, and if she wants her car back, she can find the impound lot." I eyed him. "Please don't argue with me and just do as I ask."

"Absolutely, sir," the valet said, and I turned to walk into the entrance of the badass skyscraper my dad designed for his firm.

I walked in and was greeted by the security at the front desk before using my card to get to the top floor. The more and more I thought about it, the more I was entirely done with owning this company that had been dropped into my lap. I tried to work with Jim, having Mitchell and Associates take it on, but Alex was right: there was shit Jim and Alex couldn't do. The vice president we'd trusted—because my dad had trusted her—had taken advantage of her position.

Alex tried to manage this place, but he was running two massive, billion-dollar companies between this and Mitchell and Associates. His main priority, however, was Mitchell and Associates. Brooks Architectural Firm was something he oversaw to keep the *machine* running, and he did that for me. I'd be making a lot of decisions within about thirty minutes, though, and I was so furious about everything that'd happened with Elena that I didn't know if those decisions would be good or bad, keep friendships or destroy them. I didn't fucking care either.

"You," I said to a young woman with dark blonde hair, sitting outside Tatum's office. "What's your title?"

"Well, I was hired a month ago by Ms. Adams as her personal secretary." She pulled off her black-rimmed reading glasses and suddenly seemed a bit irked as I remained quiet, studying her. "You'd think *I* was vice president, though, which I shouldn't get annoyed about. I graduated at the top of my class at NYU to get in this position. At least I'm close enough to taking Tatum's place when she becomes president."

"New York? That's an excellent and prestigious college. However, I believe you've been misled somewhat."

"What do you mean?" she asked.

"It appears that your current boss had misled you to think you'd be taking her position after she was promoted, I assume."

"That would be an understatement. I was told I was interning, and then my pay would match the job I left before I moved out here."

"Come with me. Give me a rundown on your resume, Miss—Mrs?"

"Miss Grant." She smiled at me, her youthful glow adding to her attractive appearance. "I was the Senior Marketing Director for a firm in New York. I moved out here, knowing the history of Brooks Architectural, and I was excited when Tatum—I mean, Ms. Adams—hired me after…"

All I was hearing was that this place needed a fucking overhaul from top to bottom. The woman trying to keep up with my long strides was downloading a resume that should've had her replacing Tatum a long fucking time ago. So glad I'm responsible for allowing Tatum to have this much control and pulling shit over Alex's eyes.

I walked into a conference room where an HR rep, Alex, and Tatum sat, a perplexed Miss Grant at my side. I ignored the bewildered expressions and asked Miss Grant to take a seat while I picked up the phone, sat casually in my chair, and met Tatum's daggers with a blank expression of my own.

"Yes, it's Dr. Brooks," I said when the records department answered. "I need records emailed to me and Mr. Grayson immediately. They'll be the resume and whatever else we have on—" I covered the receiver to the phone. "What's your first name?"

"Jacey," she said, and I nodded.

"A Miss Jacey Grant, please."

"Right away, sir."

I hung up and stared at the silenced room. "Turns out, you're fired." I widened my eyes at Tatum's meek expression first.

"Just like that?" she said.

I pursed my lips. "Well, if you'd like, I can call for the reports on you. We can dim the lights and have the videos of your hostile work environment and sexual harassment case shown on our large conference screen if you don't understand why you're terminated."

"Listen," she tried to speak nicely to me, "this isn't what you think."

"Ma'am," the HR representative spoke before I could, "with the contracts you've signed, and Brooks Architectural Firm's zero-tolerance policy on *any* harassment in the workplace, we are here as a formality to confirm the owner complies with your termination."

She looked at Miss Grant. "Why are you here?"

"Because she's not packing up your desk," I snapped. "Those days are over." My email notification dinged, and I pulled it up on my opened laptop, looking at Miss Grant's resume. "Holy crap," I looked over at Jacey, "you've won quite a few distinguished awards. You accomplished a great deal at your previous firm as well. It's no wonder you assumed you were going to be our vice president." I looked at Tatum. "Care to explain the lies you told this woman when you hired her?" I shook my head, disgusted. "You know what? Your voice is no longer necessary." I looked at Jacey. "It looks like Tatum was right. You were hired to replace her as vice president. Alex will schedule a meeting with you to go over the details of your new job, should you accept my offer. The monetary concerns will be addressed in all of that as well."

Her eyes nearly bulged out of her head as she looked over at Alex's pissed-off expression. I already knew I was coming in hot and that I may or may not make all of my friends angry in the process.

"Miss Adams, security will return with you to your office, and with Dr. Brooks' official declaration, you are terminated from this firm immediately," Alex said with anger and authority.

"Is that all?" I said.

"That's all we have for now," the HR rep said.

"Miss Grant," Alex said, "I request that you move forward with your day. I will be in contact with you shortly."

The room filtered out, leaving me swiveling in the leather chair my dad always filled, staring outside the floor to ceiling windows. How many meetings had that man conducted in here, and how many times must he have looked out over all of downtown, deep in thought about the next project he'd take on. This next part wasn't going to be easy.

"What the hell was that?" Alex asked, taking the chair adjacent to mine.

"That was me, handling the last of the business that I'll be taking care of as the owner of this firm."

"Coll, come on," he said. "I mean, I saw Miss Grant's resume. I'm quite shocked about her predicament, but an immediate replacement into

Tatum's VP position, and now you're acting like you're out of this firm altogether?"

"I'll be selling it. I'll ensure the new owner understands that it's merged with Mitchell, but I know you well enough to know that if I gave this burden to you, you could manage the firm and not allow shit like this to bust loose or ever happen again."

"Things like this always happen in large—"

"I know, Alex. That's why I'm out. I'll keep our family's stock in the firm, but I'm out. I can't run this place, and with the position you hold at Mitchell, trying to trust the VP and board to keep this place running, it's fucked up. So, you've got the keys if you want them—CEO and owner. Tell Jim he can hate me for the rest of his life for offering you the business, but I don't fucking care."

"What the hell happened?" he grew more solemn. "It's you and Elena, isn't it?"

"Let's say that Elena and I are officially done, and I'm getting back to what I do best, which is being a neurosurgeon and not dealing with this place. It's been bugging me for a while. Tatum's fuck up was the push I needed to do the right thing and let it go. I appreciate you and Jim carrying this shit for me, but I'm not keeping the firm. So either take the beast, or I'll sell it off."

"Okay, fuck." He rubbed his forehead. "We're not allowing you to sell it, that's for damn sure. Even if you did sell off, Jim would buy the place on principle alone. This was practically his second home growing up too."

"Then he won't be pissed when his VP leaves to own it," I said and stood. "Let me know what you both decide. I'm as serious as a fucking heart attack. I'm done here. Talk to Jim and let him know where I stand. That Jacey woman?" I eyed him and pursed my lips. "After skimming her resume, you'd be a fucking idiot not to put her in the VP position."

"After we're assured she wasn't connected to what Tatum was doing, of course."

I smiled my asshole smile. "And that's why you've got this place if you want it."

"Jim and I will discuss removing your name as owner, and we will ensure you still receive the proceeds of the company. You, your mom, and your sister."

"I can give a fuck about the endless income from this place, but I know my sister could probably use it, and even though my mother has enough mink coats to carpet her mansion and money to wallpaper it, I think her dividends are well-earned. She helped my dad start this place, so I wouldn't feel right about her not getting her share, even if she *is* swimming in gold coins like Scrooge McDuck."

Alex let out an incredulous laugh as he shook his head. He couldn't have been too surprised. The bigger surprise should've been that I attempted to hang on to this place for as long as I did.

"We'll handle it and do what's best."

I turned to leave. "The *only* reason this place has kept running without my dad is you, Alex," I said. "You know that shit too. You are the fucking reason it didn't fold, so take my offer. It's the best you'll ever get."

BEING the friends that they were, Alex and Jim handled all of my business. It turned out that Jacey Grant's nose was clean from any contamination from Tatum Adams, and she and Alex were going to work together to clean up my dad's company and move it forward.

I didn't give any of it much more thought. I was just glad that Jim and Alex didn't flip out over me, handing the firm over to Alex. Jim couldn't have been happier for his best friend, though, and rightfully so. Badass acquisitions and VP executives like Alex were primed and prepped to take over a company like my dad's or even Jim's.

It'd been about a month since Elena told me she was done, and I was moving forward no matter how difficult it was, knowing Elena and I had no hope. I couldn't fix what I broke, and if I was honest, I never wanted to see that look in her eyes again or be reminded of how she felt and how it all made me feel. My friends kept the topic dead after I went off and said I didn't want another word spoken about it.

Even though I'd gotten back to work and moved through it all reasonably well, I had my moments. Today was what I'd refer to as a dark day, a day that made me feel like demons haunted me and laughed in my face—making sure I knew that I'd gotten what I deserved for being so reckless and wild with women. These days only hit when I was stupid enough to stay at the beach house I'd finally gotten up the courage to put on the market.

"So," I heard Jake walking down to me as I stared out at the ocean, looking for serenity there, "you're really selling the place, eh?"

"I have my mom's—my ranch," I said, not looking at him as I continued to lean against the edge of my balcony, forearms resting on the top edge. "We all know I never spent that much time here, anyway."

"Well, Ash and I don't spend as much time at ours, and we still have the place as a nearby place to escape."

"I don't need the place," I said distantly. I eyed a sailboat out in the distance. "Remember when we were like five years old, and I was supposed to tie that rope—your dad was teaching me how?"

"And you fucked it up, and the wind blew the mainsail right into me and knocked me the hell out?" He laughed.

"I'm still sorry about that." I chuckled.

"No, you're not." He grinned.

"Maybe I'm not." I let out a breath. "It was that moment when I thought I'd killed my best buddy." I smiled over at Jake, still in his scrubs from working today. "That doctor who helped you—being so young, I really thought he brought you back to life."

"That neurosurgeon was an asshole," Jake chuckled. "While the nurses kissed my ass, he told me that my head was fine, and I didn't need special treatment." He laughed. "Just when I had a nurse sneak in a candy bar for me too."

I laughed at the memory. "Well, I'm glad someone stopped you from playing the system."

"What's with all of this reminiscence? Are you thinking about giving up practicing now too?"

"No," I said. "I'm just thinking."

"Well, I've let you *think* long enough, and I want to know why Elena just fired my ass as her cardio doctor?"

I rolled my eyes. "Probably searched up a hashtag on your ass and determined she didn't trust you to be her doctor anymore too."

"Miguel must be losing his shit on this," Jake said, then laughed. "Although, the way he is and that no-bullshit, Latino streak in him, I guess Elena's blood runs just as strong with that too."

"It's what made her personality so much fun." I smiled at the memories of her and I being wild together. "I definitely met Miguel's bloodline in her that day she…" I stopped.

"She made you feel like a male whore who fucked her for fun?"

I glared at Jake. "You know me too fucking well."

"It was easy to see. You have the same regrets I had when I got together with Ash and wished I never lived some crazy male-slut life before her. And what's the fucking deal with your exes not deleting old pics of you with them?"

"I have no clue." I ran my hands through my hair.

"Do you think you'll try again? You know it took *two* of you to have sex, right? This isn't all on you."

"I should've had better control."

"Fuck that noise," Jake said. "You've had nothing but control with Elena. You're so damn sexy that I want to fuck you sometimes too. Can't blame her for most likely luring you in and taking advantage of your greatest weakness with her."

"You can be so stupid sometimes," I said, not in the mood for the way Jake and I got into this routine a long time ago of acting like fucking idiots.

"Listen, whether or not you and Elena ever get through this, I know one thing I'll remain solid on."

"What's that? I'll be single and lonely for the rest of my life?"

"No," he laughed. "I won't let you carry the blame on this. I don't give a shit about what you heard her say. It wasn't all you, Coll, and we both know that."

"No, it wasn't." I rose and turned back toward the house. "It wasn't only about that, though, and that's why I'll never see her again. There's no point in trying when she's made it clear she's not thirty-two in her head and didn't want to try to be. I think it was a lot less about the sex and a lot more about not wanting to keep trying to be someone she's not. I think I'm just a reminder of what's gone, and after a while, me being around is counterproductive. I have no place with her anymore. I'm accepting that, and I'm moving on." I clapped him on his arm and exhaled. "The burden of the firm being gone has helped, and once this house is out of my life, I'll be living in a better place."

"Why do you have this place listed nearly forty million dollars over the market price?" he smirked at me.

"Because," I stopped and stared at the living room, "I'm greedy."

"Bull-fucking-shit." Jake laughed. "Hey, I'm off early, and I'm heading to the beach house to change and take a ride up the coast; you in?"

"Absolutely," I answered, feeling the adrenaline of my bike calling for me from my garage. "I'm off until Tuesday. I might just get a hotel up the coast and enjoy what I love most about it up there."

"Sounds like a great idea. Guys weekend?"

"Ash cool with that?"

"She hates it when I take her to San Francisco just to ride trollies and take tours of Alcatraz."

"Yet," my forehead wrinkled in humor, "it's what I love most about you."

"Let's get the hell out of SoCal for the weekend and enjoy the fact Jim insisted we work identical shifts."

"You think that's why this shit keeps happening?" I laughed at the fact that Jake and I were rarely off simultaneously, but as soon as Elena and I were over, his shifts pretty much matched mine.

"I *know* that's why," he answered. "Jim's always been a big brother to you too. He's just looking out."

"Thank goodness I can handle your ugly mug."

"And that I can handle your all-new, asshole personality."

CHAPTER FORTY-THREE
COLLIN

The time came and went in the blink of an eye, and before I knew it, it was officially August. I went through the motions of my life, trying to scrape together a semblance of what it used to be before Elena came into it. But I would never be the same—I *could* never be the same.

I suppose I could've gotten angry at the universe for treating me so cruelly, but when I compared my misery to what Elena must've been feeling, I knew I had no room to complain. If anything, I should've been on my knees with gratitude that I was given the gift of all-consuming love, something that most people will never have.

My sister told me that I should be grateful that things with Elena ended now instead of later—something she intended to be a comfort to me as if it's something I would've ever wanted to happen at *any* time. Maybe it was easy for people to give those platitudes because they didn't know Elena—they didn't know *us*.

To people who didn't know, there were no extraordinary circumstances. I was just a guy who'd lost the interest of a girlfriend he hadn't even been dating for a year. It seemed so uncomplicated with that logic, and I wouldn't bother to set the record straight. What looked like a whirlwind romance that was bound to fizzle out was anything but that. Elena had been my soulmate—of that, I have no doubt—but she wasn't my Elena anymore, and I'd forced myself to accept that conclusion. I wouldn't live in misery, and *my* Elena wouldn't have wanted me to, so all I could do is get on with it.

I spent the majority of my off days giving Addy and John horseback riding lessons at my ranch. Grace had been a *Return to Sender* gift from Elena, so she kept the kids busy while they anxiously awaited their new siblings, who were due to arrive any day.

The heart institute had opened last week, and that was a huge asset to Saint John's, as Jim knew it would be. All that was left now was to break ground on the neuroscience center and get the ball rolling. Sometimes I wondered how Jim kept up with all of this shit and still managed to be the ideal family man.

It was nearing the end of the day for me, and I only had one consultation left. It was with our new neurologist from a prestigious hospital in the UK, and in her two months here, this doctor was a highly impressive asset to the team.

I walked to the hospital to do a quick consult for her patient, who had a benign tumor and would probably not be a candidate for surgery, but who knew? I hadn't had a chance to read the recent brain scans or patient history before being called for a consult.

I walked briskly to the neuro ward and into the dimly lit room, knowing her patient was waiting in the hospital for her to come back with answers. I went straight to the scans and studied the brain in the 3D images of the MRI.

"Patient is Miss Elena Alvarez, and—"

"I'm sorry, who?" I looked at Dr. Moas.

"Elena Alvarez." She looked at me weirdly.

This doctor was one of the few people here who didn't know mine and Elena's history. She only knew that I was the one who performed surgery after the brain injury.

"Why is the patient in with MRIs?" I questioned, seeing the tumor I wasn't able to remove altogether had grown by quite a bit since Elena's last scans when she was released from my care.

"Headaches, nausea, and her history, of course," Dr. Moas stated.

"I wasn't able to remove that tumor completely. It's benign, but I did wonder if it would take on a life of its own after her skull was opened for the emergency surgery. Keep a close eye on it," I said. "I would recommend ordering another scan next week. For now, there are no life-threatening issues. If it grows larger in the next week, I will revisit the scans."

"Miguel Alvarez requested that you be there when I consult her."

Good God, Miguel. Why are you doing this to me?

"I assume it would be to pass the buck if the patient isn't happy that I'm not green-lighting the surgery." I smiled at her. "Well, let's hope that seeing my face will diffuse the room of any outrage."

"They were hoping for surgery," she said.

"I won't approve that," I answered after I opened the door. "Shall we, then?"

"Let's go piss off another family today." She shook her head.

"Good surgeons know the first answer isn't surgery."

"And you get to say that in the room."

I grinned, "No, I'll be present and answer questions asked of me, when asked."

"There something I need to know?" Dr. Moas asked skeptically.

"Only that this is my ex-fiancé who woke up with no memories of me and hates my ass now," I smirked at her shocked expression. "Other than that? It's peaches and cream, Mabel."

"For heaven's sake." She looked over at me. "Between women gawking and talking about you all day and your crazy sense of humor, I have no idea how we all work together so well."

My eyes widened as I gave her a funny look when we approached the conference room. "You mean to tell me you're not fascinated by the dashing Dr. Brooks? A shame."

She rolled her eyes. "Even if I *did* like boys, your cockiness would've killed it for me a long time ago," she said with a laugh. "Can we get this over with? Now I'm really afraid to meet with them."

"And you haven't met with her feisty and fun Cuban side, either." I laughed, and then we went into professional mode as I followed her into the room.

Miguel and Elena sat at the large conference room table, and Elena's eyes grew as wide a saucers when I walked in and took my seat across from her and her father. She looked at her dad, and all I could assume was nothing had changed since the last time I saw her. Now, here I was again, about to piss her off again.

I allowed Mabel to inform Elena why she was experiencing headaches and minor dizzy spells, and when she was done, that's when those bronze eyes that I'd loved so much shot their daggers at me.

"We understand," Miguel said, sadness in his voice.

"No, *we* don't," Elena shot back at her dad. "Why am I not a candidate for surgery? I have a tumor in my goddamn brain!"

Elena was more aggressive than I remembered, so her mood changes were still there, but they seemed a bit more, and I made a mental note about that. Mabel hadn't mentioned increased mood swings, but that might've been because Miguel didn't bring it up.

"I understand that; however, it is not life-threatening at the moment. There is nothing about this tumor at present that deems it necessary for a craniotomy," I said, trying to remain steady and professional against all of my instincts.

"Well, it did grow; Dr. Mabel just told us that," Elena insisted.

"We're monitoring that situation closely. If the tumor grows more by the time we order scans again next week, then we'll discuss the craniotomy," Mabel said.

"Damn it." She gripped her forehead. "I don't want to live my life on pain medication."

She sounded so much like Jamie, and my heart broke for her. Most importantly, though, the woman didn't need me cutting her skull open again within a year of her accident, especially if it wasn't life-threatening.

Miguel pulled up the x-rays in front of him. "This is the same tumor. Be sure to watch this," he advised me. "Her mood swings are far more aggressive, headaches..."

"What are you saying that we haven't already gone over?" Mabel asked.

"I'm saying things have gotten worse with Elena since the accident," he said.

"We will monitor it, Miguel," I answered. "I will make sure my schedule is ready for a craniotomy if we find that tumor has grown as much as a millimeter by next week. I understand your frustration, but I'm not risking clots, strokes, or any of the other potential complications that come with a craniotomy."

Elena burst into tears and crumbled into her dad. "He won't do it."

"We'll be back for the scheduled MRI, Dr. Brooks—"

"Can we go?" Elena interrupted Miguel through her tears.

I watched in discomfort as Miguel led Elena from the room. "Shit!" I said, believing I was alone.

"I'm guessing this is why you two aren't together," Mabel said.

I smiled over at her. "Wild guess and extremely accurate."

"Collin, have you stopped to think that this tumor could be the reason she's in pain and not fully recovering?"

I rose and shrugged. "I would be a selfish man if I cut into that woman for those reasons alone. I know that the tumor could be putting pressure on her frontal lobes and temporal lobes, amongst other places in her brain, which could very well be why I lost my fiancé. Well, aware. *But* she's alive," I said. "Maybe she's not living the life she wants, but she is walking out of here, breathing on her own, and that's a straight-up miracle after her accident."

"You're an exceptional surgeon," she said, serious. "That takes a lot."

"I know." I tried to smile, but my lips could hardly lift.

TWO DAYS LATER, I was sitting at a table with Dr. Brandt, a pediatric surgeon, cracking jokes as we ate lunch. The guy was a young, hot-shot doc, and he reminded me a bit of Jake and me in our younger days.

"How did the surgery go, then?" I asked.

Brandt's blue eyes grew wide. "The surgery went well, and I was taking her to the pediatric lunchroom in no time."

"Can't believe that adorable seven-year-old would dare be caught in public with you," I smirked at the man who had a different chick on his arm every other weekend.

Brandt was fun and relaxed, and hitting the club with him one night was probably the only fun I'd had since Elena dropped me on my ass. However, given he was in pediatrics, and I was up in the main neuro unit, I hardly saw the man. Besides, he was into the nightlife, and those days were so far in my past that I felt like an idiot being at a club at all.

"Then it came down to her mom." He gave me a look—a look I knew well enough.

"Enough of this story," I rose with a laugh. "Tell me, did you take the mom out?"

"God, no," he said. "Doctor and patient relationships stay between the kid and me. The only dates happening there are when I take them to the cafeteria for ice cream. Those kids have been through enough, and that's the end of that line."

"Wow," I smiled at him, "looks like you took a page out of mine and Dr. Mitchell's book."

My pager went off, and I eyed Brandt as my cell began ringing right after. "Gotta bounce. Good catching up, man," I said before I answered my phone.

"What's my case?" I asked, knowing this call-in number meant that my trauma unit was on standby.

The ER doctor ran down the list of everything his room had done to stop the patient's epileptic seizure, and after he ran through all of the charts and told me she was currently stable, he informed me that the patient was Elena. I felt a cold chill shoot through my chest as soon as he said it, and I didn't hesitate to have her sent to my unit at once. I ordered an immediate MRI, knowing Elena's history, trying to get a step ahead.

I looked at the scans on the MRI, and I saw immediately that the tumor had grown. The mother fucker had almost killed her once, and now, her quality of life was suffering—headaches and dizziness had reached the point of severe, gran-mal seizures.

I remained quiet while the trauma staff in the room spoke about the outcomes of what we were looking at.

"Is there a chance surgery will be taking place?" Dr. Singh asked.

"I'm watching the EEG," I said, intensely studying whether or not this tumor was indeed the culprit to Elena's seizure. I had to be sure before I made a call on this. "Is her family here?"

"Dr. Alvarez and her brother are being brought up to trauma waiting room four," he said.

"I'll bet they're both pleased to revisit that same room again," I said. "Call for them to be moved into a different room, please. Actually, forget that." My eyes were drawn to another mild seizure that was occurring, and it confirmed the only solution to the problem. Well, there could've been others, but I highly doubted that waiting any longer was the stellar choice at the rapid rate this thing was growing. "Right here." I pointed at the EEG, showing me the synchronized bursts of electrical energy firing all around that tumor. "That's our problem."

"Son of a bitch, Brooks," Singh said, looking at me in some humored shock. "Nice eye."

"Everyone says they're the most beautiful." I clapped his arm. "Everyone but that little salsa-dancing queen in the MRI machine. Get her out of there. I'll talk to her and Miguel once she's in her room."

"IS OUR PATIENT PREPPED FOR SURGERY?" I asked my OR team, who had prepped my surgical room for Elena's craniotomy, taking place first thing this morning.

I'd had two days off after the night we discovered Elena's rapidly growing tumor in the trauma unit. They were the longest two days of my life, knowing we were here again. At least this time, Elena would be awake. Even though she was a bit frightened about that, I would be able to grab this thing, and hopefully, she wouldn't have any more headaches or dizziness, and definitely no more seizures. There were so many possible outcomes for this operation, and my only hope was that Elena's suffering would finally end, and opening her skull up again would be worth it for her health.

"She is a bit nervous," the neuro anesthesiologist said, the one who would be brain mapping for me for Elena's tumor removal. "We went over everything again, and she's as ready as anyone can be before being awake during a craniotomy."

"I'll be in the room as soon as I scrub in and after I see the patient."

I walked into Elena's room. Miguel hugged me, and that was only because I knew the man was scared shitless. This was such an intricate brain surgery, dealing with the delicate parts of Elena's brain. I needed to work with the utmost precision and skill to get the entire tumor out this time.

"You were invited into the observation room," I said.

"I'll stay out with Stevie and the family," he said.

"Okay." I looked at Elena, the bed being prepped to move out once I was done, "Elena?"

"Dr. Brooks," she answered nervously.

"I know this is unsettling, but we plan to keep you comfortable as I work to remove the tumor with Dr. Nathan," I said. "Natalie has talked to you about her being at your side when we wake you up?"

"Yes," she sighed.

"All right. Let's get this out and get you well on your way to recovery."

"Thank you, Dr. Brooks."

The medication being administered was working because I was finally on the receiving end of the nicer Elena—the one I hadn't had the privilege of for a couple of months. It was time to keep this down to a doctor-patient relationship so I could do my job and get the entire tumor out.

"ALL RIGHT. Let's wake up the patient," I ordered once I was ready to have Natalie guide me to stay away from the critical parts of Elena's brain.

Elena was on the other side of the plastic barrier, making it much easier not to see her face while I operated. It was just me, a tumor, a brain that needed my help, my sucker device, and scalpel.

"Hi, Elena," Natalie said cheerfully. "Can you squeeze my hand?"

"Where's Dr. Brooks?" she asked.

I smiled. A typical question that almost every patient asked while I performed a craniotomy. They always seemed to think I wasn't around when they first were brought out of anesthesia.

"He's right behind you," I said. "Can you squeeze Natalie's hand for me?" I looked up at the computer model and then toward Natalie, who was nodding while I moved my device around her healthy brain outside of the tumor. "Keep doing that."

Natalie looked at me and shook her head.

Okay, stay away from here. I coached my way through removing the tumor and focusing on that.

"I'm sorry, Dr. Brooks," Elena said.

"Elena, can you please work with Natalie and answer her questions?" I asked, knowing she and I weren't going into a heart-to-heart while I was poking around in her brain. "And it's okay. I just rewired your brain to say that to me, so we're all good now," I said, Dr. Nathan laughing at my side. I needed to keep Elena comfortable, though, and my initial knee-jerk reaction was a bit harsh.

"I bet you've wanted to do this all along," she said.

"Elena, tell me what this card is showing." Natalie tried to keep Elena focused on the boring cards I'd stopped using a while ago, but Nat was old school, and this is how she rolled.

"It's a shoe," she said while I moved around to the side of the tumor, slowly removing it and clamping off blood vessels that fed it as I went. "Would this have helped me before?" Elena asked me.

"I can't answer that question. That wouldn't have been a reason to do surgery, though," I said. "If I did all of this to make you remember me, I would *really* be the Frankenstein doctor from the game my nephew and niece played with you and me," I smirked, and then I spoke to Dr. Nathan. "This one right here. I need this clamped, and then we'll cut here."

"That was fun," she said.

"Always a good time with Addy and John. Damn." I lowered my voice as Natalie took over talking to Elena. "This thing made itself a cozy home in here. Look at all these damn blood vessels," I said, eyeing his concerned expression. "We'll cauterize the small ones, but no wonder this thing took off."

"Found a source and just grew. Isn't the first of its kind," he said.

Natalie kept Elena engaged in conversation that I would have loved to listen to if I weren't operating on such a bastard of a tumor. The fucking thing had more blood vessels feeding off of her brain than I expected by far. They spoke about Elena's life and what she was up to, and I smiled when I heard that familiar laugh of hers I missed. I thought I'd detoxed off this woman, but she sure as hell had her way with my soul and then some.

I was six hours into this surgery before I'd successfully removed the mass, clamped off the larger vessels, and cauterized the small ones it was using to grow in Elena's brain. She would be placed on medication to prevent strokes and clots, and within three to four days—maybe less given her age and health—she'd be going home with her dad, who knew how to watch for any concerning signs.

I made my rounds after Elena was in the recovery room and was happy to see that everything seemed well and good. She was a little disoriented, which was expected, but she was free of the tumor. Hopefully, she would have no impediments, moving on with her life.

Elena's doctor, Mabel, took over in the recovery care at Elena's request, after she thanked me nicely and was sent home three days later. Thank God she was walking and talking again. In about a month or so, she should be recovered and where she was before the headaches kicked in.

·　·　·

THE REST of the week after Elena's surgery passed slowly. Ash and Avery both delivered while I was at work, and we were all blessed to have two darling little girls added to the gang.

Holding the infants in my arms and looking into each of their bright blue eyes had me at times knowing that if nothing went wrong with Elena in that accident, I would be holding my own daughter staring up at me with these curious eyes about this time too. It took us all laughing at the fact that Jim, Jake, and me were definitely up to no good, knocking the ladies up all around the same time to get my head out of the clouds of wondering what could've been.

There was something about seeing my friends so happy, John and Addy so damn excited, and the innocence of the powder-fresh babies to keep me from staying in the past that couldn't be changed. Instead of feeling sorry for myself in all my losses since Elena's accident, I felt prouder I could stay moving forward and appreciate these two angels that would one day talk and call me Uncle Collin.

I had just gotten back from my hospital visit with the babies, and finished eating before I sat engrossed in a medical article. Once finished, I walked out to the pool area, smirking at the fact that I put the place up for too high a price to sell, knowing I'd pull the listing. I wasn't selling the damn house and I knew it. It was the first place I ever bought and it really had the best views of all Southern California beaches. I wasn't that big of a bitch. Hurt or not, I had to admit I put the place up to make it feel like I'd sell it, but in some demented way, I overpriced it and kept it.

Made no sense to me, the real estate agent, or those around me, but hell, who cared. I still owned it and here I was. I was right where I needed to be, moving forward and carrying on with my life while appreciating the ocean front home and the solace it truly brought me. I would accept the things in my life that I could and couldn't change. Adapt and overcome all that had been sent my way to challenge me and I would only allow it all to make me a better man for it.

CHAPTER FORTY-FOUR
ELENA

One Month Later

𝒥 walked out of Dr. Moas' office, wanting to squeal with excitement that this was my last visit to the neurologist until my next follow-up in three months. The scans had all shown that Dr. Brooks had been successful in removing every last piece of the tumor that'd caused headaches more excruciating than the pain of trying to stomach everyone attempting to *trigger memories* of the last ten years of my life.

I walked out of her office and spotted the tall figure of Dr. Brooks, speaking with someone in the open reception area we were in. His dark blond and messy hair could be spotted a mile away. I discreetly observed him in his white lab coat where he stood, facing away from Dad and me.

So many mixed emotions filled me when I heard him laugh. I watched the two women in scrubs staring up at him, and their eyes dazzled in humor to whatever he was saying in response to a book he was thumbing through. I wasn't jealous of the interaction, though. He was a fascinating man, to be sure, and I expected nothing less from the two staff members who were being entertained by him at the moment.

"Let's go, kiddo," Dad said, and then he stopped when he caught me staring at Collin. "Did you want to say anything to Dr. Brooks before we leave?"

"No, he's busy." I smiled. "Besides, Dr. Moas told me that he cleared me to drive and resume life as a happy, healthy miracle." I linked my arm into Dad's. "I am shocked he didn't sit in on the meeting, though."

Dad and I walked out of the reception and to the exit of the neuro-offices of the hospital. "I'm sure it was out of respect for your wishes." Dad smiled at me. "Also, neurosurgeons don't necessarily sit in on consultations of patients who aren't theirs. The only reason he met with us at the hospital was that Dr. Moas requested his consultation to see if you were a candidate for surgery."

"And he turned my ass down." I arched my eyebrow teasingly at my dad, thanking God that my outbursts and horrible mean streak went away in the last two weeks as my brain healed.

"I knew he would," Dad admitted. "But I'd rather the surgeon see the tumor had grown and see if he found anything the neurologist and I hadn't seen in your recent scans."

"Well, God knows I turned him down plenty of times, so he probably enjoyed turning *me* down for once," I said with a laugh as I rolled my eyes. "I still don't understand why he would turn down operating on the growing tumor, letting it get to the point where I had seizures."

We reached the car, and Dad's expression was professional and serious. "That's because he's a damn good surgeon, Laney," he said as we got into his car. "A good surgeon never sees surgery as the first answer. I taught him that, you know."

I nudged Dad in the arm. "And you must be so proud of your prodigy of a student."

He grinned. "Let's get some lunch and head back to the ranch. You're clear to ride again, but nothing more than—"

"Walking or maybe a little trot." I smiled at him.

"Yeah. Exactly what that horse you sent back to Collin was trained perfectly to do." He shook his head.

"Don't start with me, Papi," I said, buckling up. "That horse was meant for someone else, and we both know I'm not that woman. Besides, I love riding Stormy. She's gentle and kind."

Dad nodded and sighed, and I was undoubtedly itching to get home

and finally ride the horse I'd been riding before everything went to hell
with the headaches and seizures.

"I'LL BE BACK IN A WHILE," I told Dad as he started going through the mail
at the kitchen table.

"Take it slow with that horse," he eyed me. "I'm serious, Elena."

"I'm not risking anything, especially since it's taken me a month of
pacing floors to get this part of my life back."

Stormy was saddled and ready to go within twenty minutes of me
getting to the stables, and I hoisted myself on her back. I wanted so badly
to turn the reins loose on her and feel the freedom and power I felt in the
mare when she took off, but I kept it cool. It was nice to keep her at a
walk and head up the path to the lake at the top of Dad's property. It was
the most peaceful place, and it made me feel like I was the only person in
the world.

I dismounted, took my blanket off Stormy's back, and spread the
blanket out for me to take in the beauty of the lake, the dock, the canoe,
and the birds.

A soft breeze blew against my face, and I watched as the canoe rocked
gently in the water, tied to the dock by only a rope. My eyes then
suddenly saw something entirely different.

"All right, hold still," I said. I was transported into the canoe—and back
in time—and I was looking at Collin's brilliant and curious smile.

"'Bout time you kiss me," he said as I felt myself gripping the side of the
canoe to show off a stunt I'd learned when I was a kid.

"Oh, my God." I rubbed my forehead as I saw, felt, and heard
everything as if I'd gone back in time and experienced it. "What the hell?"
I scrambled to get up.

I froze when my mind was flooded again. The beautiful view of the
ocean from here had disappeared, and I was dancing at the medical
conference. I felt so free, and I loved the song that played because it
reminded me of Miami. I held my hand up in the air, and it was caught. I
finished the spin, and I was suddenly dancing with the most handsome
man I'd ever seen. His eyes were an enchanting blue. His smile dazzled,
and he danced with me as if he were my partner for a competition. I

wondered where he'd come from as he dipped me, and my breath caught when his eyes locked onto mine.

"May I ask who you are, Sir?" I'd questioned this beautiful man as I moved the dance to become a bit more seductive. I tried to scare him off, but he didn't waver.

"Your future husband," he said, and without missing a beat, he spun me out and away from him.

I fell to my knees; what was happening to me? Did something go wrong after my brain surgery? Or was—could it be? Were these my stolen memories being flashed before my eyes before I died from a possible brain aneurysm? I was overwhelmed, nauseated, and terrified all at once. I couldn't die up here alone.

"Stormy!" I called my horse. I needed her legs.

My mind flashed to my med school graduation. I crossed the stage, shrieking in delight, and instead of being proper, I pointed to my dad in the crowd.

"I did it for you, Papi!"

I was getting dizzier and dizzier as I climbed onto Stormy's back, all while my memories were slamming into me as if I were downloading them from somewhere. They were all on repeat. All of my memories, coming back, and I didn't know what the hell was happening, but I was panic-stricken that this was the end.

I reached the house and felt like I had vertigo. "Papi!" I called out in panic.

"Right here, Laney," he said, watching me stumble into the house. He looked as terrified as I felt. "What's happened?"

"I see things, I think," I said, panting. "Papi, my memories. I remember what happened—everything. Am I going to die? Do I need to go to the hospital? I don't want to die."

I saw my dad's smile as he pulled me tightly into his arms. "Easy, Laney," he said. "No, no, no, baby girl. You are not going to die. This is completely..."

My dad's voice trailed off, and my vision changed again. I was on the beach and had been watching Collin surfing all morning. He was surfed like a pro, and I was intrigued, watching him out there, looking like a total badass.

The air smelled of salt, and I heard seagulls flying above me as the waves rolled into the shore. I watched in utter excitement as Collin danced through the water, and the next thing I knew, he was kissing me with the salty taste of the ocean on his lips. His wet suit was ice cold, and I shivered underneath him. I laughed, trying to push him off of me, but his lips remained firmly on mine while we rolled through the soft sand and kissed like no one was watching.

I finally pushed him off of me.

"You crazy man. I'm all sandy, and that water is so freaking cold," I said to him.

His smile was my favorite, and it always made me laugh because I knew he was going to do something wild and insane. He'd taken his wetsuit off by the time I figured I was safe from some crazy Collin maneuver, but I should've known better. I screamed when he threw me over his shoulder and ran out toward the cold surf. I screamed through my laughter, and then the next thing I knew, we were both waist-deep in the freezing-cold Pacific Ocean.

Collin's eyes dazzled while the sun reflected off the ocean and into them. He pulled me close while I tried to act like I was furious, but my laughter always screwed me when I tried to act angry with him.

"Hold your breath, babe," I heard him. His eyes wide and wild, and I was in trouble.

I managed to listen, and the next thing I knew, he pulled me under the water, and his mouth was on mine. I felt the cold water stinging and the electric currents I always felt inside me when he kissed me.

I saw my dad again, and I was sitting in his large chair in the living room. I started crying. "Papi, what's happening? I'm so scared," I whispered.

"Laney, I need you to be as calm as you can. Your memories are coming back to you," he said.

"Like this?" I said, looking at him in fear. "My entire surroundings are changing, and I'm being transported into them. What is this?"

"It happens in many different ways. I've had a few conversations with patients on the phone at home when it happened to them. They may come back all at once, or they may take some time. They return differently."

"This is good. Keep talking," I said, scared to get zapped off into another memory again. I needed a second to catch my breath to appreciate the miracle that was happening.

"Right," he said, kneeling in front of me. "Some people have reported that it was as if they returned in a reel, like watching a movie, but most have reported they just remembered everything. When the deep-rooted memories return, we believe those are the ones that hit the hardest. The most impact is felt with those. You're safe, honey," he said with a smile. "I want you to relax and let this pass."

"Oh, Collin. I love him, Papi," I said through tears of relief. My soul felt that more than anything.

"Close your eyes and rest. You look exhausted," he said. "Are you thirsty, hungry?"

"I'm overwhelmed," I said.

"Close your eyes. Let them come as they are. I'm not leaving your side."

I closed my eyes, and then I was lying on the couch with Collin. I was trying to watch a mystery movie, but I couldn't focus. Collin's firm lips massaged on my neck, and his hand moved over my abdomen.

"I'm never going to find out..." I laughed when Collin's hands went into my panties.

"They have sex and live happily ever after," he said, and I felt his fingers sparking sensations I loved between my legs.

"The murderer and the detective?"

"Whatever they are." He laughed, and I twisted in his arms.

"We can never get through these movies." I felt his face in my hands. His expression was so mischievous. *"You're lucky the sex is better."*

He smiled and kissed my palm. *"The sex is always better, sunshine,"* he said before he covered me with his perfect body.

The vision faded from the sofa in Collin's Malibu beach house, and I was at the hospital now. I'd just walked out of my patient's room and met up with Dr. Nathan.

"All good today, Elena?" he asked.

"Always," I felt myself smile at him.

Before I could say another word, my lower back had a hand on it, and when I turned to my right, I saw that it was Collin. He was in his scrubs, and he gave me a peck on the cheek. Dr. Nathan and I laughed as Collin kept on walking with two interns as if he'd never done anything.

"He's a mess," I said, trying to defend him to his usual resident who attended his surgeries.

"For the record," I heard Nathan say, *"that's against hospital policy."*

"You'd think he'd know that by now."

"I think my friend doesn't give a shit."

I tried to answer Dr. Nathan, but he was gone, and so was the hospital.

"Dance with me," I asked Collin after taking a sip of wine while sitting on his outdoor furniture. We'd spent the evening on a walk after our day ended, and this day was the hardest on him that I'd witnessed. He'd lost a patient to a severe stroke, and there was no saving the poor woman.

"I'd love that," he said.

I held him, and we turned on his playlist, and Otis Redding sang, *These Arms of Mine.* I begged Collin to keep the song on repeat. I loved how it drew us close in such an intimate way as we danced. I felt Collin's tense muscles ease as he danced seductively as if he were worshipping me through our favorite evening times spent dancing.

I had no idea how long I'd sat in the chair, getting my life back in the most dramatic way. Thank God that my dad never left my side.

"I have to see him," I said, sitting up. "Papi, I have to be with him."

"Collin?" he carefully asked.

"Yes," I answered. "I can't trust this will stop happening, so I can't drive. I need you to take me to him."

"You think you'll be okay?" he asked.

"If not, he's a neuro-doc, too. He'll know if something goes wrong."

Tears were streaming down my dad's face. "Sweetheart, I don't think I've ever been happier in my entire life." He let out a sob as he embraced me tightly. "Thank God, it's over. Now, let's get you home to Collin."

CHAPTER FORTY-FIVE
COLLIN

I finished eating and fell into my usual routine of opening up a medical article to read. This time I was more interested in the contents, given it was written about a patient of mine. It was a breakthrough surgery that I'd done and was still impressed with my recovering patient.

My patient was deemed permanently paralyzed before I took on his case, but he'd become a proud success. With the help of a walker, he could now move his legs after I'd removed his injured nerves, allowing the healthy nerves to signal to his brain, giving him the ability to walk again. The article was written in the patient's favor, which I was pleased to read, and the tedious medical jargon input I added was simplified. I was happy to see that this man had regained his life after trusting me to perform this particular surgery on him.

Life as a neuroscientist was a world of endless possibilities, surprises, miracles, and, in my situation, sometimes it came with sadness that couldn't change mental outcomes. Before Elena basically told me to fuck off, I'd had so much therapy that I could recite half the shit the therapists said to cope with it all. How many of my patients' lives had enormously suffered after I'd busted my ass to save them? I had a different perspective now. I had saved Elena's life twice in my OR, but mentally, I couldn't save her. I wasn't going to dwell on that tonight, though.

I had just signed off on Elena's official medical release, and I was thrilled that after a month of monitoring her scans, her operation was proven successful. I was told I had missed seeing her in the office today, and it was just as well. I was resolved to let her go. I had no other choice.

The house intercom chimed as I took a sip of beer. I tossed the magazine aside, wondering who the hell would show up and ring my house like this. Jake was known for pulling these types of pranks, acting like a jackass instead of letting himself in with the key I'd given him. He and Ash were staying down the road at their beach house this weekend, and the man probably got bored. God only knew.

I opened the door, and my eyes took in Elena's somber bronze ones. I hadn't the slightest clue as to why she was here this late.

"Collin," she said.

"Elena?" I answered when I saw tears in her eyes. "Come in."

She turned and waved off the Tesla that was sitting in my driveway.

"We have to talk," she said, walking into the house as I trailed her. I stood in the living room, watching her look around, and I was entirely confused as to what the hell was going on. She turned back to me, and her expression broke my heart. "Saying *I'm sorry* isn't enough. It's not what you deserve after everything you've done to help me only to have me treat you so wretchedly."

"I'm a bit confused," I said, standing there, wanting to hold her but fearful of what that would do. "There's no need to apologize. I understand you need to move on. I'm letting you have that."

She shook her head and bit onto her bottom lip. "My soul will find yours..." she said softly as she looked into my eyes. "It's what you would say to me, and I would feel your lips on my closed eyes."

I was paralyzed where I stood, staring into her eyes as they waited for my response, but I had nothing. She'd recited what I would say to her every time I would leave her in the ICU while she was in her coma.

"Do you remember telling me that? Do you remembering making that promise to me, Coll?"

I swallowed the sudden lump in my throat. My brain was scrambled with thoughts. She was repeating something that I had no idea she'd heard while in her coma. Was she back? Was the woman I'd loved and lost back?

"I do," I choked out. "I'm struggling to understand how you recall it now."

"I love you," she said, stepping toward my frozen body. "Baby, I remember us. I remember everything."

She touched my face, and I closed my eyes in prayer that this wasn't a dream. I turned my head to kiss her palm against my cheek.

I held her hand to my cheek, and my eyes reopened. "God, please tell me this is real, and I didn't pass out on the couch after reading that article."

"You've never slept on the couch. Even if I fell asleep, watching a boring movie that you put on, you would carry me to bed. You prided yourself in that, never falling asleep on the couch."

"I'm scared that I'll blink, and you'll be gone," I said, feeling myself trembling inside.

"Oh, baby," she sighed. "I've hurt you so badly and caused you so much pain that I completely understand your response. Will you ever forgive me? I don't deserve this chance I'm begging you for."

"You are my entire life, Elena," I said as my body jerked out of this bizarre state of paralysis. I pulled her into my arms and buried my face into her neck. The one place I found myself lost in the love of my life.

She reached up to hold the back of my neck and ran her hands through my hair as she always had when I held her like this.

I had no idea how long I stood there, holding her and feeling as though if I'd let her go, I'd lose her again. Elena and I both shed tears, and we stood here, reuniting our broken souls. I felt like life was being breathed back into my entire being. I'd imagined this scenario from the first moment I knew she had amnesia, and now that it was here, I wasn't reacting in any of the ways I thought I would. It wasn't an explosion of fireworks or spinning her around in the air as we both laughed with joy. It was gentle and so deeply soul-moving that I could hardly make a sound.

Elena released our hold on each other and took my face in her hands, and she swept the tears from my face. "No more crying," she said through her tears. "We've both cried enough for one lifetime. We're the ones who are supposed to laugh and do crazy stuff, remember?"

I grinned. "We are. We're also the couple who were ripped apart, and by some miracle from heaven, I have you back. I still—I almost can't believe it, Laney."

"I'm home, Coll," she said. "If you'll still have me, of course."

"God, stop saying that." I took her hand and kissed it again. "You know that this is your home if you want it. You know that I am always yours." I ran my hand through my hair, still having a hard time with the fact that my Elena came back to me, and she was one of the miracles we all talked about on the neuro ward. "Sit with me. My fucking knees are weak." I laughed at the fact that I'd never felt anything remotely close to this before. Maybe it was a mixture of shock and glee. All I knew was that I was overwhelmed in the best possible way.

We sat on the couch. All I wanted to do was hold her, and after a few seconds of sitting there like a jackass in shock, I pulled her onto my lap from where she sat across from me. I kissed her shoulder, her arm, her neck, and her jaw.

"Afraid to kiss my lips?" She arched her eyebrow when she shifted in my arms to face me.

I smirked. "I don't know what I am," I answered truthfully. I brushed her hair from her face, and I felt a rush of emotions of desire hit me stronger than ever before. I relaxed into the cushions, taking her beautiful face and bringing it to mine.

My lips were so urgent and hungry for her, and I was grateful that her desire for my kiss was returned with more passion than I remembered. She tasted so delicious, and I became ravenous for more of this. Our bodies found their usual position on the couch whenever I pressed for more, and I felt her react as she always did, moving so I wouldn't smother her while I lay on top of her and turned a delicious kiss into a consuming one.

Her moans, whimpers, and her fingers running through my hair...all of it was *my Elena* responding to me. I didn't want to stop with this kiss, but I had to. I had to know how she remembered and how it all came back? What did she know?

I had no idea how I did it, but I pulled away, watching Elena's beautiful chest rise and fall while she caught her breath. She smiled so beautifully at me, her fingertips running along my lips.

"I've missed your lips," she said. Her eyes stare into mine. "And your beautiful eyes. You're the best man I've ever known, and I'm the luckiest woman in the world," she said, sitting up and reclining in my arms. "I remember you coming to me while I was in the coma."

I could tell she was happy to be reunited, but she needed to talk, and it was a good thing because I wanted to hear how my woman came back to me.

"You repeated to me what I would tell you—that my soul would find yours," I said with a smile. "I was reaching, Laney. I was doing anything to get those brain waves to give me something to let me know you heard me."

She smiled. "Do you remember when you brought me to the meadow with Grace?"

"The wedding gift you returned?" I grinned, loosening up a bit so I could have a normal conversation.

"Yes," she shook her head. "I hope she's still mine?"

"Of course she is. John and Addy have fallen in love with her, but they know she's Aunt Laney's horse."

"Aunt Laney?" she smiled brightly.

"Yeah, you're Aunt Laney. Thank God you're back because I had no idea how to tell them you were no longer part of our lives."

"I'm seriously flattered," she said, tears in her eyes.

"Anyway. You were speaking about the meadow where we sat and talked." I smiled. "It was pretty much the only normal conversation we had after the accident."

"Yes," she answered and intertwined our fingers together. "The meadow, though. I didn't remember it at the time, but I now know why it was so soothing to be there talking to you."

"Why's that?" I rubbed my free hand along her legs.

"Well, while I was in the coma, I heard you." She looked at me, and I felt comfort wash over my entire being. "Baby, I heard everything."

"It's incredible. And I thought I was talking to myself most of the time." I ran my hand over her face again to feel the softness of it.

"It was so strange," she said, relaxing into me. "I remember seeing that I was going to hit the tree and couldn't avoid it, then suddenly I was in that meadow filled with yellow flowers. It was so peaceful and serene. Now that my memories have practically downloaded into my mind again, I remember hearing everything. But I couldn't talk back."

"Laney," I said, my thumb stroking along her cheek, "I'm so sorry. I knew you may or may not have heard anything while you were out. I did my best—"

"Stop." She smiled. "A lot of what I heard while I was in the coma, it's pretty fuzzy at best." She sat up and leaned her head onto my shoulder. I had to see her face, though. I wasn't ever going to be able to stop looking at the woman who'd come back to me.

I readjusted our position to where she was comfortable in my arms, kissed her chin, and smiled. "I need to see your eyes, sunshine." I smiled.

She returned my smile with a small kiss on my lips. "You came to me in that meadow, Coll," she said, and I knew my expression was blank. "Every conversation that was said by others? I mostly heard as if they were voices in the sky. It was so bizarre. But you..." her eyes studied mine, "you were there, and we sat together. I held your hands, though I couldn't feel them." She softly laughed. "Coll," her head shifted to the side, "we grieved together. Even though you didn't answer me when I talked to you, we cried together, and we held each other when you told me about the miscarriage."

"Oh, my God, Laney," I said as I held her tightly. "I hope I did everything right with her and for you."

"You did everything so beautifully, and I couldn't understand why you were doing all of it while I was out."

"I felt like I had to do whatever it took to take care of you. I had to know how you felt about the baby. How long you'd known."

"You told me that in our meadow while I was in the coma."

"I saw the butterfly you drew in your journal, and I knew you were crying when you found out about the baby. I should've been there for you."

"I cried because I knew it was an overwhelming change for you and me. We were getting married, and the next thing I knew, I was going to have to tell you, *Hey, guess what?*" she said in a silly voice that I loved, "*the honeymoon is over in a few months, and it's time to get ready for diapers and no sleep.*" She chuckled, and I laughed before she grew serious. "Would you have been upset? I know it's a dumb question after every beautiful thing you've done for our daughter and me."

I kissed her nose. "I would have loved the mother of my child that much more." I smiled. "But Josephine March Brooks is our angel now, and I have a crazy feeling she might have had something to do with you coming back to me."

"Look at you," she chuckled. "You've officially become a man who might believe in things outside this black and white scientific world of yours."

I held her closer. "You in my arms at this moment is a prime example of a scientist being completely stumped. You're not just some miracle beauty who danced into my life at that medical conference, but you're literally a walking miracle, Elena Alvarez."

"We need to fix that whole *Alvarez* thing and fast. I should be Elena Brooks by now," she said with a smile, kissing my lips.

"Courthouse?" I teased.

"I would show up at the first appointment you got."

I studied her. "I think we should do it."

"We have a lot to make up for, and I think we should start there. Then we need to find a way to get on that honeymoon you planned."

"There's a bit of a plan change on that one." I leaned her close and kissed the incision wound on her head that was healing nicely. "We can only do what I planned for the second half of our honeymoon."

"I was dying to know where you were taking me," she said. "What did I screw up?"

"El Capitan in Yosemite," I told her. "You told me it was something you'd always wanted to do. The guys and I hiked the face of that rock after we graduated college. I went behind your back and asked your dad what your experience was in rock climbing. I wasn't surprised to hear that you were perfectly primed to climb that mountain."

Her lips were on my neck. "That would have been so amazing. Dammit, you think of everything."

"All I want is to give the woman I love the life of her dreams. Unfortunately, you're going to have to settle for the second part of my surprise trip. We'll stretch out our time there, though, since you're not going to be doing wild stuff for a while."

"Tell me," she said, her eyes sparkling with excitement.

"The Maldives. One of those badass places that give us privacy, and the huts are on stilts over the ocean. It's secluded and unbelievably gorgeous. Is that something you'd be up for? I could arrange the time off, and we'd make up for missing the last months of our lives together."

"We could stay right here, and I would be delighted."

"I feel the same. There's so much for us to make up for," I said. "I'm still trying to process that this is even happening."

"Dance with me," she said with a smile. "Like we always did at night after long, stressful days."

"Have you tried?" I asked her. "Does that part of your brain work again?"

"There's only one way to find out." She popped up from my lap and started dancing a beautiful hula dance for me. "I'm back, baby, and we're wasting time."

CHAPTER FORTY-SIX

ELENA

*C*ollin and I spent the entire night talking, laughing, and, of course, having wild sex. I loved every second of his lips, savoring my body as they always had when we were together. He was a perfect man in every way, and he was right; life had ripped us apart, but we survived it, and by some beautiful miracle, we were convinced that Baby-Jo had brought her parents back together after all the hurt that they'd endured.

I felt I should apologize for using his past as an excuse to leave him in the way that I did before I got my memories back. The truth was that his past had never been an issue for me. We both had life experiences that we'd learned from, and I knew that made us who we were. Unfortunately for him, he was dealing with a much less mature version of myself, so I couldn't do anything but reassure him that nothing in his past gave me any cause for concern at any time. Luckily for me, that led to delicious shower sex.

It was so good to feel good again, to have my memories back, and to share this journey with Collin. I listened to him talk, knowing he'd been mentally beaten up in more ways than one. The pain I saw in his eyes was unforgivable, but he forgave me without a moment's hesitation, and here we were, back in each other's arms again as if we hadn't skipped a beat.

Collin worked the entire following week, but Dr. Nathan and the others worked to help take on shifts and patients and fill in for him so that we could escape the noise for a while and focus on each other.

We determined that starting the equine rehab center was not just my personal dream come true, but it was both of our way of giving back to patients suffering and going through what we both went through. In about two months, the place would be completely set up with horses brought in for rehab, and the place would be staffed with more therapists to help with patients.

Collin had revisited my brain scans more than once, and his *surgical conclusion* was met with the agreement that the tumor that'd almost killed me and forced the emergency surgery was most likely jarred, and that was the only explanation for my memory loss. Collin said it had most definitely moved into that part of my brain and caused most of my issues. He only wished he could back up that assumption, but because I'd never had a brain scan before my accident, Collin had nothing to compare where it was located in my brain before the injury.

The week had flown by, and now, here we were—the day of our secret courthouse wedding. We'd planned to get married, go back to the main house and possibly take the horses out, and then celebrate each other until we left for the airport at eleven this evening. Collin had arranged the red-eye flight on Jim's private jet, knowing we'd most likely sleep while we flew across the world, but I doubted we'd be sleeping much after Avery described the luxury of the plane. The thing was set up like some penthouse suite, and we'd most likely feel like we were in a hotel the entire flight and not on a plane. I was so excited I could hardly stand it.

THE COURTHOUSE WEDDING was fun and quick, and I squealed when Collin swept me up into his arms and announced to the people staring at us like we were lunatics that I was officially *Mrs. Collin Brooks.* I loved the sound of that more than I could express. Collin and I walked back to our car, kissing and holding onto each other like there was no one else around. We couldn't give a damn what anyone thought. We were together, married, and beginning this chapter in our life in the most blessed fashion.

When we got home to our ranch, Collin was at my door, sweeping me out of the car before I could place a foot on the ground. Our lips met as if we hadn't kissed nearly the whole way home, and once he carried me through the house and made his way to our room, he kicked the door closed behind him. Our lips hadn't left each other's, even as Collin laid me on the bed and his sky blue eyes beamed.

"Well, my handsome *husband*, what are you going to do with me now? I thought we were going to go horseback riding."

"That comes after this," he said, his lips finding my abdomen.

*Knock! Knock! Knock...*The sound of the knocks was the beat that Jake and Collin would use when they showed up at the other's house.

"He's fucking kidding, right?" Collin said with a sigh.

"Are you two dressed in there?" Jake said with humor in his voice.

"We're sort of fucking in here." Collin arched an eyebrow in humor at me and grinned.

"Careful, old man," Jake answered with a chuckle. "There are kids around."

Collin's forehead fell against my chest while I ran my hands through his hair and laughed. "Go get the door."

"He's lucky he was at my side the entire time you were gone," Collin said with a sigh.

"Watching Vampire Diaries and all too?" I laughed again. "Him and Alex, right?"

"I was in a dark place, Laney." He straightened his shirt as he stood up. "I brought them there with me too."

"Then you owe it to your best friend to open that door and see what he wants," I said.

Collin opened the door, and the next thing I knew, Jake and Alex snatched my new husband, and Coll was gone with a string of curse words hanging in the air behind him.

"We're going to steal him away for just a bit," Jim said, wearing a suit and smiling. "Congratulations on the nuptials."

He ducked out of the doorway as I sat up on the edge of the bed, and then Ash, Avery, and my sister rushed into the room with Clay and Joe.

"What the hell is going on?" I giggled, seeing Joe and Clay eye me like I was about to become their hardest makeover yet.

Lydia approached the bed. "It's a send-off party, sister." She hugged me. "That Jim guy can make some serious miracles happen."

I wrapped my arms around my sister and hugged her. "Jim did this?"

"Jim and Alex made a lot of things happen, but the crazy stuff?" Avery laughed and looked at Ash.

"Crazy stuff like kidnapping Collin?" Ash laughed, "Well, any crazy shit that goes down from now and until we get you on that plane tonight is all Jake."

I hugged Ash and Avery, genuinely grateful that I could consider these two strong and wonderful women my dear friends. The friendships we'd forged so effortlessly were precious to me, and I had more blessings to count than I could've ever dreamed possible.

"I have no idea what you all are planning, but I'm totally down for having some crazy and wild fun. I'll have to thank all of you for pulling off whatever *miracle* you have planned later," I said.

"And you'll be thanking Joe and me for our miracle, sister-girl," Clay said, pulling my hair through his hands. "Honey, you've been through a lot, and we're about to overhaul this neglect of your gorgeous hair."

"This dress is perfect for enhancing the naturally-glowing tanned skin you're blessed with," Joe said, walking over a strapless, silky yellow dress to me. "Collin loves you in a strapless dress, and your body is perfectly toned to wear this like you own it."

"Why yellow?" I smirked.

"Because of the yellow flowers in the meadow," Ash said. "There's a reason you found comfort being surrounded by yellow flowers in the field in your coma, the only place you saw Collin come to you."

"What's that meaning?" I questioned.

"Well, when it comes to chakras and healing, the color yellow has some spiritual effects. The color itself is so bright and luminous that you can't help but feel cheerful with its radiant glow. If your subconscious pulled you into a meadow of yellow flowers, then it helped you pull personal power, strength, and courage. It's such a powerful, happy, and optimistic color."

"Not to mention nothing looks better against your skin tone," Avery added with a laugh. "It enhances the beauty we always have seen in our sweet friend."

"I've missed this so much, you guys," I said, feeling overwhelmed with love. "I can't wait to get back so we can all have fun together again like we used to."

"That all comes after you and Collin make up for your lost time," Joe said, going through a bag and pulling out lacey undergarments. "Go and put these on. It's three in the afternoon, and we have a lot to accomplish between getting you reunited with Collin and on that plane."

"A send-off party, huh?" I laughed.

"There was no way the guys, your family, and we girls were letting you both off as easy as we led you to believe," Ash said with a grin.

AFTER CLAY and Joe worked their magic on me, I was blindfolded. I couldn't help but laugh—as I had been doing since the moment I woke up this morning. I couldn't help but enjoy the fun adrenaline of surprises, and it was surging through me. I was so full of positivity and love that I felt like I was vibrating.

I heard a large crowd after I'd been led from point A to point B— wherever that was located.

"What's going on?" I softly asked.

"Hey, sweetheart," I heard my mom's voice, and I jerked off the blindfold, tears filling my eyes.

I hugged my mom tightly, hardly noticing that we were in the large, renovated open area of our barn. Strands of lights hung throughout the rafters, looking like blurry diamonds as I held Mom, and then I saw Dad's smile from where he stood behind her.

"I'm sorry I couldn't get here faster. I was about to take the next flight out, then Collin's friend, Jim, contacted me. He let me know that he'd be sending a flight to pick all of us up to celebrate you being well again and that we'd be sending you and Collin off after this beautiful reception."

I cleared my eyes, Collin was still nowhere in sight, but all of my family and friends from Miami were in this room. They waved as I covered my mouth in tears and shock that I was actually seeing this. I took in the magnificent area that looked like some other-worldly and heavenly place with the hanging flowers, beautifully arranged tables, and the twinkling ambiance of this room.

I saw my girlfriends who were with me when I had my snowboarding accident, and I hugged them all and thanked them for being there for me. When I'd hugged the last of them, I looked around the room again, awestricken by everything once more.

"Clay and Joe?" I asked.

"You know it," Avery said.

Stevie hugged me tightly and stayed by my side. "Jim flew everyone in on his private jets, sis," Stevie said. "Everyone went all-out so we could celebrate our love for you, and, of course, to see you found your life and happiness with Collin again."

"You tried to sneak your way out of having a big wedding, so we decided to get to the fun part and give you and Coll the send-off you deserve," Avery said with a smile.

I felt tears again. "I don't know how to thank you all for this," I said, sniffing and smiling, trying not to ruin my makeup.

"Oh, trust us, Collin will be ensuring we feel like you both appreciate all of this," Ash said.

"Where the hell is he?" I asked.

Lydia chuckled. "He's with his *best friends*. Apparently, they had some pranks and plans for him since he tried to ditch-out on a formal wedding."

I loved how different Lydia was now. I could see the happiness in her eyes, and I loved my sister more than I ever had. Stevie stood tall at my side, and I was thankful to God that my brother had pulled it together despite my injury taking me down. He was working a stable job and busting his ass at school, and I was so damn proud of him.

I thought I couldn't be happier until a spotlight hit a stage that was created for this moment, and I heard Collin's beautiful voice start to sing slowly, "*Wise men say, only fools rush in—*"

I covered my mouth when I saw my handsome husband dressed sharply in a black suit with a microphone in his hand. I felt tears slide down the corners of my eyes as Collin sang the song with a violinist playing softly in the background to complement his perfect vocals. The song was more beautiful now than ever as I watched and hung onto every word, Collin's searching eyes finding me and singing directly to me.

He waved his hand for me to join him on stage, and I didn't hesitate to allow him to continue serenading me with that song while he gently led me in a dance. As his song came to an end, more upbeat music came on, and people made their way to the dancefloor to join in on the fun.

"I have no idea what the hell is going on." Collin spun me out, and then I twirled back into his arms. "And I'm not even pissed about it. You look beyond beautiful, baby." Everyone seemed to be having a fantastic time, and Collin and I couldn't get enough of each other, dancing like the silly, hopelessly in love couple we were.

I don't know how many songs we danced to before Jake's voice came over the speakers. Collin spun me back into him, and we fell into a perfect embrace. I rested my back against Collin's firm chest, and his chin rested on my hair.

"These two," Jake slid a hand into his pocket and casually held the mic to his smiling lips. "They've been through hell and back and have proven to all of us that love can conquer anything that tries to defeat it." He pursed his lips and shrugged. "It might sound cheesy, I know, but after watching what the past months have done to both of them, I have to say it's one-hundred percent true." He chuckled then looked out at the crowd. "We have all prayed and pleaded for these two to come together again after almost losing Elena." He looked at Collin. "I watched my best friend save her life and grieve the possibility that his soulmate was lost to him forever." He shook his head and smiled at me. "You have always had the brightest smile and the best outlook on everything. Watching you struggle as the world tried to strip that positivity from you—I have to say there are not many times when I've been at a loss for understanding why life can be so cruel, but that was one of them. I couldn't understand many things having to do with the outcome of your accident, but I look at you with Collin now, and I think I get it.

"You see, not to toot my friend's horn, but as I'm sure he'll tell you every chance he gets, he's a prodigy—you know, one of those child geniuses." Collin waved his hand out at the crowd and took a bow like a goofball as his best friend continued talking. "Being a real-life genius, however, sometimes certain details slip through the cracks, and I have to say that with all of my friend's expertise, there was an element of personal experience with these injuries that he couldn't relate to." Collin held me tighter as Jake spoke, and I felt him subtly nodding in agreement.

"Over the trials of the last months, you've both learned lessons that are valuable not only to yourselves but also to put them into action to help others who've been in your situation." Jake waved his hand around the barn that was to be the hub of our equine therapy center. "You've decided to open this place and use your experiences to help alleviate the pain of others, and, well, I think there isn't anything nobler than that. That leads me to my point."

"I have no idea where he's going with this," Collin whispered in my ear.

Jake smirked at Collin, "I think this rehab center might have to partner up with Saint John's Hospital to help reach more people; what do you say?"

"Oh, my God!" I covered my heart and looked at Collin's same shocked expression.

"That is where I come in," I heard Jim say as he spoke into a mic. "As CEO of the company who's always looking at ways to expand and enhance Saint John's, we are willing to support your rehab center monetarily and in any other way we can. We would love to help bring in staff while allowing you both to retain ownership and control, and all of that fun stuff." He winked. "We'll take on any burden of the business aspect of the equine rehab facility because it is our wish for Dr. Elena *Brooks* to focus on getting her patients well through her horses and contagious positivity."

I broke free of Collin's hold and hugged Jim, crying in his arms, knowing that the man had cemented my ultimate dream. I would now have the endless possibilities of helping those who've suffered what Collin and I went through after my injury.

"Damn it," I heard Jake whisper. "I didn't even get a hug, and I thought my shit was pretty damn good too."

"Get over here." I reached out for Jim's brother and Collin's best friend, who laughed and hugged me.

"Dry your eyes, kid," I heard Alex say.

I looked at the striking man who I'd grown to admire for his commanding air, grateful for his care and concern for Collin while I was in my coma. Alex had taken Collin into his home during Collin's darkest hour, and for that, I would be eternally in Alex's debt.

"You guys, thank you for all of this." I smiled at Collin, shaking Jim and his best friend's hand. I knew Collin was as thrilled and overwhelmed by all of this as I was.

Alex reached for my hand, used some tricky maneuver, and spun me out. "Dance with the butterflies," he said to me with a smile as the crowd watched. "Right?"

I looked at him in confusion as he released my hand, and Jim, Jake, Ash, and Avery stood behind Alex, looking at Collin and me. Two women walked up with Avery and Ash's newborn babies in their arms, Little John and Addy proudly trailing them.

I watched with happiness, my hand instinctively covering my stomach, knowing that one sweet angel was missing. Baby-Jo Brooks. I felt a tear slip out of the corner of my eye. I didn't want to cry again. I'd already done this when I first held the precious babies after first meeting them. I loved these sweet little girls with a love I didn't know I carried in me, even though I still wished we had our Josephine with us.

"If it weren't for you two, we wouldn't have that special angel, Baby-Jo, to watch over all of us. Isn't that right, Addy?" Alex asked, looking down at the five-year-old, who nodded along as he spoke.

"Yes," Addison said, smiling out at the audience to ensure they knew mine and Collin's daughter was a special angel.

Alex looked back at Jim and the gang as they smiled at Collin and me. "We believe that our angel, Baby-Jo, is a symbol of hope, and Saint John's has decided to dedicate the butterfly gardens in her name with the motto, *Dance with the Butterflies.* We will work to expand this center in Baby Jo's name for parents who've experienced the grief of losing a child. We hope that each of our donations in our angel's name—Baby Josephine Brooks— will help expand our pediatric unit. Our chief pediatric neurosurgeon, Dr. Brandt, will be working to ensure that every child who comes into the pediatric ward will know that Saint John's is much more than just a hospital. It's a place of hope and understanding."

Collin was perfectly quiet and still, even silently tearing up with me until Dr. Brandt's name was mentioned. That's when Collin kissed my cheek and chuckled. "You know that they just dedicated our daughter's pediatric unit and placed it in the care of the pediatric doctor who's the younger version of *me*, correct?"

I looked up at Collin and then over to where Dr. Brandt had walked up and smiled at both of us. The tall and handsome man was a head-turner, and when Collin wasn't on the neuro-ward but Brandt was, good Lord, there was trouble. He was a beautiful man inside and out. He was young, but my interactions with him at work had always been a blast. He might've looked and probably acted like a typical playboy, but the way he was with the kids was nothing short of heartwarming.

"I think Josephine would approve," I told Collin with a kiss on his cheek.

"I'm sure you both wondered why the dapper Dr. Brandt was invited to this barn-wedding," Brandt said with a chuckle after he was handed a microphone. "I want to say it's always an honor when I'm working with the two of you during the times I've needed Brooks' opinion on a surgery or Elena's counsel for a patient and their families. You are both exceptional doctors and people. If you choose to accept Saint John's pediatric ward being named in honor of your daughter, I will say that I am honored to be one of the surgeons who will be working there, knowing your little angel is watching over the children."

At this point, I was too overwhelmed to speak. Collin and I had been to our daughter's memorial site, and I'd seen the beautiful plaque that was made for her. When Collin told me about it in my coma, I'd imagined it precisely as I'd seen it. It was beautiful, and the gardens were always so serene. To learn that our friends were dedicating the garden *and* the pediatric ward in Baby-Jo's name, I was speechless.

"Wow," Collin said, taking the mic and hugging Dr. Brandt, saying something to him that made the handsome doctor laugh while he stepped back. "Well, Laney," Collin exhaled, "all I expected was this amazing send-off, but never anything more." He looked at our group of friends, standing there with smiles on their faces as the rest of our friends and family looked on. "You all are blowing my mind right now," he chuckled. "I believe I speak on behalf of my wife and me," he held his hand out to me, "that we humbly accept all of this." He pinched his lips together, "Wow. Yeah, everything."

"Uncle Collin," Addison stepped up, "it's okay to cry, you know? Just say thank you." She smiled.

"Thank you." He brushed his finger over her nose. "I think Baby Jo would love all of this, wouldn't she?"

Addison nodded. "She's the angel who made it all happen, I think."

I watched, loving the innocence of sweet Addison. "I know she is," I said as I bent down to hug her. "Thank you, Addy. Uncle Collin and I are so happy."

"We are too." She smiled at me. "Can we eat your beautiful cake now?"

After the incredible gift and words from Collin's friends and Saint John's, knowing the board must've approved this idea Jim and Alex had proposed to them, Collin and I were seriously at a loss for words.

We enjoyed a beautiful celebration with our friends and family, who'd come to honor mine and Collin's love. Jim had a driver bring us to the airport, and hot damn, Avery wasn't lying when she said we wouldn't even know we were on a plane.

We boarded and had flight attendants appear from out of nowhere to serve us champagne. We took off, ate a delicious dinner that'd been prepared, and then Collin dismissed the attendants.

Collin stood, and he swept me into his arms. "We have plenty of time to tour this jet," he said as we walked through a living room and past multiple rooms into another world on this plane. "But we need to pick up where we left off after our courthouse wedding."

"This plane is off the charts," I said. "Where are we?"

"This is the private quarters. There's the master suite, kitchen, and couches, all that shit. Jim had this luxury jet designed for him, Avery, and their family. I think I'll hit him up with all his generosity of today and ask to keep the damn thing." He laughed.

"Baby, I'm the happiest woman alive," I said. "Did all of this happen today? This is still real life, right?"

"Yeah, it sure as hell did." He smirked. "Now," he grabbed me and called for the plane to play *our song*, "let's dance, baby."

I fell into his arms, and we slowly started dancing to our Otis Redding song. We danced the night away, laughing and loving each other, and when we could take no more, it was time to do what we both did best... worship each other, body and soul.

Our worlds had collided so fast, and just as quickly, they'd been torn apart most devastatingly. But we survived it all. We struggled, and we felt pain as powerful as we felt love and passion. Through it all, our souls found each other again, reaffirming that we were bonded in a way that proved we were born to love each other in *sickness and in health*, and, of course, in fun-filled adventures and in happiness. Our love was stronger than ever, and I wouldn't ask to start my life with this man in any other way.

MR. GRAYSON: BOOK 4 SNEAK PEEK
BREANNE "BREE" STONE

I sat perfectly still while my best friend and makeup artist, Cassie, did a complete makeover on my face. My mind was reeling with how I would handle this night—the night that Mitchell and Associates celebrated the merge of two highly-acclaimed architectural firms.

I wanted to chew my dad's ass out for being charmed by Alex Grayson —letting the perks of Grayson's investment company seduce him into allowing this merge—but that would be impossible since Dad's Alzheimer's took a turn for the worst two years ago. Dad had set up this merge without telling me, just like he waited until the last minute to tell me about his diagnosis. I supposed he was trying to protect me, but his lack of faith in me was a tad bit soul-crushing. Why couldn't he trust that I'd keep Stone Architects Group moving forward and expanding globally without the help of Mitchell and Associates?

It didn't matter anymore because Mr. Alex Grayson no longer worked as the vice president for that company anymore, anyway. Now, Alex would be my *partner* because he'd recently become the owner of the architectural firm that was intended to merge with mine. My partner. God help me. I should've taken more time to research this man, but I was too busy losing my London deal instead. Another story for a different day.

"All right," Cassie said, stepping back and taking in her artwork. "The highlights in your hair were needed big time." She tapped the back of her makeup brush to her glossy lips. "The eyeliner works," she paused and arched her eyebrow in some kind of warning, "only because it's an *evening party*. This shade of eyeshadow makes your green eyes pop too."

"You're acting like I'm walking a red carpet, Cass," I laughed.

"You are. The fact that this celebratory event is being held at the Beverly Wilshire makes it so," she said, grabbing my silk gown. "All right, then. The pale color of this strapless dress sets off the hints of red in your auburn hair." She helped me into the gown and stepped back after ensuring it fit as if I were one of her models that she was prepping for their photoshoot. "Yeah, you're lucky your boobs don't sag because you're not wearing a bra with this dress. We can't have lines."

"Hold up," I sighed. "What if the spotlight falls on me while I'm on that stage? Have you thought of that? This dress could be see-through, and I don't need my *high beams* becoming Mitchell and Associates' newest headline because they're throwing this unnecessary merge party for Brooks Architectural Firm and us."

"James Mitchell would never allow that," she said, more worried about ensuring the dress hugged every curve in my body. "Perfection." She smiled. "Now, you're ready to show your new partner how lucky he is to help run your company."

I arched an eyebrow at her. "I think you have that one backwards. I'll be helping him run *his* company."

"You'll both be running the company together," my assistant, Nicole, spoke up with a sigh. She sat cross-legged on the sofa in my dressing room, scrolling through her phone. She pulled her reading glasses off and eyed me. "Sheesh, if you can't accept this merge by now, all you're going to do is make the man hate you, and then neither of you will be getting anywhere with two great companies merging."

"Yeah, yeah," I exhaled. "I'm the artistic one, and he's the businessman."

"Exactly," Nicole said while she shot me her usual smug grin. "Keep that in mind tonight, please."

"Hard to do when Theo and I have been the ones running my family's company since Dad left," I answered, grabbing my clutch. "But I'll be a good girl and do my best to accept Alex Grayson as my new business partner."

I left my best friend and assistant in a rush, knowing I was pressed for time already, and I headed straight to the elevators that led out of the luxurious apartments that my dad helped design years ago.

I loved my home. It would've been nice to have a place near the beach, but that wasn't in the cards since I didn't want that crazy of a commute to work. I would rather stay close to my business and fully immerse myself into the company—that I suddenly felt I was losing in this merge.

Shit, don't think like this, I had to remind myself, knowing I was already missing the first part of this event, and showing up late was *not* what I'd planned on for first impressions while meeting my new business partner.

Buzz! Buzz! Buzz!

I glanced at my phone, knowing I was minutes away from the Beverly Wilshire where the party was taking place. "Hey, Theo," I answered my vice president and the man who was as close to me as a brother. "I'm almost there. An accident jammed-up traffic, and now I'm seriously late, I know."

"For God's sake, Bree," he said. "Why would you choose tonight—of all nights in history—to be late to something? Why?"

"No shit. I'm sorry, but I don't control the traffic. Also, I had a client go over this evening, and I wasn't about to drop them because of a company merge that would happen whether or not I was at this stupid party. Besides, we both know this is just a bragging event for Mitchell and Associates. The official merge is when we start collaborating on Monday."

"Damn it, Breanne," he practically growled. "I know you're deliberately avoiding this, but you've screwed yourself by not getting your ass here when the press was snapping pictures of us all walking in. You also missed the *official* announcement that Mr. Mitchell made to all those cameras for business insiders. The best part came when I had to stand in your place alongside Mr. Grayson while the man was forced to make a speech in his *new partner's absence* tonight. Well done, you've officially dodged all the important reasons for this event."

I felt a knot tighten in my stomach. Theo had every reason to be pissed at me after all the work that'd gone into this. "All of what you just said is the reason I hate this. It feels like they slipped this all under my nose. It's like every other thing that's happened with this freaking merge."

"Listen up," Theo said. "I know the *personal* reasons why you're not mentally on board with this, but you need to snap your ass out of this fast.

You're never late to *anything*. Ever. You're the face of Stone Architects Group, and it was sort of a slap in everyone's face that you weren't here for the kick-off of this merge."

I felt tears of frustration start to surface, and I *never* cried. This was the last thing I needed. "Well, I didn't realize they'd make the *official* announcement tonight," I said, trying to defend myself and keep the tears back.

"That's because you're in denial," he said. "You've been avoiding this all month. Now, you missed your time to show them they are fortunate that Stone is merging with Brooks. And let me reiterate the fact that you're not just a little bit late. Dinner has come to an end, and the dancing has commenced." He exhaled. "You know what? I'm done lecturing. I'm exhausted. Just get here, Bree. I think Mr. Mitchell already took off, and Grayson with him too."

I sensed his frustration, but what was I supposed to do? Did he expect me to get out of the car on the gridlocked freeway and run there? I had to defend myself and lack of professionalism. "It looks like the traffic has forced me to meet Mr. Grayson on Monday, which was when I genuinely believed this would all be considered official."

"I want you to listen to me when I tell you something. Okay?"

"Okay," I sighed, pinching the bridge between my nose.

"This merge is a good thing for you, us, and our company. Primarily, it's a blessing for *you*. You're our imaginative and overly creative dreamer; you always have been. That part of your happiness in this field was stolen when your dad was diagnosed, and we lost him soon after that. You not only had to grieve his death, but you also had to ditch your dreams of designing amazing shit when you had to take over the business side of everything. Mr. Grayson will take over in those areas, and you will be free to go back to your first love of creating, imagining, and engineering again. It's a gift, and you keep kicking it in the balls."

After tipping my driver, I stepped out of the car, and I glanced up at the magnificence of the Beverly Wilshire Hotel. "You're right," I said. "I'm sorry I let you and everyone down tonight. I am Theo."

"Just get your ass in there and mingle a little bit. The big guys are gone, but that's not who you are anyway. You're the one who sees eye-to-eye with the employees who are the core of our company. Enjoy being with them and show them that you are just as *thrilled* about this merge as they are."

"Get my ass *in there?*" I questioned. "That sounds a lot like you're not *in there* as I speak to you. Don't tell me you left, too?"

"I handled all of your important business. You know, making excuses as to why you weren't here for the ceremony and shit like that? My part is done, and I'm leaving now that you're here to take over. I have a headache, and I told Stanton it's his turn to rub my feet after the night I've had. He's already drawing my bubble bath, waiting for me at home."

"God, I feel like I wasted Cass's time with this whole dress-up stuff."

"There are still some suits here with eyes on everyone. Flash that pretty smile of yours at them, and do your part."

"Go enjoy Stanton and your bath. I'll do my part." I rolled my eyes, looking for the signs that led me to the ballroom. "I'll see what I can salvage after being Mr. Grayson's flaky new business partner tonight."

"That's my girl." Theo laughed. "Owning up like she always does. See you tomorrow at lunch."

"See you tomorrow," I said, ending the call.

I WALKED IN, music playing loudly. For the first time since Dad passed, I felt almost anonymous in a room full of peers. At least, it didn't appear as if I were running one of the best architect firms in Southern California, and I didn't feel like the woman who ran the company. I was a—

Nope. Get out of your head. You're Breanne Mother-Fucking Stone, and even though you're late, you're still one of the executives. Time to woman-up, I thought, hating that I'd put myself in a position to look bad at this event.

Instead of cowering, I raised my chin and smiled. I wasn't going to allow being late to break me down in front of mixed company—Brooks Architectural Firm employees and my very own employees. I was a tenacious woman who ran a badass firm, and I was late because I wasn't about to tell a client they were interfering with my party time.

Sphere Company was expanding on the coast, and I needed them as my clients. They would be my gift and show of strength that my company carried with them into this merge. I worked overtime, showing them my plans and visions for the hotel resort they were planning to build in

Malibu. I was their girl, and I landed the deal—I just needed to seal it. That's why I was walking in late.

It was a shame that Alexander Grayson couldn't be bothered to hang around a little longer to meet his new partner. That was on him, and I'd question his priorities with this *partner* stuff when I met the man on Monday. The fact that he left early tonight was a slap in my face, actually. Would he have treated a man with the same lack of respect? Doubtful. But that was the price of being a woman in a man's world. Unfortunately for him, the *patriarchy* could kiss my ass. I deserved my spot at this table.

Theo was right. These employees were *my people*, the ones who were the core of the company. I wasn't a stuck up *suit*, and I didn't act like one either. Now, it was time to interact with these new faces and enjoy mingling with the employees who kept these two firms running. You know, the important ones behind the curtain that business executives never gave too much credit. People like Alexander Grayson, my new partner, who left early, would differ from me in this merge. He'd be the stuck-up jerk in a suit, and I would be the down-to-earth boss they all could relate to.

AFTER AN HOUR OF LAUGHTER, new faces, and meeting the lively group who'd received the exclusive invites to the event tonight, I felt quite satisfied that I'd done my part. Everyone enjoyed themselves, and after the room started to empty, I felt the need for a stiff drink. I remained at the party with the small group who'd stayed behind for the free drinks and dancing, and I found myself at the bar.

I ordered a gin and tonic, with no desire for my usual martini. After the stress of this night, I downed my cocktail faster than I expected and called for another.

Damn, I needed this drink like a month ago. I felt my nerves unwind with the first cocktail down the hatch, and it was the most relaxed I'd been since finding out about this merge.

A slight buzz washed over me just as I spotted my ex-fiancé with an animated, leggy blonde hanging on his arm.

Of all the times and places. What the hell is he doing here? I thought, knowing I wasn't ready to see this man again. I would *never* be ready to see this man again.

I squinted my eyes to be sure. Yep, it was Max.

Oh, hell no. He was *not* seeing me sitting at a bar and drinking alone. I had the upper hand on this jerk since our split, and I wasn't about to lose that.

Yet, here I was. And there he was with some beauty on his arm—it was as if the devil himself had sent my ex to ensure this night was a complete failure.

Maybe I was getting payback for the way I called it off with Max? I *did* ditch the bastard at the altar on our wedding day, but it was after I saw a video of him cheating on me, so I figured I wasn't the monster in the situation, but it's not like blaming him made me feel any better.

Now, here he was with a perfect-looking broad? She was stunning and dressed in a tight black dress, complete with bouncing boobs nearly spilling out of it. Seeing them together made me feel sick to my stomach.

Why the hell do I suddenly care about what this miserable prick does and who he does it with? It was a year ago, Bree. You're over this loser, I reminded myself when I saw him beaming, and then they turned and moved toward my direction.

Goddammit. He can't see me drinking alone. That asshole would just fucking love that. No way. Think of something, Breanne. You're creative. It's what you do, create shit.

When Max smirked like a cocky asshole when our eyes met, I reflexively turned to my left and saw a young man. I sized him up quickly. He was about my age and dressed sharply in a crisp white shirt, suspenders, and a bowtie.

This could work, I thought as he ordered a bourbon sour.

I was running with enough liquid courage that I did something that my sober mind would have never considered. This wasn't creative; this was beyond being desperate to hold my own against my ex, who was currently heading my way.

I grabbed the man's sleeve. When he turned to me, my eyes widened when I saw how out-of-this-world beautiful this guy was.

"Oh, Jesus. You are quite handsome," I spoke the truth out loud like a crazy woman.

He smiled at my bluntness, thank God.

"Breanne Stone," the striking man said with a grin that made the liquor in my system fuel this insane idea even more. "Lovely to meet you."

His assertive voice carried a deep scratch to it that was as hot as he was.

The liquid in my system told me I didn't have time to gawk.

My proper mindset told me just to walk away.

Buzzed Bree didn't listen to her practical mind, so I accepted the man's gesture and pressed on.

"I'm happy you feel that way," I answered with a rushed smile. "Listen, I don't have time to explain, but I need you to do me a huge favor and go along with me on something," I begged, turning to see that Max and the blonde's pursuit to the bar had been interrupted by a brief, passing conversation. Max's eyes moved over to where I was again, and I was not letting this asshole have the upper hand of happiness on me.

I turned back to the guy who seemed pleased to meet one of the new partners in this company merge. "Okay. Question. Do you know that man over there? The one in the burgundy button-down and gray slacks with that blonde woman on his arm?" I asked.

My victim's humored green eyes peered around me as he took a casual sip of his drink. "I'm not sure about the gentleman, but the blonde woman he's with works for Mitchell and Associates."

"So I assume you work for them as well?" I asked. "Please tell me she doesn't know who you are."

"No," he chuckled. "At least not that I'm aware of." He eyed them, playing along with whatever in the hell I was doing to his poor, handsome self at the moment. "I just know that she's new to the company."

"Good, then you're my boyfriend." I locked eyes with his wide and playful ones. "Can you go along with that lie for me? I promise I will make this up to you somehow, but that's my ex, and it's quite a long story." I cringed at what I just asked of the guy.

As I took the time to reflect on the fact that I was obliterating any chance of this divine man ever thinking I was a normal human being, his lips turned up into the most deliciously devilish grin. I had to admit that I loved the fact that he might play along with my immature, liquor-driven idea.

The shadow along his cheek and jaw created a razor-sharp chiseled face that I couldn't help but stare at. His face was well defined, and his hair was cut longer on the top than the back and sides. He must've been a model, hired to be a seat-filler at this party. Mitchell and Associates had models that covered their magazines, and I knew for sure this guy wasn't one of my employees.

"Bree?" I heard a familiar laugh come from behind me.

Max.

"Hey," I said as I turned around. "Why are *you* here?" I thought I'd play it cooler than cutting right to the chase, but apparently not.

"My girlfriend. Bree, this is Haley. Haley's company invited her to attend this event," Max said, smiling at the woman. He looked at me smugly, like the fucker he was. "Drinking alone, I see. It looks like you've turned into the lonely CEO I'd always knew you'd become, huh? As they all say, must be pretty lonely at the top."

I sucked in a ragged breath, but I suddenly calmed down when I felt the dreamboat of a man beside me pull me into his sturdy side. "My lady, a lonely CEO? Hell no," the man I'd pleaded to roleplay with me scoffed at my dumb-ass ex. "I would hardly call what we have going *lonely*, would you, Breanne?" The man's voice was authoritative, mature, and confident.

He was perfect for this, and I owed him big time.

"Hardly lonely..." I looked back at my savior. *"What's your name?"* I mouthed, and he smiled some cheeky grin in return to me.

"I'm Logan," he announced to Max as he pulled me closer to him and extended his hand to shake my ex-douchebag's hand. "I worked at Mitchell for a time," he said, looking at the blonde who was just as taken by this stone-cold fox as I was. "You've been pretty high-spirited tonight that you work for them. I've heard you talking about it."

"Oh," she snickered as she blushed. "I love it there. Do you still work for the company too?"

Dreamy eyes looked at me. "Not anymore." He arched an eyebrow that would make any woman melt and smiled at me. "Now, I'm Breanne's number one man, and soon to be..." He stopped. "Should we tell them, darling?"

Darling? I smiled, then turned back to my ex and his arm ornament. "Why not?" I ran my hand down the center of dreamy eyes' shirt. *Damn!* All muscle. I pulled it together and smiled and Logan's sexy grin. "Logan and I are going to be tying the knot?" I looked back at Max. "Poor Logan had to deal with me turning him down a couple of times—you know, due to all the past traumas and insecurities I have from being cheated on—but in the end, I said, yes." I smiled sweetly at Logan, who was watching me ramble.

"You're still not over that?" Max asked defensively. "Three years ago and—"

"She is now," Logan spoke for me.

Max eyed Mr. Hotness. "How long have you two been..." he stopped watching me with some cowardly look.

"God," Logan said with a dramatic sigh and a shit-eating grin. "It certainly has been in the works for a while. Call me a sappy romantic..." He locked eyes with me. "Nonetheless, since the moment we announced the engagement, the time has practically flown by." He took a sip of his amber drink and looked at Max. "Now, it feels as though this festive event is pretty much celebrating us," he said and clinked his glass of bourbon to mine. "Cheers to us, Breanne."

"Cheers." I grinned at his excellent response.

I turned fully to him, my eyes thanking him for the fact that he was going along with this charade for my benefit.

I certainly didn't expect a demon from my past to join me in my night of fuckery after showing up late to this important event, and I didn't expect for it to have *this* effect on me either. Max was a worm, and I *knew* my sober self would've walked the hell out of here without a word. But here we all were. Thanks a lot, gin.

"I heard you are working with the former VP of Mitchell," the blonde said, cutting through the silence of my locked-up thoughts and the tangled mess I'd pulled myself into. I looked back at her. "Sounds like you're the lucky one," she said. "From what I understand, Mr. Grayson is pretty hot." She wiggled her eyebrows, making me furrow my brows in response before I looked at Max.

I hope she cheats on your ass, too, slimeball.

"What?" Max questioned, stepping up to the bar and guiding the blonde to sit next to him.

I almost answered, but instead, I looked back at the poor guy I'd roped into my drama. I hoped I never saw him again. This scenario couldn't have been any more humiliating. What happened to the bold woman I was? Where the hell did she go? I was so out of character that I couldn't think straight, and my buzz was propelling me further into this flaming pile of garbage. So, naturally, I downed the last of my third cocktail.

Bad idea? Meh. Fuck it.

"Hello? Are you still on the planet with us? God, you still space out like a weirdo, Bees," Max insulted me with the name I hated most. "Are you jealous of my new girl?"

"You have seen the man she's spending the rest of her life with, right?" Logan said about our fake engagement. "I hardly believe jealousy is what is on my girl's mind."

"Then why are you acting so fucking weird?" Max asked.

"It's been a long night with the company merge..." I started.

"Rumor has it that you weren't even here and that Grayson dude had to do your job too," Max clicked his tongue after he cut me off. "Bad timing on that unprofessional slip-up."

All of my witty comebacks, which were usually at the tip of my tongue, were frozen by the fact that this was getting messier and uglier and more mortifying by the second.

"I'm sure Mr. Grayson will forgive me for working late tonight." I smiled. "You wouldn't know the first thing about working, much less working late, though, would you, Max?"

Max rolled his eyes. "We weren't here for Mr. Grayson's announcement, but word is floating around that he expected nothing less from a woman like you."

I felt my fists ball up in response. "I was certain Mr. Grayson was especially happy Bree was late," Logan said. "In fact, after seeing him tonight and listening to him speak, I'm going to worry about that man working so closely with you." He looked at me and pursed his perfect lips. "Alexander Grayson is quite the catch, and I can't lose you completely to that appealing businessman."

I smiled, somehow my nerves chilling under this man's steady gaze. "Kiss me," I softly said.

Did I just ask him to kiss me? Was my drink spiked? What the hell am I doing? Self-sabotaging?

"Kiss you?" Logan softly questioned, capturing me with his daring smile and perplexed expression.

Max and Beach Barbie were distracted by her cosmopolitan not being made to her liking, and I was in awe of the perfection and beauty bottled up in this man in front of me. I was confident I must've been possessed earlier and didn't realize it until now—possessed by the old, wild and daring side of me that'd been stifled since my parents died and I had to become the responsible CEO.

Between losing my parents and Max's final nail in my coffin, I'd turned into a stiff businesswoman with blinders on, but at this moment, I felt like my old self. The fun, friendly, silly, goofball. The alcohol was the culprit for taking it to extremes with a stranger, but there was no turning back now. The guy seemed like he might *actually* kiss me, so I pressed for more, not even remembering the point I wanted to make with the gesture.

"Yes. I said, kiss me." I arched an eyebrow at him, my eyes playfully drifting back to my idiot ex.

He took a sip of his bourbon sour and nodded. "Do you want a peck or a show-stopper that'll rid you of the douche bag who's starting to piss me off with all of his derogatory comments at your expense?"

My eyebrows rose with my smile. "I mean, when you need to make a point, it seems like you *have* to go with a show-stopper. Like it or not, I guess."

His laughter was infectious, and I couldn't help but join in happily. I hadn't been silly and laughed about something so frivolous in…well, way too long.

"The sacrifices we have to make sometimes, right?" he said, sliding the corner of his mouth in between his teeth and eyeing Max and Beach Barbie.

"So, when's the *big day* for you and Logan?" Max asked snottily, obviously seeing right through my stupid little game. Then he laughed, "You can stop acting like you both are together now. You look like an idiot, Bree." He looked at Logan. "Sorry, dude. She's sort of an odd one."

"Listen," Logan said, taking my hand in his, "your insults prove that you're the one having difficulty losing this beauty on my arm."

"You can't be serious?" he questioned Logan while I felt the need to run the hell out of here after asking him to kiss me, and now Max saw right through my game.

"I am," Logan said, steadying me on my feet, one arm gracefully sliding on my back and the other holding my hand. "I'm also serious when I say that you're a dick too."

"Bree, you're really marrying this asshole?"

I couldn't answer. My brain was mush, I was livid, and I was embarrassed.

"We're taking off," Logan answered for me. "I think my lady has had enough of her asshole ex questioning her. Hey, I know you don't work for either company present tonight, but it's a known fact that no one questions Breanne Stone. Goodnight."

"What the hell did I just do?" I said, feeling more clearheaded as we walked outside into the fresh night air. I looked at Logan's tall frame as he followed me out. "I swear to God that I'm not *that* immature in real life. I don't do shit like this *ever*. And—oh, my God—if you work for me? Totally unacceptable behavior to ask you to kiss me." I walked away from the front doors of the exquisite hotel.

"It was hard to resist, but if you caught my eye when you first walked in tonight, I'm quite sure all eyes were on you at that bar tonight too. It was for the best that nothing happened," he said, trying to make me feel more comfortable about my pathetic idea.

"Well, I'm sorry anyway," I answered. "If you work for me, that could—"

"Technically, I work for Mr. Mitchell," he said.

"Great. You're one of his models, aren't you? I knew it. This is right up there with the lamest way I've ever behaved in my life," I said, finding a bench and sitting on it.

"Well, I must say that finding Breanne Stone nearly fall victim to a complete douche bag tonight was not something I imagined her doing when I had the privilege of first meeting her."

I was so spun out. I was pissed at my lack of professionalism, the weakness I didn't realize I still had concerning Max, and this entire fuck-up of a night. There was no backing out of this and nothing to excuse my behavior.

"Listen, Logan, I don't know what article you may have read about me or what that man, Mr. Grayson, said about me tonight to put that in your head, but I'm human too. Human's crack sometimes." I leaned back, pressing my fingers against my forehead. "My God, what possessed me to fall apart like this? I'm so humiliated." I kept my eyes closed, willing this other-worldly, gorgeous model to leave and never see me again. "Please, God, can you keep this between us?"

I gained the courage to look over at him as he sat at my side. "I'm not the one you should worry about. It seems like your ex might have something to say about you wanting to kiss your handsome fiancé."

I grimaced. "I'm sorry I brought you into that and my demons from the past. There's nothing I can say to get you to respect the woman I *really* am, but hell, this has most certainly been a night I wish I could restart."

"Nothing wrong with wanting to kiss your future life-long partner," he smirked. "I'll keep it between us." He rose. "Hey, will you be okay? That man was a bit off-color in the way he should treat a lady."

I laughed. "I was a bit off-color the last time I saw him." I looked up and took in the man's muscular figure and what must've been all six-foot-four or so inches of him.

"Strange, but I can't imagine that from you."

"Neither could any of our wedding guests."

"That sounds like a story I want to hear," he chuckled, and it must have been because of my expression.

"Yeah, and I wish it was a story I could forget," I said, shaking my head and not wanting to get into it any further.

"Then I hope, for your sake, one day you will." He stepped back with a smile. "It was lovely to meet you, Ms. Stone."

"Hey," I called out as he strode away like the runway model he was. "It was nice to meet you too. Thanks again for roleplaying with me tonight."

He stopped and turned back. "You're going to be a damn fine partner for Mr. Grayson."

I stared at him as he walked off like he owned the world, and I couldn't muster the courage to chase him down. I could've used a night of letting that god kiss away all of this shit, but it was for the best to let him walk on. God only knew what the rumors would be on Monday if that man talked about what I had done.

SNEAK PEEK: Part II
   Bree

"THE SUITS ARE HERE," Nicole, my assistant, proclaimed while I sat in our conference room, waiting impatiently. "Five minutes early, unlike you, who—"

"Nicole," I snapped, pulling my blazer down. "Thank you. I understand I was late for the gala. The entire room is aware of it, as well. We don't need reminders."

"Got it," she cringed. "Sorry."

"Don't apologize, just lead them in."

All right. Moment of truth. Time to meet my new business partner, who I needed to start appreciating for allowing me to go back to my focus on design and engineering.

"Are you ready to start the beginning of something new and exciting?" Theo asked, taking his seat next to me.

"As ready as I'll ever be." I smiled at my right-hand man. "Are you?"

"After I saw the smile that was plastered on your face at brunch on Sunday," Theo chuckled, "I'd think you'd finally—"

"Met her life-long partner?" a familiar voice rang out as a group of crisp suits walked into the room.

I looked up to see Logan. His smile was as radiant as mine must have been after telling Theo my dark secret of how I handled Max's unexpected cameo at the conference.

I observed Logan in his three-piece business suit and stared in confusion as to who the hell this man *really* was who was sitting across from me—because he sure as shit wasn't a model if he was in this meeting.

Mr. Mitchell remained standing and announced himself, but I couldn't peel my eyes away from Logan.

"Logan?" I finally questioned, lost in his dazzling smile highlighted by his gray suit and black tie.

I looked at Mr. Mitchell after he softly coughed out a laugh. He was as handsome as Logan was. For a brief moment I had to wonder where the hell these impossibly gorgeous men came from.

"Did I miss something?" I asked, seeing Mr. Mitchell was suddenly amused after I greeted Logan.

"And that's my cue." Logan rose, buttoned his suit jacket, and I didn't miss the humored eye contact he gave Mr. Mitchell.

I felt ice-cold panic shoot up my spine at the thought that the man I'd roped into an elaborate roleplay, ending with forced sexual advances, was a goddamn executive. What had I done? This couldn't have possibly gotten any worse.

"Good afternoon," Logan greeted us, his voice still that sexy deep rasp. "Most of you already met me when I introduced myself at the gala." He looked at me. "But for those of you who were late, allow me to introduce myself." His face was commanding, and I suddenly felt played. "I'm Alexander Grayson..."

That's all I heard after the ringing in my ears made me fucking deaf. Seriously. For the next hour of him talking, I couldn't focus on one single word. I felt like my head was in a barrel, and everything was muffled. How—of *all people on the planet*—was this man Alexander Grayson?

Pre-Order Here Mr. Grayson to continue this new exciting story of Alex and Bree.

Made in the USA
Monee, IL
01 March 2021